THE FLAMING SWORD

The Day of Atonement
Volume II

THE FLAMING SWORD

A Novel of the End

BRECK ENGLAND

Mango Publishing
CORAL GABLES

Cover & Layout Design: Elina Diaz & Jermaine Lau

For permission requests, please contact the publisher at:

Mango Publishing Group
2850 Douglas Road, 2nd Floor
Coral Gables, FL 33134 USA
info@mango.bz

For special orders, quantity sales, course adoptions and corporate sales, please email the publisher at sales@mango.bz. For trade and wholesale sales, please contact Ingram Publisher Services at customer.service@ingramcontent.com or +1.800.509.4887.

The Flaming Sword: A Novel of the End

Library of Congress Cataloging
ISBN: (print) 978-1-63353-972-3 (ebook) 978-1-63353-973-0

Library of Congress Control Number: 2019932092

BISAC category code: FIC022080 FICTION / Mystery & Detective / International Mystery & Crime

Printed in the United States of America

TABLE OF CONTENTS

PREFACE

And the Lord God placed at the east of the garden of Eden Cherubims and a flaming sword, which turned every way, to keep the way of the tree of life.

—Genesis 3:24

A unique, high-tech, high-security energy field known as "Flaming Sword" encloses the famous Temple Mount in Jerusalem, the storied site of the Tree of Life in the Garden of Eden, of Solomon's Temple, and of the Dome of the Rock, which is revered by Muslims everywhere.

Why this exceptional need for security?

Because the Temple Mount is the most dangerous place on Earth. Three great religions—Islam, Judaism, and Christianity—all claim this holy spot as their own. Despite an edgy truce among them, the slightest shift in the status quo could bring war to the whole world.

In *The Day of Atonement* Volume 1, a radical Pope dies brutally, and a most sacred artifact is stolen. Thrown unwillingly together, Ari Davan, an Israeli intelligence agent, and Maryse Mandelyn, an Interpol art expert plagued by a violent past, detect in these events the dim outlines of a conspiracy that threatens to destroy the holy mountain.

Independent of each other, Ari and Maryse discover a startling image on the ceiling of the Papal Chapel in Rome, a sign that leads them to the mysterious Cathedral of Chartres, where they decipher a countdown to apocalypse in the famous Labyrinth.

Then, as they leave the Cathedral, Ari notices something strange about a statue on the façade and leaves Maryse stranded there. What did he see? What does it mean? Where will it lead?

Now Maryse is left alone to make some sense out of the fragments of evidence she has collected—a pair of gold rings with an enigmatic inscription, an ancient Tarot card with the same inscription, an illogical spatter of blood on the Papal Altar, a missing DNA sample, the disappearance of a holy icon that had not been moved in a thousand years.

She doesn't believe what the tabloids say, that "the world will end on Monday"; but she can't shake the feeling that the menacing hour is coming around at last.

And now, *The Flaming Sword*, Volume 2 of *The Day of Atonement*…

CHAPTER 1

THURSDAY, OCTOBER 7, 2027

Hotel St. Regis, Rome, 0515h

Just before waking, she dreamed of the face of Christ withdrawing slowly into the silver petals of a cloud, then of a city of domes and towers vaporized in a flood of brimstone, grainy and white rising against the sky.

The city is a cauldron. It shall be laid waste, the altars made desolate.

By a dim nightlight, Maryse Mandelyn stared at the flowered plaster of the ceiling overhead and recognized it as late nineteenth century. She smiled at David Kane's influence, how he was able to find her not just a hotel room in the rapidly filling city, but one of the best.

She had hoped to astound her old mentor—and current Interpol boss—with the story of the inscription on the rings, but he had only said he was "satisfied she was making progress." It hurt just a little; but then again he was right. Simply uncovering the meaning of the inscription had brought her no closer to the Acheropita. She could still make nothing of the disappearance of the priceless icon of Christ, stolen in plain view of a crowd of people and a battery of television cameras.

In reality, the problem had only deepened.

The city is a cauldron. A passage from the book of Ezekiel. *It shall be laid waste.*

Certainly, Rome was a cauldron. With the violent death of the most controversial Pope in a millennium, the city boiled over. Massive street fights raged within sight of the Vatican. Right-wingers attacked crowds of gays, female priests, and other partisans of the late Pope and his revolutionary Vatican III, who rallied and hit back hard.

It had been five hundred years since Luther and the schism that tore the Catholic Church in two, the news panels were saying. Five hundred years before that, the Great Schism had divided the Western from the Eastern Church. Would the cycle repeat itself? With half the Church accusing the other of sodomy and apostasy? Could the Church even survive this time?

Flying back to Rome, Maryse had watched the news for the first time in days. She had not realized the extent of the struggle that was now gathering force. The Ecumenical Council was calling itself back into session without waiting for a new Pope. There was video of the bull-like Irish Cardinal Tyrell denouncing Vatican III. Some cardinals were calling for a conclave to select a Pope to begin immediately after the funeral; others were refusing to participate until a decent period of mourning for Zacharias had passed. There was open talk of two conclaves.

She had looked around to find the airliner filled with clergy, mostly French, some of them women wearing the collar, talking agitatedly among themselves. They were all making their way toward the eruption.

She had closed her eyes at this and thought of the Carmelites in their little retreat near Paris. She knew none of this would touch them. Even if the Church were torn in two, they would continue their prayers as they had for centuries inside those walls that were like rock in a stormy sea. Fitfully, she tried to retreat mentally and sleep, but could not.

Ari Davan had left her at Chartres. She had caught the strange look on his face as he examined the statue of St. Peter on the North Porch of the Cathedral. He said he needed to return immediately to his headquarters at Jerusalem. He would not stay for Jean-Baptiste's elaborate lunch. She watched him walk briskly down the hill toward the station.

This is what men do, she had said to herself. When they leave, they leave abruptly.

Jean-Baptiste had been quiet at lunch. He had given Maryse what she needed and then withdrawn into fragmentary remarks about the food. When they returned to his house, he had sat down at his desk and written a few sentences on a paper which he then sealed up with red wax. It was the seal of the order of Malta.

"*How unfold the secrets of another world perhaps not lawful to reveal.* We think you are ready—both Milton and myself." His wide smile had thinned as he gave her the envelope. But the answers she had found at Chartres led only to more questions.

As a boy, Shin Bet Inspector Ari Davan had barely endured the long hours of *shul,* the intense study of Torah and Talmud he had to undergo to become, as his father put it, a man. At that age he had been more interested in the black eyes of a neighborhood girl staring down from the women's gallery than in the black-on-white words he was required to decipher and recite endlessly.

Right now, though, those words mattered very much.

It had come together for him on the porch at the Cathedral of Chartres as he had looked up at the statue of the man the Christians called Saint Peter— the first Pope. What struck Ari was the figure's dress. It reminded him of an engraving in an old illustrated book in his father's library. He had to see it again.

Before sunrise, he had arrived at his parents' house, touched the mezuzah at the door, and found his father awake in the small study of the West Jerusalem house. The room had not changed; he was familiar even with the dust. Among the grainy pictures of forgotten relatives that crowded the walls was a heroic photo of Moshe Dayan looking like a benevolent pirate in his black eye patch, and next to it a large portrait of a bearded Chaim Weizmann, the first president of Israel. His father had served under Dayan as a very young soldier. The silver menorah, the only thing his family had kept from before their first days in the land, shone yellow in the low lamplight.

His father found the book for him, a crumbling antique, and he knew exactly where the picture was. The illustration was still as brightly colored as the day it was printed. He had already, on his flight home, called up a hundred images like it on his GeM, but this page was worth more than all of them.

The caption read *Aharon ha-Cohen*: Aaron, the high priest of Israel, vested in the linen robes of the priesthood with the breastplate of twelve shimmering jewels, each of them representing one of the twelve tribes of Israel.

As he had done as a boy, he took a pen from his pocket and traced the words on the page with it:

> *And thou shalt make holy garments for Aaron…a breastplate, and an ephod, and a robe, and an embroidered coat, a mitre, and a girdle… and thou shalt make the breastplate of judgment with cunning work…*

and thou shalt set in it settings of stones, even four rows of stones: and the stones shall be with the names of the children of Israel…every one with his name shall they be according to the twelve tribes.

As he read, childhood returned. Then, as now, his father would wind phylacteries around arm and forehead and mourn aloud, this man who even then had always seemed to him as old as Sinai itself, over the destruction of the Temple; and when as a little boy he had learned to cry over a loss he did not understand and lament an uncleanness that could not be washed away, he had barely comprehended the grief of the Jews, the peculiar suffering they could not escape. And he also came to resent it all.

He had often idly wondered why he had become a Shin Bet man. Now it came clear for him. It was a way of purging the helplessness of his father and the impotent shadows of the generations before him, a people marched off again and again like animals to the slaughter. He had tried to break away while holding on at the same time. No high priest could exorcise the history that was in his blood.

Reb Davan was startled to see his son at that hour, and he was even more surprised at the questions Ari asked—warily, just as he had done years before. Ari knew better than anyone about his father's wish for a scholar son who would one day read aloud in the synagogue; there was all at once a sad new eagerness in the pious eyes. Wandering frantically through his books, he nearly burst with erudition on the subject.

But it was all plain enough.

> *Thus shall Aaron come into the holy place…he shall put on the holy linen coat, and he shall have the linen breeches upon his flesh, and shall be girded with a linen girdle, and with the linen mitre shall he be attired: these are holy garments…*

> *And he shall take of the children of Israel two kids of the goats for a sin offering…Then shall he kill the goat of the sin offering, and bring his blood within the veil, and he shall sprinkle of the blood upon the altar eastward with his finger seven times.*

Blood sprinkled on the altar again and again, in waves. Within the veil of the Holy of Holies. In the Sancta Sanctorum.

> *In the whole world there is no holier place.*

His father had nearly wept as he described the great Day of Atonement. "The Sabbath of Sabbaths," he had called it. As a boy, Ari remembered, he had sweated through the long warm holy day without a bath, without a morsel of food or a sip of water, listening to the keening prayers of his father and the others in the massive cubical shadows inside the synagogue. He was not permitted to put on his shoes. One Yom Kippur afternoon he had stared endlessly at a television screen that showed only a still picture of flowers and a flaming candle; and at the breath of evening he had shot out of the house up a sand hill to get fresh air into his lungs.

Now, however, his father's every word was important. "Yom Kippur is the day of cleansing, when all Israel makes atonement for sin, when we fast and mortify ourselves before Ha-Shem because of our impurity."

"And the blood, the altar, the priest?"

"That was in the days of the Temple," his father explained. "Two goats were selected to bear the sin of the people. One goat was *l'Adonai*, for the Lord, and the other *l'Azazel*—for the Devil. The blood of the Lord's goat, slaughtered by the priest, was taken solemnly into the temple and sprinkled upon the ark within the veil. Only the high priest was permitted in the Holy of Holies. Then he laid hands on the other goat—the scapegoat—to transfer upon its head the sin of Israel. A red cord was tied around the goat's head and it was led away to a place of shame in the desert, the place Duda'el, where it was thrown from a cliff."

"We don't do these things now."

"Ah, no," the old man nodded. "Without the Temple, there is no altar, no sacrifice. So, as Rambam taught, until the Temple is rebuilt, the atonement must be made on the altar of every Jewish heart. It is why, on the Day of Atonement, we sing *kol nidre* in the synagogue." Ari was well acquainted with the ancient song that implored God to forgive unfulfilled vows.

"Will the Temple ever be rebuilt?"

Even in the dim light of the study, Ari could see his father's eyes darken. "Not by human means. We cannot rebuild it. It is death for any Jew to set foot on the Temple Mount."

"Why?"

"Because, as Torah says, only a high priest of Israel may stand in the *qodesh qodeshim*—the Holy of Holies. Any Jew impertinent enough to walk there is guilty of the grossest sacrilege."

"But one day...?"

"One day, son. One day. Ha-Shem Himself will redeem the Temple Mount. As Malachi the prophet wrote, the priests shall be purified and offer sacrifice once again in righteousness. But beforehand will come a time of trouble, the *chevlay sh'l Moshiach,* the birth pains of the Messiah. The ten days between the New Year and the Day of Atonement.

"Then the Messiah will bring in *Ba ha-Olam*—the world to come—and the righteous will sit down together to study Torah forever."

Ari's father looked thoughtful for a long while and then, abruptly, blinked at the study window. "It's dawn." Almost automatically, he bent to the bureau and removed from a drawer his box of phylacteries and the velvet pillow that held his skullcap and *tallit*, the worn prayer shawl he had used since boyhood. He stood, hesitated, and offered them to Ari. A silent invitation. After a moment, Ari took them from his father and followed his lead as the older man put on another *tallit* and phylacteries.

Through the window, the first sun glimmered from the eastern hills.

Lion Gate Street, Old City, Jerusalem, 0945h

The shopkeeper could not take his eyes off Nasir's gun. The shopkeeper's wet, warm smell filled the shop as the sun struck at the corrugated tin awning. Nasir had followed him into the shop before giving him a chance to open the shutter door; he felt sweat irrigating his own back, but he wanted the man to stew a little longer.

"What did you tell the Israeli police?" he asked finally.

"When?"

"Please."

The shopkeeper suffered in the heat. "Let me turn on the fan. It's so hot."

"What did you tell the police?"

"I told them nothing."

"What did you tell the police?"

Nasir's voice did not change. He simply smiled insistently. The shopkeeper glanced from the gun in Nasir's hand to the fan on the ceiling and wiped his face repeatedly with his forearm. At last his eyes blinked hard as if he were about to faint.

"What did you tell them?" Nasir repeated.

"I told them only what I knew. Only that I knew Talal Bukmun. That he was my mother's lodger."

"What else?"

"Nothing. They already knew…"

"They already knew what?"

"That he was a weapons dealer. I told them nothing they did not already know."

"What did they say to you?"

"What did they say to me?"

"It's going to be very hot in here after I leave and lock the shutter behind me. From the outside."

The shopkeeper, not a quick man, considered this and replied. "They told me to say nothing to anyone."

"About what?"

"They said they would shut down my shop, intern me."

"They told you to say nothing to anyone about what?"

"Please. They are watching me. Perhaps listening…"

"I am watching you, too. And listening."

"I would not betray Talal."

"You would betray your mother for a *shekel*. What did they want to know?"

"They asked me if I knew a man named Ayoub."

"Who?"

"Nasir, I think it was. Nasir al-Ayoub."

"Do you know such a man?"

"No. I don't know him."

"Why did they ask you about Nasir al-Ayoub?"

"They say he killed Talal."

"You know that I am Nasir al-Ayoub."

"No, I didn't know."

"Don't lie to me. They showed you my picture."

The shopkeeper blinked at the sweat in his eyes, as if willing himself not to see.

Nasir smiled grimly at him. "I think you killed Talal. I think you stuffed him in that hole."

"No, no. I had no reason."

"You owed him money."

"No!"

"He wanted you to pay him. You thought no one would miss him, so you killed him."

"No!" The shopkeeper stared miserably at the gun as Nasir held it a little higher. "You are his friend? I was his friend, too. I gave him a place to live. A place to hide."

"He gave you money."

"He gave me some money, yes."

"So you killed him rather than paying him back. You lured him here and left him dead inside that hole where he would never be found."

"No! He came here by himself."

"Why?"

"I don't know why."

"You know. He wanted to use your shop. You told him about the tunnels. Why did he come here?"

"I don't know."

"You know. He came to meet someone. Who?"

"I don't know who."

"What did he tell you? He didn't crawl through that filth for nothing. He wanted to get into your shop. Why?" For the first time Nasir raised his voice.

The shopkeeper trembled as if with cold. He wiped his face again and again; the hair on his forearm was like mud.

"All right. He was angry. He said someone had betrayed him, and he was going to make him pay."

"Who?"

"Who?"

"Please. The man who betrayed him. Who was he? Did Talal say it was me?"

"No! I don't know. I don't know." The shopkeeper moaned over and over.

Nasir was satisfied. He knew it wasn't likely that Bukmun would have confided much to this sopping jelly of a man.

But then the jelly surprised him.

"I think it must have been the man who bought the rockets from him. But I don't know who he was," the shopkeeper whispered. "It was the man in Rome, he said. The man in Rome."

"What man in Rome?"

"A man he saw on the television."

Seconds later, the shutter was open to the cooler air from outside and Nasir was gone.

***

Down the street, in the white van, Toad watched Nasir walk briskly from the shop. "He's had quite a discussion with the shopkeeper," Toad reported from the driver's seat.

"What's the story?"

Toad was relieved to hear Ari's voice from the other end. "You're back?"

"Came in last night. I'll put you in the picture when you come in. What's the story?"

"He was drilling the shopkeeper to find out how much he knew, how much he might have told us."

"And?"

"He talked. He told Ayoub that we had his picture. Said Bukmun was in a stew over a 'man in Rome' who betrayed him, a man he saw on television."

"So Ayoub and the shopkeeper don't know each other?"

"Apparently not—only from the photo. At least that's what we're meant to believe."

Ari chuckled. "Not everything people do is a ruse."

"It's possible that Ayoub didn't know we were listening...or didn't care," Toad replied dryly. "It's also possible Ayoub did not kill Bukmun and is really trying to find out who did. But start multiplying possibilities and the product is less and less certainty."

Back in the headquarters building, Ari smiled at this; he knew that Toad thrived on low levels of certainty. He was the only man Ari knew who could keep a thousand possibilities in his mind at once without paralyzing himself. Most of his colleagues were too quick with theories—Toad, on the other hand, very slow coming up with a certainty. With Toad, it was partly that he had been trained in the severest tradition of the *yeshiva*, and partly that he believed in nothing.

"So if Ayoub did kill Bukmun, he was just trying to find out how much the shopkeeper knew. But what's the connection with a 'man in Rome'?"

Toad thought for a moment. "Pictures of Ayoub's meeting in Rome have been on TV for days. Bukmun may have caught sight of Ayoub and realized he was the man who bought the Hawkeyes. The man who betrayed him."

"Betrayed him?"

"I haven't worked that out. It's new. Shop Man was a little more open with Ayoub than he was with us."

"Could Ayoub have entered the shop Tuesday night through the tunnels and got out fast enough to show up at the front door?"

"Yesterday we found a tunnel grate in the next street that showed evidence of recent entry. A person could crawl through that tunnel from the shop, get out into the street, and walk around the corner to the front door of the shop in about five minutes."

"Where's Ayoub now?"

Toad checked with the agent following Ayoub. "He just walked through the Damascus Gate. Looks like he's making for home."

Salah-eddin Street, Jerusalem, 1000h

"After today," Hafiz al-Ayoub thought, as he lay on his couch and rubbed the ring with his thumb. Its worn gold felt like part of his body. "There will be no more heat, no more blood. Only a green and quiet peace."

For a second day, the old sheikh had eaten no breakfast. He felt he would never eat again. He wished only to lie quietly and enjoy for as long as possible the diminishing breeze that came through the window of his room. From the table by his couch, he picked up his book of Shirazi's poems. Hafiz did not believe in the legend that this book could be used for divination, but he enjoyed the game; he would ask himself a question and then open the book to find the answer. These days his question was always the same.

He opened the book at random and read:

> *Dim, drunk, I crawled the years along*
> *Until, wiser, I locked away my passion;*
> *Then I rose a Phoenix from my dust;*
> *I closed my story with the bird of Suleiman.*

Satisfied as always, he closed the book again and contemplated the verses he had read. Outside his window the morning birds had gone quiet from the heat; they would not be heard again until sunset. Tonight, the sword would pass into his son's hand and then he could rest.

For forty years he had guarded the sword with its streak of fire, although he had seldom taken it from the hiding place and the tapestry sheath. He had carried it in his heart along with Jamila—perhaps that was why he had lost her—and he had carried it through the long legal wars in courts from The Hague to Jerusalem. For a long time he had carried it in trust for Nasir and perhaps for his son after him, although he now had no hope of seeing Nasir's children. People who thought the sanctuaries were safe for all time were as deluded as those who expected that the Israelis at any moment would take it in their heads to do the worst they were capable of. He had walked the careful path of Suleiman, refusing to acquiesce to the inner rage, staying watchful in the courts—at times even revealing a glimpse of the blade—until the day when the Rightful One would claim his own.

His duty was ended now. After tonight, he could sleep.

Nasir came into the room. "I got Amal to school."

Hafiz stirred, pulling himself up on his couch. "You should have a word with the teacher in the *madrassah*," he said wearily. "Amal is likely to hit him one day."

Nasir gave a loud chuckle. He wanted to keep things light while he scanned the news on TV. With the sound on mute, the screen would not bother Hafiz, who was becoming noticeably less wakeful the last few mornings.

"Why are you watching television in the middle of the day?" his father asked from the couch.

"I want to see the news."

Hafiz settled back motionless again. Using his GeM to control the flatscreen, Nasir scrolled quickly through frozen images from a dozen news broadcasts of the last few days. Like train windows, the images flashed past of the dead Pope sprawled on a staircase, of suitably solemn world leaders, of authorities both PA and Israeli deploring what had happened; and then of lesser figures and lesser stories.

There it was. He had paid little attention to it. The others at the station had made fun of him. Tuesday, 1000 hours—the item's first appearance. He scrolled through several more appearances during the day and stopped to study one of them.

When Hafiz awoke again, Nasir was gone. It was not right to say he had been sleeping—only dozing. He had been thinking of Nasir's mother, of

Jamila; he had locked her away in his heart so long before. His uncle had questioned the wisdom of the marriage, of the passion Hafiz felt for Jamila, in light of the work Hafiz was to do. But his uncle needn't have worried, because Hafiz did his work strictly and seriously. When a child was not forthcoming, he had adopted one, reared him, and trained him. He had now added forty years to the eight centuries of peace on the holy mount: no new Crusade had been allowed to form, even in the worst of times, even amid worldwide *jihad*.

He had managed the repercussions of the attack on al-Aqsa, which had nearly brought him to the grave. In truth, Hafiz smiled to himself, it *had* brought him to the grave. Drunken with rage, the others were demanding the worst. The practice of diplomatic delicacy had exhausted him to the point where the carrion birds in his blood freed themselves and now preyed steadily on him.

It was martyrdom of a sort, he smiled to himself.

One day his uncle Haytham had made the ultimate sacrifice, which he had expected to do. Consumed by two wars, worn out by the insistent pull of martyrdom, he died in the first Intifada. After the one-eyed Zionist general in 1967, Munich in 1972, the disastrous Egyptian attack in 1973—but the Intifada was a new thing. Haytham was exhausted by the frenzy, the stones in the air, the decapitations, and the red craters in the mud. One day he had collapsed in the street and died under the wheels of an IDF van—an accident, they said.

That was the beginning of the forty years. From that day, he had carried the weight of the gold ring on his hand.

The world continued, a cancer in remission one day and fulminating the next. A Jewish dentist murdered worshipers in the mosque at Hebron. Palestinian children blew themselves up in the markets of Jerusalem and Tel Aviv. Rabin was assassinated. Rockets flew over Gaza and Israel. Between outbreaks, Hafiz struggled to keep a lock on his anger. It was beyond comprehension. The Americans lavished money on the Zionists, moved their embassy to Jerusalem, and refused to open their eyes. The Zionists talked themselves deaf about their liberty and their security. It was as the Prophet had said—God might as well have given the precious treasures of the Torah and the Gospel to an ass. In time, there was the excursion to Norway—on a private airplane—and at last Jamila awaiting him as he floated to the ground at Amman. It was compensation enough.

Jamila's father kept a peacock in his garden in East Jerusalem, and Hafiz had heard the peacock's cry many mornings from his house. The families had long known each other; it was only natural for Jamila's father to agree to the marriage, even though Hafiz's father had lost his property. Among the leading families there was an understanding about Hafiz, and the family of Jamila welcomed him. Although she had traveled widely, had attended university in New York City, the instinct for home was strong in her. The peacock, the bird of Suleiman, had brought them back together, he joked.

He took walks with Jamila in the evenings among the sedative trees of the Mount of Olives, and she came to understand hazily why he wore the ring and why he kept his eye on the *Qubbet*. Above them, the Dome receded into the sunset; at these times, the oath he had sworn melted from his memory with the last rays of day. Then, on a blue afternoon in the fall, when he was walking there with Jamila, an explosion slashed the air from the direction of the city. The Israelis had decided to open an ancient tunnel along the base of the Temple Mount, and there was rioting in the Muslim quarter. Many bombs followed that one; for months, he worked harder than ever before, but then the Second Intifada began, and with it his wife's long decline and the painfully sweet adoption of Nasir. She could not have children, but she had desperately wanted Nasir—if only to fill the emptiness that was coming for Hafiz.

For forty years, he had worn the ring while the darkness gathered and deepened around him. King Suleiman had used his ring to summon the *jinn*, enslaving them to build his great mosque. The cry of the bird of Suleiman would announce the Last Day, it was said. *It was time now*, thought Hafiz. It was past time. Martyrs prepare themselves for forty days; surely forty years was more than enough.

Hafiz had put on his uncle's ring just before he buried him and had never taken it off. But he had wanted Nasir to have a new ring. There was too much blood on the old one. He had told Nasir to bury him with the old ring and thus bury the old blood. Hafiz had hoped to wear it until the Day—now that hope was in his son.

Simon Winter Centre for Genetic Research, Technion, Haifa, Israel, 1015h

Joseph Rappaport closed his eyes for a few moments. At last the chaos caused by Emanuel Shor's death was settling—files closed, police gone, himself appointed temporary Director. He had spent the morning putting his electronic signature on documents, including dozens of applications for information from the Cohanim database, all from America. As soon as possible, he would shunt this duty off on the assistant directors. The whole thing bored him.

Rappaport had never understood Manny Shor's obsession with the old Cohanim database. It had been well picked over for years by snobs, genealogists, and medical people researching obscure diseases.

To Rappaport, the monoamine oxidase project was so much more compelling. To experiment with the genes that made people violent, that moved them to hatred—monoamine research promised to get at the root of this ancient curse. Some of Rappaport's distant cousins from Venice had been transported and exterminated in the closing days of the Holocaust. Even growing up near New York, he himself had felt from some people an occasional coolness, the barest hint of disapproval of his face, of his name. Then, late one day in the time of Trump, he had gone from the lab to his tiny office in the Life Sciences building to find a drawing of a swastika hanging on the door. At first he felt afraid—he had looked around in terror at the darkening corridors—but then curiously fascinated. From that hour he was determined to find out what might be locked in the human codes that controlled the temperature of the heart—from cold looks to flaming fanaticism.

But Manny had shown little interest in the monoamine project that now funded most of the laboratory's work. The Cohanim thing brought in a big donation now and then from an American Jew who wanted to know if his ancestors were priests. Rappaport wondered why Americans, so proud of their independence and individualism, still needed to make these links. Leaving America for Israel had caused him no concern at all—it didn't matter to him where he lived, so long as the project he worked on was interesting. He felt no more connected to Haifa, Israel, than he did to his old neighborhood in Elizabeth, New Jersey. This linkage others felt to a land or to a people or to a story—or to a God—was a mystery to him. He looked around his desk at the photos of Ernst Schrödinger, of Watson and Crick, of Stanley Cohen—these were his heroes, the people who explained life instead of romanticizing it. As a boy, he had read Schrödinger's book *What Is Life?* and knew that he would spend *his* life answering that question.

He had once asked Manny how he envisioned the world to come, and Manny had told him that, for a Jew, Heaven would be to sit peacefully in a garden with a *minyan* of brothers who love one another, learning and discussing Torah for eternity. Although the agnostic Rappaport had smiled at this, the vision suggested something to him. He would not admit it to anyone, but it moved him in the same way as the still meadows and waters of the Twenty-Third Psalm, which was the only part of the Bible he remembered.

Although Rappaport did not believe in the world to come, he began to envision a world here and now where people would no long fear each other, but would sit down in peace and put their minds to work instead of their hatreds. To gain dominion over those old foes—prejudice and violence—surely that was worth his life's work. Rappaport was not one of those geneticists who looked for more and more specialized diseases to conquer; he was interested in the universal disease of hate.

Thus, the monoamine project. As a young scientist, he had read about a dozen men from the same Dutch family sent to prison because they were uncontrollably violent. One was a notorious street bully, and another had raped and knifed his own sister. All the men had a mutation on MAO-A1, a monoamine oxidase gene. He began to wonder: could violence and hate be genetically conditioned? Could a few manipulations of the human genome put an end to prejudice, terror, crime—perhaps even war? Could the very nature of humanity be changed?

His goal was never articulated that way, but Rappaport spent the next twenty years working on it. The best work was being done at Technion; thus, he had come to Technion. He had reduced herds of animals to docility, tracked and manipulated the DNA of hundreds of criminals, and was reasonably sure that he knew how to proceed. As usual, however, the ethicists got in the way of the kind of experiments he wanted to do. He was more bemused than disappointed; after all, even the great James Watson had at one time called for a moratorium on DNA research out of fear that plagues might be accidentally unleashed. Still, he found it ironic that the Ethics Committee should stand in the way of making people more peaceful.

Manny had laughed at his ideas. "Peace is not just the lack of violence," he had said. Rappaport had not known how to respond to this; to him, the elimination of violence seemed contribution enough. The director's lack of interest in the monoamine project had hampered progress, but now Rappaport saw his way clear. A tragic death—in Rappaport's world, Manny would not have died this way—but the past was Manny's business, the future Rappaport's.

There would be no more excursions to Jerusalem to wait alongside Manny Shor while he stared at King David's Tomb. Many times the old man had coaxed him into coming up to the city with him, primarily because Manny was not a confident driver. He would chatter about *Moshiach ben David* and the world to come, about the royal priesthood and lineage, about the ludicrous prospect of digging for King David's DNA. Long meetings with puzzled officials always ended with a pilgrimage to the Tomb, a marble monolith jammed into a little building on the south end of the city. It did no good to tell him again that it was not the Tomb of King David, that it was a Christian monument dating to the Crusades. He knew that as well as anyone; he went over and over the dilettantish archeological diagrams that pretended to show the location of the real tomb, needling the historic-preservation people about this or that possibility, checking to see who was digging where.

Rappaport always held back at these meetings, pretending as hard as he could to be the chauffeur, staring deliberately at his fingers. The officials he met, wary but respectful of Manny's reputation, bit their lips and tried to listen. "The Messiah of David will carry the DNA of David," Manny would explain. "We need those bones. Nothing is more important than isolating this strain. If the genome were available, the Messiah's lineage would be immediately recognizable. Don't you understand the urgency…the importance…?" And then he would trail off in realization that the officials he spoke to wanted nothing more than to see the back of him. His campaign to get the Israeli government to crack open the marble sarcophagus in the Crusader church—in the desperate hope that everyone might be wrong—went nowhere. Still, he would beg Rappaport to take him there.

The old man always stood covered before the Tomb and always prayed the same prayer, over and over— *"May he come into his kingship in my lifetime and in my days and in the lifetime of the whole family of Israel swiftly and soon."*

The drives back to Haifa were long and dispiriting. Uncharacteristically quiet, Manny would sit behind him poring over worn-out maps of Mount Zion or reading some new article that promised a breakthrough. But the remains of King David remained undisturbed—wherever they were.

In the final few months, Rappaport had noticed a new energy in his colleague. Even though he rarely came to the lab, Manny was excited about the prospect of triangulating on the Aharonic genome—the genetic profile of the first great high priest of Israel, Aaron, brother of Moses. Of course, without a bone or two, there could never be certainty. But mathematical possibilities became probabilities as Manny studied and compared the profiles of thousands of Cohanic descendants. Rappaport cooperated politely, waiting for the opportunity that would inevitably come.

And now the old fool was gone and he was at last Director of the Centre—even if temporarily. It would soon be permanent, he was sure. He stood up and looked around at the lab through his glass office walls; with the past taken care of, he would spend the afternoon planning the future. He hoped that, if Heaven existed, Manny had found his discussion group.

A lanky young woman, one of the lab technicians, was crossing toward his office with an electronic notepad in hand. She was an intriguing case—a carrier of Tay-Sachs, she had joined the lab hoping to work on a therapy for it and turned out to be quite competent. He had come to rely on her, and in fact had just given her a highly confidential assignment.

"What do you have for me, Sarah?"

"We finished running the profiles the police wanted. Here are the results."

Rappaport glanced at the data. "What's the story?"

"We compared the sample we got from Rome with the Cohanic profile. It's a very pure strain—95 percent match."

"Hm. But nothing on sample 3111."

"Sorry. As you know, we don't keep printouts of the Cohanics—that one's gone. Unless it's in one of the old control studies. Still, there's something else I thought you'd find interesting." She scrolled quickly to a stop on the luminous blue screen of her handheld. "Here," she pointed. "And here. Mutation at this point…this point…"

"MAO-A1 defect—severe, too. Whoever our Roman is, you wouldn't want to get on his wrong side. Thanks, Sarah."

She turned to leave.

"Wait. Where do we keep the backup files on those old control studies?"

Queen Helena Street, Jerusalem, 1000h

Ari was glad to have his team around him again. The squat little detective he called Toad stood as usual in the corner, hands in pockets, while Miner—an engineer with a peninsular nose and a gift for detail—towered over piles of evidence laid out in plastic bags on the table. In Miner's lab, they could get some work done. Ari had scattered photos and a diagram of the Sancta Sanctorum on the table.

"See?" Ari gestured at the diagram and measured the air with his arms. "The Pope never gets closer than two meters from the altar. First, the chest shots—big arterial splash on the floor. Then a head shot, a smaller spray mark here. Then a long blood trail to the exit. And now we know the blood on the altar isn't the Pope's: it belongs to Chandos."

Miner was excited. "But Chandos falls where he shoots himself, too far away to get so much blood spray on the altar."

"But that's the point," Ari said. "He couldn't have shot himself. There must have been a third person in that room. Either somebody shot him and moved him, which isn't likely because there are no drag marks; or somebody carried his blood to the altar and scattered it there."

"What possible reason would anyone have to do that?" Miner asked.

"That's what I've been trying to figure out for the last two days." Ari boosted himself up on the table and sat to compose himself, trying to decide how to make sense to his team.

"Why scatter blood on an altar? To make atonement. To pay for transgression. It's all in Leviticus—the priest slaughters the sacrifice, collects the blood, and sprinkles it on the altar. It was done in the Temple of Solomon."

Miner interrupted, smirking. "So, your idea is this—the killer breaks through an impenetrable cordon of police, draws on the Monsignor and the Pope, shoots the Monsignor and collects his blood to perform some ancient ceremony, shoots the Pope as the only witness, and then escapes—again, through an impenetrable line of police who are rushing the place. Oh, and all within about five minutes."

To himself, Ari added, "And while carrying a big wooden icon in a fifty-kilo silver frame." He looked silently at Miner and made a face, hesitating. "All right. I'm waiting to hear *your* explanation."

"Simple. Just what the police said. Chandos shoots the Pope and, while standing next to the altar, shoots himself, spraying blood across it. He staggers a few steps and topples where they find him."

"You don't 'stagger a few steps' with that kind of injury: you drop where you are. Even the police admitted that. And there were no staggering footprints and no blood trail. Your theory doesn't work."

"It's more likely than yours...a mysterious third party in there carrying out some bizarre ceremony."

"Sha. Just let me finish. The killer sprinkles blood on the altar, which makes the whole thing a ritual murder. There's more. The killer then removes the Monsignor's red sash from his robe and wraps it around his head. Now, why would he do that?"

"Chandos did it himself," Miner shot back. "After firing at the Pope, he decided to hang himself with his sash. But the Pope escaped from the room. Chandos realized he had no time, so he shot himself instead."

Ari considered this, examining the photos of the chapel that lay on the table and slowly shaking his head. Miner's view was plausible, but wrong. The photos were not clear enough to show this, but Ari had seen the chapel for himself. The Monsignor's blood on the altar was not like the wound sprays he had examined so many times before—it had been flung there.

"All right," Miner said. "Tell me why the 'killer' would wrap the Monsignor's sash around his head."

"It's another ritual. I checked this with my father this morning. The ancient priesthood would choose a goat to carry away the sins of Israel—they called it the scapegoat—and they tied a red cord around its horns to symbolize the blood guilt of the people."

"Therefore," Miner picked up, "our ritual murderer not only killed the Pope but also transferred his own guilt to a scapegoat and sacrificed him, too?"

"Not quite. There's tension in the Catholic Church over this Pope. According to some, he was a heretic. A betrayer of the faith. He changed a lot of things, like allowing women to be priests and so forth, and a good many people have made a row over it. Maybe somebody thought he needed to be stopped. Chandos was the Pope's man, and maybe that same person thought Chandos would make a good scapegoat—you know, in the ordinary sense. To make it look like Chandos did the deed."

"So...a religious nutter is behind everything."

Ari jumped from the table. "How many times have we dealt with this sort of thing? We live in the center of it all. You know the Jerusalem Syndrome...a perfectly ordinary tourist cracks, gets up on the Old City wall and declares he's the Messiah. A nun sits in the Via Dolorosa and gouges her hands and feet until she bleeds like Jesus. A crazy businessman from Jakarta sets himself on fire to protest the infidels in Palestine. We're surrounded by it. We even have a special hospital for religious cranks."

"And these things add up to what?" Miner was a little impatient. "How does any of this help explain the murder of Emanuel Shor and the theft of the whatsit?"

"Two things. Both victims wore gold rings with the same inscription."

"Right. 'Until he comes who has the right to rule.' "

"Suppose there was some cultic connection between them. Everything I saw in France points to it."

"An Orthodox Jewish scientist and a Catholic priest? That's some cult," Miner snickered.

"That's the second thing. A missing DNA sample belonging to someone named Chandos—the *only* missing sample from a locker our victim probably entered minutes before the murder. And it happens to bear the name of our Catholic priest."

Miner looked chastened. "It doesn't make any sense."

"Maybe it does. When I was in France I saw a sculpture, a statue of Saint Peter, the first Pope. He was dressed in the robes, not of a Pope, but of the *cohen gadol,* the High Priest of Israel. The special breastplate with the twelve stones, the turban. Look at this." Ari flicked at his GeM and up on the wall came the image of the high priest from the Tanakh. Then a photo of the statue of St. Peter on the North Porch of Chartres cathedral.

"The same costume."

Miner shook his head. "What are you getting at?"

"I think I understand." Toad spoke for the first time, and Ari looked at him hopefully. "Catholics see the Pope as the successor to the high priest of Israel. The statue shows that. But according to Torah, the high priest must be a *cohen,* a direct descendant of Aharon ben-Amram. If Chandos believes he is himself such a person, he considers Zacharias illegitimate."

"Thus the DNA sample in the Cohanic collection," Miner concluded. "Sara Alman is typing the Monsignor's DNA at Technion right now. I wonder what she's found out." He made a call on his GeM and stepped out of the room.

Ari and Toad looked at each other. "I didn't know he was still in touch with her," Ari said. "She's at Technion?"

"She's working on the Tay-Sachs problem."

"I guess there's always hope."

Toad smiled without humor, and Ari left the subject.

"So…you've been quiet."

Toad gazed at nothing for a few moments, and then asked, "Why would a Catholic priest want to know if he's a *cohen*? What difference would it make to him?"

"I don't know. All I know is that somebody carried out a Jewish ritual in that chapel—which, by the way, is called the Holy of Holies. Blood was strewn on the altar. The scapegoat was marked."

"It could be. It is intriguing." Toad's bland face hid the workings inside. He was neither surprised nor disappointed that the answer was not simple. In his experience, crime involved the most complicated of motives. No crime was simple.

"Think about whoever did this. Everyone is guilty but you. You're the real victim. The world is a standing violation of everything you cherish. You're a soldier."

Toad hesitated. Ari was surprised to hear Toad expound like this, but any entrance into his mind was worth taking. He leaned forward to listen.

"Think about how you carried out the shootings: all of them commando-style. To you, these were not murders—they were acts of war." He paused. "What we have to figure out is, what is the nature of the war?"

Miner came back in the room. "They've just got the results on the Monsignor. Hold on—you won't believe it. The profile of Peter Chandos shows 95 percent on the Cohanic scale."

"The Monsignor was a Jew?" Ari cried.

"Not only a Jew, but what a Jew. An almost pure match to the *cohen gadol* haplotype, whatever that is."

"A haplotype is like a fingerprint," said Toad. "The man who died in that chapel was one of the priesthood of Israel…"

They looked at each other, wondering.

"So?" Miner asked, "What difference does it make? There are tens of thousands of Cohanic men in the world. Why should it matter that much to him? Could it have been some kind of…hobby?"

"Shor removed the sample without going through procedures. And on a high holy day." Toad pointed out. "Why would he go to all that trouble for a trifle? Why the secrecy?"

"He's protecting somebody. A client."

"A very important client. So important that Shor is willing to do *aven* and break the law."

Miner spoke up. "Maybe Shor knew Chandos. Maybe he was doing him a favor by profiling his DNA for him against the Cohanic type, then saw the news and decided he wanted nothing further to do with him. So, he grabbed the sample and erased all references. Simple."

"And then casually went out to be murdered?" Ari asked sarcastically.

"Why should Shor's murder have *anything* to do with Chandos? It happened elsewhere. Different building, different crime. We should be looking at the robbery instead of this religious mumbo-jumbo. Isn't 99 percent of police work about following the money?"

All three were quiet for a moment. A draft of air from the building's useless cooling system ruffled the piles of evidence on the table. The laboratory clock hummed overhead.

Ari wondered for a moment if chasing these ancient ghosts could end up as a fatal detour. Maybe he and Toad were overcomplicating things. Maybe the nature of this war was totally clear, and the oblique connections they had made were simply fog. Maybe it was the same old story—not a new one after all.

"Well, if Miner's right, we've been going down a cul-de-sac. For argument's sake, let's leave off Chandos for a minute."

"Wait." All at once Miner was looking puzzled at the GeMscreen in his hand. "There's another message from Sara. It looks like Chandos also had MAO-A mutation." He spelled it out carefully and looked up at Ari, who shrugged.

"Let me see that," Toad asked for the GeM and examined it carefully. "MAO-A mutation pre-disposes a person to aggression and violence. The head of the institute told me that. It's their main research project right now."

"You're saying that killing might have come naturally to Chandos?" Ari was surprised. "I thought the man was a saint."

"And there is still the eyelash. And the inscription on the rings," Toad reminded them.

Miner sighed and took back the GeM. "I guess we won't be leaving off Chandos."

Magisterial Library of the Order of Malta, Via Condotti, Rome, 1000h

The sealed letter from Jean-Baptiste Mortimer was more than Maryse needed. The Director knew what was wanted before she asked for it and had prepared a small, elegant study for her use. A man known to her by reputation as a retired historian—and an eminent one—he closed the door silently behind him, seated her at the table, and opened a cabinet in the wall with an old-fashioned iron key. From this cabinet he drew a book, one of the most ornate she had ever seen, and carefully laid it on the table in front of her. The leather cover featured scrollwork illuminated with four figures—a lion, an ox, an eagle, and a winged angel.

The administrator smiled tensely and locked the door as he left. Maryse took out her magnifying glass and went directly to work. The book was old and broken-backed. She learned it had never been digitized and existed only in this form. Most of the writing had faded long ago. The further back in time, the more fluid it was, until it became nearly unreadable, but there were some fresher entries dating from the late nineteenth century and into the twentieth.

"Chandos...Chandos," she murmured, her nose and eyes itching at the veil of dust that hung over the book. She was grateful for the cotton gloves that protected her fingers from the old binding. The light was dim and the script too small to read easily, so after an hour or so of examining the book she leaned her head back against the chair and rubbed her head, eyes closed, thinking through the willowy descent charts she had been studying. There was no coherent story, but the fragments of Latin next to the illuminated names were beginning to come together for her.

HIC RICARDUS CORDIS LEONIS REX ANGLORUM…

King Richard the Lion Heart of England, who in 1193 quit the siege of the Temple of Solomon. …Robert de Sablé, Grand Master of the Soldiers of Christ and of the Temple of Solomon, his knight companion…

HIC DOM. GULIELMUS CARNUTENSIS…

Monseigneur William of Chartres, Grand Master of the Soldiers of Christ and of the Temple of Solomon, knight companion, 1210…

So, this Lord of Chartres was Grand Master while the Cathedral was under construction.

HIC DOM. IACOBIMUS MOL…

Monseigneur Jacques de Molay, Grand Master of the Soldiers of Christ and of the Temple of Solomon, who in 1293 paid homage in secret to King Edward as companion-in-arms as his predecessors had done. The last of the Grand Masters to do so. In 1314, burned at the stake at Paris falsely convicted of heresy…

Of course, the story of de Molay was well known. The execution of the last Grand Master of the Templars was a medieval scandal. She seemed to remember that someone had uncovered a document in the Vatican not many years ago, said to be a pardon from the Pope for Jacques de Molay. What she hadn't known was that the Grand Master had paid homage "in secret" to Edward of England as a knight companion. Another piece in the puzzle fell into place.

King Edward III and his son Edward the Black Prince, who in 1348 instituted the Most Noble Order of the Garter with twenty four knights companions…

Sir John Chandos of the Garter, companion to Edward the Black Prince and hero of the Hundred Years' War. Although as strategist of Poitiers he had won vast territories of France for the English King, he was honored even by his enemies as a peacemaker. He died in 1370 of battle wounds at the Chateau Mortemer. The Chronicles of Froissart said of him, "It was a great pity he was slain, for he was so wise and full of devices, he would have found some means of establishing a peace between France and England"…

She would have liked to photograph the pages, but they had politely taken her GeM from her. So she took a few notes. Genealogical lines continued for generations, occasionally diverted down unexpected channels by revolution, sterility, or murder.

She had not anticipated following so many royal lines. A dried-up sinecure passed over centuries from one old aristocratic lion to another, until the twentieth century brought things to a crisis point.

At last, she arrived at the end of an errant string of names that looked promising:

> *Major Sir John Chandos, KCB, DSO, MC, Royal Dragoons Guards.*
> *b. Derby, April 13, 1908, d. Beirut, May 31, 1987. Mentioned in*
> *dispatches from the Levant Campaign, 1941.*

That was all. A Knight of the Bath, a holder of the Distinguished Service Order, the Military Cross—a British officer of some accomplishment. This information she wrote down carefully. It was not as extensive as she had hoped, but the regiment and dates were useful. Here the line ended abruptly.

A page had been removed.

She contemplated the blank book for a moment, then grasped that she had gone as far as she could here. She reached for her GeM before realizing it was in the librarian's hands.

A few minutes later she was in the Via dei Condotti, walking quickly past the high-fashion shops toward the Spanish Steps. In one of the vitrines, a digital projection of a model danced, wearing a dress priced at 17,000 euros. Shopping all around her were women who looked as if they too had been electronically projected into the street, women wearing the blistering gold and orange of autumn, trailing perfumes, admiring their own airy skin in the window glass.

Maryse caught sight of herself. Her face looked red and Irish and irritated in the cold morning sun. So intent for so long on the spirit, she was startled by her flesh; so she walked faster toward the shade of a small café looking up at the famous Steps.

She ordered tea with lemon and concentrated on a GeMsearch, reading rapidly through screen after screen.

Royal Dragoons Guards. Took part in the 1936 peacekeeping mission to Palestine. Withdrawn in 1939, evacuated from Dunkirk, recommitted to the invasion of Germany. Thousands of names scrolled past. Every medal awarded, every soldier, every serving officer for the past century was listed.

But her search requests found no mention of Major Sir John Chandos of the Royal Dragoons. Not a whisper. She squinted at her notes again to make sure of the dates and the spellings. It was odd that there should be nothing—he had, after all, been a Knight of the Order of Malta as well.

She called up her electronic dossier of Peter Chandos. *Born in Besharri, Lebanon, 1985. Mother called Rafqa Chandos, father unknown. Attended Maronite schools. Ordained 2007.*

Abruptly, Maryse looked up at a cluster of priests passing the café, all young men in black cassocks and white bands, arguing about the forthcoming conclave. Their Italian was too loud and fast for her to follow. One of them caught her looking at him and grinned back at her, making a wry face—he was slender, his skin the smooth color of clay, his eyes a clear brown.

It was getting warm. She took off her coat and breathed in the air of the piazza, seeing all at once the swift life coursing around her.

Cohen Brothers, Yavne Street, Tel Aviv, 1220h

"Shimon Tempelman to see Ivan Luel."

The office administrator was a squinting young woman whose face glowed blue-green in the low light of the corridor. She was surrounded by cabinets that shone like steel. Her computer screen lit up the cosmetic glasses she wore; a really good—and younger—policeman might be able to read that screen in her eyes just by getting into an attentive conversation with her, Tempelman thought. He wondered how much easier it would be if he had proper eyesight. As Director of Security for the Technion University, he tried to keep to himself the reality that his eyes were fading.

"Mr. Luel will be with you directly. He's telephoning." She mirrored his English accent with one of her own—she was clearly one of the top form of secretaries. "He will have only a few minutes for you, Mr. Tempelman. He has an engagement with a client."

"Thank you. My business will take only a few minutes."

He looked around at the glassy walls and the fluid-looking art and thought about the sums of money that flowed invisibly through these law offices. Patent law, he knew, was a form of the old protection racket—you pay enough and no one will raid your claim. His old mother had wanted him to be a lawyer because she admired professional men who never got their hands dirty, unlike his father who had been a jeweler down a lane in South London. An open invitation to thieves, the old man's shop was a warren of caged bracelets and watches covered in carbon dust. He always complained that the inventory never moved. Well, it moved whenever the local villains paid a call, Tempelman chuckled to himself. He had learned a good deal from those men, his father's most faithful customers—enough to become a policeman smarter than most. Smart enough to stay out of actual police work and lead a comfortable life "protecting" other people's treasured secrets from the kind of villains he had known in his youth.

Now here he was again. It was his profession, he had to admit: one sinecure after another won by allowing important people just enough of a glimpse of his considerable intelligence to be satisfied of his reliability. He was too smart to require much—pettiness was the best defense against customer revolt, he had learned—and too smart to reveal much. He had found that people were more threatened by enigma than by certainty. He gained his ambassadorship by dropping hints to a junior Cabinet minister about some artworks trafficked through back channels out of Britain. Alas, the art was never traced. But he had done a creditable job, and the references he carried in his GeM were impeccable, ready to be beamed to the chief partner of the Tel Aviv office of Cohen Brothers.

In the past, he had often debated with himself about the kind of return he would accept for his investments. Sometimes it was a position, sometimes a promotion—with a few off-the-books benefits. Police officials were always looking for clever men and willing to provide extra incentives. In this case, however, there was no debate. He knew exactly what he wanted from Mr. Ivan Luel.

Just a small share. Nothing noticeable. Just enough to provide for a comfortable retirement on a Greek island with a nice golf course. Crete, perhaps. A minuscule share of what was coming—that was all he asked. Hardly worth discussing. He was not ambitious.

Ambition was for others. He knew he would have made a remarkably good policeman—but to what end? What was the return on good police work? The best police end up acclaimed and poor. Or acclaimed and dead. At least he had been smart enough to do the job without bypassing the opportunities that came his way. Most of the people he had worked with were hopeless. This lot investigating the murder of Emanuel Shor—they were either stupid or seriously distracted. Clearly the Levine woman was behind it all; she had cooked the patents so she could sell the rights to the highest bidder on the side. She had duped her uncle into letting a contract killer into the lab and had probably arranged for the instrument itself to be sold to yet another bidder. A dangerous game, the double cross, but common among greedy criminals who imagined they could play it and then escape the consequences.

He had done his research on Cohen Brothers and was reasonably sure she was playing solitary. She would go down for it tidily. Thus, everyone who deserved to would win—the old law firm would maintain its credibility, and he would be set up for life.

Still, there was the odd business of Shor's visit to his genetics lab just before the murder. Tempelman didn't like unexplained details. Shor had been utterly Orthodox: it was unthinkable that he would go to the office on the Sabbath. The old man was undoubtedly duped into opening the Nanotechnology Center, but why go to his own laboratory? To collect an electronic key? No, the key he used for the genetics center was coded for his brother's lab as well. There was the police theory that Shor had removed a DNA sample from the lab. Why would he break the Sabbath and a Holy Day for that, unless he were protecting someone?

Tempelman had pondered all of this while working on a hard turn in the fairway at the Caesarea golf club. Sometimes when the ball goes wrong into deep rough, he thought, it isn't worth the trouble to go looking for it. Was this one of those times? But he didn't have the leisure for worrying about it now—Catriel Levine was about to leave the country, Interpol had identified the eyelash, and he had to move quickly. Crete was calling.

At one time it had suited him to become Israeli rather than British. A certain deputy minister of state at Whitehall had encouraged him to emigrate "to prevent a serious hindrance to his career." He had played on the minister a good deal and had, unwisely, crossed a dangerous threshold with him. But the minister was Labour and had scruples, so Tempelman was allowed to leave Britain freely and even to carry the minister's highest recommendation for future employment. Israel was open to any Jewish person; there was need for good security people; and the climate was perfect for golf. Judaizing his name eased the way into the country.

But now there would be no need to stay. With enough money, he could find refuge on a small acreage overlooking the Mediterranean, maybe an olive orchard, perhaps a pool. He would have time to work on the flaws in his golf game.

Still, something was wrong. His thoughts kept returning to Shor, to the detour to the genetics lab. Shor was an odd man, it was true—obsessed with his Judaism, dressed day after day in the same sloppy white shirt with the cords of his *tallit* flying around him—but he had never broken any security protocols. Lots of the eccentrics at Technion had amused themselves at cat-and-mouse with Tempelman over security systems, playing graceless jokes he had come to expect. But never Shor. It wouldn't have occurred to him. The man had no joking in him. If he had been fooled into opening the Nanoelectronics lab, might he have been fooled into recovering something incriminating from his own lab? The Shin Bet wouldn't tell Tempelman whose DNA sample had gone missing—perhaps it was the killer's? No. If so, the case would have been closed by now. Anyway, he knew that the missing sample was from the Cohanic collection, hardly controversial in contrast to the much more sensitive MAO-A collection. Again, the return on such a remarkable investment seemed troublingly small to him. There was something unclear about all of this, something blocking his mental line of sight.

But whatever the complications might be, the man behind the office door would undoubtedly be glad to make a small investment of his own to satisfy Tempelman. That was simple enough and all he cared about. For Tempelman, the details of a case were interesting only as far as they hinted at some advantage to himself. After today, he would be totally focused on burying himself in superb isolation.

"Mr. Luel should finish soon," the woman with glasses said. "I'm taking my lunch now. When he rings, please go in." She stood and walked past him, the skin of her face and amazing long legs shining green in the glow of the windows. His eyes followed her out the door.

Just as she promised, after a few moments, a small buzzer sounded on the desk. Tempelman picked up his case and pushed open the office door.

The man in the chair was not Ivan Luel; he knew that straightaway.

Kibbutz En Gedi, Israel, 1220h

Ari missed the cold weather he had left behind in Europe; here he felt throttled by the heat. Jammed into his little car, he and Toad and Miner sped along the road between the Judean cliffs and the baking blue Dead Sea. They passed few vehicles on the road; the heat was too intense here at the lowest place on the planet.

Passing the Qumran historical site where the Dead Sea Scrolls had been taken out of pocky caves in the cliffside, they could see the unlikely green groves of En Gedi flowing over the escarpment overhead. Soon the kibbutz gate opened for them.

A welcome breeze met them as they got out of the car, and Ari reflected that this must be the only cool place in the whole country. The waterfalls of En Gedi looked shrunken, but a faint freshness hung over the hilltop. A male ibex, its horns curving nearly into its back, stood under a tree nearby watching them. I could live here, Ari thought; in this place, even kibbutz life might be all right.

Jules Halevy and his wife emerged from their tiny house to greet them. "Shalom, shalom, welcome!" Halevy repeated as he ushered the three policemen into the house. "Air-conditioned, you see." Halevy grinned at them and offered drinks, which the three men accepted thirstily. Ari introduced the others.

"Thank you for seeing us. I'm Inspector Davan; this is Mr. Kara and Mr. Sefardi." Both Halevys shook hands vigorously, smilingly. Although Toad had questioned them briefly several days before, they didn't seem to remember him.

Looking around, Ari noted that the walls were covered with woven hangings, some of an abstract design, others with bitmapped pictures of palm trees and bearded prophets. It was comfortably cool in the room, and Ari sat back to assess the host. Halevy was stout, short, and dressed in what looked like homemade clothes: a tunic with no shape and trousers in the tannish color of raw linen. Barefoot, he folded himself into a ball on a low sofa and rubbed rapidly at his brief beard the color of fog.

"Now, how can we help you?"

Toad and Miner looked bemused at Ari. It had been his idea to come here. Back in Miner's cellar, they had conceded to him that religion might have had something to do with the death of Emanuel Shor. Neither man was religious, and Miner was positively allergic to it. Toad's convictions, if there were any, had never been discussed.

"The inscription on the rings is the key," Ari had said.

"The key to what? You say it comes from a Bible verse, I can't remember what…"

"Until he comes whose right it is to reign," Toad had reminded them; then he had picked up a photo from the pile of evidence on Miner's table and displayed it to them. The model of the ancient Temple of Jerusalem that sat on the grounds of the Holyland Hotel. And, on the back of the photo, six Hebrew letters scrawled by hand:

עבאלהם

"Did you ever find out what these letters refer to?" Ari to Toad, who had shaken his head.

"I asked the brother and the niece—they said they didn't know. But now I wonder…"

Ari had run out of the room to his office, the other two behind him, to look in the big Hebrew Bible on his desk. It was hard to take the stairs and study his GeM at the same time, but he found the Latin Bible verse he had photographed in Chartres.

…DONEC VENIRET CUIUS EST IUDICIUM.

Then the same verse in Hebrew. At last he had found it, with Toad and Miner looking over his shoulder.

"A, B, A, L, H, M…" Ari breathed:

עַד־בֹּא אֲשֶׁר־לֹו הַמִּשְׁפָּט

Ad-bo asher-lo ha-mishpat

"It's Ezekiel. It's the same. 'Until he comes whose right it is'," Ari translated. "Let's go talk to Shor's friends."

So they had driven an hour from Jerusalem to the hills of En Gedi.

Ari held up the photo and read off the inscription.

"I'm afraid I can't help you there," Halevy said, smiling. Ari had been through this before. "It's a passage from Tanakh, you say? Echezquel?" An odd sort of accent.

Ari decided to take a back route. "What was your relationship with Emanuel Shor?"

"Long, long relationship. Friends for years now, with Emanuel and with his brother Nathan. My wife virtually raised his niece Catriel."

"How did you meet?"

"Common interest. We both came to the Holy Land about the same time, he from Russia, myself from France, both from Orthodox families. He escaped from the nasty Soviets, I escaped from a government high-rise outside of Paris. There was a small synagogue and a kosher food store, a little Jewish island in a sea of Muslims. I was always afraid, and so was my father. Afraid of the Muslims, the Arabs. They were moving in. So we moved out."

"And, you were saying, a common interest?"

"Oh, yes. Well. I went to university, the Technion, you know. I studied particle physics. I became a physicist. And Emanuel Shor was there too."

"He was biology, you were physics. The common interest?"

"No, no. Not that. The common interest was…Rachel here."

The woman seated in the corner smirked at this. She sat upright, both hands around a sweating glass of tea, her face like a tired peasant's. She was dressed in a light sheath that echoed the intense, athletic brown of her hands and feet. "It's not true. He likes to say that, but Emanuel Shor was not interested in me. He teased me; we were friends. No," she said, smiling painfully, straightening even more in her chair. "No. The common interest was the Temple."

"The Temple. You mean, the ancient Temple."

"Yes," she replied in a quiet, yielding voice. "We met Emanuel at meetings of the Mishmar, our group that is devoted to rebuilding the Temple. Without the Temple, we can never truly see the face of God, as Moses did. We can never welcome his Messiah."

"Let me explain," Halevy interrupted, smiling humorlessly at his wife. "We believe that the Messiah will not come until the Jewish nation rebuilds the Temple. It is preordained."

Rachel spoke again. "Every year, three times a year, we gather and march to the Temple Mount. At Passover, at Shavuot, and again during the High Holy Days. We do it to show God that we have not abandoned Him, that we remember the commandment. That there are still Jews who have not bowed to Baal. We know that it is not possible to build the Temple now with the Muslim shrines in its place. But we want to show God that we are willing, that we remember. And that is why we prepare."

"Prepare what?"

"Let me show you," she whispered, as if sharing a secret. The three policemen stood as Rachel went to a large covered wicker basket in the corner of the room. Jules Halevy stayed in his chair as if frozen.

She opened the basket and pulled out heavy, shapeless folds of fabric. At first Ari thought it was a set of curtains, but she held up a piece. It was a large tunic, creamy white, woven in a peculiar fishbone pattern. "Pure linen. As required by the Law."

"What is it?" Ari felt he shouldn't touch it.

"This is the robe of the *cohen gadol*—the High Priest of Israel. It is the robe he will wear when he enters the Holy of Holies on the great Day of Atonement, to cleanse all of Israel. When the Temple is rebuilt."

"Why do you have it here?"

She smiled and laid the robe carefully over the basket. "It took us years to construct it. I am a weaver—a docent at the National Museum. I show tourists how cloth was woven anciently. But even I couldn't reproduce this. We had to study and pray and try again and again. At last we built a loom big enough to do this work, and now…Well, we have paid the price."

"The price?"

"All things must be in readiness for the Messiah when he comes. We must prepare carefully in order to merit the blessing. Someone must do this." She leaned into the basket again. "See? Here? The priestly cap and the shoes," she said, holding up three amorphous pieces of the same linen fabric.

"It should be under guard," Toad spoke suddenly. Everyone turned in surprise to look at him, but that was all he had to say.

Rachel Halevy carefully folded the priest's wardrobe and returned it to the basket. "I keep it here. No one will take it. No one is interested in it," she sighed.

"I am very interested in it," Ari offered. "Mrs. Halevy, you mentioned the *cohen gadol*, the high priest of Israel. Was Emanuel Shor looking for such a person?"

"Looking for him?" She seemed surprised at the question. "Of course, he was looking for him. We all are. There can be no sacrifice in the Temple until an authentic *cohen*, a genuine descendant of Aharon ben-Amram, the brother of Moses, comes forward to take his rightful place."

"Did Emanuel Shor find him?"

It was Jules Halevy's turn. "Dr. Shor had a theory that he might be able to narrow down the genome of the original Aharonic family. Enough to isolate a pure haplotype. Then it would be a matter of locating an individual who fits. But I don't see what any of this has to do with his murder."

"It may have nothing to do with his murder, Dr. Halevy, but we have evidence that the Cohanim project might have a bearing."

"The Cohanim project?" Halevy blustered. "I thought Shor was killed over the lattice."

"The lattice?" Ari looked at his friends, who shrugged almost imperceptibly.

Halevy nearly choked. "You mean, you don't know..." He rolled his eyes and collapsed back into his chair.

"The thing that was stolen from Levinsky's lab, right?"

Halevy had no more to say on that subject. He simply stared at them. Ari turned again to his wife.

"Did Emanuel Shor find the *cohen gadol*?"

"I don't know." She pressed her lips together and looked away. "Candidly, I don't. In all honesty, I never understood him very well. He seemed to want everything we wanted, but then..."

Ari was silent, waiting for her to continue. Suddenly she cried out, as much to her husband as to him. "Emanuel Shor was a peaceful man! Peace was all he really wanted. He went through the remains of dead bodies like a healer, like a saint. Then for him die as he did—it was blasphemy. A curse. Everything has gone wrong…"

Sobbing, she left the room.

Libris Café, Yavne Street, Tel Aviv, 1230h

Catriel Levine, chief patent attorney for the Technion University, sat down at a table on the pavement and ordered tea. Even in the black suit she wore, the heat did not touch her. Catriel could not remember being warm: her bones always felt cold inside, and today her thin skin bristled easily in the drafts from the sea. She checked her silvery GeM. The job would be done soon, and then she could leave for the airport.

A circle of young men stood nearby, Orthodox Jews, the threads of the *tallit* hanging from their white shirts, arguing playfully about something: a point of Talmud, or maybe a bus schedule. She looked at their straight, thin backs and the coils of youthful beard and wondered again at the gulf between herself and the life of the street looping around her.

That life, which she had never wanted but still watched from a distance, was now closed to her firmly and finally. What she had done about her uncle had been necessary, although no court would ever see it that way. In Tanakh, a woman named Yael lured the destroyer of Israel into her tent and hammered an iron spike through his head while he slept. Was what she had done so different? Wasn't the Temple of God worth it? Why did she not feel the triumph of Yael? Why did she feel instead like King David after he contrived the death of Uriah—a calm despair at what she had done? And now she was about to add to the pain.

She stirred the tea and drank, longing for its warmth. This café was a refuge, an old bookstore with a tea bar, the kind of place where time meant little and there were books instead of blazing, blaring screens. A book lay open in front of her, one of those Russian novels that her uncle was always encouraging her to read. But today she hadn't read a word.

She needed to harden herself. The events of the next hour would all take place out of her sight, but she would be there anyway—and in her mind she would be there from now on. This task, although unforeseen, was necessary too. Tempelman had brought it on himself. He was a sly, distasteful character with no family. He would not be missed—indeed, the world would be better without him. Still, she hoped she would not be able to visualize it, or at worst that one day other visions would crowd it out. It would be soon. Already the picture the police had given her of her uncle's death was beginning to fade.

He had not suffered, they said. A bullet to the head, apparently—they had been vague about it. Quick and final. That night in her bathroom she had looked at herself in the mirror and, for an instant, saw a thing, not a person—a murderer. But then reason flowed over the impression. Emanuel Shor, the uncle she had loved all her life, a traitor. Not only that—he had tried to enlist her as well. For a long time, he said, his eye had been on her as his "disciple." When she began to understand his meaning, it immobilized her heart; her kindly uncle changed into a creature with hair over his eyes and lips, with a chemical odor and an expertise in deceit. He was just another treacherous man after all.

And men did not have hearts. Certainly not her father, Nathan Levinsky—nor her Uncle Emmanuel, contrary to what she had always believed. Even Jules Halevy, their closest friend, a blustering doctrinaire who couldn't distinguish between talk and action. She had been vague with him about the money and the Texan, and he had gone around with an inflated head ever since, delighting in the secret as if it had been his idea. And then one of the partners at Cohen Brothers had liked her—a tall, physically beautiful man named Ivan. For him, she had felt nothing but contempt. Ivan used the law miraculously, like an alchemist who could charm gold out of bare rock. He enriched himself almost effortlessly, and his methods were very useful in achieving her agreement with the Americans. But she could visualize herself manipulated by such a man and grew sick at the thought. When he looked at her, his eyes narrated the complex and tedious dance he would lead her through to its inevitable endpoint.

No, no one would best her. She would not be stopped—certainly not by a smarmy little blackmailing policeman like Shimon Tempelman.

Yet, as Talmud says, in the death of one man, all humankind dies.

Never mind. She would fly to Dallas, secure from this minor threat. Unpleasant, but necessary.

The Arab wasn't troubled; in fact, he seemed unsurprised, even serene about it, as if he had known it was coming. Strange how much she could tell about him, even though he had never shown his face to her. She had not even tried to figure out how he managed to leave his little signals unnoticed, how she would find a crumpled envelope or a sweet wrapper near her place at the café and suddenly see a pattern in it. She knew she had passed him on the street more than once, but did not know him from any other unshaven Palestinian sulking his way to work. All that she really wanted to know was that he guaranteed results—with finality.

She remembered when she put out feelers for such a person and was surprised at how quickly she found him. Once or twice she had the vague impression that he had been looking for her, not the other way round. He wanted to be known only as "the Arab," as if there were only one Arab in the world. He had persuaded her, although she had not thought she needed persuading, that violence was as neutral a thing as diplomacy—as useful for good ends as for evil ones. And, he insisted, he served only good ends.

They had first met at dusk on a bench in the terrace park overlooking the Baha'i monument in Haifa. She never saw his face, only his reflection in a darkened street lamp. He did not like electronic communication, he said; it was not ephemeral enough for him. There would be no phone calls, no messaging—only talks, in the shadows. He told her to watch for small wads of paper, which she should then destroy. Would there be a code of some kind, she asked? He laughed quietly and said she would understand.

And she did. Walking in the park as instructed on the afternoon of New Year, she found a rutted, crinkly note on that same bench. Unfolding it, she recognized the Hebrew word for "finished" in the creases of the paper. She would not forget the view of Haifa from that bench that afternoon. A hazy, hot October day, the park filled with picnickers, and her heart frozen.

There was more. Where to find the object, how to pay him, how to contact him again if she needed him. He was like an accommodating auto repairman, and the fees were reasonable.

The aftermath was as she had predicted. She had iced herself against the police and remained quiet, even in the face of the reptilian little man from Shin Bet who appeared to know what she was thinking. Far worse was the agony of her father. The only way to deal with her own heart was by candid refutation. Not murder but pre-emption; not a breaking of law but a carrying out of law. Her father would understand if only he were able to bear understanding.

Then Tempelman had come along with his sneering inferences. Again, she was surprised at the Arab's promptness answering her call—it was a little chilling. A paper napkin carelessly folded under a cup of hot tea. Only two questions: Who, by When. No Why. Again, a few whispers on a warm evening in the park. Closure guaranteed.

This item of business concluded, she would be able to board the plane leaving nothing pending. First to Paris, then the long flight to Texas. There would at last be the kind of power only unlimited money can buy. Catriel felt around in her bag and was reassured at the touch of the small GeM-like device she carried. Soon the world would be flooded with such devices, and soon after that the Temple would begin to rise on the holy mount. For this, she reasoned against reason, her uncle needed to die.

She looked at her little silver GeM clock and realized that it was past time. A signal would be waiting for her in the lavatory at Cohen Brothers. She had felt it unnecessary, but the man had insisted. He always closed his accounts, he said. Catriel paid for the tea, returned the book, and walked down this street of cafés and legal offices toward her chambers. People were scarce on the pavement because of the heat. It was mid-afternoon, but the city seemed ghostly, almost deserted. It was the High Holy Days.

Cohen Brothers—New York, London, Tel Aviv. She paused and touched the brass plate in the lobby of the high-rise—surprising herself, as she had never felt anything for the firm. Still, she would not be coming back. She had left a message for her father and for the Halevys; she would not miss the jowly old men, and she didn't believe they would miss her; only Rachel would weep a little. The cataract of money would astound them. Jules Halevy would figure out what to do with it eventually. Her father she would not be able to face. But maybe the day would come, after he was gone, when she could return to see new construction on the Temple Mount.

The lift opened into the cool glassy corridor that led to the chambers of Cohen Brothers. Catriel was relieved that everyone was at lunch and the office was quiet; she wanted to get in and out quickly. Pushing on the lavatory door, she glimpsed herself in the mirror.

It was then she realized she was not alone.

Cimitero degli Stranieri, Rome, 1200h

Only a few people were allowed into the cemetery for the committal of Monsignor Peter Chandos. It had rained intensely only minutes before, but the cold clouds opened and the sun turned the stone of the new tomb into a watery mirror. Maryse shaded her eyes. Three policemen in black uniforms and black gloves stood at a distance. The only other participants were the Commendatore of the Vatican Police, the Archpriest John Paul Stone, and Fatima Chandos, Peter's wife. The funeral car standing nearby was unmarked, the gates of the cemetery locked.

Officially, this ceremony was not taking place.

It was a small, shallow tomb of black stone, unnamed, the lid open to receive the coffin, which the policemen had lowered inside. Stone read the service in English so that Fatima would understand it. His cavernous American voice was made for a much larger congregation than this one:

Our brother Peter has gone to his rest…May the Lord now welcome him to the table of God's children in Heaven. With faith and hope in eternal life, let us assist him with our prayers. Let us pray to the Lord also for ourselves…

Maryse thought of the last funeral she had attended, and her throat constricted. Hundreds of people had come. Their shocked keening could be heard from the Priory Hall throughout the night—even after Maryse thought she had fallen asleep on her father's bed, she could hear it. A moan filled the Vale of Glendalough that she could not distinguish from the continuing echo in her mind of her own cry at discovering her father dead.

And such a death. She had brought it on him. If he had not been with her, if he had been at home where he should be, it would not have happened.

At her father's funeral, old boys from the Priory School brought their wives. People from town walked because of the long stream of parked cars along the lane, a persistent train of mourners in all shades of black, elderly veiled women from the farms, aged men who could hardly walk. They had all embraced her. Pure bad luck, they said, echoing the TV. Everyone said it. But it wasn't. Only David Kane had known how she felt; only he had the cold facts of what had really happened. Strangely, he was the only one who had given her any comfort at all.

He had arrived in his helicopter, landing a mile down the road; and she watched for him walking up the lane with the others, taller and still formidable. It was the only time she had ever seen him wearing black. And it was the only time he had ever put his arms around her.

She was no further use to him, she had known that. Even if the publicity had not spun out of control, the hum of shock in her mind made her powerless to carry on. There was no strength left.

The days that followed were like a drawn-out eclipse of the sun. She had not seen Glendalough in green since then. The house belonged to the school; the head's books were packed and donated to the school library; the only books she took were the ones her father had given her. And then she left. Every year on the anniversary of his death, she opened one of the brick-like art books just to look at it. She did not hear his voice or feel his presence, but she liked the pictures he had left her.

Our true home is in Heaven, and Jesus Christ whose return we long for will come from Heaven to save us...

Grant that our brother may sleep here in peace until you awaken him to glory, for you are the resurrection and the life. Then he will you see you face to face and in your light will see light...

As we bury here the body of our brother, deliver his soul from every bond of sin.

These words jarred her back to consciousness. A few paces away, Fatima Chandos stood like a pale, shuddering leaf between the sturdy figures of the Cardinal Archpriest and the Commendatore. Both seemed kind, able men, but Maryse knew that they were not really present to Fatima. She knew about the terrible, fateful tolling that Fatima heard in her imagining, about the shadow that stifled all her thoughts in her wakeful moments and suffocated her sleep.

Nevertheless, unlike Maryse, Fatima had something to awaken to in the morning, after the farewell. There would soon be a welcome. She was carrying the Monsignor's child.

You raised the dead to life; give to our brother eternal life.

"Lord, have mercy," Maryse whispered.

You promised Paradise to the repentant thief; bring Peter to the joys of Heaven.

"Lord, have mercy."

Our brother was washed in baptism and anointed with the Holy Spirit; give him fellowship with all your saints.

"Lord, have mercy."

He was nourished with your body and blood; grant him a place at the table in your heavenly kingdom.

"Lord, have mercy."

After the Our Father, Fatima knelt slowly and kissed the coffin. Her face was drawn and dry as she stood. Then the policemen came forward and slid the cover into place over the sarcophagus.

"In this corner he will not be noticed," Fatima said to Maryse, who had put an arm around the smaller woman. "That is a good thing."

"It'll remain unmarked for a while. We think that's best—at least until some of the excitement dies down," Stone responded. The Commendatore nodded.

"What will you do now?" Maryse asked Fatima.

"Go home. Go home and prepare for the child." A little smile trembled on her face, and then was gone. "He will be fatherless, like his own father."

"But he—or she—will have you," Maryse tried to comfort her.

"Yes. He will have only me."

They walked slowly together toward the gates with the men following.

"My mother left me when I was very young. My father was more than enough for me," Maryse said.

"Was he? Was he really?" Fatima looked up at her, searching. The face looked unnaturally old, tired but hopeful.

Maryse answered with finality. "Yes, he was. He fed me, he taught me, he inspired me. He did all of that."

"Then I can do all of that, too."

She had known Fatima Chandos only days. A simple heart, she thought. Fatima's touch warmed her hand, and she squeezed back.

"I can do it for both of us. We are at one now, you know. Peter and I. One flesh." Fatima stopped to look back toward the tomb, now lost in a small city of tombs. The noon had grayed over again, and the glassy wet marble of the hundreds of monuments looked dull again.

Maryse spoke softly. "I won't let it lie. If I can help it, there will be no stain on his memory."

Fatima gave her a doubtful smile. "I hope so. He was a good, good man. I know this if others don't. Every thought, every action of his was goodness. The last thing he did on the last morning of his life was for the children."

"That last thing he did?"

"Yes, the shipment. He wanted the Pope to bless the shipment before it left."

"What shipment?"

"Books, furniture, clothing, school uniforms for the children in my town. In Besharri."

Maryse looked questioningly at the men.

"For the Antonine school he attended as a boy. And for the orphanage," Stone clarified.

"In Lebanon."

"Yes. There were two vans." Stone saw that Maryse was suddenly intrigued. "It was a project of Peter's, to give something back to his home town. The Pope blessed the vans only a few minutes before the…the end."

Maryse made sure she understood. "Two vans blessed by the Pope, heading overland to Lebanon—and they left the piazza that morning?"

"Just so," Fatima responded, giving Maryse a querying look.

"I'm sorry." Her face flushed with shame; here she was, interrogating the widow at her husband's funeral.

But Fatima hadn't noticed. She was gazing back again toward the tomb of Peter Chandos.

Director's Office, Shin Bet Headquarters, Queen Helena Street, Jerusalem, 1445h

"What is the lattice?" Ari demanded to know.

He had requested a formal meeting with his superior. Tovah Kristall was mildly impressed at this; it had never happened before. Unlike some other operatives she detested who were forever submitting "formal requests" for this or that, Ari was the informal sort. She knew why he wanted this one. Everything would be recorded so that future reviewers would not be able to blame him for things he was ignorant of. So Alexa 3, the digital pyramid in the corner, now tracked their words.

Kristall looked into the dark brown eyes to gauge just how far off she could put him. In chess, patience was crucial. Her lips tensed. There was no leeway this time.

"Where did you hear of such a thing?" she snapped at him.

"From Jules Halevy," he threw it back at her.

She reached for her GeM and barked at it. "Come in here."

Her stick-thin assistant with the big eyes entered. "I want Jules Halevy's clearance revoked immediately. I also want him brought here for questioning. Now."

The assistant nodded and started out. "Not yet. Here." She scribbled a note and handed it to the little man, who read it and left.

Then she turned fiercely back to Ari, but he was not intimidated.

"I'm not cleared to tell you anything about it," she answered his gaze and lit a cigarette. She knew he hated smoke.

"Why don't you take a chance and tell me what I'm supposed to be investigating."

"You're the one who hangs from cliffs, not me."

"All right. For the record, this is the situation you and your superiors have put me into." He stood and paced the room, thinking for a moment, then speaking loudly for the computer's benefit.

"Here are the main results of our investigation. Emanuel Shor, Monsignor Peter Chandos, and the Pope himself all died the same day. Shor and

Chandos both wore finger rings of the same type with identical inscriptions, acronyms for a Biblical verse: '*Until He comes whose right it is to reign.*' Emanuel Shor also carried a photo of the ancient Temple of Jerusalem with the same verse scrawled on the back, only in Hebrew.

"Shor entered his own laboratory minutes before his death and removed all trace of a DNA sample belonging to someone named Chandos, a Cohanic sample that shows lineal descent from the high priests of ancient Israel who officiated in the Temple. The DNA of Peter Chandos is of a nearly pure Cohanic strain, and a hair matching that DNA profile was found at the Shor death scene. Finally, we know Shor, his brother and niece, and the Halevys were mixed up with an extremist group that wants to rebuild the Temple."

Ari looked straight at Kristall, who was staring back at him through a thick screen of smoke; he took a breath.

"So, I believe with reason that a religious fanatic—or a group of fanatics— are engaged in some kind of plot regarding the Temple Mount."

"With what object?"

"I don't know, but I believe it's connected with this 'lattice,' whatever it is. Unless you *tell* me what it is, I'm at a dead stop—and that's what I want on the record."

Kristall flicked ash into a paper coffee cup. The briefing room was blue with smoke. She looked up at Ari, considered him for a moment, and then said only, "Peculiar story."

"Jerusalem is a peculiar place."

"So you would connect a fairly straightforward technology theft with the assassination of the Pope?" She inhaled deeply from her cigarette. "That's just bizarre."

"Bizarre it may be, but straightforward it is not. There's more."

Kristall nodded for him to continue.

"Chandos and the Pope died in a remarkable room. It's called the Sancta Sanctorum, or Holy of Holies, said by Roman Catholics to be the holiest place on earth."

"Holy of Holies. The *Debir*? I thought that was a feature of Solomon's Temple. Where the Ark of the Covenant was kept?"

Ari was surprised she knew this; he had always thought of Kristall as totally nonreligious. Unconsciously, he had gone back to his natural tone of voice. "Apparently, Christians envy the Temple of Jerusalem. They've always wanted something like it, where God's presence dwells...thus, this Roman chapel. It's perfectly cubical, like the *Debir* in Solomon's Temple.

"Anyway, a good deal happened in there that morning. Someone wrapped Chandos' official red sash around his head—like Jewish priests did anciently with the scapegoat. Someone also collected Chandos' blood and used it to spatter the chapel altar—the same thing the high priest did in the Jewish Temple on Yom Kippur. And someone stole a valuable art object—a silver icon of Jesus of Nazareth that they believe represents God on earth."

Kristall shivered at this. She was enough of a Jew to abhor the idea of picturing any man as God. "Someone's been very busy. I hadn't heard any of it...but then the Vatican are professionals."

She inhaled smoke again. "It's intriguing. Still, the connection between Chandos and our Technion problem is tenuous. A stray eyelash that Shor himself might have dropped; after all, Chandos might have been a client of his lab, and he could recently have been in contact with him. A finger ring any number of people might wear—maybe just a souvenir from some religious shop."

Ari was looking at her skeptically—it wasn't like her to dismiss important evidence so readily. She went on:

"No, I can't tell you about that thing...that object. It's classified at the highest levels. But I can tell you that its value is beyond estimating, and worth whatever trouble the thieves go to screen themselves. It's just possible that all this hocus-pocus is meant to distract us long enough so they can get what they want."

"And what do they want?" Ari gave it back.

"Money. And loads of it. I admit it's a new angle, but ritual murder might be just the kind of angle they want us to pursue. In the meantime, here's another angle I want *you* to pursue." She beamed a message to him.

Eagle went off the grid at 1107. Last seen westbound Ramla checkpoint.

"Who's Eagle?"

"That's our designation for Nasir al-Ayoub. Somewhere outside Ramla, our key suspect disappeared a few hours ago. He could have gone to ground there. I want you to find him."

"The lattice?"

"You talk about that at your own peril. Our discussion is recorded per your request and regulation. And ended." The pyramid said goodbye politely and went to sleep.

Angry, Ari turned and left the building. Choking on smoke, he cursed her all the way to his car, then pulled out his GeM and rang Toad.

"You've been tracking an Eagle?"

"Eagle. Yes," Toad replied. "He's disappeared. Our people lost him at the Ramla checkpoint...found his car in a car park nearby."

"He must have known we were tailing him."

"Best to assume that. They're still looking, but it's been since before noon."

"What about satellite?" Ari asked.

"They never got a visual fix on him."

"Why 'Eagle'?"

"His name is Nasir—Arabic for eagle."

"Oh. Kristall wants me to take this one over. Got any ideas?"

"We followed him this morning, on foot through Damascus Gate to his house. After a few minutes he motored out and we traced him electronically this far. None of our taps give any indication of his agenda for today."

"He wouldn't be broadcasting it, would he? Any known contacts in Ramla? Women?"

"He is hooked up with a woman, a Dr. Adawi, who lives in Nablus."

"Wrong direction." Ari turned and saw something on the driver's seat of his car. It was a note. He picked it up and scanned it quickly.

"Um...Toad, something's come up. Keep me in the picture, will you? I'll ring you later."

Jaffa Gate, Old City, Jerusalem, 1545h

The last thing Ari expected to see in his life was Tovah Kristall playing the tourist. She stood just inside the Jaffa Gate wearing white capri pants and a blue-and-white striped shirt, sunglasses, and a sailor's hat. That skin the sun had rarely touched gleamed a fishy yellow. She was arguing with a street vendor over the price of a cheap alabaster chess set that she held with one hand while waving her cigarette with the other.

"Look, I collect chess sets. I could buy one of these from anybody in this town. There are a hundred places. But I chose you. I'll give you seventy-five euros."

"You're killing me. A hundred."

She looked up at Ari, who now stood smiling next to her. "Can you imagine? This cheap little man. I offered him seventy-five euros…five times what he paid for it." She turned back. "Keep it. I won't deal with a pirate."

Kristall grabbed Ari by the arm and led him away. The vendor followed, moaning "eighty…eighty…"

"Why don't we go up to the Wall now? I've wanted to do that for such a long time," she said a little too loudly. She headed for the entrance to a staircase nearby, where for a few *shekels* a tourist could mount the steps and walk about half the circumference of the Old City Wall.

"So now you're Mata Hari, the famous tourist?" he whispered.

"Come on."

At the ticket window he waited for her to pay, but she just looked at him; then he pulled his GeM from his pocket and paid both their admissions. Halfway up the steps, she stopped to cough. It was a noise like pebbles and sand in a cement mixer. He put his hand on her arm to steady her.

"It's all right, Davan." She shook it off and continued up the stairs.

From the Wall, they could see the roofs of the Old City dominated by the Dome of the Rock, rising into the air like the sun. They walked slowly in the heat along the parapet.

"I didn't know you were such a chess enthusiast."

"Everything is chess, Davan."

He paused. "I'm here, as you asked. You were quick getting here yourself. What other tricks do you do?"

"I like to play spy now and then, don't you? It reminds me how *fun* this job is."

"You like to get out into the field, get in touch with reality." It was quiet sarcasm.

"My friend, reality is back in that blue hellhole of mine." It was true; he had rarely seen her outside of the hazy blue-paneled situation room. But she was not convincing; he knew that she liked it there at the center of things.

They stopped in shade beneath a stone tower in a corner of the wall. The blinding gold Dome seemed near enough to touch. She turned and spoke quietly:

"You think there's some kind of plot concerning the Temple Mount."

Ari was surprised—he thought she had dismissed the idea. "Yes?"

She gazed again at the Dome. "I knew Shor was connected with a group that wants to build the Temple." Gnawing silently at her cigarette, she breathed smoke in and out while Ari waited for her to surface again from her thoughts. Then she started speaking, as if to herself.

"This mess is deep. Religious crazies. An itinerant Palestinian contractor. And a new kind of weapon...." She caught herself and looked at Ari. "I couldn't, or rather didn't want to, get into this after you forced me to record our conversation. In certain circles, it's best to dismiss this sort of thing."

She crushed her cigarette on the ground.

"Any threat to all that Vatican over there I take seriously," she said, pointing to the Temple Mount. "I take it very, very seriously. These people who want to rebuild Solomon's Temple—they are the worst enemies we have."

"Why do you say that?"

"Because, Davan, no two objects can occupy the same space at the same time. Look at it." She gazed again at the Dome. "The Mosque of Omar. Built thirteen centuries ago on the rock where Mohammed went up to Heaven. Go back thirteen centuries before that, and the Temple of Solomon stood on the same spot. Built on the rock where Jacob ben-Isaac laid his head and announced, Surely this is the House of God."

Again, Ari was startled at the things the irreligious Kristall knew about religion.

"Obviously, to build the Temple, you have to remove the Dome. And that brings catastrophe. The whole Muslim world would rise up like one person—one very *angry* person—and they're no longer the pitiful army our grandfathers routed sixty years ago. For decades they've looked for any excuse they can find to 'eradicate the Zionist Entity.' They mean it, Davan. I've looked in their faces.

"So the very last thing we want is a religious paranoid-delusional blowing up the Dome of the Rock to make way for some fantasy of a Temple. It's been tried before. One of my first cases. A man named Solomon Barda. A lunatic, an Israeli who lived in the States for a while, joined some mad cult, and came back here to start his own religion. A bizarre concoction of Judaism, Islam, and Christianity. He had splendid success—three followers as crazy as he was—who believed they could coax the Messiah down from Heaven by destroying the Dome. They had got hold of enough dynamite and C-4 and Semtex to turn it into rubble."

"What happened?" Ari asked.

"It was forty years ago. No, more than that." Kristall's voice had hardened. "We caught them in the act. They all went to prison. All but one...the one who escaped.

"And that's why we have paid to put up the best 24-hour security system on the planet around that Muslim shrine. 'Flaming Sword.' No one, nothing gets through it undetected. Weapons, explosives easily spotted. But a missile—that's something else. In August, we came awfully close to disaster. If the Synagogue hadn't burned..."

She trailed off again.

"If you think my idea is so laughable, why are you going on like this?" he asked her.

"No one's laughing, Davan. I brought you out here to talk it through with you because no one else wants to talk about it. Not the Prime Minister, not anyone. They all think we're invincible. I told him, there are two billion Muslims in the world, and the number is rising fast. There are five million Jews in this country, and the number is going down."

Ari interrupted her. "What's the new weapon?"

She was quiet for a moment, but took a rattling breath and went on as if she hadn't heard him. He knew then he would get no answer.

"To make things worse, there are all these fringe groups who are tired of waiting for the Messiah to come. They all believe the Temple has to be built first, so they want to speed things up a bit. To give God a nudge and force the Almighty's hand by blowing up the Dome."

"I've heard about all that. Do you think this Mishmar of Emanuel Shor's is involved in that sort of thing?"

"I'm not concerned about them. We've been watching them for years. As for Dr. Shor…well, never mind. They're not on my mind right now. It's this Palestinian, this Ayoub."

Ari frowned. "Why would a Muslim want to destroy the Dome?"

"Doesn't it occur to you that the best way to push Israel into the sea would be to get the Muslim world angry enough to attack us in force? What would motivate the combined armies and air forces of twenty Islamic countries to come at us all at once? What kind of an event might prompt ten million Muslim boys to wade through oceans of their own blood to get at us? The destruction of this Dome would do that.

"Davan, unlike you, I'm not a *sabra*. I wasn't born in this country. I didn't grow up with Hebrew on TV in a nice West Jerusalem neighborhood. I grew up in Ukraine, where we were *zhids*—the cause of everybody's problems. Everything bad in life was because of the *zhids*. You don't get paid enough? It's the *zhids*' fault. You lost your job? The *zhids* took it. Our neighbors hated us."

Ari had never heard Kristall talk like this.

"At school, in the marketplace…it didn't matter. It wasn't what they said or even did. It was how they looked at me. Sometimes I wished they *would* say something to me. I dreamed they would, so I could smash their faces.

"When my family wanted to leave, the government laid an 'emigration tax' on us, supposedly to get back the money they had spent 'educating' us. It took everything we had, but we left for *eretz* Israel, and for a while it did feel like a new world.

"It didn't take me long to find out that nothing had changed. We were still surrounded."

The air was pale with heat and the exhaust of the streets, the reflection of the dimming sun spreading like a reddish stain over the Dome. Below the Wall, the evening auto traffic was pressed into a noisy, slow-moving wedge. Ari and Kristall looked out over the Old City, its trees and dusty roofs quiet in contrast with the world outside the Wall. Kristall absently pulled out a cigarette, looked at it, and threw it back in her bag.

"I want you to take responsibility for this Ayoub," she said. "The Eagle is yours."

At that moment, her GeM sounded from the bag. "What is it?" she snapped a tiny receiver into her ear and then was listening intently. Somewhere, over the noise of the traffic, a peacock gave a faint call. At last she rang off and looked up at Ari.

"You were saying something earlier about 'ritual murder?' "

"If I remember right, you used that expression, not I."

"How did the Pope die?" she asked. "And Shor?"

"Commando-style—one shot to the head, three to the chest on a horizontal axis."

"The ceremony continues. You have two more. Died the same way, this afternoon. In an office tower in Tel Aviv.

"Who?"

"Shimon Tempelman and Catriel Levine."

French Room of the Adolphus Hotel, Dallas, Texas, 1200h

Four playful cherubs danced down from a blue heaven trailing a tinselwork of flowers. The ceilings and walls, bright and mellow at once, flowed with ribbons of colored light. Through an arch of gilded plaster, a window revealed a row of bank buildings across the street, but softened the traffic sounds from the abyss below.

"Roast venison with rosemary potatoes." Pastor Bob Jonas grinned decisively at the waiter, and then looked triumphantly around the table. "Six-shooter coffee with that," he added in a loud whisper.

"I'll have whatever Chef says," Lambert Sable dismissed the waiter.

"Yes, Mr. Sable," the waiter bobbed. "I'm sure he'll want to greet you himself."

"Tell him not to bother."

There was a tricky silence. Then Pastor Bob laughed. "Not very often a servant of the Lord gets to eat in a place like this. Might as well leverage the opportunity."

"You mean, to share a table with sinners?" the reporter asked.

"I don't see anything wrong with eating lunch with the Dallas Morning News. Jesus ate with the publicans and the sinners."

"Mr. Sable," the reporter asked, "we've been trying to get an interview with you for a long time about your support for Pastor Bob here. What made you agree to it now?"

In his inelegant suit, Sable looked utterly out of place in the restaurant. Nothing fit him quite right. His clothes were expensive, but the shapeless body couldn't fill them. He had never finished high school, a Marine at eighteen, a software billionaire at forty, never quite sure what other people were about. Two wives were unaccountably gone; his children errant and immersed somewhere in Las Vegas, addicted to this and that. But his mother had raised him on the Bible; it was the one thing he counted on. And now, he was hopeful, the long confusion of his life was over.

"Because people need to be warned. My board wanted me to stay away from you—you'll understand why—but there're only a few days left, and I've got a burden for all these people." He gestured around the room.

The reporter took stock of the other guests, mostly women branded with the Neiman-Marcus logo and murmuring over champagne and salads of tiny, expensive greens. She turned back to Sable.

"You're quite convinced, then."

"Oh, yes, the winding-up scene is only hours away now." The reporter was an attractive woman. Sable cursed his sweating habit; he felt his scalp dripping and dabbed it with his napkin. "So I said, to heck with the board, you media folks can help us get the word out before it's too damn late."

"Maybe you can help me understand why you feel this way."

"That's why I asked Pastor Bob to join us," Sable said anxiously. "He's got it all figured out. He can explain it a lot better than I can."

The pastor crossed her hand with his. "First of all, Olive, are you saved? Are you a Christian?"

"I'm Jewish."

Pastor Bob grinned at Sable. "We got work to do with this young lady, Lam."

The reporter explained. "The News sent me because they think I can take a more objective approach to this story. Maybe you could start from the beginning, just for me."

"From the beginning?" Pastor Bob glanced up at the pink cherubs overhead and appeared to say a little prayer. "Okay. Here goes. The Bible says that before the end of time, 'the Lord himself shall descend from Heaven with a shout, with the voice of the archangel, and with the trump of God: and the dead in Christ shall rise first: Then we which are alive and remain shall be caught up together with them in the clouds, to meet the Lord in the air.' We call this the Rapture of the Church."

"So all the Christians will, what, fly away? Rise up into the sky?"

"Something like that. All we know is that one moment you'll see us, and the next we'll be gone."

"Leaving people like me—Jews, non-Christians, nonbelievers—behind?"

"That's right. What follows will be seven years of tribulation. The devil will rule the earth, and God will pour out his wrath until he makes an end of all wickedness. At that point he'll establish his kingdom finally and forever."

"But how do you know this Rapture will take place on Monday?"

Pastor Bob put his palms together as if in prayer. "Simple mathematics. The Jews measured time in jubilees—periods of fifty years. The earth will only last six thousand years, or 120 jubilees. According to the ancient rabbis, the 120th jubilee will mark the final deliverance from all sin; now, Monday is the Jewish day of atonement and also the end of the 120th jubilee."

"But the earth is billions of years old. Where do you get this notion of six thousand years?"

"My dear, the *Bible* says the earth is only six thousand years old, and that's good enough for me. Just add up the genealogies in the Bible—it's as simple as that. Now the Lord doesn't want his saints to suffer through the seven years of tribulation, so up we go. Mr. Lambert Sable here and I are flying all the folks who want to go to Jerusalem to meet the Lord personally on Monday."

"So, what becomes of the people who are left behind?"

Pastor Bob stopped smiling and put both hands flat on the table as if he were going to push himself up. "Bible prophecies couldn't be clearer about that, ma'am—Daniel, Joel, Zechariah, Malachi, John the Revelator. And you need to hear it because it involves you and your people. After the Christians are gone, the Jews will come together at last and build the Third Temple right where the Dome of the Rock is in Jerusalem.

"This will infuriate the Muslims, who surround Israel on all four sides. The demolition of that Dome and the rebuilding of the Temple will ignite the greatest war the world has ever seen. Millions of Muslims will converge on Jerusalem, slaughtering every Jew they can find until the city is nothing but a cup of Jewish blood. It'll make the Holocaust pale by comparison.

"Only then, when his own crucifixion at the hands of the Jews is avenged, will Jesus Christ make his final appearance in glory."

After a difficult silence, the reporter turned to Sable. "So...you're buying this? And you've actually willed all of your property to...um..."

"I call it the Left-Behind Foundation," Sable answered. "It's to fund the evangelizing of all the people left in the world after the Rapture."

"So there is some hope for us?" she asked.

"Oh, yes. Many people will be saved during the Tribulation; I want my assets to go into helping them." Sable was eager.

"But it'd be oh, so much better for you not to have to face the Tribulation, dear lady. You need to come with us, Olive. You really do," Pastor Bob said, reaching across the table for her hands. She drew back.

The Pastor beamed at her and looked at his watch. "You've got about eighty hours to change your mind." Then he saw the waiter approaching and dropped his napkin in his lap. "And here comes my venison with rosemary potatoes."

"And certainly We created man of the essence of clay... Then We made the seed a clot... Then We made the clot a lump of flesh."

The green robes of the circle of brothers had long since dimmed into undifferentiated black. The only light came from a pale lamp the white-robed Sheikh used to read by, and the other three witnesses sat, all in white, at the remaining compass points. The sword lay on its tapestry on the ground before the Sheikh, who chanted from the book propped on his lap, stopping after every phrase, aching for breath.

"As for those who led the way, the first muhajirun... God is pleased with them... He has planted for them gardens streaming with running waters, where they shall have eternal life... This is the height of exaltation."

A barefoot young initiate, all in black, stood in the center of the circle. The Sheikh paused while the initiate cupped his hands in a fountain. He washed his hands, face, and feet, breathed in the water and washed his mouth. Then the circle of men arose to begin the night prayer.

As the prayers closed, the initiate remained on his knees, hands spread before him as if holding an offering of incense or cupping the light from the Tower. The Sheikh continued:

"We caused to grow gardens of palms and vines for you... And a tree that grows out of Mount Sinai that sheds oil."

One of the witnesses stood and opened a vial of olive oil, then slowly poured the oil over the head of the young man, who looked up at the sky, at the faint golden light reflected on the remains of the Tower, and shook his rich, wet, black hair. "You are anointed as the Black Stone is anointed, the cornerstone which fell from the garden of Heaven."

"We made a covenant with Adam, but he forgot it, and We found him lacking in faith. And when We said to the angels: 'Bow down before Adam,' they all bowed themselves down except the Shaitan, who refused.

" 'Adam,' We said, 'The Shaitan is an enemy to you... Let him not turn you out of Paradise and plunge you into affliction...

"But the Shaitan whispered to him, saying: 'Shall I show you the Tree of Immortal Life and an everlasting kingdom?' ...

"The man and his wife ate of its fruit, so that they saw their nakedness and covered themselves with leaves of the Garden. Thus did Adam disobey his Lord and go astray...

"Whoever you are, death will overtake you, though you are in lofty towers..."

The Sheikh stopped for breath. He leaned back and closed his eyes, his head surrounded with the stalks of white star flowers. It was not a large garden, but a very old one, set with low walls and flagstones, watched over by the medieval ruin of the White Tower and hemmed in by an olive grove. A single lemon tree near the fountain was about to bloom; the hot night had allowed a limp breeze with a trace of lemon flower.

The Sheikh sat up, rubbed his eyes, and continued: *"Then his Lord had mercy on him; He forgave him and rightly guided him...*

"Go hence," he said, *"and may your offspring be enemies to each other."*

Panting, the old man leaned forward and picked up the scimitar. The fiery lightning ran the length of the blade. He elevated the sword in both hands and went on reading:

"This is the Verse of the Sword—*When the sacred months are over, slay the idolaters wherever you find them. Hold them, besiege them, lie in ambush everywhere for them. If they repent and take to prayer and alms, let them go. God is forgiving and merciful...*

"How can there be a covenant between idolaters and God and His Apostle, except those with whom you made an agreement at the sacred mosque? So as long as they are true to you, be true to them; surely God loves those who carefully do their duty... God will not call you to account for what is futile in your oaths, but He will call you to account for your deliberate oaths."

The initiate bowed to the Sheikh, took up the sword in its tapestry, and then returned it to the Sheikh's outstretched hands.

"The sword is the symbol of the covenant you make on this gathering day to do your duty. Do you accept?"

The young man nodded, and the three witnesses stood and approached him. They unfolded a long white robe and dressed him in it and put a white turban on his head. The old man then laid over the robe an ancient green stole and said in a stern voice, "We invest you with the *khirqa*, the robe God gave Adam in the Garden of Eden. Wear it so you may find the sweetness of faith. We bind your head with the royal turban. Wear it as a crown in token of your throne and kingdom. Its virtue will accompany you to your grave."

Then the Sheikh set down the sword and toiled to his feet with the help of two brothers at his side. He took the initiate by his right hand. "This is the *bayat*, the taking of hands—whosoever gives his allegiance to this band of brothers gives it to God Himself. The Prophet established this order when he allowed his most trusted followers, the first *muhajirun*, to take his hand and commit themselves to infinite loyalty to God and His Messenger. It is the link in the chain that connects you to the light of the Prophet, peace be upon him. It connects you to the chain of all the prophets, Adam, Noah, Abraham, Moses, and Jesus."

He enfolded the young man in his arms, touching him with the hem of his own robe, saying, *"Those who are keepers of their covenants and who keep a guard on their prayers—these are they who are the heirs, who shall inherit the Paradise."*

"You are the true Son of the Eagle," he whispered in his ear. "May you be the last."

CHAPTER 2

FRIDAY, OCTOBER 8, 2027

Interrogation Room, Shin Bet Headquarters, Queen Helena Street, Jerusalem, 0030h

Jules Halevy sat on one side of the table. He rubbed his wet face and beard. "Doesn't the air-conditioning work in this building?"

"Not well," Kristall answered from the other side of the table. The interrogation room was buried in a labyrinth of hallways where no air from the outside could penetrate, and she was smoking with unusual energy. A glass of boiling hot coffee stood at her elbow. Kristall had no sensitivity to heat.

"So. Here we are. What can I help you with this time?" Halevy smiled without humor.

"We're grateful to you for coming tonight," Ari said from his perch on the corner of the table. He didn't like bringing people in for questioning in the middle of the night; he put himself in their place and resented the Service for it. Usually, he thought, it was unnecessary.

Kristall gave Ari a harsh look. "Dr. Halevy, one question. Tell us everything you can about the Mishmar." She sat back in her chair and exhaled smoke.

"One question, madam? One question? One question like that will take a long time to answer. Why don't you ask me another question...explain nuclear physics, for example?"

She took a long draught of coffee and put it down.

Halevy sighed and answered in a weighty French accent. "The Mishmar? We are patriots. We are a patriotic group. We are Zionists."

"Who want to build the Temple on Mount Zion."

"Yes, that is one of our aims."

"And how do you plan to carry out this aim of yours?"

"With the help of God." He answered her stare with his own.

"You don't contemplate helping him along with the job?"

"What do you mean?"

"I mean plotting to remove the Muslim shrines on the Temple Mount. To make God's job a little easier?"

Halevy reared back as if slapped, then began to laugh.

"You can giggle later. For the moment, I want you to answer my question," Kristall said in a ragged voice. Halevy stopped laughing.

"You take me from my house and my wife in the night. You bring me to this 'office,' this torture chamber. And then you demand my respect."

"Professor, I'm prepared to keep you from your house and your wife in this torture chamber, as you call it, for many more nights. As soon as I have what I need from you, you may go home."

Halevy grimaced. "No, no. Of course not. There is no such plot. Our group exists to keep the hope of the Temple alive. To prepare for the day."

"The day?"

"The day that Israel takes back what is rightfully ours. In 1967 our troops took the Temple Mount and then the secularists in the government turned it back to the Muslims. It was treason. So we march, we protest, we raise money, we prepare—but everything we do is legal, peaceful, within the law."

"So…what do you plan to do? Offer the Waqf enough money and they turn their *Haram al-Sharif* over to you?"

"We plan to continue what we've been doing. That's all."

"And so you've prepared priestly costumes, ritual items like the menorah and incense burners—all this just *in case* God decides to sweep the Muslim shrines off the Mount and give you a building license?"

"We propose to bring about the Temple through peaceful means."

"Such as? How do you propose to 'peacefully' erase the Dome of the Rock?"

Halevy was tired. They both knew there was no good answer to the question, so he stared at her impatiently.

Kristall reached for an evidence bag and pulled out Shor's photograph of the Temple model. "And you know nothing about this writing?"

"Nothing at all, as I told your friend here earlier."

"What do you know about the gold ring Emanuel Shor wore?"

"It was a gold ring. What is there to know?"

"What does the name 'Chandos' mean to you?"

"You're joking. Chandos? You mean the man who killed the Pope? Who *doesn't* know that name?"

"Why was Emanuel Shor in the nanotechnology center on Sabbath? On a holy day?"

"I've asked myself that question a thousand times. And so have your people."

"Why did Shor have a red circuit on his GeM?"

"What is a 'red circuit'?"

Kristall beamed a photo of Nasir al-Ayoub from her GeM onto the table. "This man...do you recognize him?"

Halevy barely looked at it and shook his head.

"Dr. Halevy, you are a dry fountain."

"Then may I go?" He stood; his shapeless linen clothes were creased with sweat.

"Not yet. I have one more question... Now you may explain nuclear physics."

Irritated, Halevy arose and went to the door. It was locked.

"I'm quite serious, Dr. Halevy. I want you to explain to the officer here about the lattice," she indicated Ari.

Halevy sighed. "I suppose you have cleared this."

"Inspector Davan is now on the need-to-know list."

Ari looked up in surprise; Kristall had changed her mind. But he leaned forward intently.

"All right, Inspector. If it will speed things up." Halevy stood by the door, looked at Ari with contempt, and began speaking rapidly. "The lattice is a nanoelectronic device composed of quantum dots wired in cadence to each other within a silicon matrix..."

"We can stay here all night, Dr. Halevy. Some people think I live here, and it's very nearly true," Kristall said.

Halevy sank back into his chair and closed his eyes for a moment. "How do I explain this to a dolt?" He was quiet; then he seemed to gain new energy.

"Levinsky and I became interested years ago in what are called 'designer atoms.' The idea is this: an atom is made up of a nucleus of protons and neutrons surrounded by orbiting electrons. The number of these particles dictates the kind of atom it is. The lowest number of electrons occurring in a natural element is one—hydrogen. The maximum number that occurs in nature is 92—uranium. Atoms that heavy are unstable and give off particles in the form of radiation.

"Suppose, however, that you could trick electrons into orbiting an artificial nucleus. Then by adding and taking away electrons you could change any element into any other element—like changing lead to gold and back again.

"Such an artificial nucleus is called a quantum dot; we can create it in the laboratory." Halevy stood. "And that's what we call a 'designer atom.' "

He held his hands up to the bare lamp hanging from the ceiling and laced his fingers together. A cross-hatched shadow fell on the table. "Now picture a lattice made of silicon threads, woven like a basket, with many of these designer atoms embedded in the spaces between the threads. You flood the lattice with, let's say, seventy-nine electrons per dot. The result?"

Ari answered immediately. "Gold."

Halevy was delighted. "You know! You're not such a dolt after all." He wiggled his crossed fingers and laughed. "Gold! Number seventy-nine on the periodic table of elements. The lattice turns to gold! You can pump electrons in and out of the lattice, changing the number at will many times a second."

"You mean, you can turn silicon into gold?"

"Or any other element you wish, although you'd be wise to create the ambient temperature the element needs to remain solid—hydrogen, for example, dissipates into a gas at room temperature."

"Which is why Levinsky's laboratory is kept freezing."

"Exactly. Certain elements such as phosphorus are extremely unstable, even explosive, if it gets too warm."

"And you've built a lattice like this."

"Just a few of them so far."

Ari was impressed. "It's fantastic. The value of it..."

"Is beyond calculating. We can create elements undreamed of. Superconducting materials. Batteries that last a decade. Solar cells thousands of times more efficient than the ones we have now. But we didn't build the lattice to make ourselves rich. Catriel Levine has ironclad patents—the rights belong to Technion...and..."

"To the Mishmar," Kristall interrupted. "Enough money to persuade a good many people in high places to, let us say, align themselves with your way of thinking?"

"The Jewish people need the Temple, and we will do whatever we can—legally—to bring it about."

Kristall shook her head wearily. "Dr. Halevy, the Israeli people don't want the Temple. Ninety percent of us are secular. All we ask for is a little peace, to live our own lives and let our neighbors live theirs. People like you disturb our peace. You scratch at old wounds until they bleed and turn septic. In August somebody fired a rocket at Al-Aqsa and nearly brought the wrath of twenty Islamic nations down on us."

"Others would come to our aid. America."

"Doctor, now you're making *me* laugh."

"And God."

Kristall put out her cigarette and stood. She was tired of this. She whispered to her GeM and the electronic lock on the door released itself with a quick hum. "Dr. Halevy, I sincerely hope your intellectual property is as secure as you think. Today there was a break-in at the offices of your solicitors in

Tel Aviv. Two people were murdered, one of them the superintendent of security at Technion."

"Security? You don't mean Tempelman?" Halevy murmured.

"I do. The other victim was Levinsky's daughter, Catriel Levine." Kristall fingered another cigarette and walked out. "Take him upstairs, Davan," she called over her shoulder. "I want to talk to him again in the morning."

Halevy suddenly looked a hundred years old. His eyes shrank in his head, his hands and legs shook as he crumpled to the floor, and a high wail rose softly and hung in the air.

Ari watched with revulsion as Tovah Kristall disappeared down the corridor.

Palace of Sant'Uffizio, Vatican City, 0530h

The cobbled square below his window was unusually dark. Night lasted longer now, and the lamps that ordinarily lit up the City were kept low in mourning for the dead Pope. Cardinal Tyrell stood at the window and watched for his visitors.

As he waited, he prayed. There can be no compromise with evil, he said to God. Evil can be stopped. Noah stopped it, Moses stopped the Midianites, Elias stopped the priests of Baal. The Lord Himself cast out evil spirits. He can cast evil from the Church. He sent Peter Chandos to remove Zacharias; He must now finish His work.

Two figures emerged from the darkness and sounded the bell. Tyrell called for them to be let in.

Shedding his cloak, Cardinal Estades came in moaning about the early hour and his arthritic legs. "This day will be far too long. The funeral goes on for eternity, which is fitting, I suppose. And then if the conclave begins immediately…"

"The conclave will not begin until the end of canonical mourning," said John Paul Stone, the cardinal archpriest, who stood like a giant in the entryway. He stepped forward, removed his cloak and laid it carefully down, sitting uninvited in an armchair. He sat still and rocklike.

"Is there coffee?" Estades asked. Tyrell rang for coffee to be brought, and Estades leaned back with relief on the settee. "Well. Here we are, Leo, as you asked. Father John Paul has a busy day ahead, you know."

"I know. We all have a busy day ahead."

"I need to see to final preparations," Stone said. "It's not very convenient, so let's get to business."

Tyrell looked at Stone with distaste and spoke abruptly. "I want your assurance that you won't oppose the calling of an extraordinary conclave immediately after the funeral."

Stone realized that, despite the bullnecked strength of the man, Tyrell was deeply exhausted. He knew he had been holding telecons day and night with cardinals in South America and the Far East, lobbying hard with the conservatives for the election.

"The camerlengo's office won't permit it."

Tyrell snorted. "The camerlengo will do as we tell him."

Stone didn't want the conclave rushed; he needed time to put the opposition case to these same cardinals.

"At any rate, I'll give you no such assurance. Not until after a decent interval of mourning for Pope Zacharias."

Tyrell braced himself with a swallow of coffee. "Let's be realistic, Father. You know that a dozen Latin American bishops are ready to leave the Church. The same is happening in Africa and China, Japan, Korea, the Philippines. The archbishop in Manila is refusing to ordain women, and so is Nunes in Sao Paulo."

"If they disobey the Pope, they can be replaced," Stone shrugged at this.

"Replaced with whom? People who think as you do? You have no constituency—just empty cathedrals in Europe and the coastal archbishoprics in the USA"

"Being right is enough. Justice and fairness are enough. The Holy Spirit assists the conclave—that's enough of a constituency for me."

"And the Holy Spirit assists perversion and sodomy in the Church? In the priesthood itself?"

"*In Salutem Ecclesiam*. The encyclical…"

"There will be other encyclicals," Tyrell snapped.

"You can't switch these things on and off like a light bulb. The magisterium of the Church is at stake."

"Brothers," Estades interrupted. "If there is a conclave on Monday or not, it isn't the end of the world. What are a few weeks in a two-thousand-year-old Church?"

It could be the end of that Church, thought Tyrell. He was desperate to move now; he calculated having a bare majority in the Council, but many were wavering. Once the Cardinal Archpriest and the energetic young men around him began their offensive, a few weeks could make all the difference. He sat down heavily in his vast swivel chair.

" 'Brother.' It's a good word," Tyrell intoned. "We are brothers, you and I, priests of Christ after all. So, Brother Stone, I would really like to know why…I would really like to understand…why you are so eager to open the Holy Sacraments, even the priesthood itself, to unconfessed sinners. To people who practice the most abominable perversions."

Stone smiled and shook his head. "It's very simple. I don't consider them sinners. God has made them what they are, and they are my brothers, too."

"For two thousand years…before that, from Sinai, from the angels who destroyed Sodom, God has decreed death as the penalty for these sins."

"It was the times, Brother Tyrell. At Sinai, death was decreed for many things—for marrying a Gentile woman, for adultery…Would you have all adulterous Catholics stoned in the streets?"

"They choose death. God administers it."

"But God loves them…"

Tyrell rose from his chair. " 'God will not withhold justice even from those he loves.' Saint Augustine."

" 'The anguish in our neighbor's soul transcends all doctrines. All that we do is a means to an end, but love is an end in itself, because God is love.' Saint *Edith* Stein."

Estades interrupted again. "Stop. All morning you will throw quotations at each other like rocks. Leo, I don't know why you asked me here, except that I'm reminded of the old steers my father kept among the bulls to calm them so they wouldn't gore each other. I suppose I'm the old steer, so I'll do my work."

"Manolo, you are the perceptive one, as usual." Tyrell put his fingers to his forehead and rubbed hard. He looked at Stone. "As senior man, I will put the question to the others directly the funeral is over."

"Then there will be a breach between us. A breach in the Church."

"It's happened before," Tyrell waved them away.

Police Headquarters, Dizengof Street, Tel Aviv, 0630h

"Apparently they've embedded this lattice into a GeMscreen. You can turn it into whatever element you want, even some that have never been heard of before. They have an app that turns the screen into a high-definition hologram projector. Another one turns it into a 99-percent efficient solar cell, so you can set your GeM in the sun for five minutes and not charge it again for years."

They were both waiting outside a dingy conference room for Kristall to call for them. Miner was fascinated by the rough sketch Ari was making on a notepad. "And you say it could be made into a weapon?"

"That's what Halevy said, but he wasn't very forthcoming about it. I got an idea he wasn't sure what to say."

"How could he be?" Toad interjected. "If the thing can be turned into any one of an infinite number of elements, he could never know exactly what it was capable of."

Ari had explained everything to Miner; Kristall would have known he wouldn't withhold anything from his team.

"And now everything points to the Arab... I mean, the 'Eagle'?" Miner asked.

"He's the intersection. The eyelash, the murder scenes. And now we've tracked him here."

"When did he surface? I thought they lost him yesterday."

Ari laughed. "We had a hundred people looking for him from Ramla to the coast. Then the airline rang this morning to tell us 'our man' had just booked a flight to Rome on the Internet."

"In his own name?"

"Right. He's planning to waltz onto an Alitalia flight at 0800 just as cool as you please."

"I suppose it's really him."

"Oh, yes. He's already at the airport—arrived two hours early, like a good customer. Either he doesn't know that we're onto him or doesn't care. Plus, he's flying business class."

Miner was puzzled. "Are we going to let him go?"

"Yes. Kristall wants me to stay with him. She's intrigued."

"So...any idea why the two vic's in Tel Aviv?"

"The woman was involved in patenting the thing... There's so much at stake here that the killer might have wanted her out of the way, maybe to make it easier to steal the rights. Tempelman...I don't know. He was shady. Obviously he was involved somehow."

"What's in Rome?"

"Nobody knows. Maybe Eagle's going there to hand off that very special GeM to somebody?"

Miner brightened up. "That makes sense. No better way to smuggle the, um, item out of the country than as a perfectly ordinary GeM."

"That's Kristall's way of thinking."

"So you'll be on the flight too."

"Yes, and I've got something for you to do while I'm away."

Toad stood in a corner of the cramped morgue and watched as the examiner measured the gaps between the wounds on the body of Catriel Levine. The long white corpse was punctured once in the forehead and three times in the chest. If the three points were connected, they would form a straight line. The examiner had already measured a similar pattern on the body of Shimon Tempelman, which lay covered on an adjacent table.

Toad felt cold inside and out. He was used to the role of observer. Sometimes he felt as if he were not arms and legs and head, but just eyes, looking out at a world that he was not spatially a part of. He put no trust in people's descriptions of things until he saw them himself. Now he saw under the lights the dead body of Catriel Levine and submitted to a reality he had only imagined. For an instant he felt like he was drowning—a sudden burning in his eyes, a contracting throat. She'd been remote, contemptuous; still, it felt like his own life had been lost.

The examiner covered the body and beamed his data to Toad. All the statistics of Catriel Levine's mortality poured digitally into his GeM; he stared at the image on the screen and wondered why it had such power over him. He thanked the examiner and left for the briefing.

He went into a choked little conference room as a group of city police came out, grumbling about Shin Bet. GeM projections played on the walls: Kristall, Ari, and Miner were showing a schematic of the Cohen Brothers offices to a big white-haired man in an elegant suit. Another man Toad did not recognize sat looking desolate in a chair too small for him while two impassive Shin Bet operatives stood behind him.

Ari pointed at the wall and turned to the seated man. "When exactly did you leave your office for lunch?"

"I don't know exactly. Do you know exactly when you had *your* lunch yesterday?" He was tall and trim with a grand chin, but the little chair made him look like a gangly child. He was also very unhappy.

Ari gave him a cool stare. "Then approximately."

The man sighed and fingered his tie. "It's hot in here."

"It's hot everywhere."

"I left the office about 1130, actually. I had a lunch meeting with a client and was to meet with this man Tempelman at 1230, but my paging service rang to tell me he'd be late, so I stayed for another drink. Look, the police know all this."

Kristall turned to one of the agents, who reported: "We've got onto the paging service. The call to them came from a woman—not Tempelman's voice."

"I don't know who it could have been," the tall man said. "My assistant takes her holiday every year at this time, so I've been handling my own appointments."

"We've vacuumed," said the agent, "so we have some leads."

Kristall was impatient. "We're done with you for now." The two agents tapped the tall man on the shoulder and escorted him to the door. He turned. His face was reddening.

"Cate was my whole life. You find who murdered her." He trembled. "You find him."

"We'll do our best," Ari responded.

Toad leaned into Miner's ear. "Who was that?"

"His name is Ivan Luel. He was the dead woman's boss."

In his mind, Toad saw Catriel's body again and felt the stab of the bullets. He had never before connected with any human being, even in his imagination. This pain was new to him.

"Sefardi, tell us about the profile of the shooter," Kristall asked.

Startled, Toad fumbled with his GeM. All at once an image of the perforated head and chest of Shimon Tempelman covered the wall. Toad manipulated the GeM and a luminous gridwork appeared over the shot pattern, the wounds describing a nearly perfect triangle.

He then superimposed a similar image of Emanuel Shor's body, maneuvering the two images until they fell into line with each other. The distance between the gunshot wounds was virtually identical on both bodies. Finally, a bleak white picture of Catriel Levine overlay the other two, revealing the same pattern again. Toad looked down and said flatly, "It's possible we're dealing with the same shooter in all three cases."

"What does the pattern indicate to you, Sefardi?"

"It's common enough." He paused, then coughed repeatedly, his hand over his eyes. Ari and Miner looked at each other questioningly, but Toad went on. "Anyone trained properly knows how to stop a subject this way—three shots across the mid-chest are instantly disabling. The shot in the head ensures a kill. It's typical of IDF training, commando training, that sort of thing. Uncommonly good shooter, though."

"And the gun?"

"Same nine-millimeter configuration, although the lab hasn't said it's the same weapon."

"A remarkable shot. Astonishingly accurate," the white-haired man muttered to himself, as if in admiration. A little louder, he asked, "Does this shooter fit profiles you've got?"

"We're trying to get service records from the PA on Eagle," Kristall said. "As backup, we're looking through our own database of sharpshooters."

"Where was Eagle during the shooting?"

"We don't know, unfortunately. He went off our grid yesterday around midday and didn't surface till this morning. But he disappeared near Ramla, which isn't far from here."

"Then you have no fix on this case except the possibility of Eagle?"

"For now, that's true," Kristall sniffed at the white-haired man. "But they've vacuumed thoroughly; I imagine the scene will be giving up some interesting data shortly. Meanwhile, Davan here will be keeping Eagle company on his jaunt to Rome."

"Your vacuum cleaners might not be equal to this suspect." The big man rose and gave Ari a sharp look. "As it happens, I'm flying to Rome myself. For the papal funeral. May I drop you at the airport? I have my own transport, but I can take you to your terminal."

"That'd be very welcome, thanks."

Everyone but Toad left the conference room. He opened his GeM and stared once more at the three corpses digitally overlain on the wall, at the black holes in the bare white skin. His throat cramped again. Coughing hard, he shook himself as if trying to stay awake in the middle of a long and desolate night.

Maryse reached for the GeM on the night table and shut off the alarm. Again, she watched the cornices of the ceiling coming into focus as she remembered where she was.

She had dreamed of Glendalough, of the velvet-green valley and the rocks rising on all sides. She was a girl again, and there on the cliff a boy was climbing. He was not from the glen; of course, rock climbers came from everywhere to try the cliffs. It was that strange April when the weather turned hot, and she escaped the heat in a little cove of rock with a spring not far from the Priory. Trees like cascading robes veiled the cove so that she could see the valley without being seen. From here, Glendalough looked as it must have a thousand years before—the lake, the enigmatic forest pierced by the gray tower of the monastery.

It was said that St. Kevin himself had built the tower. A prince of Leinster, sick of the world at only fifteen, he had abandoned his lover, cast off his titles, and put on the hair cloak of a pilgrim. Wandering Ireland in search of a solitary place where he could devote himself utterly to finding God, he had come to this glen, to a cave in the cliff where, like St. Bruno, he lived in deep contemplation for seven years. He was tortured by the memory of Kathleen, the princess he had escaped, and her eyes of unholy blue. Still he sought his peace in the cave, waiting for the Lord, his only company the squirrels and birds who fed him with berries and fish from the vale below.

Word of this miracle spread and eventually reached Kathleen, who made her way to the cave and found him asleep. Quietly, she watched him, weeping, until the rising light woke him. At the sight of her eyes he struck out, flinging her from the rock and into the lake far below.

In Maryse's dream, she saw a boy mounting up to Kevin's cave. Even from far away, she could make out the brown cords of his arms and legs, the ribbons of muscle in his brown back, as he wrenched himself straight up the cliff. From her cove she had seen many climbers, admiring their daring—she herself did not deal well with heights—but most of them clambered slowly and deliberately, patiently gauging each handhold. This boy moved like a tawny animal, as if hunting the creatures that lived in the cracks of the mountain.

When he arrived at the cave, he sat for nearly an hour on a rock under the overhang, cross-legged, motionless, while Maryse gazed at him, frozen in fascination. He was grand, she thought—monumentally alone, like a young king on his throne.

It was a frequent dream. She wondered if she had really seen the boy climber at some time, or only imagined him. She didn't know why the dream kept returning, why that distant face she had never clearly seen stirred her in her sleep, and why tonight she had dreamed it again and again.

Ari Davan told her he was a rock climber. Perhaps that was it. But she also remembered having the dream at the Carmelite house. The boy on the cliff long ago—he was the first that had awakened something in her. She had never seen him but once, and from so far away.

She wondered what Ari was doing, what his abrupt return home meant. Something had occurred to him there on the cathedral's north porch, below the statue of St. Peter. They had worked out much more than either could have done separately. Now that she knew the stakes were so high, she resented his running off without a word, as if she were no longer needed.

The men she had known lived alone in those dark hollows. They felt they had to put everything right, to mend all uncertainties, to repair the broken world, all by themselves. Men were obsessed with finding answers—too often with war as the ultimate answer.

She remembered a morning when her father took her on a long walk—so long they hadn't returned until the evening. Unlike Kane's battles with the forest of Glendalough, Ian Mandelyn's walks were contemplative, slow, centered on ruins like the remains of the old chapels that had grown up around the cult of St. Kevin and then crumbled. They would take a lane like a cleft in the crowded trees and there, buried in the moss, would be an old foundation, the worn stones thrown down by the Danes or the English or just storm and time. Her father loved sketching the ruins, and she would play on them until it was time to go home.

The longest walk was soon after her mother left them, and she sensed that morning's walk would be different.

After several hours, they had stopped by the road that entered the vale of Glendalough and, after some poking through the hedges, her father found a slab of stone with a curious engraving—a labyrinth of concentric circles. He told her that it was very old, much older than the remains of St. Kevin's chapels, and that its meaning had long been forgotten; but he thought it might have something to do with the planets navigating their circles through the sky, with puzzlement over their motiveless turning, and with the need to understand the end from the beginning. Whoever carved the labyrinth, he had said, had no more answers than we do—only faith in the order of the heavens.

The light grew, bringing her back to the present, and soon she could hear the scramble of hotel people in the corridor outside her room, bringing breakfast to the guests. It was the day of the Pope's funeral; the hotel was filled with dignitaries, and they were all taking their coffee and rolls at the same time. The smell of food got her out of bed.

She dressed and went down to the breakfast room, where she worked over her report on the GeM. She wanted to be ready for Kane when he arrived. Photos of the scene that morning when the Pope blessed the consignment that was heading to Lebanon. Close-ups of the white vans. Bills of lading filed with the Vatican charities office and signed by Chandos. Emails from the Antonine school in Besharri. The transcript of a phone conversation with the headmaster.

At length, she snapped the lid shut and sat back to drink her coffee. There was more she wanted to discuss with Kane. More than an icon had been taken from the Sancta Sanctorum.

The glory of the Lord departed from the house because of the men that devise mischief, and give wicked counsel in the city.

The city is the cauldron…it shall be laid waste, the altars made desolate. Desolation and war shall sweep the land of Israel.

Near Ben Gurion International Airport, Israel, 0730h

In the swift, silent car, seated next to the President of Interpol, Ari tried to quell his nerves by focusing on the job—after all, the man was only giving him a friendly lift.

"That's a heavy coat," Kane observed, smiling. Ari had determined he wouldn't freeze in the European cold this time, and carried his new anorak with him.

"It's like winter in Rome."

"Yes, unseasonably cold."

So Ari got to talk about the weather with David Kane, and that was all. He could see the Airport City around them; soon, he would be on his way. But then Kane spoke:

"Davan, is it? I understand you connected with one of our agents in Rome this week. Mandelyn?"

"Yes."

"What did you think of her?"

"She seemed very knowledgeable, very avid to find the item she was looking for."

"So she let you in on that, did she?"

Ari wasn't sure, but perhaps he had just made trouble for Maryse. However, Kane was still smiling, his eyes on the outline of the driver beyond the dark glass wall in front of him.

"It's important to our case, too," Ari replied. "We need to know all we can about the connection between our murders and the...events in Rome."

"Naturally. It's an odd connection—those rings, that DNA business. What do you make of it? Any theories?"

He thought about opening up his theory to Kane, but it would take time—and it was presumptuous. Kristall wouldn't like it.

"Well, sir, right now my job is to track Eagle, because he's our best lead."

"As you say. You know what he might be carrying."

"Yes."

"Best not to disturb him on the flight, then."

Ari chuckled, then realized Kane was no longer smiling.

"I had my doubts about allowing him on a commercial airliner with that thing," Kane said. "Extremely unlikely that Eagle plans to do any mischief in transit—he seems methodical, and there's enough money likely to be waiting at the other end to dissuade anyone from suicide, right?"

Ari thought the topic morbid and said nothing.

"But there's always a risk," the big man answered himself, and looked out the car window. "Mandelyn is back in Rome."

"She is?"

"I'm meeting with her before the funeral."

"I don't suppose I'll be seeing her."

"No." Kane fell silent again as the car approached a secure entrance to the air terminal. He tapped on the glass and the driver stopped the car so Ari could get out. Ari sat for a moment without moving.

"Mr. Kane, you asked me if I could connect these dots." He paused, then went on. "Have you ever felt you could see something so clearly, something no one else could see—and if you didn't share it, you'd go crazy?"

"What do you mean?"

"I mean there's something very important going on here. Possibly a plot to destroy the Dome of the Rock."

Kane frowned passively out the window, then turned to Ari. "Go on."

"Point one: Shor in Haifa and Chandos in Rome die the same day, both wearing rings with identical inscriptions—a Biblical verse about the coming of the Messiah. Point two: Shor carries a postcard of the ancient Temple of Jerusalem with the same verse handwritten on the back. Point three: DNA proves that Peter Chandos belongs to the family of the *cohens*, the ancient priests of Israel who were the only people allowed to officiate in the Temple. Finally, Shor, Levinsky, and Catriel Levine were all of them mixed up with the Mishmar—a fringe group that wants to rebuild the Temple."

Kane's frown deepened. "And these points add up to a plot to destroy the Dome of the Rock?"

"The key might be the lattice. It can be made undetectable because it can be turned into any substance, but for the same reason it can also become a powerful explosive."

"So anyone could carry it past the Flaming Sword—a fake tourist, for example—and detonate the device inside the Dome."

"Anyone—or someone from the Mishmar."

"And why eliminate Shor? Or Levine and Tempelman, for that matter?"

"To protect the plan. Nobody who knows about it can be allowed to live—the risk of a breach is too great."

"You think Tempelman found out about it?"

"He might have been tailing the Levine woman. Or maybe he was going to spill what he knew to the patent lawyers."

"Or maybe he was blackmailing someone."

Ari smiled; apparently Kane knew Tempelman—and he was listening.

"It's tantalizing," Kane said. "So you think this organization, this Mishmar, is planning to destroy the Dome and rebuild the Temple in its place, and the killings are to keep the plan secure."

Ari nodded.

"How do you see Eagle's role in this?"

"I thought about that last night." Ari leaned closer. "Two possibilities: he might have gone private, as a contractor for the Mishmar. Second, he might be a countermeasure. We know he's PA intelligence—maybe they're onto the Mishmar and working underground to stop them."

Of course, there was a third possibility: that Eagle was himself the threat to the Dome—which would involve a big talk with Kane, and he didn't how far to drag Maryse into this.

Kane seemed to consider Ari's words as he watched an airliner rising overhead. "If your second theory is correct, then you ought to be on his side," he said quietly. "The State of Israel would not want to deal with the consequences of an attack on the Dome."

"I'm aware of that."

"Perhaps not fully. I met privately with the Prime Minister this morning. He's young, he's a saber rattler, and he doesn't seem to appreciate that he's no longer the only nuclear power in the Middle East."

Ari nodded goodbye, smiled grimly, and got out of the car. As he walked away, the darkened car window opened.

"Davan," Kane called after him. "Thank you for your thoughts."

***

At the departure gate, Ari had no problem identifying Eagle. Even in this unearthly heat, the man wore a heavy black turtleneck pullover. And the little gold ring on the fourth finger of his right hand was unmistakable.

Relieving Eagle's previous watcher, Ari took his place in the queue behind the man as they boarded. Eagle looked fit, he thought, and traveled light—only a small black carry-on bag. Ari sat a few rows behind him, close enough to watch him but not close enough to be noticed. His little buttonhole camera picked up everything and transmitted it home.

He thought about his conversation with Kane. He had expected to feel awkward talking to the head of Interpol and was surprised that he had not. The man didn't look the sort who invited confidences; still, Kane had listened. Maybe his theory wasn't so brainless.

But Ari knew there were infinite ways to connect the dots of this story. As he leaned back in his seat, he fought sleep and tried to focus. Was there a Jewish plot to wipe the Muslim shrines off the Temple Mount? Or an elaborate Palestinian provocation? Or was it just a simple bloody conspiracy to get control of the lattice? And what did the death of the Pope have to do with any of it?

He drifted off for a moment and saw in dream a golden dome shining, then burning, then turning to vapor above the blistered remains of the Holy City.

Al-Anbiya Madrassah, East Jerusalem, 0945h

Imam Abu Rushd was not happy about the morning recitation of the *shahada*.

"*La ilaha il-Allah, Muhammadun rasulu'llah!*" he called out. The heat of the morning was unblinking—not the wavering heat of the past few days, but a sickening heat like a blanket over everything. It exhausted the boys. Maddened, they had torn their tight white caps from their heads, and sweat yellowed their white clothes. The imam gasped for air between his teeth, and shouted again, louder. "There is no God but Allah and Muhammad is his prophet!"

Amal bin-Ayoub shouted back as hard as he could, in hope that the imam would be satisfied. At last the teacher surrendered.

"The Shaitan," he said. "Today's subject is the Shaitan. We will study the devil."

The tired boys looked a bit more interested. The devil always gets them, thought the imam. Studying the reference chalked on the wall, they flicked open their books and chanted aloud:

> *God said to the angels, Bow to Adam. They all bowed except Iblis, who said, Shall I bow to him whom Thou hast made of dust?*
>
> *He said, Is this the one whom Thou hast honored above me? If Thou wilt leave me alone till the day of requital, I will most certainly bring eternal death to his children.*
>
> *God said, Depart! For whoever of them follows you, you shall have your full reward with them in Hell. Deceive whom you can, send your horsemen and armies against them, buy them up with your treasures, promise them what you will, but the promises of the Shaitan are lies.*

"The enemy of man is Iblis the Shaitan. He was one of the Jinn, a being of pure fire who was cast from Heaven because he would not bow down to Adam."

"Why is he called Iblis?" a boy asked.

The imam was ready. "Iblis means 'the one who despairs.' Because he has no hope, he seeks to drag all men with him into a hopeless hell. He is the leader of the godless West, the great Shaitan; he whispers in their ears that there is no God, that there will be no day of requital."

"Young men!" he raised his voice. "The heat you feel today is nothing compared to the burning of Hell. The unbelievers—the Jews, the Westerners—who follow the Shaitan will burn in despair."

He wrote a reference on his slate board. "Recite with me!" The boys scrambled to find the page:

> *God has said: As for those who disbelieve in Our teachings, We will drive them into the fire; as often as their flesh is thoroughly burned, We will give them new flesh to burn so they may suffer their punishment. Truly, God is mighty and wise.*

"Teacher, does that mean they grow new skin?"

"When the skin of the damned burns off, God replaces it in an instant with tender new skin, which burns off again. An infinite number of times each second, for an infinite number of years. The pain never ends. Never, never."

"That is not the only pain that never ends," Amal muttered to himself as he glared up at the clock.

After the lesson, Amal rushed home to get lunch for his father. Ordinarily, he would have stayed at school, but the old man had become much weaker these past few days and needed him. Amal exhaled heat as he clambered up the stairs to his father's room, his shirt soggy and his pulse beating hard.

Hafiz was sleeping under a light sheet on the sofa in his room; a small air-conditioner buzzed wearily in a window without much effect. Amal thought it might be better to help his father down the stairs to the kitchen, where it was cooler. Hafiz sat up, groaned, and allowed the boy to support him to the table. Amal laid out figs and fresh oranges from the refrigerator. It was too hot to eat anything else.

"You were out very late," Amal scolded his father. "When I went to sleep, you were still out."

Hafiz gave him a frail smile through two days' growth of beard. "You were still asleep when I came back."

"Where did you go? Were you with Nasir?"

"It's not important where we went."

Amal forced a slice of orange on his father. "Where did you go?" he insisted.

"*Jameel*. We went to a meeting." The old man sucked faintly at the orange to get at the juice. "That's where we went."

"An important meeting, to take you out all night."

Hafiz smiled again. He knew the boy was worried about him, and put his hand on his shoulder.

"And how was the fearsome imam this morning?"

"What will happen to unbelievers—it's terrible." Amal shook his head. "The fire."

"The only fire is in the heart. And they who will feel it, feel it already." The old man was suddenly dizzy and tired, drained by this attempt at theology.

"I will never understand, Father. Not like you."

"What makes you think I understand?"

"You are Hafiz. You know the holy book by heart."

"Knowing a thing and understanding it are not the same."

He massaged the muscle in the boy's shoulder and admired the long young body arched in the chair next to him.

"Where is Nasir this morning?"

Hafiz hesitated. "He had to go away. He was called away in the night."

"I wonder why Nasir always wears black. It is so hot," Amal mused, spooning cold yogurt on figs.

"It has to do with his calling, I think."

"I wish he wouldn't smoke. It endangers your life, you know. My science teacher says it is foolish to smoke."

"Listen to your teachers."

"I try to."

Hafiz lay his head on his hands on the table because the darkened kitchen was in a slow spin.

"Are you all right, Father? Should I get you some water?"

"Yes, thanks."

Hafiz raised his head and sipped at the water glass. Amal watched the old man struggle to swallow and fed him another orange slice. He decided not to go back for his afternoon classes.

"Father, when my uncle died, did his soul go to the cool garden? Or to the fire?"

"It would be as God wills. And God is merciful."

"The imam says all the Jews will go to the fire, and all the Americans, and all the Westerners."

"The imam is not God."

"But it's written…"

Hafiz sat up and toiled to his feet. He was quite sick now, needing to release the tight hard bubble in his chest. Over the kitchen basin he coughed a fine spray of blood.

Alarmed, Amal wet a cloth and held it to his father's lips, embracing him to keep him from falling.

Hafiz opened his eyes to the boy's troubled face near his, the curious black eyes and hair, and suddenly realized that he had two sons. He had neglected this one—shamefully. He had played with him, loved him, but never taught him.

It was time. Past time.

Church of Santa Maria Maddalena, Rome, 1100h

"Maybe the biggest security operation ever," Intel was saying.

Kane replied, "Yes, I could see that when I helicoptered in. I doubt any dead body in history has been as well protected as this one."

"Fifteen hundred uniformed police and who knows how many undercover. Gunboats on the Tiber. An entire armored division of the Italian Army ringing Vatican City with anti-aircraft missiles."

"An elephant for swatting gnats."

"Plus Flaming Sword technology around the Basilica itself."

"It's a good thing. They should be worried about Eagle now. Where is he?"

Intel hummed musically for a moment. Kane admired the voice. "He's on a bus to the city. An airport shuttle from Fiumicino."

Kane chuckled. "A bus? He'll be a long time coming. I could see it from the copter—this city's gridlocked. He's got a Shin Bet man stuck to him. I've asked St. Helena Street to patch through his buttonhole camera for you, so keep an eye on him."

"Copy."

Kane cleared his throat. "And our other trace?"

"Passing the Pantheon as we speak."

"Thanks. Out." Kane's voice-activated GeM blinked off, and he sat contemplating his image in the mirrored barrier between himself and his driver. He leaned forward to examine more closely his smoothly cut white hair and immaculate Royal Marine blazer with its insignia. He was satisfied with the sturdy figure he saw—sixty-five years old, wearing the same coat he had bought in Lympstone at age twenty.

Nodding at the Interpol driver, who leaped to open the car door, Kane took a breath of the cold air and looked up at the wedding-cake façade of the church of Santa Maddalena. Inside the nave was turquoise and gold with pillars like a garden of giant flowers. No one else was in the church, so he walked tentatively down the aisle to kneel at the tabernacle and then examined the famous statue of Mary Magdalene that stood at the foot of the high altar. It was rusty rosewood, with a mournful face scarred like the stem of an ancient tree.

He turned when he heard the door to see Maryse entering, her auburn hair blown by the wind, her face pink with the cold.

She gave him a slanting smile and sat down to unpack her bag.

"Any progress?" he asked, taking a chair across from her.

"Good morning to you, too," she said, looking around at the grand church. They were alone. "Why here?"

"Convenient. And I've always loved this church. Not as important as some, but it's a jewel."

She was already working the screen on her GeM. She scrolled through several pictures of the vans that had left the Piazza San Giovanni for Lebanon the previous Saturday and laid out for him her theory that one of them might have carried away the missing icon.

He cleared his throat. "Why aren't you in Lebanon then?"

"Obviously, the icon could have been dropped off anywhere along the way. Our people are already interrogating the drivers—we'll probably know something soon."

"Still, I wonder what would have motivated Chandos to send the icon to Lebanon."

"I don't know." She switched off the projector. "Besides...something much bigger than the theft of an icon is going on here."

"So I've heard," he replied. "Your friend Davan briefed me before I flew out this morning."

"You met Ari?"

"I gave him a lift to the airport. He's got two more murders on his hands. Seem to be related."

"*Two* more?"

"Something to do with the death of the genetics expert in Haifa."

"What do you mean, he briefed you?"

"Says there's another dangerous angle to all of this." He sketched out for her his conversation with Ari.

Drawing her hair back, she looked at him and then shut her eyes, trying to gather her thoughts. "A threat to the Dome of the Rock?"

"Yes," he said. "The holiest, most coveted piece of property on the planet. Sacred to three religions. An attack on the Dome would bring down the full fury of the Muslim world on Israel. We've lived for three generations with Islamic terrorists, but everything we've seen so far is a pinprick compared with what would come if the Dome were destroyed."

"What do you think would come?"

"The imams have nuclear weaponry and the will to use it."

"They wouldn't destroy Jerusalem. It's holy to them too."

"No, not Jerusalem. But Tel Aviv, Haifa…"

"Israel would strike back."

"Undoubtedly. But don't forget…there are only about six million Israelis and 600 million Muslims in the surrounding countries. One or two bombs and Israel is finished. The Islamists have two advantages—they're a hundred times more numerous and could absorb the blow, and many of them welcome death. It's an automatic pass into Paradise."

"The city is the cauldron," she murmured. *"Desolation and war shall sweep the land of Israel…"*

"What's that?"

"It's a quotation from Ezekiel. In the Bible."

"And quite fitting, too."

They were quiet for a long time. "This is maddening," she finally said. "Two wholly separate crimes that threaten to tear the world apart—only they're not separate. They're linked. Something connects them."

"Right. What does Rome have to do with Jerusalem?"

"*Quid Roma Hierosolymis?* The same question St. Augustine asked. I wish I could talk to my father...he might have known how they're connected."

"Your father might have known, yes." Kane looked up cheerlessly. "I respected him."

"He respected you. He thought of you as his greatest success." Her voice came out softer than she intended.

"A far cry from my own father," Kane murmured. Maryse was surprised at this; she had never heard him say a word about his own family. She knew nothing of him before Priory School.

He saw the curiosity in her face and smiled. "His name was Leonard Kane. He played tennis at New Haven...at Yale. The French Open, Wimbledon. That's where he met my mother. She did like him—big, athletic sort. Grew up in Manhattan. He followed her round England.

"But he was one of those men who have no future. Athletics take you only so far. There was some trouble, and my mother's family... Well. I met him a few times. He floated round for a while. He wasn't impressed with me; but my mother's money—*that* impressed him."

Kane looked at his GeM clock and stood. "At any rate, I'm sure your father thought of *you* as his greatest success. I'm due at the funeral. I don't know why they want me there; it's a diplomatic thing. You going?"

"I thought I would. It's a Pope's funeral. I'll watch from the piazza for a while and then get back to work."

Idly, Kane stepped up the aisle and pointed at the brownish statue next to the high altar.

"It's Mary Magdalene. Your name sounds like hers. Medieval, made of wood. To think they built this entire church around it."

Maryse came forward. They both looked up at the curtains of rococo marble high over their heads, and the angels and apostles, figures like gilded sugar rising on terraces above the altar. Through the dusty windows in the rafters bloomed an odd orange light.

"The sun is trying to break through." Kane turned to her. "Oh, by the way, Davan is in Rome again."

Maryse tried to hide her surprise—she didn't know why. "Is he? What is he doing here?"

"He's the agent attached to Eagle…which means he won't be in control of his whereabouts."

"I understand." She felt unaccountably embarrassed and afraid that her face showed it.

"Let me drop you at the piazza. I have a car waiting." She followed him down the aisle, but paused when her GeMphone rang.

There was a jolly voice at the other end. "My dear, it's Jean-Baptiste. Are you still in Rome?"

"Yes."

"So am I. You must come sit with me in my box. It's such a show."

"You're here for the funeral?"

"Oh, yes. Wouldn't miss it. Pomp and panoply, you know. Takes me back to the world I prefer—the Middle Ages. Won't you come? And you can brief me on the Via Condotti."

St. Peter's Square, Vatican City, 1200h

The shadows of wet, cold clouds darkened the Basilica of St. Peter to a watery gray as the funeral of Zacharias II began. Maryse had never seen such a crowd. Thousands of umbrellas spread and then fell with the irregular rain. Vast viewscreens hung at intervals from the colonnades, and the people packed in around them reminded her of waves in a windy sea. Harbored by the colonnade, a group of mostly elderly men and women in black-and-red robes clumped together in one of the rank of reviewing stands surrounding the square. They were watching the screen overhead.

Maryse maneuvered through the crowd toward the stand, which was decorated with the banner of the Order of Malta. She was surprised to see Jean-Baptiste in the front row, splendid in a black cape lined with crimson velvet and a black tunic trimmed with medals. He also wore an absurd cocked hat. Vigorously he motioned her up the stairs and into the box.

"This is my friend Maryse Mandelyn!" he shouted to the little knot of people sitting by. They were a smiling lot, courteously introducing themselves. The death of Zacharias II apparently hadn't grieved them much: they could have been celebrating a win at a test match. Everyone had a grand title. Here was the Grand Chancellor of the order, the Grand Master, the Grand This and Grand That. Only later did she fully realize these were some of the most important people in Europe.

"Look! There's the King of Spain," Mortimer pointed like a child at a parade. "And over there, the Prime Minister of Palestine. Looks like a taxi driver. Directly across from him, the President of Israel. Lovely irony. And you have something for me?"

Maryse felt in her bag and found her handwritten notes from the Via Condotti, which she put in his gloved hand. He smoothly folded them into his breast pocket.

"The end of the papacy of Zacharias II—Zacharias, who died between the porch and the altar." Mortimer gave her a knowing look. A delicate music rose and fell in the distance. "Pie Jesu from Fauré's Requiem," Mortimer sighed. "At least the late Pope had taste. And the spectacle begins." He gestured up at the viewscreen.

The little drama taking place far away on the Basilica porch came into high definition. Surrounded by Swiss guards with lowered swords, a simple coffin lay on the steps. According to tradition, it would eventually be swallowed up in a coffin of lead and then a coffin of cypress. Old clergymen, magnificently robed, clustered together against the cold, stood behind the casket. There was not a woman among them, thought Maryse; they looked very much like the old church, except for the giant black figure of the Cardinal Archpriest, whom she recognized. He stood at one side of the company, Cardinal Tyrell at the other, an Irish curate's fierce look on his face. A gaunt man known as the Cardinal Dean presided between them.

The choir began singing in Latin, which Maryse automatically translated in her head:

Blessed be the Lord God of Israel who has visited and redeemed his people,

And has raised up the horn of salvation for us in the house of David his servant,

Just as he said by the mouth of his holy prophets from the beginning:

To save us from the hands of those who hate us;

To show mercy to our fathers; and to remember his holy covenant,

The oath he swore to Abraham our father, that he would grant to us

Liberation from the hands of our enemies, that we might serve him

Without fear and in holiness and righteousness all our days.

"Apropos," Mortimer whispered loudly. "The Canticle of Zachary. Traditional for funerals. Particularly fitting for this one."

At length they draped the coffin in red silk and intoned, "*Usque ad sanguinem effusionem*—even unto the shedding of blood," and then it was slowly paraded around the plaza, a scarlet thread of cardinal priests and bishops following.

※

Buried in the crowd, Ari Davan was silently panicking.

"I've lost Eagle," he said in a whisper to his GeM. The mass of people was overwhelming; he couldn't see the man anywhere. "I need a better view."

From various cameras hidden atop the gigantic elliptical colonnade, images flashed past his GeMscreen. A red rectangle showed Eagle's last position, near one of the great columns. Ari cursed himself; Eagle had obviously slipped outside the plaza and all the cameras were turned inward.

He had followed Eagle without incident all the way from Ben Gurion Airport. The man had slept through the flight, walked carelessly through the da Vinci Airport, made one GeMphone call, and picked up an ordinary express bus. Then a slow progress through the crowds of souvenir shoppers and mourners toward the Vatican, finally joining the onlookers in St. Peter's Square. When it became clear he was heading for the funeral, Ari had connected with the Vatican police and their surveillance system. Eagle had made it almost too easy.

There was only one thing: he had shown interest in the endless line of helicopters landing inside the City, following them through binoculars as they disappeared behind the great dome of the Basilica. But once the ceremonies started, he had stood quietly, respectfully, in one place near the edge of the crowd, Ari watching him at a comfortable distance. Then, without warning, he had darted out of view.

Ari made his way as fast as he could toward the colonnade, whispering vigorously into his GeM at the man on top. "Turn that north camera around. I can't see outside the square." He wished he had dropped a GPS tracker on the man while he had slept on the plane, but didn't risk it. Eagle was obviously no play-actor.

Finally reaching the colonnade, he jumped a metal barrier that closed off the Piazza and found himself in an empty lane. This was where Eagle had disappeared. Ari scanned his GeMscreen and saw only himself looking around in a foolish panic. Another curse: by turning the camera, he would have missed Eagle re-entering the Piazza.

"Reverse the camera!" he shouted into his mouthpiece. The image staggered wildly and refocused on the crowd below. It was hopeless: a hundred thousand people had raised umbrellas as the rain splashed down again on the processional and on the blood-dark coffin that moved as if by itself through an ocean of black.

Ari began running helplessly along the colonnade, glancing at the GeMscreen and scanning the crowd at the same time.

※※※

Maryse watched the coffin as it passed. Like a bleeding trail, the cardinals followed, Tyrell among the first of them, almost parallel to the viewing stand. She wasn't sure, but she thought those iron eyes were looking straight at her. The choir continued the Canticle of Zachary:

And thou, child, shalt be called the prophet of the Highest:
For thou shalt go before the face of the Lord to prepare his ways:

To reveal the knowledge of salvation to his people,
of the forgiveness of their sin,

Through the heart of God's mercy, from which the Eastern Star
from on high has come,

To enlighten those who sit in darkness and in the shadow of death, to direct
our feet into the way of peace.

"They're singing about John the Baptist, you know," Mortimer smiled. "My namesake."

"Yes, I know," Maryse replied.

"John the Baptist prepared the way of the Lord. I like to think I'm doing a little of my namesake's work."

It was a curious thing to say, but she let it pass. The cold was becoming uncomfortable, and she had work waiting for her at the hotel. "I think I'll excuse myself now," she said to Mortimer, who smiled, picked up her hand in his elegantly gloved hand, and kissed it.

At that instant she saw it—an almost microscopic point of red-hot light sweeping over her hand. Before she could warn him, Mortimer leaped from his chair, his eyes wide, and collapsed on the floor. Maryse fell on top of him and buried him under her own weight.

People crowded around her, shouting. "*Fuori! Fuori!...* Give him air." "Heart attack!" someone shouted. A tall man with hands of steel pulled Maryse off Mortimer, a German doctor who had been introduced to her as head of the Order's medical mission.

"It's not what you think," she whispered into the doctor's ear. "He's been shot."

The man looked up at her in surprise, and then turned back grimly to his work. Two Order sisters knelt next to the doctor.

He murmured to the nuns, "Get these people away. There's danger." They seemed to understand intuitively and began to usher people away. Police had converged on the viewing stand and were moving the distraught members of the Order down the steps.

By this time Mortimer was blinking awake, and then almost as quickly his eyes fluttered shut. Puzzled, the doctor searched through his clothes and found nothing. He turned on Maryse, "What is this? He has not been shot. He is not wounded at all. Stroke or heart attack, it must be." He motioned for the police to bring a stretcher.

Maryse was stunned. Had Mortimer really winked at her just now?

***

Across the Piazza, Ari noticed the disturbance in the viewing stand. It was his only lead. "Punch me up the camera on the south colonnade." The picture came into focus. Black-clad police were clearing everyone off. Was it possible? And was that Maryse Mandelyn coming down the stairs?

Ari pushed his way through the crowd. By this time, the processional was moving back toward the Basilica, and people had drawn back from it. He was across and following Maryse on his GeMscreen as she trailed behind a clutch of police who were carrying something—a stretcher?

The GeM fixed her face in a square white halo and then he was at her side. She was startled to see him. Her face was bloodless, trembling.

"What's happened?" he asked, nodding at the stretcher.

"Jean-Baptiste Mortimer. He was just shot…I think."

"You think?"

"The doctor couldn't find a wound on his body. I want to go to hospital with him."

"Who would want to kill Mortimer?"

"I don't know," she whispered. "I was sitting next to him, he was…he was kissing my hand, and just then I saw a targeting laser."

"Kissing your hand?"

"Look, I've got to go with him." They had reached the edge of the crowd and an ambulance was backing toward them.

"Wait. I can't leave here. Did you see anyone? Where did the shot come from?"

"It must have come from the other side of the plaza. Long-range, from the laser sight. Up there?" She pointed to the top of the northern colonnade, which was ringed with police, small figures in black alternating with giant white statues of saints.

"Maryse, they might not have been aiming at Mortimer at all. It might have been you."

"I know that," she whispered as he put his hand on her arm. "Stay. I'll call you from hospital."

He helped her into the ambulance and then whispered into his GeMphone. "I want to talk to everyone on the north colonnade. Now."

Piazza Citta Leonina, Rome, 1315h

"Absurd. I have a hundred agents up there. No one without authorization was admitted. No one could have taken position on the colonnade without being seen."

Staring over the shoulders of his technicians, Bevo never took his eyes from a bank of flat viewscreens. He had not once looked at Ari, who stood in the entry to the police van parked in a piazza beyond the colonnade. From here, Bevo could see everything: there were a dozen panels filled with umbrellas; on another panel, a purplish electronic grid surrounded St. Peter's, which filled the screen like the stump of a black tree.

Ari insisted. "The shot must have come from the colonnade. The vector, the line of sight..."

"You don't even know a shot was fired. The old man you speak of had a heart attack, I understand."

"I told you. There was an Interpol agent in the box seated next to the old man; she saw the laser sight."

Just then the Commendatore of the Vatican Police came breathless into the cabin. "I just heard. We've lost track of Eagle *and* a shot was fired?" He bent over one of the technicians who was rapidly entering data into a computer.

Bevo was fixated on the screens. "We'll find Eagle, but only if we stay on the job. I've got every man in the square looking for him." He muttered, "I wish you'd keep your Middle Eastern madmen to yourselves."

"And the hospital? The ambulance?"

"My men are in the ambulance, and we're securing the hospital as we speak. Your old Knight of Malta is in no danger now—if he ever was."

The Commendatore broke in. "Your man here has just replayed the feed and analyzed the line of fire Mr. Davan described. The processional was passing at that instant, and several of the cardinals were under the shooter's sights—including Cardinal Tyrell."

For the first time Bevo looked up. "You're saying someone shot at Tyrell and *missed?*" Relieved and disgusted at once, he thought of the headline that might have been: "Leading candidate for papacy dies under the eyes of incompetent police."

"We've got to locate this Eagle of yours," Bevo snapped, turning back to his monitors. "If he has been firing a gun, nothing's to stop him from trying again."

"I'll get the Cardinals out of there," the Commendatore sighed and left the cabin.

"There's another possibility," Ari spoke up. "The Interpol agent next to Mortimer. She might have been the target."

"Why? You mean..." Bevo glanced at the contact list on his Gemscreen, "Mandelyn? The woman who speaks Latin? Why her?"

The story was far too long and delicately woven to tell this man. "It's only suspicions. She's chasing the Acheropita. Maybe she's getting too close."

"That thing? The frame has been melted down by now—why would they risk killing her for thirty kilos of silver?"

"There are precedents," Ari murmured.

Bevo turned on him. "*Ebbene*, Mr. Davan. Since you are close with Miss Mandelyn, I suggest you contact her again and find out the truth about this shooting."

***

"I am so surprised to be included."

"Be quiet, Manolo. Stop acting the fool," Tyrell whispered.

Six cardinal princes of the Church sat on benches in a darkened alcove of St. Peter's Basilica. Before them, behind a blue and gold illuminated window, Michelangelo's Pietà shone like a white diamond—the Virgin cradling her crucified Son in her arms.

"I had forgotten how beautiful she is," Estades said, smiling serenely at the view. "Years since I really looked at her."

Several Vatican police officers stood around the small group, watchful, waiting. Chanting from the funeral outside filled the nave with echoes.

"How long will we be kept here?" asked the elderly archbishop of Zaragoza of no one in particular.

"The Commendatore said to wait until he came back for us," Tyrell called loudly; the Archbishop was notoriously deaf. "Ridiculous, if you ask me."

"I agree," said John Paul Stone, who stood and then paced around the columns of the alcove.

"We've lost one Pope. Let's not lose another," murmured the ambitious Archbishop of Manaus. He looked around at the others, who were giving him disapproving glances. "It will be one of us—we all know it. That is why they are hiding only us in here."

Little LaSalle of the Ivory Coast stretched up to speak in Tyrell's ear: "And it must be you. And soon!"

Stone glared at them both.

"It will be as the Holy Spirit chooses," sighed Manolo Estades, who was still admiring the grand Pietà behind its thick veil of bulletproof glass.

Tyrell stood and approached Stone. Quietly, he said, "I've talked to the others. There will be a conclave, and it will be tomorrow."

"Impossible."

"The Secretary of State and the Dean have agreed on the grounds of cost. Since the time of Pope Francis, budgets matter. The Camerlengo has no objection, as I anticipated."

"I've been talking to people myself. You'll be facing a fight, I promise you."

"Unseemly, Brother Stone."

"Unseemly! What did Hamlet say about serving funeral-baked meat at a wedding? Your conclave is an insult."

Cardinal LaSalle's round face came up between them. "It was God who removed Zacharias, and God will put Cardinal Tyrell in his place," he hissed. "Zacharias was a heretic."

Repulsed, Stone turned his back on them both. Tyrell followed and spoke low in his ear.

"Listen, Brother Stone. I don't know how this will go and neither do you. But, in a few days, you may be Pope yourself."

Stone snorted with contempt.

"Promise me," Tyrell's voice turned to a plea, "promise me that if that happens you will reconsider the Encyclical. That you will let the Council re-open the issue. If you will promise to do that, I will do my best to follow you."

Stone turned to him with a tight smile. " 'The Church must no longer withhold its blessing from those whom God has blessed with love.' That motto hangs by a silken thread over my desk. You must understand this, Tyrell. I believe in this motto, I believed in Zacharias II, and I believe that *In Salutem Ecclesiae* is of the Holy Spirit. I do *not* believe that the Holy Spirit 'reconsiders.' "

"Then I will be against you."

"Your Eminence, there's nothing new in that."

In the silence that followed, they could hear the mournful tones of the Cardinal Dean's voice echoing through the doors of the great Basilica, but they could not make out the words.

❊❊❊

The Commendatore spoke to Ari in urgent, twisted English. "I have arranged. We talk to Bevo's men on the colonnade."

Bevo sat watching as the computers continued to scan suspect faces in the crowd, automatically comparing images to a ghostly template of Eagle's face. "Go. Talk. But I think they would already have reported a shooter standing by their side. In any event, keep quiet, please."

Ari had at last got through to Maryse, who told him that the left side of Mortimer's chest was black with a heavy bruise.

"What's wrong with Bevo?" Ari asked the Commendatore as they walked quickly to the stairway that would take them to the top of the colonnade.

"He is terrified. The shooting of the Pope—it was his job to prevent. Now another shooting? You see?"

"What did you do with Tyrell?"

"I put him in the Basilica with the other *papabili*."

"The other what?" Ari called as they took the staircase two steps at a time.

"*Papabili*. The cardinals most likely to be elected Pope." He panted, laughing. "I would like to be in that room right now."

As they reached the top, the great funeral mass was continuing in the square below. The two of them moved as discreetly as they could down an aisle overhung with titanic statues of apostles and saints. There was a police officer in nearly every alcove. Ari checked his GeMscreen for the point where he estimated the shot had come from, but the nearest policewoman couldn't help. She pulled off her helmet with its glassy mask, revealing a torrent of blonde hair, and answered the Commendatore in quick, gruff Italian.

"What did she say?" Ari asked him.

"She saw the disturbance across the piazza, and she called in—but so did others. She saw no shooter. No one but police up here."

Ari frowned. "No one but police. Do you personally know all of these people up here?"

The Commendatore immediately saw where Ari was going. "No, of course not. They are mostly Roma police, Bevo's special detail."

Ari ran to the end of the colonnade and began photographing each agent with his GeM. As he flashed his ID he pulled down the smoked-plastic mask on each face. The Commendatore did the same, moving up the aisle from the center. No one resisted.

"These photos are going to Bevo," Ari shouted as he clambered down the stairs behind the Commendatore.

"Do you recognize everyone in these files?" Ari asked Bevo as they reached the van. Bevo turned to one of the viewscreens and studied the faces as they flipped past. He nodded at each one.

"Yes, I know them all. They are members of my detail."

"Then how many are there?" Ari took control of the viewscreen and rapidly counted. "Forty, forty-one, forty-two."

The Commendatore intuited what Ari was doing and commandeered one of Bevo's technicians. They muttered in rapid Italian at each other, and soon a video was flying backward across another of the flatscreens.

"This is a camera sweep of the colonnade only minutes before the shooting," the Commendatore grabbed Ari and they counted together once. They counted again to make sure.

"*Quaranta tre?*"

"Forty-three."

They stopped the recording and studied it for a moment. "Zoom in on that one," Ari shouted. The Commendatore translated.

The screen narrowed and swooped in on a figure in nebulous black, a lean, helmeted shadow resting against the pedestal of a saint.

"Our missing man," Ari whispered.

"*Aquila?*" asked the technician.

"*Possibile*," the Commendatore said. "Eagle. Could be." Then he turned to Bevo, who was examining the image curiously, and spoke in a short burst.

"There are police in the Basilica with the *papabili*. I go to check on them. I will ask Bevo to put out an alert," he told Ari. "And I want to talk to everyone on the colonnade again."

But Ari was already on his GeMphone.

"Maryse. He's disguised as a policeman. Don't let any police near Mortimer...or you."

Policlinico Gemelli, Rome, 1500h

Maryse was not watching the medical team. They were agitated, yelling at each other in an Italian she couldn't follow—a word that sounded like *maglia* over and over—but she was satisfied that they were mostly grandstanding. Mortimer's breathing was regular and his heart rate robust; she could tell that much from the monitors that clinked and beeped

109

overhead. She was keeping her eyes on the curtains, on the black shapes of the police motionless beyond the glass walls of the surgery.

It had all come back to her. That day in Dublin, looking down from the top of a building outside the National Museum, the day the Ardagh Chalice burglar escaped her trap. Five years had passed since then, but she still couldn't think about that day—she could only see it, hear it, hold her breath over it until she felt like never breathing again.

She had been unconscious of it, of the same mad cycle repeating itself all over again. She missed her own father so badly that she had set Mortimer in his place—and then watched helplessly as another bullet had nearly taken Mortimer. Now he lay on a hospital bed with a broken chest because of her. Because of her. She had tried to quit, to put the whole business behind her, but now it all came round again like a returning nightmare.

It was to have been the summit of her career—catching the perpetrator of the most notorious museum robbery of the decade. The Ardagh Chalice, Ireland's national treasure, a cup made holy by early Celtic Christians, discovered by two farmers in a potato field centuries later. It had simply disappeared from behind carefully designed security barriers in the Museum's Treasury. The robbery had required extreme agility and timing to the nanosecond, and it was only by luck that she had stumbled on the thief's method of operation and enticed him into a meeting.

The day after the robbery, she and Kane had been working through a digicam recording of the adjacent hallways. After a tedious two hours watching nothing happening, she noticed a tiny, grainy light on the wall that she had not seen before. An obscure tracking thermostat next to the Treasury had lit up in the minutes before the robbery. They both ran to look at it to find that it had recorded a dramatic drop in temperature; thirty minutes of freezing cold had come and gone without notice in the night. The thief had wired the air-conditioning system and had rendered the hall so cold that a mist generated by a simple CO_2 aerosol can would hang visible in the air at ceiling level. In turn, the mist would reveal the exact path of each of the random laser firings that secured the room.

A thief this shrewd would not have been stopped by the window alarms, but it remained to work out how he had made his way from the window along the ceiling of the Treasury. Even if he could see the laser beams, he would still have to dodge them while crawling along like a spider in defiance of gravity.

She knew about burglars who could walk on walls and ceilings—wearing boots carpeted with carbon nanotubes a thousand times stickier than a fly's foot—but she had never heard of one so agile. Still, she followed up with the few manufacturers who could produce this kind of nanotechnology. Strangely, she now thought, they were mostly Israeli firms. It was one of these that had given her the lead: a search of their orders turned up a single oddity—an order phoned in on a telephone-card number and charged to a Chinese import company that no longer existed.

In the end, it came down to a simple telephone call. She left a message at the number on the chance that the thief had not simply thrown the phone card away. In retrospect, she should have known better when he returned the call. It had been too easy.

There's a pub near the National Museum.

Bring the money and I'll tell you where it is.

All right.

It usually worked out that way. Art thieves were mostly extortionists; a famous item could not be easily disposed of, and only rare eccentrics intended to keep the valuables they stole. Mostly they just wanted cash on delivery.

She had invited her father to stay with her in the city after a mild crisis with his blood pressure, although his uncharacteristic depression provided her real motive. He had resisted going, but she had come to the door of the Priory, packed him up, and brought him down to Dublin. Packing had been simple: only his cardigan and a book or two. That day she drove him to the doctor and should have taken him back to their flat, but secretly she wanted him to take part in her triumph—to be near when she potted the headliner crook of the decade.

The plan was to meet, find out where the chalice was, then tag the financial transaction with a code hidden in the GeM beam. The thief would not be able to access the money without revealing his exact location. She would park the car in Molesworth Street near the Museum and leave her father safely behind for the few minutes it would take to complete the transaction at the pub.

But it didn't happen that way. A sudden laser sight: a bullet pierced the windscreen at a high angle and her father was dead before she let out the involuntary scream that still resounded in her head five years later.

111

Afterward, she had climbed to the roof of the Museum with Kane. They both stood exactly where the killer had stood. "That bullet was for me," she remembered saying again and again. Numb, dizzy from vertigo, staring down at the rectangle of police tape that surrounded her car, she cursed the lethal trap she had set for her father and the career she had never wanted. Until then she had dealt rationally with people in a business that was unorthodox but still operated according to the basics—opportunity, risk, investment, profit, sometimes loss. It had never occurred to her that a thief would come after her. It was irrational. Where was the profit?

The thief had never been found and the chalice remained lost. David Kane had pleaded with her to stay in the service, but the entire concept of a career with its vectors of success now was meaningless to her. Her father with his art books: she would now live that life out for him.

Or so she had intended. Recovering the Acheropita—it had to be done. But also there was David Kane. And Fatima Chandos. And Jean-Baptiste: the laser sight on his cloak had hit her heart like frozen lightning. She looked at him on the bed and knew she needed now to stay well away from him, for his own safety.

And Ari Davan. She had not realized how bitterly cold the world was until she had felt his arm on hers.

A nurse came up and spoke to her in bemused English. "The gentleman is awake and resting now. He is very clever. If you would like to speak to him."

The medical team withdrew from the room, smiling at her and congratulating themselves—and Mortimer. She waited until the door was firmly closed behind them. Keeping her eyes on the windows, she walked around the bed and glanced down at Mortimer, who was grinning like a child.

"It works!" he whispered, starting from the pain in his shoulder.

"What?" She shook her head, uncomprehending.

"My new vest! *La maglia!*" He opened the neck of his gown to reveal a thin web-like fabric underneath. "Latest in protective clothing. Made of nanotubes—catches a bullet at the first pressure. Light as cashmere, but relative to weight, much stronger than steel. Still painful when hit, though. Be quite dead without it."

"Why? Why were you wearing a protective vest?"

Mortimer's grin dissolved. "Oh, my dear, I'm sorry—you thought the bullet was for you. As with your father. Probably upset you awfully. No, I can assure you…the bullet was for me."

Interrogation Room, Queen Helena Street, Jerusalem, 1600h

The blonde woman answered every question in a graceful monotone.

"I don't know anything else. I was paid—that's all I know."

Two thousand euros had slid out of nowhere into her bank account for a simple half-hour's work. An electronic transaction with only one end. The other end was not only untraceable, it didn't even exist. Even the money tracker from the Institute was baffled, which impressed the unimpressionable Toad.

An employee of one of the higher-toned, unadvertised escort services in Tel Aviv, the woman had taken an "order," as she called it, by telephone. She would be paid two thousand to walk into an empty reception hall at noon Thursday, greet a certain Mr. Tempelman on behalf of a Mr. Luel, put him off for a few minutes, and then leave immediately after allowing the man into the office. That was all.

Everything about the woman indicated that she was telling the truth. The telephone call was easily traced—it had come from a public telephone at the bus station, paid for by a nondescript telephone card never used before or since. The woman was considerably older than she looked, Toad thought after she had peered at him uncertainly for twenty minutes. Myopia, he decided. She probably wouldn't be able to identify her employer even if she had seen him. He let her go.

"I've seen a few transactions like this," the money tracker had said. An accountant with a big belly and old glasses from the 2000s, he was nevertheless highly respected for sniffing out criminal sources of cash. "The sort of thing high-end arms dealers or art thieves do. Or have done for them. Odd, though—such a big maneuver for such a puny sum."

The money tracker waddled off in search of arms dealers and art thieves. Toad suspected the man's reputation was based on persistence rather than intellect, as was his own. Toad had solved many tough problems for the service and been praised for his brain; his own view was that mental focus and a closed mouth—along with a quiet place to think—were more important.

"Ari's lost the Eagle," Miner announced as he shuffled into the interrogation room. "Disappeared from view, and then a few minutes later someone took a shot at someone from somewhere."

Toad gave him a look that meant he would like to hear more particulars.

"They think the shooter was disguised as a Rome policeman. Looks like he was aiming at a group of higher-ups, but he hit an old man instead—one of the public. How did the blonde work out?"

"Nothing new there," Toad replied.

"So you think the Eagle's just a contract killer? One of those jet-setters you see in films? I've always wanted to run into one of those—I never thought they actually existed."

"No, I don't think he's just a contract killer."

Miner was surprised at the quickness of Toad's answer. His partner usually gave noncommittal shrugs at questions like those.

"I've been doing a little reading about our Eagle," Toad said quietly. "Adopted out of a Lebanese orphanage. Mother dead, father a very big name in the PA, but also a very private one. Everybody defers to him, but you never hear about him. He's never held any particular office, but he's in the background of lots of official photos. 'Hafiz al-Ayoub.' Never anything else. Just a name in a hundred photo captions."

Miner was impressed. Toad was the only one he knew in the Protective Service who had bothered to learn Arabic—for Miner, the little squiggles of their writing held no interest whatever, but Toad could read it as easily as Hebrew or English.

"Maybe he's just a *well-connected* contract killer."

Toad shook his head. "I've been thinking about what Ari told us. About the Temple Mount. There's any number of people with the motive to do some damage there; they all want to bring on the Apocalypse. We have cranks of our own—starting with the Mishmar—and then there are fringe Muslims and even Christians. Years ago, some religious nut from Australia tried to burn down al-Aqsa. And a cracked little Jewish-Christian cult got awfully close to blowing up the Dome back in '84."

"Ages ago."

"Well, we're not the only Protective Service. They've got one too."

"You mean, the Waqf? You mean that maybe we and the Eagle are on the same side?"

"Look at what was done with Bukmun. We know he had some connection to the blow-up this summer, the hole in al-Aqsa and the Synagogue fire. Maybe Eagle liquidated him for that."

"Then why is Eagle shooting up Emanuel Shor? And that lot in Rome? He makes far more sense as a contractor. Shoot anybody for a reasonable fee."

Now Toad gave his noncommittal shrug. He couldn't deny Miner's logic.

"And there's more." Miner held up a silver GeM in his long bony hand. "This is Catriel Levine's. Nothing much of interest here—except for a boarding pass for a flight to Dallas-Fort Worth via Paris—scheduled for departure yesterday at 1700 hours."

Toad's eyes focused hard on the GeMscreen.

"When she didn't show up, they gave her first-class seat to an American exchange student flying standby. He probably enjoyed it very much. By the way—there's no return ticket."

"I don't suppose Tempelman had a ticket."

"No. Tempelman's GeM is boring." Miner produced another handheld, this one battered and black. "Golf scores. Links to restaurant reviews, porn vids. However, there are also scans of patent documents regarding a certain nano-something-or-other and the rights of the Technion."

"I suppose you've got the lawyers onto those."

"As we speak. Here's how I figure it: Catriel knows all the paperwork. Now she's got hold of the technology and she's running off to the USA to sell it to the highest bidder. Tempelman finds out about it. He either wants to stop her or cut himself in on it—the latter, I'd say, based on those choice gems on his GeM. And someone decides to put them both out of the way. Who stands to get it all in the end? My bet's on Luel."

"You figure Luel bought Eagle's services to get the technology in the first place and then get rid of Catriel and Tempelman?"

"Voilà."

"It's very neat," said Toad. And he meant it. A neat, conventional solution to a very conventional problem. Follow the money—the first principle of criminal investigation. "But wasn't he in love with Catriel? Wasn't he going to marry her?"

Miner held up the silver GeM. "No texts in the last three months? No phone calls from him? Believe me—it's all pure business. She wasn't taking any messages, thank you."

Toad smiled, which surprised Miner considerably. "Then let's get Luel down here for another talk."

Miner shuffled off. Toad waited, then picked up the titanium shell of Catriel's GeM and scrolled avidly through its contents.

Miner was right: the digital leavings of her life were uniformly impersonal. Not a note of music, no history of videos or games. No apps, whimsical or otherwise. The remnants of obscure e-mailings back and forth to lawyers' offices, nothing to or from Luel. A mass of legal documents, a contact list consisting almost exclusively of other attorneys.

With one very interesting exception.

He switched on his GeM and spoke into it a name from her contact list. *L. Sable.*

Salah-eddin Street, Jerusalem, 1915h

"The child's name was Yusuf bin-Ayoub. Joseph, son of Job, born in Tikrit, now in Iraq. He was surrounded from birth by power, although he was not born to it himself. His uncles were generals who quarreled among themselves while the infidels held the holy places.

"Now, like Joseph of old, he was sent into Egypt as a boy and by a miracle became sultan. When the great king Nureddin died, he became also master of Syria. And thus he held the holy land between his hands, like this."

Hafiz held up both hands, trembling, as if to clap at a fly. Amal sat close to him in the darkness of the kitchen, his head on the old man's shoulder. Against his forehead he felt the old man's beard, and he could smell warm blood on his breath. As a child he had listened to his father's stories, but it had been years; this story, he sensed, would be different from those.

"Nearly a century earlier, the Kaffirs had come. The Crusaders. Here, in al-Quds, the sacred city, where Muslims and Jews and Christians had lived in peace for centuries, pouring through the Damascus Gate they came with their great horses and their great broad swords. The Muslims gathered on the Haram, the Temple Mount, to defend themselves. There the Crusaders slaughtered everyone—children, their mothers, everyone—ten thousand Muslims. Because many of them had swallowed their gold to protect it, the Crusaders tore their bodies open. As they entered the Dome of the Rock on their horses, they rode in blood up to their knees, as if the shrine were a cup of wine.

"Then they fell on the Jews in their great synagogue and burned it.

"No one was prepared for this. The believers who survived were banished from their homes; the Crusaders brought wives and their servants and set up their own kingdom and built fortresses.

"In their ignorance they thought the Dome was the Temple of Suleiman, so they didn't destroy it—but they lived like swine in al-Aqsa and desecrated the Mount by stabling their horses there.

"Our people were helpless. The sacrilege was strong, and the people were weak. There was no unity, only disarray."

The old man coughed hard, and Amal gave him water which he struggled to drink.

"But the holy Rock cried for deliverance," he went on. "The Rock from which the Prophet, peace be upon him, ascended to the presence of Allah. And the cries were heard. The Lord sent a deliverer."

"Yusuf bin-Ayoub," Amal said, nodding.

"Yes. He was known as *an-Nasir*, the Eagle of God, and fighting under golden banners trimmed with eagles, he destroyed the Crusader army and descended on the Christians who still held Jerusalem."

"Nasir," Amal echoed. He grinned at his father. "Like my brother."

"Like your brother."

The room was cooler and nearly dark now, as Amal could no longer see his father's face. He pictured the Arab army like a golden ring around the city, ready to grasp the Kaffirs by their necks, and the great king with his brother's name commanding them.

"And he slaughtered the infidels?"

"No, he did not. He offered the Christians safety if they would yield the city to him, which they did rather than die. And he entered the city through the Damascus Gate, just as the Crusaders had done—but he came in peacefully, swearing the Christians would not be harmed and their holy places would remain open. It was the twenty-seventh day of Rajav, 584 years to the day from the Prophet's ascent to Heaven.

"The great sultan removed the images the infidels had set up in the Dome of the Rock and cleansed it with rose water and rose petals in memory of the bodies of the thousands of Muslims martyred there."

Hafiz closed his eyes against the darkness. His voice had become a murmur. Worried at the grating sounds of his father's breathing, Amal shook him gently and coaxed him awake.

"Why are you telling me this story? You haven't told me stories since I was a child."

"Because it is your story," the old man murmured, drowsing. "And it's time you knew it. It is the story of our family, of the sons of Yusuf al-Ayoub— of Saladin."

"Saladin? We are of the family of Saladin?"

"He was called *Salah ad-Din*, the Justice of the Faith, and from the time he held the world in his hand until now, the family of Ayoub watch over the sacred temple, to prepare for the Day."

"The Day of Requital." Hafiz grasped for the water again, drank, and smiled in the dark at his younger son. "When Prophet Isa—Jesus of Galilee— returns to the temple of Suleiman with the army of Heaven to carry out the *salah*, the judgment of all mankind.

"Many false Saladins have arisen since—madmen like the Mahdi of Khartoum, or fools like Nasser of Egypt or the murderer Baghdadi of Daesh or Saddam of Tikrit, whom the Americans hanged." The old man chuckled weakly. "Saddam Hussein saw himself as the new Saladin. But none of these could hold the world in their hands."

"Father, what must we do to watch over the sacred temple?"

Hafiz' voice sank to a whisper. "Your brother…Nasir…it is his place. May he be the last."

"And how must we prepare for the Day?"

But the old man was tired. Amal knew he would have to get him into bed, that the story was over for now, and he toiled up the stairs, nearly carrying Hafiz to the couch in the upper room. With the window shutters closed and the little cooler buzzing, the room was bearable, and Hafiz' hands and feet were unnaturally cold. The warmth would be good for him.

Amal pulled off the old man's slippers and laid him on the bed, then sat next to him until the quiet snoring grew regular. He switched on the viewscreen on the wall and muted it, settling back to watch for a while. Arabic titles ran rapidly over images of war preparations. Israeli warplanes cruised diagonally across the screen. Soldiers of the lands surrounding Israel marched past, their oily new guns at the ready; sleek missiles rattled on trucks across the desert; banners of red, green, and black flew. Amal had seen images like these all his life, but there was one thing he had never noticed before: the black eagle on every banner.

His father stirred next to him. "Amal." His eyes were still closed. "You asked me how to prepare for the Day."

He paused; Amal waited and at last decided Hafiz had gone back to sleep. But then he heard him murmuring.

"There's a poem. Hafiz al-Shirazi… *Rose petals let us scatter… And fill the cup with red wine… The firmaments let us shatter… And come with a new design.*"

Interrogation Room, Shin Bet Headquarters, Queen Helena Street, Jerusalem, 1920h

By seven o'clock, when Ivan Luel showed up for questioning, Toad knew everything about the man that phone and text records could tell, and by seven-twenty, he knew everything else.

Sex, money, and influence—they summed up Luel's life. The lawyer had talked a stream since he entered the room. His face glistened like a magazine cover; he had unbuttoned the two top buttons of his white silk shirt, and the way he sat on a green chair in the interrogation room revealed that fear was his signature emotion. Toad knew that Luel had women up and down the coast from Yafo to Haifa, women in New York, London, and Sydney. He also knew from the messages he had read that Luel could not speak to a woman without gaming her in a tone of voice that Toad had learned to recognize from years of interrogations; he had wondered idly why so many women were vulnerable to it. He now had no doubt, however, that Catriel Levine had not been among the vulnerable ones.

Looking apprehensive, Miner sat in the corner while Toad questioned Luel. Yes, he had known about the lattice and its potential value. No, he had not been involved with Catriel's work and was now frankly surprised that she had done what she did to secure the claims. Yes, he had lied about Catriel and himself—there was no engagement, it was all business—and self-flattery. No, he knew nothing about her ticket to America, and pouted in a bewildered way when he heard about it. And the less he knew, the more he had to say.

"And Lambert Sable? What do you know about him?"

Luel looked stupidly at Toad. "Sable? The Gemster? What everybody knows. You mean, the CEO of GeM, right?"

He knew nothing about Catriel and Lambert Sable.

Toad began to lose interest in Luel. The man was all surface, no purpose. Precisely the opposite of the person they were looking for. He tried to imagine the contempt Catriel Levine must have felt for Luel and enjoyed the imagining.

While Luel babbled, Toad wondered what drained such a man of intelligence. He mused momentarily about the discovery of the MAO-A gene in Peter Chandos; was it really possible that some people might appear harmless and yet lack the gene for a normal human conscience? It would explain a good deal, he thought. The man seated in front of him seemed to have an overactive gene for superficiality.

Toad glanced at Miner, whose genetic makeup was benign until paired with a woman of the same genetic makeup; combined carriers of Tay-Sachs disease, they would produce offspring doomed to an early and painful death. Then he thought about his own genes. What was there in the conjoined spirals of his DNA that had produced the cold unseen carapace he lived in?

His thoughts turned to the person they really were looking for. Whoever it was played no games. No surface—all malevolent purpose. A rapid-fire killer. At once painstaking and quick, timed to perfection, this person carried out his operations as if performing the most delicate surgery.

What struck Toad about the killer was the sterility of his work. Not a single biotrace at the Shor murder scene, except a hair that in his opinion had been planted. So far, no identifiable traces at the double murder scene at Cohen Brothers. Such a performance was not impossible, but required superior planning. Add the speed and precision of execution, and this killer became easily the most formidable opponent he had ever faced.

Surfaceless. Traceless. In a way, invisible. Toad knew something about invisibility. All criminals sought it; it was their failure to achieve it that brought them down, and Miner and people like him had grown so sophisticated that nearly everything was now *physically* visible.

What Toad knew about was psychological invisibility. To render the self unseeable—he had worked at it forever and understood the mechanism. The key was Edgar Allan Poe's stolen postcard: hide where you are. Become faceless, unmemorable, put out no psychic signals at all. Stare at the floor in a lift; enter only doors that are open. Focus the mind on solitude.

The more one is absorbed in the self, the more invisible one becomes, Toad realized. He himself was so completely captive to his own thoughts that the thoughts of others rarely entered in. And when it happened, the shadow of his own thinking soon covered the landscape again.

He realized then he hadn't heard anything Luel had said for ten minutes.

Then Ari's signal came across his GemPhone.

"Please excuse me a moment," he said and walked out the door. Luel turned to talk to Miner, who by now had also lost interest in the lawyer.

"I've lost Eagle," Ari was saying.

"I'm not surprised," Toad said.

"What?"

"Nothing. Go ahead."

"I lost him hours ago at the Pope's funeral and I can't get help. Everybody here is completely territorial. Now that the funeral's over they don't care about Eagle, but I don't think he's finished. You know what I need."

Toad did know, and he copied the coordinates Ari gave him as he took the lift to the underground communications room. He didn't know the officers there, but it didn't matter; Ari's voice on the GemPhone was enough for them. Toad stood in the shadows of the darkened room as they brought up the day's digital feed from one of the Eros-Z satellites, the government's high-resolution eyes on the globe.

Given the right coordinates in time and space, the imaging officer brought up an iridescent blur on an overhead viewscreen—the blur became a vortex of light, and Toad had the sensation of falling through the middle of a cyclone. Then, all at once, the image slowed into something recognizable: the vast piazza before St. Peter's Basilica in Rome. The image was strangely bluish, but the audience that filled the piazza was visible as a squirming black mass flecked with red.

"Why the blue cast?" Toad wondered.

"The new camera sees through clouds, but they cause a shift in the color spectrum," the officer replied absently. He was getting a fix on the north colonnade, which bloomed into focus so close that Toad could see police officers strung like a line of black ants along the top.

"Can you see this?" Toad asked Ari over the GemPhone.

A long pause that was filled with tinny, grunting music; then Ari answered. "Great. I've got it projected on the wall."

"Where are you?"

Ari shouted over music. "I'm in the men's room of a disco in the Piazza Navona."

The officer laughed. As he ran his finger over a small crystal-like pad, the image zoomed dizzily in and out. "What are we looking for?"

Ari was counting audibly. "Twenty, twenty-one, twenty-two…there he is! Zoom in on the middle of the colonnade—the nineteenth person from the end."

The image telescoped over the head of a figure in black violet leaning immovably against what appeared to be a great statue. "Fast forward," Ari commanded. They could almost see the figure's rapid breathing as they watched for about a minute. Then all at once the man sprang to life, fired a weapon toward the crowd, and slipped under the canopy.

"Back up! Mark him!" Ari cried.

"Eagle," Toad murmured.

The officer swept his hand over another touchpad, backed up the image, and grabbed the figure inside a pulsing red circle. "Mark!" Toad knew that the computer had analyzed the figure to the millionth of a pixel and would recognize him even in a swarming crowd of people—so long as he stayed visible.

But the red dot did not reappear. The image zoomed out and forward, faster and faster every second as the officer searched for it. The blue marble of the colonnade brightened and darkened as the clouds varied overhead, the funeralgoers vibrated at high speed like molecules under a microscope. The time code buzzed along: thirty, forty minutes, but no signal.

Suddenly there was a loud ping from the computer and the red dot pulsed to life again; fifty meters or so from where it had disappeared, it emerged again from the east end of the colonnade. Toad watched in fascination as the man sauntered away from the Basilica through the square titled PIAZZA CITTA LEONINA on the screen.

Ari exploded through the phone. "He walked right past me! See that van? I was inside that van at that moment trying to get some help!" Toad decided he meant the rectangular trailer parked alongside the pavement with cables running in all directions. It looked like a bacterium waving its tentacles at the tiny red intruder.

Toad remembered that he had an interview waiting upstairs.

"You've got your suspect," he said softly into the GemPhone. "*Mazel tov* with that. I'm off to talk to Miner's suspect." And he shuffled to the lift.

But then, glancing back into the interview room, Toad saw that Luel had reduced Miner to near catatonia and decided to leave them alone. He continued down the corridor toward his office.

Surfacing Eagle had confirmed an idea in Toad's mind. Of course. The killer was got up as a policeman. Unseeable, like himself. Part of the permanent security presence. Like a tree on the avenue or a cloud in the sky—just there, as he should be.

Did a fake policeman trick Shor into taking the Chandos DNA sample and visiting his brother's laboratory? What would cause Shor to commit *aven* and break the law unless he were trying to help the law? Who but a security person could get into Cohen Brothers' locked offices without being challenged?

Of course, that work had already been done. All of the security people in both locations had been carefully identified and interviewed, so the killer was good at insinuating himself into the flow, mixing with the others on the colonnade and then disappearing. He had to have precise information; thus, someone was feeding it to him. Toad knew that Eagle was well connected, so that fit; it would be interesting to know who exactly those connections were…particularly at the Vatican.

Eagle had met with a lot of people in Rome. Toad had evaluated all of those he could identify—including Didi Mattanyah—but they might be worth a deeper look. He must have linked up with someone in particular. Who was networked between both the security conference of the prior week and the security for the funeral? Many of these would be obviously be the same people: the head of the Swiss Guards? the head of the Vatican detachment of Rome police? Who else? Who was commanding in this mysterious war?

Toad found himself back at the lift and decided to drop into the black room again to check on Ari's progress.

He walked into turmoil. Over the heads of the excited technicians, a vast grid of Rome onscreen was going dark, but a bright red signal was blinking rapidly across the city: it was a taxi. Ari's voice could be heard shouting over the speakers, but not at anyone in the room—he was shouting at his own taxi driver. He was in pursuit.

The red signal raced along a straight diagonal toward the lower right-hand corner of the map, the map twirling and zooming to track it. Suddenly it slowed and stopped. In the darkness the red circle filled with green light— the satellite was now tracking a heat signature. Eagle was on foot.

"He's stopped." Ari cried. He was in traffic, well behind the signal. "Where is he? Where did he stop?"

The officer punched up the location on the screen. PIAZZA SAN GIOVANNI IN LATERANO.

"It's the Holy of Holies," Ari breathed.

Global eManager Headquarters, Plano, Texas, 1200h

"Lunch again, Lam?" Pastor Bob Jonas strode into Lambert Sable's office, rubbing his hands. "What's on the menu?"

But Sable was grim. "We've got a serious problem."

The pastor looked around the office; it was virtually empty now. Photographs, mementos—everything was boxed up for Sable's departure. The telescreen walls were blank. The only thing on the desk was Sable's tablet.

"What's up?"

Sable wiped his eyes with the back of his hand. "Our contact from Tel Aviv never showed up at the airport. I just found out she was murdered yesterday. We've lost control of 1317. Nobody knows what's become of it—not the Israeli government, not Interpol—nobody."

Pastor Bob smiled and fell into one of the cream leather chairs. "Have you thought maybe that's what the Lord wants?"

"What do you mean?"

"The anti-Christ is destined to control the world through the 'mark of the beast.' If your little gizmo is part of prophecy, nothing y'all can do is going to change that."

Sable paced the office. "But it's a nightmare. It can be mass-produced. You realize anyone who controls those designer-atom devices can pretty much do what he wants to anyone he wants? He could destroy cities or make a single individual disappear without a trace. There may be no limit to what he could do, now that everyone in the world is dependent on their phones."

"Sounds like fulfillment of prophecy to me, Lam. The Tribulation *is* a nightmare."

"I'm still going to try to stop it."

Pastor Bob chuckled. "That's noble of you, Lam. But it's not really your fault, is it? Y'all didn't invent the thing."

"No. It wasn't my idea. Lawyer came to see me representing the inventors—Israeli scientists—and I got excited about it. She wanted it kept very quiet. Then I got to thinking about how this thing could be used and wanted to stop it, but it was too late. They'd already built one. So I made a few inquiries and got put in contact with a group called the Flaming Sword, some Arabs who have it in for the Israelis, and who said they'd get the thing for me. Then I'd cut off the funding and that would end it."

"I want to make sure I understand this," the pastor said, amused. "You contracted with the Israelis to build the thing; then you contracted with an Arab terrorist to *steal* the thing."

"Yes. I know it sounds ridiculous."

"But terrorists, Lam! 'The Flaming Sword?' What were you thinking?"

Sable shook his head. "I got assurances."

"Assurances. '*God drags away the mighty; they have no assurances.*' That's in the Old Testament…somewhere. Obviously, your Arab friends have stiffed you." The pastor looked around the office. "By the way, why are you packing all this stuff up?"

"Well, I thought I should put it in storage."

"For what? You're not returning, and your little mementos aren't likely to survive what's coming."

"No, I suppose not."

Pastor Bob fingered the tablet on the desk. "Did you see what our new friend has written about us? And to think we bought her lunch."

"She bought her own lunch," Sable sighed. "And she's made me look like an idiot."

The pastor stood and read paragraphs in a dramatic voice: " 'Sable seems completely taken in. He's underwriting an exodus of believers to the Holy Land this weekend. Expecting never to return, he has willed his share in GeM to the 'Left-Behind Foundation,' which the End-of-Time Church controls.

" 'The money is supposed to go to saving those of us who eat our supper without saying grace and therefore will miss out on the Rapture. Thus, Sable's stock holdings valued at some $300 billion will fall into the hands of whoever is left behind at the Church. Presumably the Church has designated non-rapturees (lawyers, of course) prepared to carry out these terms automatically when (or if) the mass lift-off actually occurs.

" 'Of course, when all the good folks are gone, only the baddies will remain—and we all know what happens when naughty folks get hold of that kind of money. Personally, I can't wait!

" 'Meanwhile, the rest of us need to watch our step come Monday. You won't want to be caught on the freeway when all those Christian drivers get raptured. Like old Lambert Sable himself, the engine's running, but ain't nobody driving.' "

Pastor Bob set down the tablet and laughed. "A Jew columnist in a Texas newspaper. Incredible."

Piazza San Giovanni, Rome, 2015h

The great Cathedral of St. John Lateran was darkened in mourning and only security lights remained to guide passersby around the piazza. Although his line of sight was dim, Nasir was pleased—he had his quarry trapped. He knew that there were no exits from the building in front of him; the man he was following would have to come out the way he came in.

Nasir decided to fall back a little so he could surveil the entire structure. In the center of the plaza, an obelisk rose to a point crowned by a great cross that reflected the murky yellow light. Keeping the building in sight, he strode across the intersection and took a position in a cornice of the pedestal next to a statue of a lion. It was a good place to hide and still see everything. He estimated the target at about 170 meters, well within the range of his Russian-made AS rifle.

He repeated in his mind the vow he had made. It was serious now. He had reached the mission. The preparation, the years of training and planning, the inherited burden of the family of Ayoub—at this moment the weight of it all fell on him. He felt he might as well be trying to ward off the twilight; yet it had to be.

Into his mind came the image of Rabia al-Adawi—the light olive skin, her morning face under a scarf like a rainbow. In his heart he had always known that there could never be a wedding, so he might as well stop thinking about her. Staring at the ring on his finger, he forced his brain into careful estimates of the elevation of the gun needed to remove this threat.

How can there be a covenant between idolaters and God?

A woman an idol? Unquestionably. The most compelling of idols.

He would leave her behind for the sake of the covenant he had made. *God will not call you to account for what is futile in your oaths, but He will call you to account for your deliberate oaths.* He had made a deliberate oath and would live by it and die by it.

***

"See where Master Cosmatus signed his name to the stonework. Eight hundred years ago. Remarkable!" Jean-Baptiste Mortimer straightened up and took a sharp breath.

"Are you all right?" Maryse asked.

"Shoulder feels like it took a bullet." He laughed as he softly rubbed at his collarbone with his good right hand. The other hand was cradled in a sling. He was still dressed up as a Knight of Malta, although the silly hat had disappeared.

"Lovely place, after all." He looked up admiringly at the four beasts glowing on the blue ceiling. "I'm particularly fond of the winged creature—he humanizes the picture. You know, originally they had nothing to do with the Four Evangelists. The idea that Luke is the ox, John the eagle, Mark the lion, and Matthew the winged man—that's all Medieval allegorizing. In ancient times, the four beasts were the guardians of God's throne."

Maryse nodded impatiently. The Sancta Sanctorum chapel was freezing, and she was holding her arms firmly crossed inside her overcoat against the chill. Crime-scene detritus still clogged the floor; only one bright light shone from a police scaffold. Getting inside had been a bother; the guard at the top of the stairs had no respect for her Interpol ID and it had taken a call to the Commendatore to convince him to open the gate. Furthermore, she had no idea why Jean-Baptiste had wanted to leave the hospital, where he was relatively safe, and come here.

Of course, his safety was only relative anywhere. They had taken a back exit out of the hospital and traveled in an Interpol car to get here; still, no one who really wanted to follow them would have been thrown by any of that. It was probably best to keep moving, but she became more uneasy by the minute. Mortimer had wanted to see everything. He had run his hands over the great door of the San Lorenzo chapel, carefully counted the tableaux in the fresco that circled the Sancta Sanctorum, peered closely at the blood spray on the altar, and taken the measure of the white spot in the limestone wall where the Acheropita had hung—all while she stood there trembling from fear and cold.

"Now I see," he murmured, still staring at the ceiling. "I'm quite sure there were only two men in this room when the Pope was shot."

"But the blood on the altar. You can see for yourself that Chandos couldn't have been anywhere near the altar when he was shot, yet that's his blood. There had to be a third person here."

"Then I suggest you talk to the medical examiner about time of death. For both Chandos *and* the Pope."

"Time of death?" Maryse was surprised. "Everyone knows the time of death. The video is plain—the Monsignor entered the chapel with the Pope. Five minutes later they were both dead."

"So it appears…"

He was going to say more, but then looked at the exit as if he had heard something.

Maryse too had an abrupt sense that someone else had come into the building. A dull hard thump—unmistakable. Someone had been hit and fallen. The guard. Her heart punched at her ribs.

"We've got to get out of here," she whispered. "We're trapped; the only exit is the way we came in."

"Happy to oblige you, my dear," he whispered back. Now he looked genuinely frightened. They crept toward the open gate.

Just outside, the guard lay as still as a toppled statue on the marble floor. Instinctively, Maryse stepped in front of Mortimer, shielding him with both arms—the vision of a side street in Dublin flared in her mind.

The Holy Stairs receded into gloom at their feet. A staircase on either side— which to choose? Should she choose any of them? She had never felt so helpless. Someone was in the building, probably behind them now, waiting in one of the myriad alcoves to ambush them. For the first time in five years, she wished for her nine-millimeter.

"We'll back down the middle staircase," Mortimer whispered in her ear almost imperceptibly. "Backs against the wall." It was decided.

For a fleeting second she worried about the blasphemy of going down the Holy Stairs backward, but that way the line of sight was clear. Who knew what was waiting in the side staircases?

They backed slowly along the marble wall, eyes fixed on the illuminated gate of the Sancta Sanctorum, expecting the black-clad shooter to appear at any instant on the landing. She kept Mortimer shielded with her body and he made no protest.

Maryse forced herself to count the stairs to keep her nerves under control. Each step took them toward the open air. There was just enough light that she could see the stormy fresco of the Crucifixion on the arch overhead; under it, the landing stayed empty.

Icy with fear, she felt intensely the presence of ghosts, numberless ghosts toiling up these steps on their knees, hooded in penitence, climbing toward Calvary.

When she counted step twenty-two, she began to breathe again. They were nearly there.

Then a hand lightly touched her arm.

"Ah, Davan. A relief to see you," Mortimer whispered. It was Ari.

Holding one hand tightly over his mouth, he pointed up the staircase and nodded at them. Time to move.

Maryse grabbed Mortimer and swung him around a pillar at the base of the staircase; Ari followed, flat against the pillar, his gun ready. She glanced at it—a futuristic Tavor bullpup, a high-end Israeli weapon with homing sights.

A statue of Christ stood between them and the piazza. Ari motioned to Maryse to get herself and the old man to safety beneath its pedestal; they crouched and crept around the base, putting it between themselves and the sanctuary.

Breathing at last, Maryse peered over the pedestal at Ari, who stood rigid against the wall glancing from one staircase to another. He clearly knew someone was up there, but it was impossible to tell which staircase held the shooter. The two side entries were dark and the Holy Stairs barely illuminated—still, she could see more than Ari and could alert him.

Then, stunningly, the point of a red laser appeared on the pedestal next to her head.

Someone had her in a gunsight—someone behind her.

She ducked instantly and pulled Mortimer down with her. She watched the laser sweep around the pedestal and disappear in Ari's direction; he would be in plain sight.

"Ari!" she shouted. "He's not in the building. He's behind us. In the square!"

At that instant the world exploded. A single shot screamed over her head from the square—from the sound, it glanced off the Holy Stairs. She heard Ari fire again and again into the piazza at the source of the laser sight. In the corner of her eye she saw bullets sparking off the giant obelisk in the center of the traffic circle.

The bursts stopped. A lone taxi was slowing toward the nearby traffic light.

Fighting the urge to see what Ari was doing, she realized her first duty was to Mortimer's safety. She hauled him up, crouched, and ran, keeping the taxi between herself and the obelisk. Grabbing the door, she snapped a quick order at the driver and pulled herself and Mortimer into the car.

She stole a look out the back windscreen and watched as the obelisk shrank in the distance. Although grateful for the warm presence next to her, when she thought of Ari she felt cold again.

CHAPTER 3

SATURDAY, OCTOBER 9, 2027

Headquarters, Servizio Polizia Scientifica, Rome, 0010h

Dr. Silvia Malemanni was disgusted at being called into the morgue at midnight. Bevo had shouted down the phone at her, forcing her out of the after-opera party she had been looking forward to for a week. The old orderly Ancona shuffled toward her with her white tunic and cap, but she elbowed him away and made her entrance in the tiara, lime opera gown, and jeweled slippers she had worn for *Tosca*.

The body of Nasir al-Ayoub lay covered, except for the head, on the table in the center of the room under a knifelike white light. Sweating despite the cold, Ari Davan stood out of the way next to Bevo and the Commendatore of the Vatican Police, who were whispering violently at each other. Malemanni pronounced a few indecipherable curses and started her GeM recorder.

With an imperious wave, she went to work with her digicam. Ari's GeM pinged him.

"It's Eagle all right," Miner's voice came into his ear. On his GeM screen Ari could see his own texted image of Eagle's still-handsome face imposed over a grid from a life photo—both images were of the same man. The search was over.

"Thanks. Davan out."

Feeling vacant, Ari tried to gather his thoughts. He had not wanted to kill Eagle—more than anything, he had wanted to talk to him. The end of Eagle had not only failed to resolve anything, it had raised more problems.

Although it had been tracing Eagle in the darkness and through clouds, Eros-Z had surprised Ari by losing the target. He had never known Eros-Z to fail before. Eagle was supposed to have been in the Sancta Sanctorum, not hiding nearly 200 meters away in the middle of the roundabout. The guard had been found unconscious in the north side chapel, so Eagle must have come in by one of the stairways, taken the guard down, and waited for his chance at Maryse and Mortimer; possibly Ari's own arrival caused him to flee. Granted, the satellite could not have tracked Eagle after he entered the building, but it certainly should have signaled Ari when he left it.

He reversed the Eros-Z recording to the moments before his arrival at the Piazza and slow-played it again. No...no signal had been given. He watched as the red dot disappeared under the loggia of the Sancta Sanctorum, but from that instant until the end of the recording it remained hidden.

Ari shut it off and picked up the GeM he had found in Eagle's pocket. After a minor squabble between the Vatican and the Rome police, he had been allowed to keep it long enough to download the contents to his headquarters. Bevo had fought the Commendatore on this, but while the argument proceeded, the data flowed.

To Ari's chagrin, the entire content was in Arabic. Toad would read it for him.

But there was one unusual feature: a red-circuit button hidden in the base, like the one in Emanuel Shor's GeM. He touched it to see what would happen.

A recorded voice answered. It was speaking another language—not Arabic, Ari thought—it sounded French. He switched off the GeM.

He wondered why, despite the cold, a sheet of sweat had formed over his body. The smell in the room, the light, the confusion—whatever it was, he was beginning to feel sickened by this place.

Again his own GeM pinged and he answered. It was Toad.

"Initial review of Eagle's files. Not much...looks mostly to be email from PA police."

"What about the red circuit?" Ari asked.

"It rings a private number listed to the National Library of France, Rue Richelieu, Paris. A machine voice asks for a code, then switches off after thirty seconds."

"National Library of France," Ari repeated. He had been there with Maryse. How many days ago? They had met a man who knew about Tarot cards. "The National Library. I was there."

"When?"

"Was it Tuesday...?" Ari shook his head—he couldn't remember.

After a pause, Toad's voice: "Are you all right?"

"Yeah, yeah."

"You met with someone."

"Yes. The Tarot card man. Insufferable snob."

At that moment, Dr. Malemanni gave a cry and held up the dead man's hand. She was pointing at the golden ring on Ayoub's finger.

"Hold it," Ari said to Toad. "It's another of those rings."

"On Eagle's finger this time." It was not a question.

"Yes." Ari inspected the ring as the doctor splayed the man's fingers for him. "DVCEI, exactly like the others. Only new. Our Eagle must have just joined the club." Ari snapped a photo and forwarded it to Toad, who rang off.

The door swung open and two young men in business suits came into the examining room. Ari recognized them as Interpol—just behind them were Maryse and David Kane, the President of Interpol himself.

Maryse grabbed both of Ari's hands. "You made it out," she murmured, looking into his face. "But you look a fright!"

"You're welcome. What do you mean, I look a fright?"

It was true, of course. He hadn't slept in thirty-six hours, his clothes were filthy, and he hadn't eaten since the flight...it seemed a lifetime ago.

"You're shaking."

"I suppose so." He grinned at her. For good reason, he thought—he hadn't been in a firefight since an encounter with a drug seller in Tel Aviv years before. That was nothing compared to the Piazza tonight.

Kane shook Ari's hand and looked at him as if he were a new car he was considering buying. "Thank you, Davan," he said. "Thank you for saving a very precious asset."

"I'm not an *asset*," Maryse grumbled happily. "I'm just glad to see you standing." And she gave him a tentative hug. "Thanks from me, too," she whispered in his ear.

"This is Eagle's GeM?" Kane asked, picking up the battered handheld. "Has it told you anything?"

"They're reading the files now at Queen Helena Street. It's all in Arabic."

"Find anything else of interest on the dead man?"

Ari nodded at the doctor, who held up the finger ring with triumph in her face. "A real mystery, eh, Signore Kane?" Malemanni was amused and excited.

"Ah," Kane grunted, and approached the examining table to take a closer look. Malemanni smiled broadly at this important man, and they spoke to each other in Italian. Maryse inspected the ring, but did not touch the dead hand.

Then the Commendatore and Bevo came forward correctly to greet Kane.

"How did you get out of there?" Maryse asked, turning to Ari.

To Ari, her voice was like an echo. He tried to remember. "After you left in the taxi. It all ended. There was no more. So I watched the obelisk through the scope for a long time—the Tavor detects fire but didn't pick up anything. I had called the Commendatore there and his people were on the scene in, ah, minutes…" He shook his head abruptly to clear it.

"Ari, you've got to lie down."

He looked up at her questioningly. "Maryse, I didn't know you would be at the Holy Stairs. What were you doing there? And Mortimer—I thought he'd been shot at the funeral." But he could hardly keep his eyes open.

"You really must."

As if he understood what Maryse was saying, the old orderly shambled over to them and pointed to a side door that was open. Just inside the door she could see a cot, probably kept there for long nights like this one. The old man smiled gently and led Ari away.

***

When Ari awoke, he didn't know how long he had slept. He had no idea at first where he was or if he had hallucinated being shot at and firing back into the night at a great Egyptian obelisk. His head seemed to be slowly rotating on his neck.

He checked his GeM clock. 0123. Not quite an hour, unless he had slept through a whole day and into the next night.

No, it had all happened. Eagle was dead. Whatever threat he posed was over. He heard Kristall's voice in his mind: *Why would a Muslim want to destroy the Dome of the Rock? Doesn't it occur to you that the best way to push Israel into the sea would be to prompt ten million Muslim boys to wade through waves of their own blood to get at us?*

It was an ingenious theory—that Nasir al-Ayoub, on his own or on behalf of someone else—had wanted to provoke a cataclysmic attack on Israel.

But, in sudden clarity after sleep, Ari realized the theory now made no sense. Why would Eagle hunt Maryse—an Interpol agent looking for a stolen Christian artifact? Or Mortimer, an old Foreign Legionnaire? Or was he more than that…this cryptic, poetry-spouting old man. Had he served in the Middle East at some point? Had he offended someone there? Ari imagined an obscure vendetta between Mortimer and some snarling Arab prince—no, it was laughable. And what had any of the day's events to do with the murders in Israel? He couldn't work it out.

It wasn't over at all.

He opened his eyes again to a sharp crack of light from the door and the sound of Malemanni's voice speaking staccato into her GeM recorder. Opening the door, he saw the examiner washing up at a basin in the corner and Maryse uncomfortably asleep in a metal chair. The others had gone.

"She insisted. She waited for you," Malemanni said. She had put on her white gown after all; it dripped yellow and red from the gruesome work she had finished. "Now you can go home with her."

"It's not like that," Ari replied drily. His mouth felt like sand.

"Would you like a drink?" The examiner's mood had lightened now that her work was done, and she produced glasses and a small bottle of Amaretto from a cabinet. He wanted the drink very much.

The ringing of glasses woke Maryse; she smiled to see him and welcomed a glass of the liqueur. Ari looked around awkwardly for the Tavor, which he found cached in a large plastic evidence bag on the shelf.

"We will need your weapon for ballistic analysis," the examiner said in her thick English. Ari nodded and swallowed the Amaretto; it blazed in his throat.

The doctor shouted for the orderly and, when he appeared, flooded him with Italian. He turned and left. "Now Ancona will call for a taxi, and you can go to your hotel."

Ari gave Maryse an embarrassed look, but she didn't see it.

"Dr. Malemanni," she said, "I know it's very late…"

"It's very early," the examiner gestured at the clock.

"We have the time-of-death data for Monsignor Chandos. Would it be possible to get the same for the Pope?"

"I don't understand," Malemanni replied. "Everyone knows the time of death for the Pope. It was obvious."

"That's true. Still, Interpol needs the data."

Malemanni snapped her head back, tossing her opulent hair to one side. "For that, Interpol will have to speak to *il Vaticano*."

She glared at Maryse for a moment, but then turned to Ari as she shed her tunic and pulled on her dress coat. "I congratulate you, Signor; you are *tiratore magnifico*."

Maryse smiled. "She says you're a great shot."

Ari was surprised at this; he was competent with a gun, but no expert. In fact, before tonight he had never fired the Tavor except on the practice range.

"Adequate, maybe."

"Oh, far more than that," Malemanni waved her hand. "And at 170 meters, I hear. *Esatto*. What is your word? *Accurato*. Accurate. Precise. You see?"

Malemanni swept the white blanket off the corpse on the table, and Maryse drew back. Ari could not believe what he saw.

One puncture exactly in the center of the forehead. Three punctures, equidistant from each other, in a horizontal line across the chest.

Palazzo Malta, Via dei Condotti, Rome, 0245h

As if alone in a nightmare of beauty, Maryse and Ari dashed across the deserted pavement past the delicately luminous Spanish Steps, past Gucci and Fragonard and Versace, their gorgeous windows barred and darkened. For Maryse, they could not run fast enough. The Palace of the Order of Malta loomed up at the end of the Via de Condotti.

She shook the iron gate, but it was locked. In the courtyard inside the gate, they could see a circle of light around a wall fountain pouring from a lion's mouth and, above it, the spiked red cross of the Hospitallers. They both rattled the gate, and Ari pushed repeatedly at the bell.

After a few minutes, a tall, efficient-looking man, all in black except for his brilliant white gloves, warily approached the gate.

"Interpol!" Maryse shouted, waving her ID through the bars. "We telephoned. I must speak to Mr. Mortimer."

The man hesitated and then put a mobile phone to his ear. Soon a uniformed guard appeared. Ari pulled Maryse back as he advanced to unlock the gate, but he was short and fat—surely not the unknown policeman they feared.

"There are uniforms everywhere," Maryse panted to Ari as they entered. Then to the tall porter, "We've tried to ring Mr. Mortimer, but he doesn't answer his mobile. This is Inspector Davan of Israel Security." The porter carefully studied both sets of papers they produced. "We're on official business!" Maryse barked. "Mr. Mortimer may be in danger."

"So you said on the telephone," the porter declared in precise English. "I have taken the precaution of calling the police as well."

Ari cursed; the police were the last people he wanted to see—there was no way to tell if a uniform could be trusted. And he didn't want to have to waste time explaining the situation to the Rome police. He extracted Bevo's card from his pocket in hope of warding them off.

"Would you please check on Signor Mortimer *now!*" Maryse asked.

The elegant porter led them into a corner of the courtyard and disappeared; clearly, people of the street were not easily admitted to the Palace of the Sovereign Order of Malta. Ari kept his eyes on the gate, waiting for the Rome police to show up. At last a man and a woman in street clothes came out of the darkness beyond the gate and buzzed; the security guard let them in.

The woman looked genuinely put out; under a cheap furry hat she wore her hair in two stone-hard buns, and her lips were enormously red. "Polizia di Roma," she snarled when Maryse extended her hand to her. They pumped hands once. Ari understood nothing as Maryse and the woman spoke soft and halting versus loud Italian. Silent, the man with her looked on sadly, his face unshaven and his overcoat wilted with wear.

Ari checked the time. He and Maryse had been running for an hour, stopping taxis, trying to make their way through the unfamiliar maze of Rome at night to the Palazzo Malta, where Mortimer was staying. She had rung Mortimer's mobile number at least twenty times with no answer, and a call to the palace operator had produced nothing but this officious porter.

At the same time, he had been trying to work out what must have happened at the Piazza San Giovanni. Malemanni was certain: "Four bullets. No more." Ari knew he had fired a good many more than four bullets at the target, spraying them at the target but certainly not in any elegant pattern. It was obvious that he had not brought down Eagle; someone else had, and that someone else was still out there and possibly still hunting.

But hunting for what? For Mortimer? Maryse had said little; she was too breathless. Apparently, Mortimer feared for his life because of a threat he had received—something to do with his legionnaire days. He had been wearing one of the new nanofiber tunics that stopped even high-power bullets; Ari knew of the tunics from the Shin Bet special ops teams. Eagle could have used one tonight. What he couldn't work out at all was—who besides himself would be hunting Eagle?

His first reaction had been to ring Miner. It had been hard to make himself understood while loping along the pavement in Rome's unending traffic, and Miner was sleepy.

"Three across the chest and one in the head? Were they entry wounds?"

"Yes."

"Well, um…obviously, if Eagle was facing away from you at the time, this unknown was firing from the opposite direction. If not, then he was either behind you or between the two of you."

"Obviously. What I need from you is ballistics. Get our people on with the Italians and work out where those shots came from. And another thing. We want a comparison of the time-of-death data on the Pope's killer, Chandos, *and* on the Pope. You'll have to get the Pope's data from the Vatican."

"It's 3:30 in the morning…"

Ari hung up, then rang Toad and briefed him.

"Here's an anomaly for you. Eros-Z tracked Eagle into the Holy Stairs building, but didn't track him out of it. He was almost 200 meters away from the building when he was brought down."

Toad was quick. "Then you weren't following Eagle at all. You've been following an unknown subject since the funeral."

"That's what I think too, so get on Eros-Z and see if we can still find the profile."

"They switched off the trace after you told us Eagle was down."

"Maybe they can pick it up again."

"I'll try."

"Another thing. I want everything—and I mean everything you can find—on this Jean-Baptiste Mortimer and his connections to the Middle East." Maryse had glanced apprehensively at him. "Google's worthless on this. You'll have to go deep."

"Got you."

His third call had been to the Commendatore's private number. "The Unknown might still be hiding in the building," he told him. The man was fast and professional: "We will secure the Santa Scala immediately."

Now he was facing the Rome Police detectives, who wanted to know why they had been rousted from a warm station in the middle of the night to freeze in the courtyard of the Malta Palace. "Someone is in danger?" the woman asked, as if accusing Ari of causing the danger himself. He was showing them his credentials and Bevo's card when Jean-Baptiste Mortimer appeared in the palace entryway with the attendant.

His arm still in a sling, Mortimer wore an elegant black-silk dressing gown and slippers and wiped his eyes with one hand like a child awakened from sleep. Maryse threw her arms around his neck.

"It's all right, my dear," he patted her on the hair. "I'm terribly sorry. I had turned off my mobile. Pain pills made me drowsy. Come in. Come in, both of you."

Following Mortimer inside, Ari shrugged at the porter, leaving him to deal with the police officers. The porter and the woman detective squawked at each other; then the two police officers made for the gate, the woman dragging the man by the lapel.

"Like an old married couple," Ari muttered.

"Co-workers are often far closer to each other than married couples are," Mortimer observed, leading the way through a darkened lobby into a side room filled with comfortable chairs. " *'With one sad friend, perhaps a jealous foe, the dreariest and the longest journey go.'* Shelley."

The attendant reappeared almost immediately, carrying a tray of cups and a pot of steaming tea. Maryse and the old man sat.

"Mr. Mortimer, I have several questions for you," Ari said stiffly. He did not like the old man's cryptic smile, nor the ordeal he had caused Maryse.

"Try to help if I can, my boy. I'm frightfully drugged, though."

"I'm asking as a police official, Mr. Mortimer, not as a tourist. My questions aren't casual."

"As I said, I'll try," the old man replied, peering up at him through narrowed eyes.

"Maryse told me you were the target today—of two attempts on your life. Because of something to do with your Foreign Legion days. Tell me about that."

"A very old story. Can't it wait until morning?"

"Mortimer, I haven't slept in two days. Today I've pursued a criminal suspect from Tel Aviv to Rome, chased across this city two men who apparently wanted to murder you, and been shot at myself. I'm not waiting one minute more to find out why."

"All right. Have some tea. Sit, for goodness' sake."

Reluctantly, Ari sat down and took the tea, which he drank thirstily.

Mortimer sighed. "Twenty years ago. South of Lebanon. After one of the countless bloody little battles against your plucky little country, the French government sent me there to do a bit of administration. Through friends I met a Filistini—Palestinian—doctor named Adawi working there. Gifted fellow. Very pleasant.

"Skirmish broke out between some villains and your lads. The villains had casualties and radioed for Adawi to come help them. I refused to let him cross the line of fire—for his own good, I say. A few died. PLO—Hamas—Hezbullah—whoever they were, they've been after me ever since."

"That's it? They've sent a professional killer to Rome to take you down over a twenty-year-old grudge?"

Mortimer shrugged, yawning broadly. "Twenty years is yesterday to them, as you well know. They renew their threats periodically, but I take precautions."

Staring at Mortimer, Ari shook his head. It didn't fit. "It's not enough. There's got to be more to this. We were caught in the middle of a firefight tonight between a ranking Palestinian policeman and someone unknown—an incredibly skilled marksman."

"Perhaps the Palestinians are fighting among themselves. Been known to happen. One faction trying to stop the other?" Mortimer looked at Ari as if to ask were there any more questions. Maryse twisted uncomfortably in her chair.

But Ari was not satisfied. "I notice you weren't surprised just now when I said there were two gunmen in the plaza tonight."

"Actually three, including yourself. I knew about the one in the stairway—caught sight of the flashes from his weapon, despite the inhibitor. Gas-powered, I'd say, and silenced."

Maryse was stunned. "You said nothing to me."

"Thought you'd seen it too, dear." Then to Ari, "Chap in the street wasn't at all interested in us. Could have picked us off like pigeons. No, he was firing away at the person on the stairs, who evidently overmatched him."

"Who could it have been?" Maryse asked.

Ari's GeMphone beeped. He listened to Toad for a moment, said thanks, and rang off. "Our satellite lost track of him. No way to find him now, unless he's still in the sanctuary."

"Doubtful," Mortimer yawned.

"One more question."

The old man closed his eyes and waved his hand; he was falling asleep.

"There's a red circuit on the dead man's phone. It connected tonight to a number listed to the National Library in Paris—the same place you once sent us. Do you know anything about this?"

"What's a red circuit?" Maryse asked.

"It's a private global uplink," said Ari. "Costs the earth, usually untraceable."

Mortimer's eyes trembled open. For the first time, Ari thought, he looked unsure of himself. "The name of the dead man?"

Ari checked the screen on his GeM. "His name was Nasir el-Ayoub."

Staring at his empty teacup, the old man shook his head almost imperceptibly.

"Mr. Mortimer?" Maryse asked gently. "Jean-Baptiste? Are you all right?" She glanced at Ari. "I think that's enough—he's exhausted." And she coaxed the old man up and shuffled him off to the custody of the porter.

Alone now in the waiting room, dizzy with fatigue, agitated, Ari didn't know what to do. His eyes felt like sandstone, so he shut them, tired at last of trying so hard to see through clouds and night.

Palazzo di Sant'Uffizio, Vatican City, 0530h

Cardinal Tyrell finished his private Mass with an ardent prayer for the Conclave that would begin in a few hours.

Burying Zacharias II the day before had been most satisfying—and symbolic, Tyrell thought. The years of captivity in Babylon were enough; now it was time to bring the Church back from exile, from depravity and distortion, from the sewer of sex and the abandonment of the vows that made the

Church holy. Today they would begin the return journey—if he had any influence at all.

He took off his liturgical vestments, washed his face and hands vigorously in cold water from the tap, and was about to call for his morning coffee when the telephone rang.

It was the Commendatore of the Vatican Police. Evidently, the suspected assassin who had fired at the funeral crowd was still at large after all—he was to stay in his rooms until the guards came for him. Fine, fine, yes. Tyrell was secretly glad at the news; it meant that the Conclave would be carefully locked up and watched. He did not want Cardinals wandering off just now.

Tyrell was not afraid of any assassin. He knew he was the unofficial leader of the Catholics who wanted to cleanse the stables of the Vatican; doubtless, a good many of the deviates in the Church and their dupes would like to see him out of the way. As a youth in Belfast he had heard gunshots at night, he had seen death. And again in Beirut in the 1980s. Death was no terror; but that sin should reign in the Church, in the priesthood itself—that he could not bear. So, he had to live awhile.

He sat down to coffee and hard rolls with jam. Across the piazza, at the St. Martha house, a hundred Cardinals were taking their own breakfasts; he was glad he was not among them. He wanted to make a solemn entrance, to hold himself apart from the others when the time came.

Gulping coffee, he switched on the screen in his breakfast room to see the now-familiar glossy woman with the dome of St. Peter's behind her.

"This unusual step of convening to elect a new Pope so soon after the funeral of Zacharias II is causing great controversy."

The background changed to a street in Rome and marchers with rainbow banners calling for immediate sainthood for the late Pope: *ZACCHAREO SANTO SUBITO!*

"According to some of the cardinals, this step is a cost-saving measure—as they are all here in the Vatican, why not proceed immediately to Conclave instead of waiting the customary two or three weeks?

"But others are whispering that the real reason for haste is to suppress the very significant and time-consuming lobbying effort that might be required to elect John Paul Stone, the American who wants to carry out the liberalizing policies of Zacharias II—and perhaps go even further down that road with the next generation of Catholics." In the background, Stone was eagerly greeting a group of youthful priests in rainbow-colored vestments.

"By contrast, the conservatives feel they have a better chance of electing their acknowledged leader, Leo Cardinal Tyrell, if they move quickly. A wave of reaction to Zacharias's policies has swept over the College, policies such as lifting the ban on divorce and abortion, ordination of women and gays, and marriage for priests and gays. The bishops of Vatican III, a narrow majority of whom voted for these policies, have gone home, leaving the decision as to who will guide the future of the Church in the hands of the Cardinal electors. The Vatican establishment has agreed the Conclave for today—and that means they are probably behind Tyrell.

"What difference will it make?

"If Tyrell is elected, he will campaign strongly to reverse the reforms of Zacharias II, and a reversal would touch off Church-wide protests, possibly even schism. There could be two Catholic churches a year from now. That's why this papal election is perhaps the most significant in the history of the Church—it may take many weeks, or it could be over in a few hours."

Tyrell switched off, grumbling with admiration at the woman. He supposed there was no way to keep these things from the press—and she articulated the crisis well, but so openly that it seemed almost dishonorable to do what he was doing.

Still, he was not convinced there would be an upheaval in the Church if the pernicious policies of Zacharias were reversed. Faithful people can't be reasoned speciously out of their faith, he thought, and most Catholics had faith in the Pope. If there were two churches a year from now, one of them would be a tiny group of deviates shrieking like the devil on the side, really no church at all, while the great vessel of the Roman Church sailed on like Noah's ark.

But only if he himself were at the helm. That was the work of today. He had allies, some younger men, such as the keen little Ivoirien Lasalle, who had no patience with evil. Tyrell's strong Irish voice reminded everyone of the anchor the Celts had always provided the Church against barbarians; men like Lasalle fell quite naturally behind him.

Once elected, he would move aggressively. In the ninth century, the corpse of the wicked Pope Formosus was dug up after his death, seated on the Papal throne, tried, and convicted for his crimes in life. Tyrell knew he would have to do the equivalent: to maintain the faith of the Church in papal infallibility, he would have to impeach Zacharias as Formosus had been. He would have to create the impression that Zacharias had been taken out of the way by the action of God to preserve the integrity of the Church.

It wouldn't be impossible. After all, as far as the world could see, the executioner of Zacharias had been an exemplary priest, serving the Pope out of duty, but ultimately choosing to serve God out of faith. Caesar, a menace to the Roman republic, had his Brutus—so Zacharias, who threatened to pervert the Roman church, had his Peter Chandos.

Tyrell looked up at a framed photo hanging on the wall, of himself and Peter Chandos, and his thoughts traveled back through decades. Peter as a thin brown child, with the clean smell of dirt on his body. Peter's mother, her eyes of acute blue filled with the sharpness and inevitability of loss. The clash within his own heart. Those first months in Rome with that beautiful boy and his inexplicable bursts of rage. The years of fulfilling an obligation that had unexpectedly turned into joy and heartbreak.

Then, like a desperate angel, Peter had put an end to the corruption at the heart of the Church.

Shin Bet Headquarters, St. Helena Street, Jerusalem, 0700h

Toad awoke in a cot that had been put up for him in the Black Hole. He had slept restlessly, getting up to gaze at the Eros-Z screen and then falling asleep again. In a dream, Catriel Levine sat on the edge of his cot; he dreamed of her long neck and head hovering over him, her long arms stretched and pointing to the viewscreen as it turned into a flat map of blood vessels, veins and arteries projected on a universe of black.

He awoke and the veins became roads and sea lanes in a night view of the Italian peninsula.

"Anything?" he asked the technician, the third replacement of the night.

"Nothing," was the reply.

Ari's unknown subject had left no trace since disappearing inside the Holy of Holies in Rome. At this point it was unlikely he would be found, but Toad was not impatient and the satellite didn't need sleep. He slumped back into the cot, running scenarios through his mind as if testing combinations to a lock.

The Unknown was either the same shooter who had killed Catriel, or another one with the same skills. Commando training produces people like that, but few with the level of skill to get such a result at 170 meters. The best in the world, even. And such a person must have left traces somewhere. British, Israeli, or American commando schooling, most likely.

"Search this combination: Who are the best long-range marksmen in the world? Where are the best commando training units in the world?" he asked his GeM, and the little brain went to work.

He carefully scrolled through the results: lists of Olympic shooting medalists, competition results, military schools and training camps. But no obvious intersections.

He asked again. "Who is the best long-range marksman in Italy?" More lists—some of the same Olympians, members of competitive shooting clubs, biathlon winners. Strange to combine skiing and shooting in one sporting event, he thought; but then he had never understood the attraction of any sport, despite being hauled off to football matches by Miner. He drilled down on some of the likelier names; nothing surfaced.

After this, he sent the GeM off on another search. "Who was Catriel Levine?"

It was a question he had asked the GeM many times. Her images appeared—a professional photo of a professional woman with a quarter-smile on her face, the same photo again and again; pictures of the Cohen Brothers offices in New York, London, Tel Aviv; the graduating class of some American law school. Official accounts of legal proceedings with "C. Levine" listed among a score of lawyers' names. Nothing about the Mishmar, nothing about the Temple. The GeM knew little about Catriel Levine, Toad realized. It knows little about anyone.

He balanced the sleek silver handheld between his fingers. A portal to all human knowledge; that was the promise.

He tested it again. Touching the panel, he asked, "Why would anyone kill Catriel Levine?"

Of course, he knew it would tell him nothing; he could ask the GeM who, what, where, and how—but never why.

He sighed and closed his eyes, but just then Miner came in and sat down heavily next to his cot. "Any trace yet?"

"No."

"Got the ballistics report from the Italians." Miner's voice was scratchy with fatigue. "Ari's Tavor didn't touch Eagle; the shooter used fairly ordinary nine-millimeter bullets, but they were fired from a gas-powered rifle."

"Silent. Lethal."

"Given the accuracy, he must have used a flash-sensing scope."

"Latest military spec." Toad yawned

"You know this changes everything. There's another shooter out there besides Eagle."

"I know." Toad was thinking aloud. "Actually, five people are involved. Eagle, the shooter, Ari, the woman from Interpol, and her friend, the old Foreign Legionnaire. Now you have all kinds of permutations."

"Could be one Palestinian hunting another. They have their factions. Hamas and Fatah?"

Miner fell quiet when Toad didn't respond. Toad was not asleep, though; he was far too methodical a thinker to go off brainstorming at random. The best theories account for all the elements, he knew, so he tried to think through each element independently.

Miner was right. Eagle could have been the target from the first. There was Kristall's theory about Muslim plots to destroy the Dome of the Rock and incite the Islamic world to attack Israel. Maybe the shooter was after Eagle in the piazza today and at last caught up with him at the Holy Stairs. But which would be the plotter? Which one needed to be stopped—Eagle or the shooter?

Then there were the Interpol agent, Mandelyn, and her elderly friend. He knew nothing about the agent, but the shooter had hit the Legionnaire; what would link the old man to Eagle? Their worlds were so different—why would they both be targets?

He heard a bell from Miner's GeM. "Here's something interesting," Miner said. "About time of death."

"Whose?"

"Chandos and the Pope."

"Everyone knows their time of death. It was all on TV."

149

"They supposedly died within minutes of each other, didn't they? Then why, my friend, was there a two-degree difference in body temperature?"

Toad sat up. "Which one was lower?"

"Chandos. It might mean nothing. After all, it was a cold day and Chandos died inside the chapel, while the Pope made it out into the sunlight."

"It might mean everything. One degree translates into one hour; Chandos could have died as much as two hours before the Pope did."

"But the whole world watched the Pope go into the chapel *with* Chandos."

"Or with someone who looked very much like Chandos."

All at once the quiescent map on the wall buzzed like an angry insect, and a red speck vibrated into view next to the word FIUMICINO. It hovered near the green line that marked the Mediterranean shore.

"The airport," the technician shouted; the screen collapsed on itself and the red speck grew into a blister underneath the words AEROPORTO LEONARDO DA VINCI.

Toad and Miner were on their feet. "Can you fix on that?" Miner asked.

The techs were already bent over their screens. "He's moving—from a car in the road toward Terminal B—lost him." The red marker disappeared inside a building.

"Fix on the car," Toad muttered.

One of the techs grabbed a car moving from the curb. Another was on the phone to the Rome Airport police. Toad admired their speed of reaction; the marker had been onscreen for less than five seconds, but everything that could be done was done.

"Terminal B is the international terminal," one of the techs muttered. "Too bad. It has two piers—there's no way to tell which one he'll use."

If he uses any of them, Toad thought. For anyone as skilled at evasion as this unknown, allowing himself to be seen going into the departure level at the airport was certain to send the police off looking in all directions. He had only to find a blind way out of the terminal—through a parking garage, for instance—and then drive away again.

"It's a taxi. We've stopped it."

"Impound it," Toad commanded in a quiet voice.

Over the loudspeakers he could hear the frustrated shouting of Italian voices, and suddenly a video uplink appeared on the screen—a pursuer's eye view from a collar camera of aluminum-and-glass corridors and crowds of passengers.

Toad looked on, irritated. "We don't even know who we're looking for." He leaned over a tech's shoulder. "Tell them to watch for uniforms, particularly police uniforms." But he had little hope.

They were looking for an image without a face—a uniform, a helmet. Was it a mercenary's face? A religious fanatic's? Was it a male or a female face? Toad recalled the video of the shooter vaulting off the colonnade of St. Peter's, nimble but not adolescent, quick and watchful at once. It was something, but not enough to form a theory, as he had no access to any other image. Except, perhaps...

The best theories account for everything, he said to himself again as he watched the backs of a half dozen black-clad airport police jogging ahead of him on the TV screen. In his mind he played back the video of the Papal assassination: the Pope and the Monsignor climbing toward the sanctuary, the black tide of police surging up the stairs, Zacharias tumbling headfirst covered in blood, the corpse in the chapel. Was it possible the shooter was also in the picture? How else to account for two degrees of difference?

And then, all at once, he knew who he was looking for.

Palazzo Malta, Via dei Condotti, Rome, 0745h

Ari awoke alone in the dark with no idea where he was. For a moment, he was genuinely afraid—there was no light except for formless reflections on glass or stone, he couldn't tell which. The dense air smelled of nothing. The solitude of the place unnerved him; utterly disoriented, he had no sense of where he had been or where to go.

But then he had been alone for a long time—it felt like forever. All he could see ahead was more empty isolation. The tethers that held him to the world seemed brittle: his father and mother, his few friends. Elena was gone forever. Strange, he thought, what blazes of realization cross the mind when all that can be seen is darkness.

Then the GeMphone droned in his ear and he remembered where he was. The little screen threw a blue light over the waiting room of the Palace of the Order of Malta, where he had passed out from exhaustion hours before in an enormous leather chair.

"Yeah," he croaked. It was Toad.

Minutes later he stumbled through the towering doors of the lobby practically into the arms of a tall, elegant individual who was carrying a tea tray. "I had hoped you'd be awake by now, sir," the man said in English without a trace of an Italian accent. "I brought you tea." Surprised, Ari took the cup and sipped at the hot liquid, staring suspiciously at the reflection of his own face in the silver pot. He was a bristly mess.

"I need to see Mr. Mortimer. And what happened to, um, agent Mandelyn?"

"The lady was taken to her hotel. As to Mr. Mortimer, he has not rung yet this morning; he asked us to mind you while you were here."

"Thanks, but…"

"Would you care for some breakfast?"

Ari realized he had eaten nothing in nearly two days except for peanuts on an airline flight and two cups of tea. The attendant piloted him into a marbled room where brioche and butter, tomatoes, pale cheese, and foaming cappuccino were laid on a table dressed in linen. Not bothering to sit, Ari grasped at the food. "Call me a taxi, please?" he asked between bites.

But when he turned around, the attendant had disappeared and Jean-Baptiste Mortimer stood in the doorway in white shirt, blazer, gray flannel trousers, and a red silk bowtie.

"Good morning, Monsieur Davan," he announced, and walked eagerly to the table. "Why don't you sit down?" The old man sat, flourished his napkin, and gestured Ari into a majestic Italianate chair. Ari noticed there were three places set at the table.

"Are we expecting someone else?"

"We are. She'll be here momentarily."

Conscious of his rumpled anorak and scruffy hair and beard, he hesitated, then sat. This man had answers he wanted to hear.

"Did you know there was a problem with the time of death?"

"Didn't know it. Surmised it," the old man said as he put a generous lump of butter on brioche. "What exactly was the discrepancy?"

"Two degrees."

"Ah. That helps. That helps immensely. I wonder if they have jam…" He rang for the attendant.

"And how did you, uh, surmise it?" Ari muttered at him.

The attendant came in and whispered into Mortimer's ear.

"No jam? Oh, well. After all, it's not a hotel. And here's our friend Maryse Mandelyn." Mortimer got to his feet as Maryse came in, shivering from rain and wind. Beneath her topcoat she wore new denims and a cream shirt, and she carried a black travel bag. She lightly embraced Mortimer and took the third chair, with a quizzical smile for Ari. Belatedly, he stood and then sat again, confused.

"Brioche, dear?" Mortimer asked, offering her a plate. "Thank you for coming back. Thanks to both of you. I think it's time we cleared a few things up." He nodded to Ari.

"You asked how I surmised that there were two shooters? Couldn't be simpler. Your shooter couldn't be Peter Chandos, if Peter Chandos was dead in Rome in the morning and committing murder in Haifa in the afternoon."

He took a sip of the cappuccino and dabbed his lips with his napkin.

"Now, the police had swept the Sancta Sanctorum twice—the previous night and a couple of hours before the service—then they closed off the chapel. No one could have been inside; ergo, your unknown shooter must have entered the chapel with the Pope."

"Someone who looked like Chandos?" Maryse asked.

"Exactly. Chandos was already dead and had been for roughly two hours."

"How do you know that?"

"Mr. Davan here told me. There was a two-degree difference in body temperature between Chandos and Zacharias. One degree per hour…"

Maryse exclaimed to Ari, "That's why you wanted time-of-death data."

Mortimer nodded. "I wasn't clear at all how he worked it out, so I had to visit the Sancta Sanctorum myself. Hadn't seen it for many years. Must have been tricky for him—to get inside with the police in the morning, lie in wait for Chandos to make his final inspection at 9 o'clock, murder him, get out again, and dress up like the dead man in time for the big ceremony."

"So," Ari was fascinated. "The Unknown got inside in police disguise and waylaid Chandos. Then he was free to accompany the Pope and kill him too. But how would he get out? The police stormed the building. Unless…"

"Precisely," Mortimer smiled at Ari. "Under his voluminous clerical robes, he still wore his police uniform. He had only to disrobe, hide in the San Lorenzo Chapel, slip in among the police who were running about like madmen, and leave with them."

"Then catch a flight to Tel Aviv," Ari continued.

"To drop an eyelash next to the body of your unfortunate scientist. A busy day for our unknown adversary," Mortimer chuckled, slipping extra sugar into his coffee. "Brings to mind a film I once saw about a man who was betrayed by the DNA in his own eyelash. There are no new ideas."

Maryse broke in. "From a distance, the look-alike might have fooled the crowd, but how did he fool the Pope? Chandos worked with him every day."

"That's where some of your library research came in, Maryse. Your findings on the Chandos family after the war."

"But I didn't find anything about the Chandos family after the war. A page was missing."

"That is exactly the finding that matters. All the most recent information on Sir John Chandos and his children—gone."

Ari picked up on this; he now knew that Mortimer, like Toad, had already guessed. "Chandos had a relative who looked like him—whose DNA matched his. Who resembled him enough to fool everyone. A brother?"

"Undoubtedly. A brother—a twin—who is meant to remain incognito to the rest of the world. *So like they were, no mortal might one from other know.* Macaulay. Otherwise, why remove all trace of him from the records of the Chandos family?"

"So the Unknown killed the Pope." Maryse was relieved and troubled at once. "And his own brother?"

"To vary Orwell a bit," Mortimer said as he finished the last of the brioche:

> *"Poor little Willy is crying so sore,*
> *A sad little boy is he,*
> *For he's broken his little brother's neck,*
> *And he'll have no jam for tea."*

Kibbutz En Gedi, Israel, 0930h

The members of the Mishmar, seeking shade, trailed sorrowfully away from the graveyard and crossed the little desert road that led to the kibbutz meeting place, a pavilion with a corrugated metal roof supported by wooden pillars. Curtains of mosquito netting hung chaotically from the roof.

Even under the pavilion, Nathan Levinsky suffocated in the heat. The funeral of his only daughter had given no consolation. Bolts of anger blinded him, gutted his eyesight, reduced his reason to ashes. She was gone, murdered by a Mohammedan brute as so many others had been. Emanuel gone, Catriel gone. Murdered.

He struck his forehead with his fist. He struck it again and again. All the threats of the prophets of death to the heathen burned within him—it flamed through his frail nerves again as it had against the swinish Russians in his boyhood—it beat against his ears. *I will tread on them in my anger, and trample them in my fury; and their blood shall be sprinkled upon my garments, and I will stain all my clothing.*

It was time and past time for God to act. Some said He was waiting for the Jews to cleanse the Mount and show that they were ready for the Messiah. Others said He would act in His own time.

But perhaps God had already acted.

With abrupt insight, Levinsky looked up at the sky at the sun, the white fire of God. He knew God had put in his own hands, into Nathan Levinsky's hands, a flaming sword that could not be extinguished. A sword that could burn out the hearts of those murderous dogs who had taken everything from him.

Yom Kippur, the day of settling scores, was only one day away. He whispered the words of Isaiah from memory: *For the day of vengeance is in my heart, and the year of my redeemed is come.*

His eyes hot, he now looked around at the miserable little crowd of temple faithful keening in a circle, washing their hands in a pail they were passing from one to another. Rachel Halevy's hands were dripping with water. Levinsky could use these people to excise the abomination from the Temple Mount. But not with water—only fire would cleanse their hands. They would carry fire gladly in their hands to do so. And if God had put such a miracle in *his* hands, why not use it?

The pail came to Levinsky. He still felt in his fists the dust from a stone he had placed on his daughter's grave and would not wash it off. Jules Halevy muttered gently in his ear, "You must wash." He would not. Halevy insisted. Levinsky reached up and took Halevy by the shirt and pulled him down to his face.

"I will not," he whispered. "I cannot. The filth remains on me until they pay for my daughter and my brother. They must pay. It is time. You *know* it is time."

He felt the grating of Halevy's cheek and his stale breath as he pulled away. His friend looked stonelike at him.

Levinsky hissed, "God has put the flaming sword in our hands. You have talked and talked for years, doing nothing but taunting the authorities. They would arrest you if you were not an academic. They don't know you are a fake."

"A fake?"

"Yes. You make meaningless gestures, laying a cornerstone for a temple you know you will never see. There is no plan, there is no goal. No serious work. Your crazy wife knits vestments for a nonexistent priesthood; you march in the streets, but only on your day off. My Casha, my brown-eyed one, she died because you have been playing the fool."

He grasped Halevy again with both hands.

"She *died* for the Temple. And you? You are still living, washing your hands in filthy water, and still you have no plan."

"Nathan, it must be done intelligently," Halevy protested.

"God has been working while you have played the fool. He has put the sword in our hands! Now! Now is the time."

Halevy hugged Levinsky and wrenched him from his seat at the same time; they walked together into the sun away from the mourners, who stared at them as the two men whispered violently at each other. Rachel stood up, shading her eyes from the sun. The move alarmed Levinsky's two bodyguards standing under a wilting terebinth several meters away, but Levinsky waved them away.

Halevy insisted, "We can *buy* the Mount. I know the royals are interested. We can still take the American offer—there will be a delay, that's all…"

"You're not serious," Levinsky retorted. "You have never been serious. You want your hands on billions, fine. But billions will not buy their rotten hearts—you know that. The only thing they respect is blood."

"I miss Casha too, but…"

"Miss her? *Miss* her? She has not gone on a trip, Yuli. She is dead. They killed her! She was worth a billion of them, and a billion of them will pay." The heat soaking his eyes and face, Levinsky stumbled back toward the pavilion, but Halevy caught at him.

"I will put it to them," Levinsky whispered hoarsely in Halevy's face. "And at least one of them will go up the Mount. One of them will—it only needs one. You'll see. I have a GeM left, a working prototype. It will be so easy for one boy just to speak into it, to say one word—*one word*—and God will take him and all of us into His hand."

Levinsky turned to the mourners, now standing silently and watching them. Any one of a dozen boys among them would volunteer without a thought, he knew. He stared into their thin brown faces, streaked and unshaven in their mourning, and thought with satisfaction of their young bones melting like candle wax as the Dome turned to vapor and disappeared into the sky.

Leonardo da Vinci Airport, Fiumicino, Italy, 0930h

David Kane hauled himself into the small jet and took off his wet coat. Grimly, he surveyed Maryse and Ari, who were already seated in the cabin, and then motioned out the jetway for the two pilots to come aboard. He flung shut the curtain that separated the cabin from the cockpit and took his seat facing Maryse.

"The tower says the weather will break in a few minutes; we'll take off then," he told them. "In the meantime, let's talk."

Ari was still cowed by the big man with the brush-cut hair, although Maryse seemed familiar enough with him. It was Kane's airplane. Everywhere the insignia of Interpol—a world globe impaled on a sword—on the curtains, on the fawn leather seats, stamped in gold on the wooden trim.

"The airport police have turned up nothing," Kane launched in. "The taxi has been impounded. They're going over it now, but the word is that it's so filthy they'll find the DNA of a thousand people."

"We're looking for only one trace, though," Maryse spoke up. "The unknown Chandos. Peter's twin."

"If there is such a person," Kane replied.

"There must be. It explains everything." Maryse leaned in energetically. "Fatima Chandos insists that the killer could not have been her husband, as does everyone who knew him. It explains how this man's DNA could be found at the murder scene of Emanuel Shor. It's the same man who's been killing ever since—the two people in Tel Aviv, the Palestinian in Rome last night. From what I understand, it's the same gunman in each instance."

Kane settled back in his chair thinking. Ari waited for him to say something, but there was silence. He didn't know how welcome his own words might be in this exchange that seemed almost father-to-daughter. An odd connection existed between these two, he realized, between this delicate, artistically-minded woman and this old Royal Marine: he recognized the massive crowned-lion ring Kane wore.

Feeling out of place, he half-wondered why he was on this plane. Maryse had already arranged to fly with Kane—she was going to investigate the transports that had been sent to Lebanon. Now, for them both, there was an even more compelling reason to go: no records existed of any sibling of Peter Chandos. Every vital record from Rome to Lebanon listed Peter as the only child of one Rafqa Chandos, with paternity unknown.

Telephone calls to the hospital where Peter was born and to the government of Lebanon had turned up nothing. Rafqa herself had been an only child, thus no near relatives. Even Fatima Chandos, who had been reached at her parents' home, was astonished at the suggestion: there was no brother, there had never been a brother.

Only Peter's mother would know the truth. Ari had to talk to her. The problem—Rafqa Chandos had suffered a series of strokes, the worst one a week before, when she learned of the death of her son. According to the doctors, she was not likely to be of much help. Still, there was a chance, it was the best lead he had, and the flight would bring him closer to home. There was no reason to stay in Italy, now that they had lost track of the Unknown.

An Interpol car had come for them, Mortimer had waved them away from the gates of the Palace of Malta with a condescending grin, and they were at the door of the plane almost before Ari could think through why he was going. On the way, Maryse had worked agitatedly over her GeM, lips tight, studying the little screen as she entered one combination after another of the words *Chandos, marksman, commando training* and a dozen others, trying to wring out of the Internet any trace of the still-theoretical twin brother of Peter Chandos. Nothing. In the meantime, his own thoughts became more and more jumbled; now he needed to pour them out to someone.

Once before, the President of Interpol had listened to him, so he leaped in. "I'm afraid nothing's really been explained."

Kane's head turned abruptly, and Ari swallowed. "You'll remember our talk yesterday morning, sir."

"Yes."

"The whole thing is still as fantastic as at the start. Why would one man— obviously a highly trained killer, probably a black-ops person—successively kill his own brother, the Pope of Rome, an Israeli geneticist and his lawyer niece, the security chief of Technion, and a secret policeman from Palestine? Ruling out a psychopath, we have utter disconnection—each case is highly suggestive by itself, but together they make no sense."

Kane grunted. "Could be a mercenary."

"In whose pay?"

"Maybe he likes the work. Wasn't it one of your reports that found this man Peter Chandos was genetically wired for violence? If he does have a brother, he'd share the genes, wouldn't he?"

Ari wished he had Toad at his side.

Then the pilot's voice interrupted them. "The weather hold has been lifted and we will leave now. We are just under three hours to Beirut. Please prepare for takeoff."

Anemic sunshine brightened the wet, cool glass of the windows. The plane shuddered toward high speed and vaulted into the air. Soon, far below them, the city of Rome glistened damp in the momentary light. Ari could now pick out the ring of St. Peter's square and then the obelisk jutting up from the piazza of San Giovanni—he would not forget the night before, caught there between two deadly unknowns.

The roar and pressure of the climb ended, and the cabin fell quiet again.

Kane turned to Ari: "What about your theory of yesterday? The plot to destroy the Dome of the Rock?"

Ari was pleased that Kane remembered and mortified that he couldn't fit last night into his theory. But then he was stunned when Kane retrieved his own argument for him almost word for word:

"Point one, you said: Shor in Haifa and Chandos in Rome, two thousand kilometers apart, dead the same day, both wearing rings inscribed with a Bible verse about the coming of the Messiah.

"Your point two: Shor had on him a picture of the Jewish temple with the same verse handwritten on the back.

"Your point three: Peter Chandos was, according to the DNA people, a descendant of Jewish temple priests.

"Your point four: Shor and his late niece belonged to a cult of some kind, dedicated to rebuilding the temple.

"Now, from your perspective of yesterday, all of this adds up to a plot—that people are being eliminated to protect this plot, which is to create a New Jerusalem out of the Old. Oh…you also said that the, um, item taken from Technion might play a part."

Ari smiled and said nothing; Maryse looked at him with wide eyes.

"It seems to me," Kane went on, "that the discovery of this new suspect might lend support to your idea." The older man looked out his window at the blue haze below and fell quiet.

Ari waited for him to continue, but he didn't. After a long silence, Ari realized that he was being challenged. "Well," he stammered, "if there is an unknown Chandos, he would share Peter's DNA and would also be a *cohen*. Thus, he might have an interest in the Temple—in protecting any plans for the Temple." His mind lit up. "Yes. The DNA sample that was taken—it must have been the unknown twin's, not Peter's. He's been trying to hide his existence from us all along. That's why it was stolen from the lab."

Maryse jumped in. "And if Shor knew him from the Mishmar and trusted him, that explains why Shor broke into the two laboratories—to help the plot along."

Kane added, "But Shor didn't realize that our Unknown was in business for himself." He paused. "It's a possibility. A satisfying possibility in some respects. But it's not sufficient."

Ari and Maryse waited for more.

Kane shrugged into a pillow, closed his eyes, and said. "There's the small detail of the Pope. What required his death? What does the Temple of Jerusalem have to do with the Vatican in Rome?"

And, picking up a blanket, he turned away from them to take a nap.

Kibbutz En Gedi, Israel, 1130h

A police car outside was the only sign of trouble, Toad thought. The Halevy cottage looked quiet, exactly as he had seen it a few days before. No broken windows, not even a broken vine on the little stone wall around the property.

"Inspector," the officer nodded as Toad entered the open door and showed his identification. The man was just closing his tablet and putting his pen away. "Looks to be simple robbery. Three items of clothing taken from that basket there. Seems they were valuable artifacts."

"Yes," was all Toad said. Although the room had several comfortable chairs, Jules and Rachel Halevy sat silent on the floor, leaning against the wall and staring straight ahead, apparently emotionless. Both were dressed entirely in dull black linen. The collar of Jules' shirt lay open, ripped from his neck to his shoulder, while Rachel's shirtwaist was torn in a mourning gesture. She wore over her hair a black batiste so faded it was nearly blue.

Without waiting for an invitation, Toad selected a cane chair and sat down in front of them. "I'm Inspector Sefardi. Thank you for letting us know about the theft," Toad said. Jules Halevy turned his head curtly; he was clearly tired of dealing with the police.

"And I'm very sorry about your loss." For once, this was more than pro forma. Toad nodded at the photograph of Catriel that dominated the opposite wall between two shaded windows; these were words he had used many times without meaning them, but this time was different.

And he understood why they sat on the floor—they were performing *shiva*, the seven days of mourning. Rachel Halevy glanced up at him with a tiny sign of thanks, then went on rocking back and forth slowly, almost imperceptibly. She was in deepest sorrow, and Toad respected it. But he needed answers.

"I understand the funeral was…quite moving," he said, uncharacteristically.

Rachel stiffened. "Yes, it was. I dressed her in my own white shroud…the one I had woven for myself." She was quiet for a moment, then looked up at Toad, almost as if he were a friend. "We buried her facing east—to greet the Messiah, you know, when he comes."

Toad nodded. From the picture on the wall, the limitless black eyes of Catriel Levine stared out into nothing. He forced his thoughts back to the job. "I know you've told the officer here about the theft, but would you mind telling me again…when did you notice the items were missing?"

Rachel spoke absently. "Not until this morning. I don't know why—I felt like looking at them, opened the basket, and they were gone."

"And the last time you saw them?"

"Was when you were here with the other men."

"So someone could have taken them…"

"That night while we were at a kibbutz meeting? Perhaps during the funeral."

"Nothing else missing?"

She slowly shook her head.

Toad stood and walked out the open door, where he found the policeman examining the windows. "What do you think?"

The officer seemed bored. "Simple. No force needed. Nobody on the kibbutz locks up. You want something, you waltz through the door and take it." Then he cocked his head. "Why is Shin Bet interested in this?"

Toad gave the man a half-smile and asked, "Did anyone notice anything?"

"They were all at the weekly meeting—about harvests, prices, all that. I'm surprised there aren't more burglaries here."

Toad called up on his GeMscreen a picture of Peter Chandos' face. "Have you seen this man in the area?"

The officer grunted. "You're joking, right? The man who shot the Pope?" He started to laugh and then realized Toad was not smiling. "I'm off now," he said, edging toward his car.

"Thanks," said Toad, and walked back into the house as the police car raced away.

Jules Halevy came out of the house, shading his eyes from the sun. He stopped as if to say something, then appeared to change his mind. "I'm going to the guest bungalow to sit *shiva* with Nathan Levinsky," he announced. "Any questions you have, my wife can answer."

Toad went inside to talk to Rachel.

"Do you have an idea who might have wanted to take the garments?" Toad asked her.

She looked up, startled that he was still there. "No. No one. They have no value except..."

"To the high priest of the Temple."

"Yes. They were made for his purpose only. It will be difficult to replace them," she said, rising painfully from the floor, "but perhaps others can be made in time."

"In time for what?"

The woman was taller than Toad, her body erect and strong under the folds of black linen. "In time for the consecration of the Temple. It must be done."

"How?" he asked quietly. "How could the Temple be built without taking down the Muslim shrines?"

"The Temple will be rebuilt. It *must* be rebuilt," she responded in a frozen whisper.

"Why must it be rebuilt?"

"Are you observant, Inspector?"

"I'm a secular Jew."

"Then perhaps you don't realize that the salvation of Israel is not in your bombs, your guns, and your secret police. It is not in playing appeaser. The only salvation of Israel is faith in Ha-Shem and in his covenant, in the command to rebuild his House. For a hundred generations we have mourned the Temple, we have stood before God an impure and an unholy people, unable to redeem ourselves from our sins. Only when the Temple is rebuilt can the Messiah come and redeem Israel at last."

"Is it up to the Jews to rebuild it—or to God?"

"The Rambam taught that we must rebuild it ourselves; it is one of the Thirteen Articles."

"But Maimonides also taught that the Messiah would build the Temple. In fact, it is by rebuilding the Temple that he will prove he is the Messiah."

"You know the Rambam? You—a secular Jew?"

Toad waved this aside. "Mrs. Halevy, was Catriel involved in any kind of... plan to remove the Muslim shrines?"

"Do you mean to destroy them? To blow them up?" Rachel replied acidly. "No." She paced around the table, holding onto chairs as if to support herself. "But she thought perhaps they could be bought. Not officially, not openly. Still, there are Islamic powers that are venal enough to betray their faith."

"And where would your movement have got the kind of money that would be needed to try something like that?"

"You should ask her father that question."

"Thank you, I will. Does the name Lambert Sable mean anything to you?"

Rachel looked confused, then shook her head.

"Again, I feel sorry for your loss." Toad turned to go. It was all he knew how to say.

As he left, Rachel Halevy stared at him as if wondering how such a nonentity—and a secular one at that—could feel anything at all.

**

Toad wandered down the little lane into the kibbutz until he found a sign pointing to the cemetery. All around him, the settlement was utterly silent, except for the cry of birds in the sulky heat. Willows shaded the lane, tall, brown, and limp for lack of water; a great terebinth tree stood inside the gate of the cemetery, its distressed branches sagging with drought, its roots pushing off to odd angles the gravestones beneath it.

Impressed by the quiet, Toad sat down on a bench in the shade of the terebinth and fanned himself with his notebook. It was years since he had felt the peace of the Sabbath, the only thing about the *yeshivah* he missed, and the welcome escape, one day a week, from the noise of the world. He listened—no farm machinery, no cars, no voices even in the distance. Utter stillness.

He remembered the Sabbath hours staring at the sterile white brick walls of the *yeshivah* where he had grown up and been schooled after the death of his parents—killed by a terrorist attack on a pizza restaurant. They had died for pizza, he had often thought, laughing shortly and bitterly to himself, leaving him alone to make his anonymous way through school, through the military where, having done poorly on the physical, he was relegated to the criminal investigation division, and then through a slow, humiliating life. His mother and father were buried in a cemetery like this one; he had visited it one time.

But once a week, after the gesticulations of the synagogue, the Sabbath meant he could stay in his room, tidy his bed, and read all day from his small, select collection of books. He read everything—the Tanakh, the Talmud, the Zohar—not because he loved wisdom, but because he read everything in reach. And the holy books were there, available. He read them many times. No one at the *yeshivah* ever noticed him, no one ever came looking for him, so he was content—and safe. It felt good to lie on his bed reading. He missed that.

At age twelve, he had picked up some books thrown away behind the library. It didn't matter to him what they were; they were new to him. One of them was a romance novel, as he later learned. It was filled with vague descriptions of passion that raised a grotesque feeling in him. He read again and again. To him, real women were unimaginably remote, as alien as some extinct and gorgeous reptile, and he had developed his acute power of observation because of his enthrallment with them. He had no interest in pornography; it was overkill. Instead, he was hypnotized by a breath or an eyelash or the tilt of a neck.

He had studied Catriel Levine microscopically—her thin temper, her olive hands, her eyes with their complex agenda of fanaticism mixed with cold control. Like a gemstone, she was hard but vulnerable, too. A rich man had found the flaw in her. A rich American with his hand on her.

But your riches shall fall into the sea in the day of your ruin.

In the middle of the cemetery he caught sight of a fresh hill of dry white earth topped by a pile of stones. This would be the new grave. He got up and walked around it. There was no name on the grave, but he knew whose it was. She had died alone and cruelly, and now that she was dead matter under the gravel of this desert, he found it harder than ever to coax up any kind of faith in human connections—they were all but impossible to make, and doomed anyway. But he ached nevertheless, and though he could not say why, he wished he could have spoken to this woman and raised a smile from her. Just once in his life.

He found a small gray stone on the ground, picked it up, and gently laid it on the pile that marked the place where she rested.

"Inspector."

Toad was startled by the voice. He turned; in the mottled shadow of the terebinth, barely visible, stood Jules Halevy.

"There is something I must discuss with you."

The Sistine Chapel, Rome, 1400h

The hymn had been sung, the vows taken, and the doors closed and locked. The preacher climbed up to the lectern and looked over the assembled cardinals, who sat in hastily constructed ranks of seats on both sides of the chapel. Michelangelo's Last Judgment soared up the wall behind the lectern, its devils with bile-colored faces herding the damned into the sulfur of Hell, while the righteous slipped heavenward through golden air as if magnetized by the colossal bronze hand of the Christ. Before this spectacle the young preacher stood, all in white like a miniature angel. Cardinal Estades had nominated him, both supporters and opponents of *In Salutem Ecclesiae* had signed off on him, and everyone was curious to hear him.

By custom, the homily that began the conclave laid out the challenges facing the Church so that the college could consider them in choosing the Pope. The honor of reading the homily was traditionally highly sought after, but there had been no time for the usual wrangling. In fact, most of the logical candidates had decided to be unavailable; the divisions in the room were so deep, it would be a mortal stroke to a career to take one side or another. The earnest young priest who agreed to do it, a teacher of homiletics in the Papal university, was to some a brave man and to others a sacrificial lamb.

"Brothers, the glorious city of God is my theme," he began in English, the language most of the cardinals understood, in a voice nervous but determined, "and the promise of the Church of Christ to the faithful in the earth. It is a surer hope than anything the tottering world can hold out. As the Prophet Isaias taught, every one that shall be left in Sion, and that shall remain in Jerusalem, shall be called holy.

"Before the Church today is the great question: What does it mean to 'remain in Jerusalem'?"

"Some passionately argue that the citizens of Jerusalem have been given over to Sodom and Gomorrah, that the rupture of ancient canons brings down the gates of the temple, inviting corruption into the holy place."

Seated near the lectern, Cardinal Tyrell nodded, turned his massive head, and raised his eyes to look directly into the eyes of John Paul Stone across the aisle. Stone stared back at him. Tyrell listened with satisfied surprise as the preacher went on to enumerate the abominations that Zacharias II had forced on the Church: divorce, "gender equity" in the priesthood, perversions of marriage, the abandonment of celibacy. Around him, he noted, heads were nodding in agreement.

"These measures, in their view, taken in the name of compassion and inclusiveness, threaten the very foundations of the Church Militant, the Church founded to war against these very evils. So, as the prophet Isaias warned, in taking these measures we might have been as Sodom, and should have been like Gomorrah."

The preacher stopped and drank from a glass of water.

"Others speak with an utterly different voice. For them, the great challenge to the Church is not in these canonical deviations but, as the prophet Ezechiel said, '*the iniquity of Sodom is pride…neither did she strengthen the hand of the poor and needy.*' God has a controversy with a Church and a hierarchy, they say, who have sold their souls for material gain and look with proud disdain on the marginal, the different, and the outcast. In the words of the prophet Isaias, '*The spoil of the poor is in your house. Why do you consume my people and grind the faces of the poor?*' We must eternally ask ourselves, was he speaking of us?"

It was Cardinal Stone's turn to stare down Tyrell. Why, he asked himself, did these old men strain at a few liberating changes made by Zacharias and continue to swallow the cruel ideologies of capitalism? Saving a world immersed in poverty both material and spiritual—that was the proper work of the Church.

The preacher took a long breath, as if suddenly uncertain what to say next. But he pushed on.

"These two parties threaten the Church, our Holy Mother Church, with schism. Some bishops have already declared with haughty outrage that they will not bow to the See of Peter in the matter of *In Salutem Ecclesiam*. Now, through an act of treachery, that See is vacant, and the proponents of the late Pope are in their turn threatening defections of their own if a new Pope should recant on the measures taken by the Council. We hear every day of unimaginable things—a new African-Latin American federation of Catholic dioceses on one hand; on the other, the archbishoprics of Canada threaten to break communion with Rome.

"It is my task to raise a warning voice. If we prove unable to maintain our unity in Christ, if we elect a Pope out of anger at each other, the Church will tear itself in two and fall under the interdict of God, as He has said in holy scripture: '*Cursed be their fury, because it is stubborn: and their wrath because it is cruel: I will divide them in Jacob, and will scatter them in Israel.*' "

"What is he saying?" the little African bishop, growing indignant, asked in Tyrell's ear. "Shush," he replied. Tyrell had heard convocation sermons before, but never one like this—so much scripture, so much candor. Regardless of where the preacher was going with this, he admired his courage. He reminded Tyrell of Peter Chandos—the zeal, the candor, the physical beauty of the strong youth in pure white.

"We must humble our lofty eyes, we must stoop from our haughtiness as men, and exalt the Lord alone, as in the day when He will come again and put an end to our contentions.

"Because that day will come, and as the prophet Isaias says, that day shall fall upon every one that is proud and high minded, and upon every one that is arrogant, and he shall be humbled."

Stone was growing resentful; he disliked the insinuation that his fervor for change was arrogance. The need for change went far beyond what had been achieved; the reforms of Zacharias merely laid the foundation for future revolutions. Stone had been studying the tools of the papacy and was fascinated by the Medieval practice of the papal interdict—the equivalent of excommunicating entire nations for disobedience to papal command. Although in the twenty-first century the interdict would have nothing like the impact it had in the Middle Ages, it would still make an enormously important statement to rich countries that refused to do more to help poor countries. He could envision laying an interdict on Britain and the USA— what a prospect! Tens of millions of Catholics putting furious pressure on their governments. What a tool for forcing change…But the election needed winning first. Stone looked around in dismay at the empty seats of the Canadian delegation, who had boycotted the conclave because of its haste. They would have been valuable votes.

"This week our brothers of the Jewish faith will set aside a day, one day of the year that is devoted solely to reconciliation, as commanded by Leviticus: *'Upon the tenth day of the seventh month shall be the day of atonement; it shall be most solemn, and shall be called holy.'* The Jews call this holiest day of the year Yom Kippur. In the English language it is called the Day of Atonement—the day when all debts are forgiven, all differences are put aside, and the people become 'at one' with each other and with God.

"Might it be possible for the day of this conclave to become a Day of Atonement, a day of forgiveness, of understanding, of embracing one another's differences—not in sacrifice of principle, but in upholding of brotherhood? Not with an unyielding mind, but in remembrance of the yielding knees of Our Lord, who Himself knelt to wash the feet of Peter and your Apostolic predecessors?"

Tyrell caught the eye of Manolo Estades, who was beaming beatifically up at the preacher, and smiled and nodded at him. The boy had been a good choice. Tyrell resolved to approach the election with humility; he would not be cavalier about revoking the acts of the previous Pope. It would be done with care.

"And so I conclude my plea with the declaration of the Psalmist: *'Behold how good and how pleasant it is for brethren to dwell in unity.'* "

For a moment Tyrell thought there might be applause as the young man descended the lectern and exited the chapel; those around Estades mutedly congratulated on him on his choice, and the huge room filled with appreciative whispers. The homily had been well received. Yes, Tyrell said to himself, he would approach the papacy in the spirit of seeking unity—but without sacrificing principle. He felt exalted, inspired.

Then, across the aisle, he caught sight of the superlatively confident Archbishop of Manaus, surrounded by his conclavists, busily writing his own enthronement speech.

Besharri, Lebanon, 1535h

The hybrid motor of the little hired car bleated in protest as it reached the thousand-meter mark. It was an old red Mercedes Tourer, and its shifting from electrons to petrol was already uncertain; but Ari willed it with a heavy foot over a hill and stopped in trees at the pedestal of the town. Above, rock houses rose in terraces toward a golden stone church, and Maryse smiled at the beauty of the place.

She got out of the car and looked upward. The town sat in a bowl beneath the colossal escarpment of Mount Lebanon. She had seen pictures of the year-round snows, but now there was no trace—the heat had scalded everything. Even this wilted grove felt like the kiln room at her old ceramics school. Fortunately, Ari had warned her about the unusual heat, and she wore a light linen top and shorts that made her self-conscious. But she was grateful she had put them on at the airport before making this expedition into this feverish landscape.

Before flying on to Tel Aviv, Kane had dropped them on the runway in Beirut, where this car had been waiting for them—a rust-red Mercedes hybrid arranged by Interpol. But it wasn't the most reliable of cars, and she was happy to let Ari drive. Their GeM navigators were useless here. For two hours they had struggled with the old car's navigation system that knew nothing about these branching, coiling roads, but at last found the town where Peter and Fatima had grown up—and where the transport from the Vatican had terminated two days before.

A police official in a sweat-tarnished shirt was walking down steps to meet them. A short man with a mustache like a small animal, he gazed at Maryse's long legs disapprovingly. She wished she had not worn the shorts after all.

"You are Interpol?" he asked in snipped French.

"Yes," she said in the same language, producing her ID and glancing uncomfortably toward Ari. They had discussed it and decided not to reveal Ari's background unless asked: the reception for an Israeli in Lebanon could be unpredictable. Ignoring the man, he was still putting his backpack together. She glimpsed his requisitioned Tavor as he dropped it into the bag.

"Yes, my colleague and I are here to trace a shipment that might have contained contraband artworks."

"Your office informed us," the official replied. "We are of course very pleased to help." He was still examining her bared white legs.

"Most grateful," Maryse murmured. "Shall we be on our way?" she called to Ari in English, who came up beside her, grinning.

At the top of the stairs was a little plaza buried in a clump of blond stone buildings. In a shaded café, three men in sand-colored working clothes drank wine; a thin policeman stood watch on them, but no one else was visible in the sun-darkened square. The official presented them to Maryse.

"These are the drivers who brought your shipment to the school. At your request I have detained them at their hotel. I have warned them to cooperate completely with you."

The policeman nudged the men and they stood, openly staring at her legs as if they had never seen anything so white. Holding her heavy bag in both hands, Maryse moved to conceal herself behind one of the cloth-covered tables; at her side, Ari stifled a cough.

All three drivers were southern Italians on their way home—but she sensed they were not too angry about the delay. The table was littered with empty wine bottles. She asked a few questions and then projected a photo of Peter Chandos onto the tabletop. One of the men hesitated, tapped at the picture, and nodded. She told the police official to let them go, and he marched the three men growling away. "Wine—finished!" he barked.

When they were out of sight she turned excitedly to Ari, who had understood nothing. "They unloaded the consignment at the school Thursday night. One of the boxes was different; it was big but narrow. The mayor was there to greet them; the headmistress and the sisters supervised everything, but while everyone was inside the school, this driver went for a cigarette. A man in work clothes approached him and handed him a bill for the narrow box. Then he carried it off to a small van."

"That's when you showed him the picture?"

"Yes. He said it was coming on night and he couldn't be sure, but he thought the man in work clothes looked like the man in the picture."

"What about the van?"

"He said it was an old beater, red, rusty, petrol engine. A Jeep. He remembers being surprised that the man didn't take the box into the school with the other boxes."

"The Acheropita."

"I think we're on track. Now we have to find that Jeep." She pulled her GeM from her bag. "Kane will take care of it. Then we have another stop to make."

Ari went into the café for two bottles of water. He had changed into a light shirt, but his climbing boots were heavy—he felt more secure in them. Wiping the sweat from his face on his sleeve, he turned to watch Maryse as she talked agitatedly on the phone. She was talking to Kane. There was an odd connection between them—colleagues, yes—but more. A pitch in Kane's voice, a cadence he had noticed, just a trace.

But then it wasn't his affair.

She was a professional, and that was all that mattered to him. She would be useful up to a point; there would be the awkwardness at the end, and it would mean little and then, in time, nothing. As he watched her leaning tensely into the phone, he took a bottle from his pocket and drank thirstily. The paleness of her arms and legs, the scattering of freckles around her green eyes, the autumn-colored hair—she had been a physical presence only as all women were, and until today, muffled against the cold of Europe. Now she was exposed, vulnerable. He wondered how she would deal with what was coming.

His own GeM rang. It was Toad.

"We've arrested Nathan Levinsky."

"What?"

"We've arrested Levinsky and several men from the Temple society. They were planning to use the, uh, item to remove it. You know. To remove *it*."

Ari made sense of this. So there *was* a plot, and Toad couldn't risk even saying the words openly.

"We're holding them at St. Helena Street. K's interrogating them now."

"How did you get onto them?"

"Jules Halevy. Here's another odd twist," said Toad. "Somebody stole the high priestly vestments from the Halevys."

"What? When?"

"Probably Thursday night while they were at a kibbutz meeting. Or possibly during the Levine funeral. Anyway, while I was at the kibbutz, Halevy approached me and told me about Levinsky's plan. He was going to send one of the Mishmar boys into the Dome on Monday."

"Yom Kippur," Ari breathed.

"I'll keep you informed. Our trace on that red circuit? The French police say the man you met in Paris has gone missing."

"His name was...um, Grammont."

"Yeah. They went to his office, to his flat—nothing. He was at the library yesterday, but didn't show today. Otherwise, co-workers are useless; they say he wasn't really on staff. Just had a carrel there. No neighbors know anything, they can't identify any relatives..."

"What about the other man—Mortimer?"

"There's another odd one. There's huge data on him as you said, far too much. Lots of traveling, lots of appointments abroad, lots of honors. One thing doesn't fit—as far as I can tell, he wasn't in Lebanon when he told you he was."

"He was never in Lebanon?"

"I didn't say that. He was in Lebanon—in the 1980s with the Foreign Legion. But he had no assignment there in '06 with the French peacekeepers."

"So he couldn't have run afoul of Hezbollah then."

"Not then. He spent '06 and '07 in New York with the UN."

"What did he do with the UN?"

"That's the odd part. He has all these assignments, but you can't tell what he's actually doing. No particular job description."

"And I used to think he was just a tour guide."

Toad was quiet for a moment. "Why would the Unknown climb the colonnade of St. Peter's in the middle of the papal funeral to take a shot at a tour guide?

"Yeah. Another good question with no answer. I'd better ring off."

Ari looked back at Maryse, who was also putting her phone away. She saw him through the café door, waved, and smiled.

Air France Flight 1620 over the Mediterranean, 1540h

Lucien Grammont closed his book for the descent into Tel Aviv. The flight had been pleasant once out of the storms over Europe, the dinner quite good—truffled chicken, excellent *haricots verts* with béarnaise sauce, and a wine he would remember. He was glad the Order allowed for his one vice, although he was not the gourmand that Mortimer was.

Grammont brushed himself off, pulled his tie straight, and looked around with distaste at his fellow passengers. Most of them unshaven, they wore sport shirts, sandals, and even short pants; obviously they had heard of the heat wave in the Middle East, but still that was no reason to dress in such a fashion in *première classe*. He was no lover of the twenty-first century, of electric automobiles, apps for everything, and the abandonment of dignity. Between a fine coffee in the morning and tea in the late afternoon, his days were spent in a courtly world of old manuscripts and books illuminated by hand. To him, the Medieval world was the ideal and the present century a Dark Age.

His Paris apartment on the sixth étage of a private hotel in the James Joyce Square was sparely ornamented with antique engravings and icons of substantial value to a knowledgeable eye; but his books were his true treasure. Fifty years of collecting had taken the place of wife, children, or friends, and he relished his library with an intensity that most men reserve for money or sex. In fact, in his university days an acquaintance—not a friend—had referred to him as a "bibliosexual." The few really fine volumes he owned—originals of Rabelais and Montesquieu and one piece of Incunabula—he kept in a bank vault; but the simple white shelves that walled his apartment shone with hundreds of old leather books immaculately catalogued and cared for. He knew each book with the intimacy of a childhood friend and could lay his hand on the one he wanted even in the dark.

Even now he held his book tight under his arm for the descent. It was a nineteenth-century edition of Shakespeare's *Henry IV*, a favorite he had read many times, taking pleasure each time in the downfall of the proud would-be usurper, Hotspur, at the hands of the dilettante prince. Grammont didn't like men who wanted to dominate the future. He hadn't the slightest interest in the future; the fertile past was his terrain, and he interred himself in it completely.

So it was ironic that he was paid so well to erase it. Although he disliked working with computers, he found it easy and the detection work interesting. He was well paid. The money meant good books and fine restaurants, so he frankly didn't mind long hours searching databases for anything that might obstruct the Order's mission or even hint at its existence.

His predecessors had done their work more concretely—at times they had been required to eliminate certain threats in person. He was prepared to do this; his experience in the Foreign Legion had left him with the necessary skills. But the work had been almost entirely and pleasantly remote, as the Library had the fastest of fiber connections and the fussiest security. Sometimes his work involved an abrupt and anonymous threat of litigation against an academic—he found them easy to intimidate because they ordinarily had little money and feared losing what they had. Usually, however, he did his work without notice. A page disappeared from a book, a Web site lost content, a newspaper archive was erased. Often money was involved, but it was never extravagant; and he had rarely met any of his "subjects."

Nor did he have much contact with his principals. They left him to do his work and cared not at all that he spent most of his time on his own collections. The flurry of calls from them the last few days was not unexpected. Only one call startled him: when he was asked if he had removed a certain page from the Great Book at the Via Condotti. He had not.

In the past year, he had twice feared that he might have to leave his eyrie at the Bibliothèque Nationale. Once in the summer in response to a rocket attack in Jerusalem, and another just this week to intercept two police officers investigating the death of one of his principals. The rocket attack had failed to raise the concerns anticipated; and in the latter case the police had come to him. They had in the end caused little trouble. Now, however, there was an undeniable need for a meeting. Death could not be escaped.

No one in the Order had required replacement during his tenure, so this meeting would be his first. For years, he had tried to imagine the Order members together and always pictured the rare meeting taking place in a sumptuous mansion with walls of paneled wood and tapestried chairs. However, it was to be held in a hotel conference room like any down-market business meeting; that had been the request, and he had complied with it. The arrangements had been easy, the expense minimal, the locus pedestrian: a tourist hotel on Mt. Scopus in Jerusalem. Perhaps it had been chosen because of the short notice; but it was more likely the ceaseless need for anonymity. Also, there was a certain humility in the choice, and humility was not in Grammont's vocabulary of virtues.

He had not planned to leave Paris until Sunday, but an insistent call at five o'clock that morning had instructed him otherwise. It was not an unwelcome call; he could postpone one of those intolerable visits to the dentist on the rue Montaigne. He was to go immediately. At the time he had wondered why he had not been contacted through the normal channel; it became clear when he realized the normal channel had been shut down some hours earlier. It worried him a bit; still, the meeting schedule had not changed. No doubt there would be fresh duties on arrival.

The lights of the airliner dimmed for landing. Grammont could see from his window the sheer line between light and blackness marking the Levantine coast. He had visited the Holy Land many times in connection with his work, but he never landed here without thinking of the ships of his Frankish forebears, Crusaders keen on crushing the infidel, armored men slogging ashore, among them the Chevalier du Grand Mont, his earliest recorded ancestor, who had died on the grim road between Jaffa and golden Jerusalem. Thirty generations had not effaced the memory of the young warrior who left his lady and son in France to expel the heathen from the temple of the Savior and Son of God.

Discreetly, Grammont crossed himself as the plane descended to the runway and the soil of the Holy Land. The lights came up. Sighing, he opened his book and re-read the first page:

> *"Therefore, friends,*
> *As far as to the sepulchre of Christ,*
> *Whose soldier now, under whose blessed cross*
> *We are impressed and engaged to fight."*

Shin Bet Headquarters, St. Helena Street, Jerusalem, 1555h

"The Arab networks are coming on with an emergency announcement," her skinny assistant whispered into Tovah Kristall's ear.

"All of them?"

"Yes. All at once. It's scheduled for four o'clock."

"Get these people out of here," she snapped at the security men and stood. Three frightened-looking boys jumped up and followed the men out of the room; Nathan Levinsky remained in his chair, trembling, unshaven.

"So you don't know anything," she shot at him. "Too shocked, too old, too grief-stricken. Just don't start drooling—then I'll be sure it's an act."

She left Levinsky in Toad's keeping, but not before calling him to the door.

"They've gone over everything at the kibbutz, correct? No sign of the missing prototype."

"Nothing," Toad responded quietly.

"Splendid," she said bitterly. "Now we have two of them out there somewhere. And Miner's going over everything with Halevy?"

"Yes."

"Briefing in fifteen minutes. I've got to find out what the Arabs are up to now."

Kristall didn't wait for the elevator. She lit a cigarette and climbed the stairs, trailing smoke and hacking all the way to the briefing room. Inside were Shin Bet's security analysts and Didi Mattanyah.

"Must be an important TV show," she said as they settled around the table to watch the big screen, where an ordinary-looking news anchor was rattling away low-volume in Arabic. A black, white, and green banner emblazoned with a black eagle rippled behind his head.

"It's a war flag," one of the analysts intoned.

"I know that," Kristall snapped back at him. She gestured at her assistant: "Get a linkup with the defense ministry."

All at once a babble of voices could be heard over the sound system; it was the noise from the defense ministry scenario room.

"Pretty loud," she said. "Whatever this is, it's going to be nasty."

Then everything went quiet as a group of scowling men showed up on the screen. One was a cleric; most of the others were whiskered and wearing open-necked shirts. One looked almost pristine in coat and tie, and he was the speaker. Everyone well knew who he was. Arabic script began to race silently across the bottom of the screen.

The translator's voice stuttered to life.

"We have uncovered a Zionist plot to destroy the holy shrines of Al-Aqsa. This plot is to be carried out on Monday, the Zionists' holy day.

"The Zionist threat to Al-Aqsa is well documented. For sixty years the Zionist entity have held the holy shrines in their hands, eating away at them, digging under them for what they call archeological purposes. They have hoped for generations that the shrines would fall of their own accord.

"But now their patience is ended. They are sending madmen to bomb the shrines using a new type of explosive, while denying all knowledge of the plot. They will insist that it is all an inexplicable accident.

"Let the Zionist regime understand clearly the consequences of the destruction of the holy shrines. They will find that the patience of the Islamic world shall also be at an end. Retaliation will be swift and massive."

The uproar from the defense ministry was long and loud. Tovah Kristall sat silently, irritated by the noise, her eyes on her frightened analysts, feeling tired and old. She had worked so hard for so many years, but nothing had changed.

Then Didi stood. "Anyone for coffee? It's going to be a horrid evening." Against her will, Kristall laughed amid the angry shouting from the defense ministry over the telephone and the mobs screaming death to Israel over the television. "Coffee, yes." And then she waited.

It took only seconds for the Prime Minister to come on her private link wanting to know how word got out about the Levinsky affair. "It's somebody in your organization, obviously."

"Pardon my contradicting you, Prime Minister," she growled, "but that isn't obvious at all. You knew about it and so did your people. We'll fly this mission together, or you can be sure we'll crash together." She wasn't certain, but she thought the politician whimpered at the other end of the line. "Now we have two jobs to do. One is to make assurances to all quarters that there *was* a crazy plot, but it's completely under control. That's your job. The other is to make sure that it *is* completely under control, and that's mine. That includes finding out who tipped off our ill-tempered friends."

"Can't we just deny the whole thing?"

"The other side clearly knows too much; if we denied it, they would host a very large celebration for the global media to trot out the evidence. Furthermore, if *you* try to deny it, I'll take it to the media myself."

She shut off the line to the Prime Minister's office in Kaplan Street and turned to her assistant. "I'll see Toad and Miner. Now."

Both had been waiting outside the door, and both shuffled in.

"All right. You heard?" They nodded. "Toad, who other than you knew about this Levinsky business?" She answered her own question. "Myself, the team here, and Miner. And Halevy and his three crazies, all of whom we have locked up. That's it. I want you to find out who at Kaplan Street knew about it before this broadcast. Miner, go find out."

The big man left with a glad sigh.

"Toad, what about Halevy?"

"He says that Levinsky came down from Haifa for his daughter's funeral last night. They put him up in the guest bungalow, and this morning Halevy had an argument with Levinsky, who apparently wanted to use the nano device to destroy the Haram shrines. Then, according to Halevy, Levinsky tried to recruit one of the younger men at the funeral to do the deed. He wanted it done on Yom Kippur as a kind of statement. As revenge. For his daughter."

Kristall tapped out her cigarette impatiently. "But what's going on with Halevy? Why did he turn in his friend? He of all people wanted to see the Temple rebuilt—why would he stop it? And might he be the one who tipped off the other side?"

Toad shook his head. "I think Halevy is genuinely against violence. He's thoughtful, a physicist; his enthusiasm for the Temple is more hypothetical than practical; his designs for bringing it about are more subtle than blowing up the shrines. He's terrified by real emotion—and that's what Levinsky faced him with this morning. Real anger. I know he struggled with the decision to talk to me, but in the end he did.

"But no, I don't think he leaked the information to the other side. He would know what their reaction would be, and as I said, he hates violence. He's also a logical man—what good would it do to tell the tale to them?"

Kristall had lit another cigarette and drew in smoke. "What good indeed? And for whom?" She paused. "Have you made anything of this Lambert Sable connection? The contact number on Catriel Levine's phone?"

"Total firewall. Nobody gets through to talk to him. Even the American FBI are helpless."

"*Especially* the American FBI," Kristall spat. Her assistant came up behind her as unobtrusively as possible and let slip a piece of paper on her table. She picked it up, skimmed it, and closed her eyes.

"Toad, get Davan back here immediately." She handed them the paper; they looked hard at it and left the room. Toad was already ringing Ari Davan.

"Or better still," she said to herself, "tell him not to come back at all."

Besharri, Lebanon, 1630h

Parked precariously at the side of the road, Ari rang off his phone and without a word switched on the car radio, scanning for an English-speaking station. His conversation had been in Hebrew; Maryse looked questioningly at him until the sense of the radio broadcast came clear. They both knew

that the consuming puzzle they were playing at was about to turn into
a war.

"I've got to get home tonight," he said. "Things are out of control."

"I understand," Maryse replied.

"It's not just this latest show. The European media are naming me—*naming*
me—as the killer of a Palestinian 'diplomat' named Ayoub."

"What? But it's not true…"

"Doesn't matter. Every Hamas hothead will be after me. As for the Service,
I'm finished."

"You're exaggerating."

"Maryse, you don't know this part of the world. You should leave me here,
get away from me, and stay clear."

She looked silently at him for a moment, and then shook her head. "Let's go.
We have work to do."

"But you're in danger, too. Take the car; I can find my own way home."

"Ari, please. No one here knows who you are; you're not even officially in
Lebanon. Let's finish this."

Outside, the peaks were turning to gold as the angle of the sun dropped.
With a nod and a curse, Ari threw the car into gear and started along
the narrow road around the town. On one side, the road shaved the
hillside, and on the other, houses protruded from the mountain stone like
natural growths.

At the foot of the road nearest the cliff, the police had told them, and at
last they came on an isolated two-story house where a worker was building
a ramp to the door. It was a ramp for a wheelchair. Outside the house,
shading her eyes as she watched the road, a woman in a pale cotton shift
was waiting.

"Fatima!" Maryse cried as she jumped from the car. They embraced; Fatima's
body felt stronger, more limber. Clearly, she liked the mountain air. She held
up a tiny gold cross she wore around her neck.

"Thank you for this." Maryse had bought it for her on the day of her
husband's funeral. "It will always remind me of you…of your kindness."

"Did you have any trouble? Getting home, I mean?"

Fatima smiled. "I arrived here yesterday without trouble." And then, soberly, "Peter's mother is inside...I know you want to speak to her. It will be difficult."

"We won't take long." Maryse motioned to Ari, who got out of the car. "This is, um, Paul. He works with me."

The young Lebanese woman looked up at Ari.

"Welcome, Paul," Fatima said, offering him her small hand. Her smile was neither bright nor sad, but accepting.

"Thanks," Ari replied, and Maryse heard relief in his voice.

"Fatima, we need to ask Rafqa Chandos a few questions and then get under way. We haven't much time," Maryse changed tone.

"Of course. There is a nurse, an Antonine sister. Let me speak to her first."

Fatima went inside, and Ari and Maryse stood in the gate. They looked wordlessly past the house and across a chasm that rose from the road's end up into the mountains; it looked as if an immense snake had filed its way through the sandstone and left this glittering fissure in its wake.

"It's called the Qadisha Valley," Ari said. "The holy valley. A place for hermits and monks. When I was in the army we did simulated battles on the plain of Bekaa—just beyond the hills there—and fought imaginary commandos in the Quadisha Valley."

Strange how often they go together, Maryse thought—holiness and warfare. But she didn't say so.

Fatima came out, her face cheerless. "The nurse says it's all right, but doesn't think you'll get much from her. The stroke left her able to hear and speak; still, what she says is not always...what is the word? Intelligible."

"Please. Let us try."

Fatima led them into a darkened room that was surprisingly cool; a window had caught a breeze from the gorge. The nurse stood shyly by a small bed. Rafqa Chandos seemed to sleep, her head slightly bowed under a white hood, her hands spread at her sides, her body draped in fluid white that reminded Maryse strangely of a wedding gown. She was not a small woman, and the bed not large enough—thus the impression of felled strength. A nutrient dripline ran from her arm; otherwise, she did not appear ill at all. Her lips stirred faintly, almost soundlessly.

"She prays," Fatima murmured. "And recites. Mostly the gospels." She looked up at Ari and Maryse. "Rafqa is a linguist—she learned English from her father and studied Greek and Latin in the religious school. Much of what she says, I think, are old lessons from the school."

Maryse approached the bed and spoke calmly into the woman's ear. "Rafqa, my name is Inspector Mandelyn. I'm sorry to disturb you, and very sorry for your loss. But I must ask you one or two questions."

There was no sign of comprehension. The lips continued to open and shut in some unknown pattern.

"Did Peter have a brother?"

The woman's breath quickened and she shook her head once. Twice.

"Was that a no?" Maryse whispered up to Ari, who looked clueless. "Ask her again," he said.

"*Tasaqat,*" the nurse said. Fatima translated: "It is a palsy. It may mean nothing."

This time a little louder: "Did Peter have a brother? A twin?"

Again, the breathing came quicker. Her eyes fluttered and she shook her head in tight little movements.

"That's not palsy. She's telling us no," Ari said. "Maybe we should go."

Maryse turned to the nurse, and Fatima translated.

"Did anyone—a man—come to the house in the last few days? Since Thursday?"

No, the nurse had seen no one. But she only moved in Thursday when Rafqa was released. It was thought she could heal at home as well or better than in hospital, and she had seen no one but the medical people and the worker building the wheelchair ramp.

No. Wait. There *had* been someone. A man. She only glimpsed him, thought he was passing by. She had seen him from the window, only his back. It was just at nightfall, and he was standing on the cliff edge near the house.

What did he look like? He was ordinary, not tall, not short. Dark hair, yes. How dressed? Dark workman's clothes, blue I think. Doing what? As I said, just standing by himself and looking out over the valley. A moment later he was gone. I thought no more of it.

"The twin," Maryse said to Ari. "This is his mother's home. Maybe he hid something there, in the back of the garden."

They started to leave the room when the muttering from the bed grew louder, more breathy. "*Phosphoros. Phosphoros.* For my sin…"

Maryse turned. "What did she say?"

"I think she said, 'phosphorus,' " Fatima repeated.

"Does that mean anything to you? Has she said it before?"

Fatima shook her head, as did the nurse.

Maryse was puzzled. "It means light in Greek, light carrier, or something like that."

"Or the element phosphorus?" Ari volunteered. "Number fifteen…in the periodic table." The women stared quizzically at him.

"Maybe it's too dark. Maybe she wants more light." Fatima switched on an overhead lamp.

By this light Maryse could see, barely opened, the elegant blue of Rafqa's eyes; she seemed to recognize something in Maryse. She struggled to raise her hand.

"*Pos exelesen ek tou ouranou…Phosphoros. Quomodo cecidisti de caelo… Lucifer…*"

Then Maryse understood. "She's quoting scripture. The Septuagint. The Vulgate. Greek *and* Latin. *Quomodo cecidisti de caelo Lucifer.*"

Maryse scrambled in her heavy bag for her GeM and tapped at its transparent face. She kept repeating the Latin phrase softly to the GeM while Ari looked on uncomprehending.

"Here it is. The Vulgate. *Quomodo cecidisti de caelo Lucifer…*'

"What is she saying?"

Maryse looked up, puzzled. "It's a passage from Isaias. *'How art thou fallen from Heaven, O Lucifer, who didst rise in the morning? How art thou fallen to the earth, that didst wound the nations?' "*

"It's just random," Ari whispered. "She's raving."

"I'm not sure. She cited the same passage in Latin and Greek. Lucifer equals Phosphoros—the light bearer." Maryse shook her head. "What is she trying to tell us?"

"Lucifer is the devil, right?"

"He's often called that. If I remember, originally the term referred to an angel that was ousted from Heaven."

Rafqa Chandos began to murmur; the words had the weight of solemn intonation: *"Erunt duo in lecto, uno unus adsumeter, et altera relinquetur... altera relinquetur."* And then, unmistakably, a sob, "For my sin."

"Did you get that?" Fatima asked. She had taken a pencil and paper and was writing heatedly.

Maryse tried to translate: "Two...there were two in one bed. And one...I don't understand. But the other was relinquished."

After a silence, Fatima spoke. "I know what it means. She used to tell us this from the Bible, in our catechism. It is from the Gospel." And she recited:

Even thus shall it be in the day when the Son of man shall be revealed.

I say to you: in that night there shall be two men in one bed; the one shall be taken, and the other shall be left.

"There *were* two," Maryse breathed. "Two of them. One was taken and the other left. Peter stayed with his mother, but the other one..." She approached Rafqa again. "Who took him? Who took the other one?"

Maryse faintly nudged the woman's shoulder, and her mouth opened: *"Leo... de tribu Iuda."*

"The lion of the tribe of Judah." Maryse repeated the text into her GeM and waited for it to answer. "This makes no sense. Now she's quoting the Apocalypse, a reference to Christ. Christ took the other child?"

Ari was rattled at this. "Why would Christ be the lion of Judah? Wouldn't the lion of Judah be a Jew?"

"Christ *was* a Jew," Maryse said simply. "I don't know. I don't think we can push her much further…" She was watching the nurse, who was worried about the stress on her patient. Maryse motioned to Fatima to follow her out of the house.

The heat seemed even heavier in the slanted light reflected from the mountains; only a random breath from the canyon below provided any relief. A new wooden ramp now led from the doorway to the lane, and the worker had left. Maryse led Fatima to the corner of the house. She had remembered from her police training that most abductions of children were by their own parents.

"Fatima, does anyone know anything about Peter's father?"

The small woman slowly shook her head. "It was never talked about. Never. Not even my parents talked about it—and they talked about everyone. I don't think they knew who the father was."

"And she always lived in this house?"

"Always. She inherited it from her father, the Englishman. He is buried in the cemetery here."

"Is there anyone in this town who would remember the Englishman… Rafqa's father?"

"Perhaps the retired priest at St. Anthony's. He is very old."

"Would you go with us to see him? We'll need an interpreter."

"Of course." Maryse kissed Fatima lightly on the cheek and looked around for Ari. He had moved to the back of the house—the "garden" as she had called it, although it was only a garden of rocks that swept precipitously toward a cliff. She knew what he was looking for: recently disturbed earth.

"Maybe he buried the item back here," Ari said as she and Fatima approached. They walked the small plot, but found nothing but hundreds of footprints.

"They had workers in last week," Fatima explained. "To mend the windows and the roof."

Leaning over a toothy old rock wall, Ari examined the cliff side and shook his head; next to him Maryse leaned cautiously over it, hoping to find a cave or a rope dangling to some hiding place. But there was nothing: only a cascade of rusty terraces and the vertical drop into darkness beyond.

All at once her stomach plunged and her eyes went dim—the cursed vertigo. She drew back too fast and her bag, dangling crazily from her shoulder, shot over the wall and landed six or seven meters below on a protruding crag, its contents spilling over the side.

Ari laughed and then stopped abruptly at the look on her face.

"I'll get it for you."

"No!" she cried. "Leave it there."

"But you don't want to lose your GeM. It's got all your notes. And I've climbed much worse than this."

"No. Please."

But he had already removed his boots and socks and was over the side, rubbing dust into his hands to improve his hold on the marl stone. It was true, she thought, watching him: He was a fine climber. His fingers and feet locked into the cracks like machinery, and he coiled and spread his body against the rock with the smooth rhythm of an expert.

A years-old image flashed across her memory as she willed him down the face of the cliff to the ledge below.

"Got it," he shouted up. The sun was gone from the gorge now and all she could see was the back of his shirt; he was kneeling against the ledge, hanging from one hand and collecting her things with the other. Fatima tightened her hold on Maryse's arm as he began to climb up again.

Police Administration, Via San Vitale, Rome, 1640h

"What do you mean by this?" The Commendatore of the Vatican Police rushed through Bevo's office door and set his tablet on the desk.

Bevo pretended to examine the panel and then sat back again in his chair.

"Won't you sit, please, Signor Commendatore?"

"I will not sit. I have no time to sit. And why will you not answer my calls?"

"I've been very busy, Signore." Discreetly, Bevo tossed a mint in his mouth and rose to shut his bureau door.

"Yes, you've been busy spreading the worst kind of disinformation."

"What do you mean?"

"This news release. 'Israeli spy kills Palestinian diplomat. Rome Police official Antonio Bevo announced today the murder in Rome of a prominent Palestinian diplomat by a functionary of Israel's security forces...' "

"The Palestine government wants to know about the dead man and the press were asking me questions, that's all. The press often asks me about important cases."

"You make it sound like Davan is an assassin. You know as well as I do that Ayoub attacked Davan, not the other way around. And that Davan didn't kill Ayoub—the Unknown did."

"I don't know that. That's Davan's version of things. The ballistics people have an opinion, I have mine. The two men exchanged gunfire in the middle of a busy intersection. Davan had followed him to Rome, specifically targeting him. The Jews and Palestinians have been killing each other for a century—why is that so unexpected?"

The Commendatore was enraged. "And you *named* him! You put his name in the news—Ari Davan. He's useless to their government now; and what's worse, he's a dead man. Ten thousand militants will be looking for him."

"Yes, I know. Apparently, this Ayoub was quite popular in Palestinian circles."

"Why didn't you release Davan's photograph as well—to make it easier for them?" the Commendatore barked bitterly.

Bevo shrugged. "He'll be easy to find. Google." He looked at the photo of himself on the wall and wondered how difficult it would be to take it down after all these years. It would go with him, along with the police flag and the testimonial plaques beneath it. He had been so young in that photo, his helmet white and pristine, his jaw like a razor.

The Commendatore rattled on. "This is the worst possible time. The tensions are as high as I've ever seen. The conclave under way. War—*real* war this time—threatening to break out any moment in the Middle East. And we've been trying for forty years—ever since John Paul II—to keep cranks from the Middle East away from the Popes. Every would-be assassin with a Koran and a pistol has wanted to make his own special pilgrimage to Rome.

"So you announce that an 'innocent' Palestinian diplomat is gunned down by a Zionist agent right in front of the holiest Catholic shrine—just when the Islamic shrines in Jerusalem are threatened. Just what are you playing at?"

Bevo looked at the man with mock innocence and shrugged again. The Commendatore was a fussy sort; he would be glad to be rid of him.

It was only a matter of days now. The opprobrium he had feared would now be forgotten; his position would be substantially better; all he had to do was cooperate. He could leave behind the hard policing, which he was getting too old for, and take on something far more prestigious and far less demanding. He had earned a few drinks. After all that had happened, he had never expected to be invited upstairs.

"I don't understand you. What do you have against Davan? That he was right about Eagle and you were wrong?" the Commendatore said.

"On the contrary, Davan was wrong all the time. Eagle was no threat. If anything, Eagle was trying to prevent a crime."

Baffled, the Commendatore said, "I'm going to issue a retraction immediately," and started for the door.

"You might think again," Bevo smiled. "I don't believe a retraction would be welcome in certain quarters."

The Commendatore looked back nervously at him and left.

"Good," Bevo said to himself. "Go."

He glanced at the clock. It was a bit early, but he picked up his private GeMphone from the desk, tapped it, and spoke politely into it.

"Is this the Via Condotti?"

St. Anthony of Kozhaya Monastery, Besharri, Lebanon, 1840h

The priest's cell was very clean and warmly lit by a single shaded lamp in the corner. The priest, Father Elias, was so old that his face looked like a thin white flower petal; although nearly blind from age, his mind was clear.

"Did I know Sir John? Did I not?" he whispered happily. He seemed pleased to see Fatima, whom he had embraced gently. Maryse and Ari were only shadows to him, but his greetings were no less warm. Tinged by French and Arabic, the old man's English was good—he had been to America, he told them repeatedly. Long ago, to go to school. He knew about baseball, but he also knew about cricket because of Sir John.

"And where do you come from, young man?" Father Elias asked Ari, who hung back silently against the door, declining to sit. After a long hesitation, Maryse spoke for him: "He's my colleague. We're with an international police team...we're trying to track down a stolen art object."

"Stolen art!" the old man exclaimed. "How exciting. I had thought perhaps you were journalists."

"Investigating the Chandos family?"

"Of course. They swarmed through like locusts days ago. But poor Rafqa was in hospital; and, as the Americans say, their span of attention, you know..." He trailed off, his smile evaporating.

"We are not journalists," Maryse insisted, and she fished her identification from her battered bag and held it up to the lamp.

The old man leaned forward politely to examine it, but then demurred. "All I can see these days is a ring of light. Degeneration of the macula. It starts in the center of the eye, a small black spot, and then the spot expands until the center of all things is darkness—but a ring of light remains. A golden ring."

"I'm sorry."

"Oh, no. It is like the vision of Dante. God Himself in the *Paradiso*, a ring of golden light—and that is what I see."

Maryse smiled up at Fatima and glanced back at Ari, who was brooding against the doorway, clutching his pack hard under his arm, still covered with coppery dust from the cliffside. It had been such a relief to see him scrambling safely over the edge, her bag slung around his chest.

"They are not journalists, Father Elias," Fatima said.

"Good. I would not want to add to her sufferings—Rafqa's. She was my parishioner for many years, and my friend. So, how can I help you?"

"We need to know about the father of Peter Chandos."

"And why do you need to know about him?" The priest was still on his guard.

"It's very hard to explain."

"They are trying to help Peter," Fatima interjected. Father Elias rose in his chair and tilted his head, listening to the quiet breathing of his visitors. Then he relaxed, satisfied.

"I can tell you nothing about the father of Peter Chandos. It was a turbulent time—there was war in Lebanon. People came and went. Sir John left the village quite often and his young daughter with him. He was quite elderly by then and he needed her. Then, one day, they returned for good with the child Peter."

"Did Rafqa have other children?" Maryse asked.

The old man shook his head. "No. Only Peter. Little *Boutro*, he was called. Shy, quiet little boy… Sir John doted on him."

"When did Sir John come to Besharri?"

"When I was very young, the French were here. And then the British, with Indian soldiers to drive out the French—that was during the war. He had been seconded from the British Mandate in Palestine. He was a general then, General John Chandos. He led his soldiers to Mount Lebanon; they stopped a while and then went home. But Sir John never went home. He stayed here."

"He married?"

"Oh, yes. He brought his wife with him. She was much younger than he—just a young woman. But she loved being Lady Chandos, serving tea in the afternoons and carrying a párasol. More English than the English."

"She was not English?" Maryse asked.

"She was Jewish," Ari called out.

Again, the old man glanced up at nothing and sniffed the air. He smiled.

"Your young man can talk, after all."

Maryse looked questioningly at Ari, who leaned on the doorjamb and looked back at her with an odd expression, anxious, unreadable. In the dusky light his eyes looked black and his legs and arms like tarred ropes; he was exhausted. She herself felt overwhelmingly tired.

The priest went on. "Lady Chandos *was* Jewish, the daughter of a chemist who escaped to Palestine from Germany before the war, but she converted to Christianity when she married Sir John. You understand, he was very handsome—dark hair, unusual blue eyes for a man."

"Some years passed, and Lady Chandos gave birth to Rafqa. She was their only child. But then things got very bad. In the old days there were thousands of Jews in Lebanon—they were happy and prosperous here and we got on well together. But soon after Rafqa was born, things got very bad for Jews in Lebanon. One day when Lady Chandos was shopping in Beirut she vanished. Abducted…killed. They found her in south Beirut."

"Sir John was despondent after that. They say he put a bullet through his own head—I think little Peter was only two or three years old—and Rafqa was left alone with him."

The old man seemed to stare into the past with his shimmering, weak eyes. "And now Peter is gone. And the Holy Father. I pray for all their souls."

Fatima knelt and held the old man's hand.

Maryse motioned to Ari that they should leave.

"You're not going," the priest protested, but Maryse reached for his hand and shook it. "You're Irish, aren't you?"

"Born and bred," she laughed gently. "The accent. It's not to be avoided."

"Well, goodbye to you," he said as he struggled to stand. "To you and your Israeli friend."

Maryse snapped around and looked at Ari. His eyes burned, but he said nothing.

"You know," the old man chuckled, "to be blind is not to be deaf. For years I have made a speciality of listening for accents while taking the sunshine in the square. Many people come to Besharri."

Maryse touched Fatima on the shoulder in farewell. On the road where they had left the car it was nearly night. A muted sun lit the cirque of Mount Lebanon just as it set; within minutes the road ahead fell into the shadow of the mountain defile. Maryse shoved her bag into the back seat of the car and strapped herself in while Ari worked through his own knapsack. She heard him stowing it behind her.

As she watched, the last of the sunlight made a pattern like marquetry along the black escarpment overhead, and then spread deep red across the stone. For a few seconds the whole world was on fire. Then the spires of Besharri's twenty churches swelled into shadows, and a few windows in the town shed golden-gray light; on a veranda across the way she imagined a graceful lady pouring tea, an escapee from hatred dancing unknowingly back into the arms of hatred. Then she saw another young woman with eyes like blue jewels carrying her baby laughing into the room where her father lay asleep—this time forever. And the image of her son lying asleep as well, his sculptured head wrapped in red silk against the whirling marble floor of the holiest place in all the world.

Fatima appeared in the priest's doorway and waved. The radical coldness of men's hearts that had blighted Fatima's life would touch her again—and her child, too—unless Maryse could change things. Her own life had turned into a formality, a close examination of stone and paint and dead books, bitter and willful in the wake of her father's death. Only now she realized she had been living in the tomb with him.

At last Fatima closed the door, and Ari came around his side of the car and slid into the driver's seat, the Tavor in his hand.

His voice was almost inaudible. "You will remain completely silent. You will not move."

Startled, she turned. Ari was holding the gun to her head.

Salah-ed-Din Street, Jerusalem, 1950h

Amal gazed at the viewscreen and wondered how he could feel so empty and so angry at once. Pictures of his brother flared again and again on the screen, framed in the black and green of the national flag. Shot to death in the street, they said, shot by the Zionists.

Shot by one of them in particular. Ari Davan.

Ari Davan. This name he would not forget, ever. An evil name. A God-cursed name. The sound of that name burst against his ears with such pain he could not hear what was being said on the television. How they could pronounce this news with such dead faces, he could not understand. A news reporter with a mustache, telling the story with his face dead and indifferent. This news should erupt like a bomb in the sky.

At last he understood what his teacher had said. On that day of requital even the rocks and the trees will cry out, "*O follower of God, there is a Jew behind me. Come and kill him!*"

Nasir, dead, shot like a dog in the street, left in the street by this Jew, this Ari Davan. His brother, dead like a dog in the street of a God-cursed western city. He would not wait for the day of requital. That day was here. That day was tomorrow. He would find this Ari Davan and cut his throat.

A door opened below and he heard people coming in the house. His father would be returning. They had called his father to the ministry to identify Nasir's body; Dr. Adawi had come for him, with many friends. And now his father came up the stairs with Rabia supporting him. She did not wail like their friends in the street; she was all in white with a sheer black headscarf, her face stricken but determined.

Hafiz sat on his bed and Amal went to him. The old man took his head in his hands and kissed him, then closed his eyes, muttering at the brightness of the lights. Rabia switched off all but one and doused the viewscreen. Through the window came an oddly vivid white light—they had set up security lamps all round the Dome of the Rock, and even at this distance the shouts of soldiers could be heard as they patrolled the perimeter of the Mount. A curfew would go into effect in minutes.

"Rabia, you must go now. The devils will shoot you on the street."

"It's all right, Amal. I'm going to stay here with your father. And there are others downstairs. You will not be alone." She was looking strangely at him.

He remembered what his father had taught him about visitors and felt suddenly ashamed. He clattered down the stairs and came back up in moments with a tray of fresh oranges and juice. She smiled.

"It's odd how much you resemble him," she said. "You look like your brother, even though you are not related."

"He is my brother."

"Yes, I know, Amal." She reached out and swept him into her arms. The boy tried to stifle his cries but could not.

His sobs intermingled with his father's clotted breathing from the bed. At last Rabia lifted his head and looked into his eyes. "You have a heavy responsibility now."

"Yes." He heard that Jew's name in his mind and it was like a hammer on his ears. "Ari Davan. I will kill him. He will not live another day."

She was suddenly firm. "No. That is not your responsibility, Amal. I mean that you have a responsibility to your fathers."

"My fathers? What fathers?"

"Hasn't he told you? About the black eagle?"

Rubbing his eyes, he shook his head.

"Not about Saladin?"

"Yes, he told me. We are of the house of Saladin. But so are many other people."

Rabia examined his face for a moment, then embraced him again.

"There is more—so much more—to tell."

CHAPTER 4

SUNDAY, OCTOBER 10, 2027

Qadisha Valley, Lebanon, 0030h

Maryse awoke. Pain flashed through the nerves in her arm. Panicking, she kicked at a layer of loose clothes shrouding her and immediately realized she shouldn't have done it. She remembered where she was—in the freezing dark, tied tightly, nearly grafted to two trees on a hillside, gagged by a hard knot in her own headscarf. Panic closed in again, an electric claustrophobia that arrested her breathing. She hovered for an instant as fear coiled through her body, and then she screamed. It was a wild, stifled noise that would never be heard by anyone but herself.

She yanked and pulled at the strips of cord that held her spitted between the trees, her wrists scratching at one tree and her frozen, dead feet strapped to the other. She struggled uselessly—her fingers had nothing to hold to, and the trees were as inflexible as iron pillars. But she kicked and kicked, mindlessly willing the circulation back into her legs, fighting the intense cold that draped her body.

At last, exhausted, she lay back to gather strength. Though fear had sharpened her eyes, she could see nothing above her but the icy stars. He had needed sleep, he said; he couldn't make the drive without sleep. He hadn't slept more than a few hours for days, and he couldn't think anymore. He had tied her between these trees and covered her with her own clothes from her bag to keep out the cold. It gets cold in the mountains at night, he had said.

Not a word more. Nothing to explain why he had held her at the point of his gun for an hour while he tried to drive the twisting road. Nothing to account for this sudden, insane change in him. Was he angry at her for revealing to the old priest and to Fatima that he was a Jew? Impossible— he had revealed it himself, just by speaking. Had she become his hostage in case the authorities came looking for him as the accused assassin of a diplomat? Or worse…

She tried to remember what had happened at the Sanctuary the night before. The man shooting at them—according to the radio, he had been a Palestinian diplomat, not a criminal. Not a terrorist. Was it possible that the man had been trying to stop Ari? From doing what? Was Ari now "the Unknown?" Had she unwittingly carried an enemy along with her, unpacking to him every detail she had uncovered, every idea she had?

Of course, she hadn't told him everything. She hadn't because she had given her word not to, and now she was glad of it. Jean-Baptiste had been right, as always.

She wished she could tell time by the stars. She had no idea how long she had lain asleep there on the ground—had it been hours or only minutes? Deep cold was inching up her legs, a rigor that reminded her of Eagle's dead body in the Roman morgue.

Soft light outlined what must be a cliff in the distance, and she realized that the moon was coming up. To keep the panic down, she focused keenly on the light, on the ring of light—on the slow revelation of the moon, on the blunted horns of the past-quarter moon, on the hypnotizing moon, willing herself into a trance, into sleep that would banish the cold and the pain.

It was no use. Again, panic struck like a convulsion: her entire body buckled with it. She kicked and kicked at the cords, ripping the skin of her ankles but not caring about that, wrenching madly at her own wrists, choking on the gag until the fear of suffocating in her own vomit deepened the panic.

Just then she saw a light flickering through the woods toward her.

It was Ari. He stumbled nearer, using his GeM as a torch, weirdly illuminating the entire clearing with its blue light. He knelt and stripped the cords from her feet and then detached her hands from the tree, pulling her up and gathering her things into her bag. But her hands stayed tied. He still held the gun in one hand.

"I'm sorry that was necessary. It's past midnight now; a few hours' sleep will have to do. Let's go."

He nudged her up the slope toward the road. Blood poured back into her arms and legs and heated her brain. She could run now, she thought. Run into the woods where he wouldn't find her, and when it got light break for the town. But Ari had the gun to her back.

Strapped down in the car once again, hands tied, she stared at him and at the gun on his lap. Now that the road was all downhill and straightening, he seemed almost imperceptibly to relax. They passed a road sign indicating the direction to Baalbek. Having studied a map earlier in the day, she now knew they were going southeast through the Beqaa Valley.

She turned to him. "Why?" she asked simply. There was no answer.

Again, "Why?"

Ari was silent, studying the road ahead with straining eyes. He was obviously heading for the border with Israel, which she estimated to be 150 kilometers away. Lebanon was a little country; by two or three in the morning they would be at the frontier. What was waiting for him there? A few hours before she had felt anxious for him, worried that he might be arrested, that his agency might cut him off—or schedule an accident for him. Now she didn't even know who he was. He was alien to her, opaque, racing forward insensibly like one of the insects that weaved into the headlights of the car.

Despite the gun, the straps around her wrists, the quiet menace seated next to her, Maryse couldn't fight off sleep any longer. She didn't want to sleep. She wanted to stay awake, staring at Ari until her gaze eroded him into speaking. She tried to focus on his face and saw instead through the windscreen the occasional light in the distance signifying that there was a world outside this abrupt nightmare. It was no use. Ahead of them, the headlights of the car defined a small, stifling universe of weeds and cracked road evolving into blind darkness that would not end.

She awoke once at the sound of a passing lorry. She glimpsed signs for towns she had never heard of: *Rayak, Marjayoun*. But mostly she hung between sleep and anxiety, willing the night to end. At last Ari stopped the car.

The clock on the dash read 03:04. Maryse looked around; there was nothing outside the car but black night, and she swallowed uneasily. What now?

Ari switched on the overhead lamp and examined her face closely; his own face was hard, bleak, fearful. The fear in it startled her.

"Are you all right?" he asked; the question startled her again. What did he mean, was she all right? She was not all right. Nothing was right.

"Oh, I'm well enough. I've been held at gunpoint for hours, tied up like an animal in the woods, driven all night who knows where by a madman. Yes, I'm holding up fine."

He studied her face again for a moment and then closed his eyes and slumped into his seat.

"We're at the border," he said. "Over that hill is the security zone. I don't know what will happen to us there."

"Ari, what on earth is going on? Why are you treating me this way?

Silence.

"Who are you, anyway?" she cried.

Eyes still shut, he spoke again. "I could ask you the same question."

"What do you mean? You know who I am."

"I do?" He sat up and looked squarely at her. "How do I know you're not one of them?"

"One of whom?"

He breathed in deeply and squeezed at his forehead with his free hand. "Do you know what it is to be surrounded by hatred all your life? To be truly despised? Spat on? To see your people murdered with enthusiasm? To live in constant fear that somebody is going to drop an atom bomb on you?

"The Rome police—our respected colleagues—put out my death warrant today. Why?

"The old priest tonight—that story—the lady with her tea parties who ran away from being Jewish just so she could live and have her family. Murdered in the street.

"Our neighbors want to vaporize us and are just looking for the right excuse. And Eleni..." He broke off.

"Eleni?" Maryse asked, more gently than she intended.

"My wife. Dead. An Arab let fly a rock on the windscreen of her car. He was just a kid, they said." Ari slumped again into his seat and added, quietly, "Just a kid, out for a lark, murdering Jews for sport."

Maryse was silent for a while, then quietly replied, "Israel has been pitiless with them."

At that Ari sat up, staring ahead. "Before the security zone, I need to know what's going on. It'll go better for you *and* me if I know."

"Know *what?*"

Ari reached into his vest pocket and held up to the lamplight a small, delicate golden ring.

His voice was dry, cracking. "It's a woman's ring. It's engraved with the letters DVCEI. I found it tonight—on a ledge—where it fell from your bag."

Salah-ed-Din Street, Jerusalem, 0545h

"Allahu Akbar, Allahu Akbar…"

Hafiz sat up in the bed as best he could for the dawn prayer. He rested against the wall, his head pitched back so he could breathe. He gasped the words of the prayer.

"I witness that Allah alone… is worthy of worship.

"Hasten to the prayer…hasten to the prayer."

At this point prayer was survival. He saw nothing in the darkness around him, wanted to see nothing, dreaded the dawn. He longed for the pure black emptiness of night to go on forever.

"Hasten to the triumph…hasten to the triumph."

He tried reasoning. Nasir had hastened to the triumph, had gone ahead to Heaven as a martyr, killed in defense of the sanctuary of Allah, blessed among the gardens and streams of Allah with all the martyrs. This quieted the bleeding in his soul, but still he could not get breath.

All the sleights of hand with which Reason tricks us here
Were tried before Moses, to no avail

"Nasir," he murmured in the midst of the prayer. "Nasir…"

And then, struggling for air, struggling for dignity, "I complain of my grief and my sorrow to Allah."

The words brought him no release. He murmured his complaint again and again and again until the gray pallor of dawn finally suffocated him.

He had heard of the panic of grief.

Now it overtook him.

It shattered his mind, choking him, the debris sprouting in his lungs, into his heart, into his fists. He struck at his chest with feral energy, willing the death of the Jews who had killed his son, his family, his people. *"O faithful one,"* the walls of his house cried to him, *"there is a Jew behind me. Come and kill him!"*

He pounded at the plasma in his lungs, felt it bubbling like lava, felt the blood welling up in his stomach, sickening him. Then it came up in a shining stream across his bed.

"Father, Father!" Amal had wakened and was holding him; in one hand he was grasping at a GeMphone. "I'll call the doctor. Please don't die. Please don't die."

Abruptly, in the plea of his son, Hafiz found his soul again. The panic ebbed and he began to cry. They both cried. As Amal held him, Hafiz murmured poetry:

> *Has anyone seen the boy who used to come here?*
> *Round-faced troublemaker…*

A photo of Nasir came slowly into sight on the wall as the dawn progressed. Hafiz found it and gazed at it, at the handsome dark face collared in a white robe, imagining Nasir in a heaven of cool springs and blue enamel domes.

> *Have you heard stories about him?*
> *Pharaoh and the whole Egyptian world collapsed for such a Joseph.*

Father and son were silent for a long time, holding one another, eyes fixed on the portrait of Nasir, while another day started to scorch the world outside. But it was dim in this upper room of the house with the shutters closed.

"You should sleep, Father," Amal said.

Hafiz shook his head and slowly raised himself back into the ritual position. The horror of loss had exhausted him. "Prayer is better than sleep," he whispered. "Prayer is better than sleep."

The boy sat respectfully on the bed, almost hypnotized as the old man muttered the *salat* again and again. Hafiz was soon lost in prayer, eyes black-lidded, while Amal continued to gaze at his brother's portrait in a trance of plotting and preparation. At length, when his father had finished his prayers and was breathing quietly, he spoke.

"I cannot pray, Father."

"Why not?" Hafiz asked.

"I'm so angry," he said softly. "To think that God would allow the Jew to kill my brother."

Hafiz was silent for so long that Amal thought he had fallen asleep again. But then he said, "If you knew what was in the prayer, you would run to it."

But Amal did not reply. Hafiz listened to the boy's mind and knew what was going on there. It was the space of silence in Heaven before the Day of Requital that was to fall upon the world. At last the boy sighed and stood up.

"I'll clean your bed, so you can rest a while longer."

Hafiz watched his son pulling the soiled sheet away, watched him moving around the dusky chamber, a thin dark boy all in white like a ghost, and saw himself making a death journey across the desert long before. The same hard fire burned in Amal that had burned in himself; only in Amal it burned hotter.

"You should eat something," he said at last to the boy. "And then we will go bury him."

"I don't want to eat."

All that mattered now was this boy, Hafiz thought. Everything Nasir had prepared for, Amal must now do. From his shattered heart he would have to piece together a new design for the boy—but first he would have to save him.

"You loved Nasir."

Amal looked startled at his father. "I loved him, yes."

The old man touched the holy book he kept by his bed. "Even in love, the devil does not lack for ideas," he murmured. "But you must listen...listen with your heart to the message of the angel."

But the boy stared back at him, his eyes constricted, his lips narrowing.

En Gedi, Israel, 0730h

The electric bus rattled slowly to a stop, and Rachel Halevy climbed into her seat. She nodded to the driver.

"You might have to find your own way home tonight," he said to her. "We're being requisitioned. They're wanting to evacuate the coast."

"But not Jerusalem?"

"No. I guess not."

She held her weaving bag tight between herself and the window of the bus and was lost in the landscape outside. Even this early in the morning, the sky was hot. To the east the earth lay under a glaze of salt where a flock of honey buzzards rested before resuming their annual southerly dash toward the Sinai—Rachel knew their departure was more than a month late. She searched the sky for any sign of a cloud, but there was nothing. The forces of Baal reigned.

"No knitting today?" the driver asked, watching her in his mirror.

"Not today," she muttered, and grasped the bag more tightly under her arm.

Guilt had nearly overwhelmed her. She ought to be sitting *shiva* now, instead of riding on the bus, but at least she did not intend to do any work. The work of this day had to be pure—nothing worldly—the simple work of calling fire from Heaven. Jules was in prison, Nathan with him. There was now no man to step forward and do it. And it needed to be done today, a day earlier than the *goyim* expected, the day of Israel's redemption.

She calculated to get off the bus at the Jaffa Gate and walk through the Old City to the Temple Mount. No one would think to stop her. She was known; her weavings were sold in the *suqs*, her face common at the prayer wall. Although she had never been to the Mount and it was closed because of the emergency, she had no doubt that the Lord would lead her to the top. It was time. After all, he had saved Israel by opening the door for Esther.

Nathan had given her the device. She comprehended little about the mechanism, but knew that it could turn into gold or silver. But today it would become lightning—a flaming, consuming pillar of fire. Just speak to it, just a word and a number. Nathan had whispered it to her as he dropped the tiny box into her bag when the police came. She had understood immediately and wrapped it unobtrusively with one hand into a skein of sandalwood linen yarn.

Now she put her hand in the bag and touched it, and began to pray silently. *Speak to the Holy Spark that languishes inside it, speak to the steel and stone, speak to the Holy Spark, see it rising up to its source.*

Loosened from the yarn, it was cool in her fingers, wrapped in its small sack of icy gel, refreshingly cool. The thought of the heat and the pain seemed distant now. As she held the cold box in her palm and rubbed it against her wrist, a welcome chill trickled through her veins and comforted her. Death would come in an instant of heat, but the vapor of it would go up and spread into the blue and then come down like water on a thirsty land. And the mountain would be clear and clean of the desecration.

Then the people of Israel, like the Maccabees, would come up and build the Lord's house, and the sacred oil would burn again and the land be purified at last. She had thought her contribution, her *tikkun olam*, would be the long, finger-wrenching weaving of the priestly garments—now that she realized so much more was required of her, it seemed strangely easy. With one word, one flash of light, the destroyers of her people destroyed. The killers of her Casha. *How are they become a desolation in a moment! They are wholly consumed by terrors.* That her own life would also be consumed—it was so little.

She would go to the Wall and say a prayer, the *t'khine* for death. And perhaps the *t'khine* for new birth as well. It was odd how she looked forward to it. The devout old people at the Wall, the ones she admired so, would be stunned. She knew the Lord would take them too, entwine them with white light and unite them with their fathers and mothers, just as the vapor of her own life would twist effortlessly up toward Him as well.

The city was in sight now. The bus was dipping into the eastern suburbs and the brazen Dome of the Rock came into sight.

She held herself back from spitting at the image in the window.

A restless quiet filled her mind as the Dome grew closer. The words of Isaiah beat a rhythm in her thoughts.

And it shall come to pass in the end of days, that the mountain of the Lord's house shall be established as the top of the mountains, and shall be exalted above the hills.

Mizpe Ha-Yamim, Israel, 0745h

Far below, the heat of the early morning was already raising a mantle of mist from the Sea of Galilee. Mountains, usually green but now withered white, cupped the shrinking lake. As Ari jogged, protected from the abrasive heat by the overhanging tamarisks, he caught sight of the lake. The shade wouldn't last; the trees along the path were dying.

He had slept only two hours but had to get out of his stifling room into the air, to breathe the coolness of the departing night. Now he needed a swim; there was no one in the pavilion, so he pulled off his clothes covered with stone dust and dropped headfirst into the clean, blue pool. After a couple of laps, he climbed out and put on one of the white terry robes that always hung on the tiled wall.

How many times had he come here with Eleni? Once after the wedding, then many times as he began to earn some money. It was his favorite place—the spa of Mitzpe Yamim, the "many waters" where he could swim and run and climb like a boy. The man at the desk had known him when he slipped in at four in the morning. Of course, there were rooms; the tourists had canceled because of the war scare. It happened all the time. The timorous tour groups from America, he said—they thought of Israel as a holy Disneyland and didn't like the attractions disrupted.

So, Ari had the pool to himself. He sat on a lounge chair and hugged himself in the soft terry and gazed out at the lake far below. It was hard to tell where the water ended and the mist began; white as the sea, the curtains around the pavilion breathed in the slight morning air. He lay back and closed his eyes, trying not to think of Eleni. Most days she didn't enter his mind at all, and he felt obscurely guilty about this. He thought about the old priest and the story he told of John Chandos' bride, the young Jewish woman who wanted only her family and peace; since then, he had not been able to shut away the vision of a windscreen traced with Eleni's blood. He had repressed it so long; now he wondered how he could live another moment with that image in his mind.

But he had to. The outlines of the threat to his homeland were at last coming clear to him—and only to him. He knew that. But it was already too much to deal with alone, and there was no telling how much more there was ahead. He needed Toad and Miner and had to get to them.

It was so fantastic a story even now he wondered if he had dreamed it. It was odd to think that history might not be as anyone had thought. But he still had the little golden ring and knew that Maryse Mandelyn was locked in a room without windows upstairs.

Still staring at the lake, he went over her story again in his mind, that fantastic story she had told him in that rhythmic Irish voice, in the midpoint of the night.

"It's only fair that you know," she had started, hesitating, staring at the golden ring he held up to her eyes. At that point, something in her seemed to give way. "Although it's been kept secret for a long time, and at great cost.

"Tomorrow evening, a meeting will be held that has happened periodically for nearly nine hundred years. Three men will meet in Jerusalem to choose a fourth member of their group. And in this way they'll perpetuate the most exclusive, the most crucial organization in the world—the Order of Cherubim."

"Order of Cherubim? I've never heard of it."

"Few people have. You know what cherubs are?"

"Little fat angels."

Maryse had actually smiled—a tired, rueful smile—and relaxed a bit. "Right. Yes. That's how you see them in paintings. But originally cherubs were guardian spirits. In the Bible, God ordered cherubim with a flaming sword to stand guard at each of the four corners of the Garden of Eden. The four cherubim were originally fearsome creatures of God, the most powerful

207

of his creatures, whose task was to protect the holiest of places from profane hands.

"Then," she went on, "over eight hundred years ago, the West was locked in a fight with the East over who would possess the Holy Land, and especially the holiest place of all… I don't have to tell you about it. You know better than I do. Shin Bet exists to protect it. It's the site of Eden. It's where Abraham went to sacrifice his son. It's where Solomon built. It's where Jesus of Nazareth worshiped. It's the center of the whole world, the most sacred spot on the planet."

"The Temple Mount," he said.

By then she no longer looked tired. Her eyes were luminous.

"As I said, all the armies of the West were poured into the fight. The Crusades were the largest military campaign a united Europe ever launched. And the armies of the East were just as strong and just as determined to hold the holy places. Year after year they fought, thousands died, until two leaders who were wiser than the others at last realized what a century of fighting had cost them.

"The King of England, Richard the Lionheart, and the Sultan Saladin parleyed one night in a destroyed village called Ramla. This was in September 1192. The meeting was so secret that no account of it was ever kept. Richard brought with him his friend, Robert de Sablé, the Grand Master of the Templar order. With Saladin was his most trusted adviser and physician, a Jew—Moshe ben Maimon, the man you know as Maimonides."

"The Rambam? He was adviser to the Muslim king?" Ari was incredulous.

"Look it up."

Ari switched on his GeM and called up the online encyclopedia. "You're right," he shook his head. "Maimonides was court physician to Saladin. I didn't know that."

"Saladin thought of Maimonides as the wisest man in the world and wanted him at the meeting. It was the strangest meeting in history. Here were the four most powerful men on earth, representatives of the three great religions, parleying in a bloody round tent in the desert, in the middle of the night, with nothing but ruin and death ahead of them. They knew it. They knew it had to stop, but that it would not stop because the stakes were too high. Possession of the Mount of God meant everything.

"But they also suspected that in truth the Mount belonged only to God, that no mortal king had any right to it, that their battle had been cursed because it was a blasphemy from the start. So they made a pact. It was to be a secret agreement among the four of them, that they would keep the peace on the Mount of God until he came whose right it is to reign."

"Until *he* came...?"

"Yes. Of course, they each had their own idea of who that Person would be. The Muslims believe that Jesus, whom they call the prophet Isa, will return and take possession of the Mount as his headquarters in the final battle against evil. The Christians believe that when Jesus comes again in glory, he will appear on the Temple Mount and rule the world from that site. And the Jews believe that before the Last Day...well, you know what the Jews believe."

"What *some* Jews believe. That the *Moshiach ben David*—the Messiah—will come to rebuild the Temple."

"Exactly. Only the Messiah has the right to reign. Thus, the motto on the golden ring, which is the sign of the Order of the Cherubim: DVCEI. *Donec veniret cuius est judicium.* 'Until he comes whose right it is to reign.' "

Ari was beginning to understand.

"So that night," she went on, "the war stopped. They took hands and swore they would protect the Mount, that no one of them would bar the others from the holy place, that they would hold it in trust for the coming of the rightful king. The Crusaders withdrew, Saladin promised free access to all pilgrims, and the Order of Cherubim has enforced the peace ever since."

"Enforced it?"

"Yes. Before leaving the tent that night, the four men swore to each other to perpetuate themselves as the highest and holiest of feudal orders. It's said that Maimonides suggested it: an order of Cherubim, an order of the powers of the earth who would guard the Mount with a flaming sword if necessary, like the angels of Eden. The Rambam spoke of the guardian spirits of the prophet Ezekiel: the lion, the eagle, the ox, and the winged angel. They saw something providential in this. Richard's standard was the Lion, Saladin's the Eagle. Maimonides adopted the Ox and the Templar master the Angel.

"They also arranged for the perpetuation of the order. Richard swore on behalf of his successors to maintain the pact; for centuries, the kings of

209

England passed the obligation from one to the other. That's why the lion became the symbol of all England. When Richard the Lionheart died, King John inherited the title of Lion of Jerusalem. John passed the obligation to his son Henry III, and so it continued.

"Saladin did the same, passing the obligation to his son, and the birthright of the Eagle remained in his family even after his descendants lost the crown. You still see the black eagle on the flags of the Middle East.

"Robert passed the duties of the Angel to his successor Grand Master, a Frenchman named Gilbert Horal, who championed peace between the Christians and Muslims in Palestine. The Grand Masters kept the pact until the Templars were destroyed in 1314."

"What about Maimonides? What about the Ox?" Ari asked.

"Maimonides' son Avraham succeeded him, and for generations the descendants of Maimonides were the heads of the Jewish community."

Ari was suddenly excited. "The Hebrew for ox is *shor*. Our murder victim Emmanuel Levinsky changed his name to Shor."

"Right. When he became one of the four Cherubim."

"You're telling me, then, that this Order of Cherubim still exists?"

"They meet in Jerusalem tomorrow night to replace Shor."

"So the King of England is coming to Jerusalem tomorrow."

"No, not the King. It's more complicated. King Edward III's heir, the Black Prince, died young, and the King had no confidence in his other sons. Instead, he secretly passed the right to the Black Prince's friend and most trusted knight—a young warrior who had won the greatest battle of the Hundred Years War for him, who had taken the place of his own son in his heart."

"And who was that?"

"His name was Sir John Chandos."

King David Hotel, Jerusalem, 0815h

David Kane looked out the window of his suite at the Dome of the Rock. His lithe young aide brought him coffee and stretched out on the floor with his GeMscreen to watch the news. Kane had just rung off Intel and was now on the phone with the Shin Bet administrator, telling her things she already knew.

"We're reasonably sure now that the device did not make its way to the States. Our connections there know that there has been interest, but no delivery. And the Unknown is completely off the grid, I'm sorry to say."

He listened to Tovah Kristall's recriminations in silence. "What good is Interpol…why the foul-ups in Europe…what good is it to put an operative in place only to be surfaced by the Italian police?"

It was no use to point out again that, unlike her government, Interpol had no satellites—no authority, even, that wasn't granted by one of the member states.

"As I understand it," he interrupted, "Eros-Z has nothing further on the Unknown. We both have operatives looking into that possibility in Lebanon. At this point, though, I'm more worried about the second device…the one Levinsky kept back."

Then it was Kristall's turn to tell him things he already knew—Intel had his sources in Shin Bet. They had Levinsky and his crowd in custody; they were saying nothing. The Technion laboratory was under heavy guard, the En Gedi site had been thoroughly searched, and every GeM in the kibbutz thoroughly scrutinized. As for Davan…he could tell she was worried about him. There had been no report since last evening.

Kane, too, was worried. He knew that Maryse was with Davan, but had heard nothing from her for more than sixteen hours. Repeated attempts to contact unanswered. He had not anticipated this.

Kristall rang off. She was competent, he thought, and imaginative. She was one of the few who could see clearly the dangers of the next twenty-four hours. The Israelis were a strange people, living as they did on the edge of apocalypse, crowded together in seacoast cities that could easily be attacked—as indeed the madman Saddam Hussein had done in the Gulf War—and mostly oblivious to the horrific forces that swirled around the Temple Mount. They were not ready for what was to come.

Intel was keeping him informed. On the west coast, people were jamming the roads to the Negev, to Galilee, to Jerusalem, while others laughed and took their morning coffee in the street bars. A bizarre sort of panic—with half the population fleeing and the other half going to work as usual—there were so many who either didn't understand or refused to understand the threat. It was just as well, Kane thought. Moving a population as big as Greater London's all at once...not a very likely enterprise.

First a dribble, now a flood of refugees was surging into Jerusalem—he could see from his window the rising smog from the west. He shook his head. They weren't ready for it: Tel Aviv-Yafo, Haifa, destroyed in an instant. But then it was hard to know how to prepare for apocalypse. The Israelis trusted their enemies not to bomb Jerusalem; even those who didn't believe in its sanctity believed in its security. He also wondered how many of them had come for the spectacle: to see the Dome of the Rock vaporized.

He had done all that could be done. Before his time, Interpol had been a laughing stock, lumbering around the world after art thieves and forgers; since his time, the agency had taken the lead against terror. He had worked hard to get ahead of these brutes, digitizing millions of fake travel documents, fingerprints, DNA samples. He had made a science of detecting invisible people. Interpol had invented the Red Notice, the virtually instantaneous signal to world police organizations whenever a known terrorist surfaced; the number and speed of Red Notices had curved up exponentially. He himself had helped catch Harun Rashid, the man behind the London bombings, when no other police force in the world could find him. He could rightly boast that the lights of Interpol headquarters had not been switched off since he had taken his job.

But he had always known the time would come when terror would no longer be contained. It was in the nature of the hearts of those who spread it as much as in their weaponry, which was now more sophisticated and terrible than ever.

At first, he had hoped to keep Maryse out of it. He had wanted to provide for her, to keep her near and safe, to focus her energy on the organization's traditional work, to grow her into leadership while he held the world together. That was the reason he had recruited her on the firing range in Glendalough when she was barely beyond freckles and braids. He had learned to plan the important things far in advance.

Her five-year retreat from the force was nothing—he had not worried about it. The mental rest would give her seasoning. And he knew she would come back when he finally needed her.

She was needed now, that was certain—and he bit his cheek, wondering where she was.

There was an abrupt growl of static in his ear and then, once again, Intel's voice.

"Considerable row at St. Helena Street. Jules Halevy is shouting about his wife. He's been trying to contact her, nobody knows where she is."

"His wife," Kane roared. "His wife!" All at once he knew where the second device was. He called to his startled aide. "Elias! Get me on to Shin Bet. And then try again to find Maryse Mandelyn."

Mitzpe Ha-Yamim, Israel, 0845h

Maryse finished writing "Help Me," grabbed the little piece of stationery and stood at the door listening. What could only be the housekeeper's cart finally rattled to a stop in the corridor outside, and she shoved the paper under the door, willing it to be seen. After a moment, she heard someone pick up the paper, and then silence. She prayed that her pidgin Hebrew could even be read.

At last the sound of a keycard, and with a soft buzz the lock opened. Maryse charged at the door, knocking back a stout little woman who fell crashing, dazed, against the corridor wall.

"*Slicha!*" Maryse threw back in a whisper and ran. "Sorry!"

She was sorry, but couldn't wait to see if the housekeeper was all right. The hall opened into an atrium with a glass-enclosed lift buried in indoor palm trees. Ignoring the lift, she looked around, found the stairway door and yanked at it. One set of stairs, through the lobby, and she would be free.

Quietly closing the door at the foot of the stairs, she looked around the corner into the lobby and saw the clerk behind the registration desk. A small man in tropical white, he was reading a newspanel on the desk and looked content to stay there. No chance of getting past him. Then the housekeeper's screams started; she had woken up.

The clerk jumped at the noise, looked around confused, and walked quickly toward the stairway. Maryse darted back behind the door as he rushed past and up the stairs. The way was clear.

She didn't look back, running full speed down the deserted driveway toward the main road. She passed the dirty red Mercedes still parked in a nook of the woods, a long charging cable attached to it; and she knew that Ari had not left her behind. He was still at the spa somewhere and would come after her—she had only minutes to evade him.

The driveway went down a curve on a steep hill, which made running easier, but the heat was so strong she felt she would pass out before getting to the main road. Her hiking boots, not made for running, felt like heavy weights on her feet, and sweat fogged her eyes. At last the road came into view, and she raced toward a small market and petrol station that stood at the corner. Squatting behind a waste bin, she watched the grove where the driveway from the spa gave out onto the road.

As she had expected, the red Mercedes reared to a stop at the foot of the drive and Ari leaped out, shirtless, wearing only a dark swimsuit. Maryse fought down an urge to call out to him. He looked around anxiously, gazing at a stream of passing vehicles slowed by a great greenish ambulance that monopolized the road; then got back in the car, swung it in a circle, and drove back up the hill. Maryse relaxed at last, sitting down in oily dirt behind the barrel to get her breath.

Inside the little grocery, a flat-faced woman in a long, faded shift stood guard on her goods. "Is there a bus?" Maryse asked in hopeful English. The woman shook her head. "All buses gone. Carrying people south." Maryse looked at pastries in a plexiglass box and juices and tins of food, realizing how hungry she was; but she had no money and knew from the way the woman stared at her that she was out of luck.

"Do you have a telephone?" she asked.

"Only my mobile."

"I'm sorry…*slicha*…but I must make an important call."

The woman's face was like stone.

Maryse knew that she could be trapped at any moment here, so she flew out the door and round the back of the shop, into a shady corner where she could watch for Ari without being seen. She wondered if he had believed her story of the night before. His eyes had softened, she thought, but he had said nothing at all to her after they cleared the border. The Israeli guards had given them little attention—to a man who was obviously Israeli and his girlfriend. The guards were tired. After that, Ari had breathed more slowly but more harshly. When they came to the place, she made out the signboard—Spa Mizpe Yamim—and, after talking to the clerk, Ari had led her in silence to the dark room where he would leave her locked in for the night.

With a roar of sliding gravel, the red car appeared again and rounded the corner, speeding off toward the south. Maryse caught only an impression of Ari; he was in a dark shirt and sunglasses. He was undoubtedly headed home. "And still carrying all my things," she thought. She wished she had stopped at the car long enough to get her GeM and backpack.

She came out of her hiding place and wondered what to do next. She knew Kane would be looking for her; it was a matter of finding a phone.

Maryse recognized it before she saw it—the clanging noise of a diesel engine, of a kind she hadn't heard in years. Down the road came a big blue van streaming smoke, its gears growling down as it slowed into the petrol station, shedding people who leaped off and crowded toward the little grocery. She couldn't count the number of people wedged inside, squirming to get free if only for a breath of air. The shopkeeper shouted greedily at the people flooding into the store for juice and water; they were saturated in sweat.

Maryse greeted the driver as he jumped from the cab, swabbing his face with a towel.

"Refugees from Metulla. On our way south."

"What's the news?" Maryse asked.

The driver looked at her incredulous. "You don't know?"

"I've been under a rock."

Looking at her, he realized he should answer. "This morning the army mobilized all along the Lebanese border—north of here. We left with what we are wearing. No more. We will not sit here to be blown up by Hezbollah rockets."

"Jerusalem?"

"As close as we can get. Let's go," he shouted, walking toward the crowd. For the first time, Maryse noticed children. "We may not have much time."

"This heat is brutal," he muttered, to her and to himself, as he pulled open his cab door and wrenched a bottle of water from under the seat. People, mostly families with children, packed themselves back inside while some climbed to the top of the ancient van and others stood on a running board and held onto the frames of the windows.

The engine snarled to life again. Spotting a space on the running board, Maryse leaped for it, and a young man in patched fatigues, his eyes streaming in the sandy wind, grasped her hand to steady her. "Thanks!... *Toda!*" she shouted over the noise. He grinned at her and turned his face away from the wind. Maryse hung onto an empty window frame and tried to shield herself from the flying dust that scoured her bare legs and arms. There was nothing for it but to hold on.

The hills of Galilee looked black to her burning eyes, heaps of coal shrouded in the particulate heat. It was as if the destruction had already come. Once she turned to look ahead, but hot dust blinded and choked her.

"Look backward," said the youth standing next to her. He had red hair and a face patched with dirt. "If you try to look ahead, you'll be sorry."

Too late for that advice, she thought. When she opened her eyes again, she could see round hillocks by the roadside and knew them to be *tells*, ancient sites that had never been excavated—the oddly smooth graves of whole towns built one upon the other until the impulse to build was exhausted. She visualized a mountain of bones and potsherds under the skin of sand.

By one of the *tells*, the bus slowed and stopped. The driver climbed out with a tank of water in hand and thrust open the engine.

"He has to add water to the radiator," the red-haired man explained.

It felt good to let go of the window frame. The men holding onto the bus with her stepped off and groaned, massaging their shoulders and legs. Maryse felt like collapsing on the ground, and her new friend held up an arm as if to catch her.

"Do you have a mobile phone?" she asked him.

"Right here."

"I'll pay for the use of it," she said, although she didn't know how she would.

"No need," he replied, handing her a grimy, sweat-moistened GeM from his pocket, and walked off toward the *tell* with the other men.

Knowing Kane's secure number paid off—he answered her call immediately. No hello. "What happened? Where are you?" he demanded to know. She briefed him quickly.

"Stay with the bus. I'll send help." And he rang off.

The bus beeped, and the dust-caked passengers clambered back onto the running board. A grizzled little man was hanging on with an old Galil assault rifle strapped over his back and extra magazines jingling from a belt across his chest. The red-haired youth jeered at him as he climbed on next to Maryse.

"Are you going to shoot the rockets down with that, old man?"

Maryse thanked him for the use of his GeM and grabbed hold of the window frame.

"Another hour," he shouted over the grating noise as the engine ignited, and they were off again at what seemed like high speed, although Maryse knew they would never go much faster than fifty kilometers per hour.

Around them, the land became flatter and the humidity increased. As the wind slackened, scrubby desert plants gave way to cornfields and orchards of wilted olive trees. In the distance, Maryse could see mountains floating as if on clouds on the horizontal plain. She knew those heights looked down on the valley of Armageddon, which lay all around her, as peaceful as an Irish dale except for the noise of the bus.

Now that there was less wind, she could hear the moaning of the children inside and the quick, repetitive scraping of the wheels beneath her feet. In her arms and shoulders, the bones ached and the muscles began to sting from holding onto the window frame. She didn't know how much longer she could continue. In the old days it wouldn't have been a problem. But she was older now; her body hurt, her skin felt like sand and metal. The pain was wearying.

Then a sign: "Afula, 15 km." A cheer rose from inside the bus.

"We'll be safe at Afula," the red-haired man shouted. "The rockets won't get that far."

Then she could see off to the right a white line, oddly symmetrical, tracing the horizon and thickening the closer they came.

"The West Bank wall," he shouted again. "Keeps the crazies inside."

It was a long concrete barrier that stretched to the south as far as she could see. For years it had kept things quiet by separating Palestinians from Israelis. Beyond it was a world of hopelessness, villages of exiles in a permanent limbo that was both physical and mental.

"That's odd."

"What?" Maryse wasn't sure she had heard.

Nodding his head, the red-haired man was staring at something. Then she could see it; a huge vehicle like a black bull astride the road at an angle. All at once the bus brakes clanged and shivered, and they rolled to a stop.

"What's going on?"

Men inside the bus moved to the front, and Maryse could see the bus driver peering down the road. Half a kilometer at least separated them from the vehicle barring the way—clearly, the driver didn't want to get any closer.

Maryse stepped down and was urged back. "You don't want them to see you," the young man hissed at her. "If it's who I think. See? Behind their vehicle?"

Nearly blinded by the sun on the plain, Maryse saw still figures in the distance, like black posts with horizontal white bands across their heads. They were like impressions on photo film. A pillar of dust rose up behind them, clouding the unceasing line of the West Bank wall.

A rustle, and instantly a man carrying a rifle appeared from the canebrake at the side of the road. Over his black mask he wore a strip of cloth marked with Arabic lettering. He stood at attention like a soldier and, aiming his weapon at the little man with the Galil, motioned for him to put down the gun.

The little Jew rubbed his stubbled face for a moment, then cautiously unstrapped the Galil from his back and deposited it on the ground.

As he straightened up, the masked man pulled the trigger of his gun. Surprised, the little man grasped his chest and fell back against the bus.

Maryse jumped to hold him and inspected the wound, digging the heel of her hand into the sucking hole that appeared in his shirt. After a shout of horror from the bus, there was an instant of stillness and then the shooter came forward to pick up the Galil. He mumbled at Maryse in English, telling her to get away from the dying man. She shook her head and looked up into the barrel of a rusting Kalashnikov.

It was no more than a reflex, she concluded later—five years of Interpol training hammered into her brain. She grabbed the barrel and thrust it right, pivoting at the same instant to the left and springing with full body force into the man's chest. His head thumped the ground as he went down. She flipped the gun around and leaped back toward the bus, keeping him in her sights and well away.

The red-haired man snorted with laughter and took her place at the dying Jew's side.

"What are you doing?" she asked.

"Former IDF medic." He blocked the chest wound with his palm and breathed calmly into the man's mouth. "Loved it," he said, looking up at her admiringly. "Just loved it."

Maryse's staccato breathing slowed a bit as she realized what she had done.

"Where did you get your training?" the young man pressed. "You know, you have us to thank for it."

"What do you mean?" she muttered, holding the terrorist firmly in her gunsight.

"Krav Maga. Israeli Defense Force stuff. For taking guns away. But I've never seen anyone use it in a real fight."

Intensive afternoons under hot lights at the Interpol school. Aikido, Brazilian judo, Krav Maga. It all swept back into her memory—the knowledgeable shredding of the opponent's joints and muscles, the science of killing with a minimum of exertion, the rational practice of disarming the irrational.

"So. What next, Sergeant-Major?" he laughed.

Despite herself, she let out a laugh too, and just as quickly realized how incongruous it sounded. She would not take her eyes off the terrorist, who still lay where he fell. The mask made it impossible to know for sure, but his short quick breathing told her he was conscious. Still, she felt the eyes of everyone in the bus on her. Then the driver was at her side.

"Why?" she gasped. "The poor old man laid down the weapon. Why shoot him anyway?"

"That's why they're called terrorists," the driver said. "They terrorize."

"What now?" she asked the driver.

He was silent for a moment and looked over his shoulder down the road. "As long as we stay quiet here, they'll assume their man is in charge."

"Who are they?"

"I can tell you that," the red-haired man spoke up again. "Saladin Brigades. I know them by the headband. Lost a brother to them," he said with an odd smile. "They have a long, long, long history of raiding up and down this valley. They find a weakness in the wall, they're over it like a shot, and back again before we know it."

"That means they can't afford to stay round," Maryse said. "What do they want?"

"I don't know. If they wanted somebody like us, they'd have taken us by now," the driver ruminated. "But they seem to be focused quite in the opposite direction." He bent over and picked up the Galil.

Gunfire clattered like gravel flung in the distance.

"They've got someone cornered. There's a red car turned over by the roadside, and they're very interested in it."

Her eyes tightened. "Red? Mercedes?"

"Difficult to tell, but I think so. A red Mercedes hybrid."

An explosion ripped the air. Already wailing from heat, the children on the bus screamed.

"From the sound, I'd say a regulation hand grenade," the red-haired man said, looking up at Maryse. "Wouldn't you, Sergeant-Major? About a hundred meters off?"

The bus driver cursed quietly.

"Look," Maryse lowered her voice, keeping both eyes trained on the terrorist who lay baking on the ground. "I'm a police officer. Interpol."

"I wondered how you knew what to do with that fellow," the driver muttered, nodding at the man on the ground.

She went on. "Get on the phone to the police. If you'll hold him here, I'll go see what's going on."

"Better not go. They've already got a target; and we can hope they won't want us. Let them finish and leave, and we'll send this one off with them. I have women and children to consider."

"I'm sorry, but the red Mercedes is important. I've got to go."

The driver looked at her curiously. "If you must. We'll keep the Galil on this one." The red-haired man grasped it quickly. "Take that," the driver handed Maryse the Kalashnikov, and she ran into the hills.

Ben Yehuda Street, Jerusalem, 1003h

When the camera shop opened, Amal al-Ayoub was waiting. Few people walked along the normally crowded street, and Amal felt conspicuous. He wondered why the street was deserted; perhaps it was the panic, perhaps it was that the Jews' holy day was approaching. As soon as the shop man unlocked the door, Amal slithered inside.

"I need to buy film," he announced in English. "For a camera."

The burly old man who kept the shop stared back at him.

"What kind of film?"

"I told you. Film. For a camera."

The shop man scraped his jowls with the back of his hand. He was not very clean. A Jew, Amal thought. Another Jew.

The man pointed to a dust-encrusted glass case at the back of the shop. Inside the case were many small boxes, yellow and green mostly, warped and faded with age.

"Not many people buy film. Only photographers—the professionals. And I keep the good film locked away for them. Are you a photographer?" He peered at Amal through sleepy eyes.

"Yes," Amal lied. "Of course."

Again, the old man rubbed hesitantly at the stubble on his face, then decided to unlock the case. Amal stood in front of the case and pretended to study each small box carefully; at last he pointed to a box that looked particularly old and dusty.

"That's very fast film," the shop man sighed as he extracted it. "Are you sure it's what you want?"

Amal did not know nor care how fast it was—only that it was old. He gave the man the money and nearly ran from the store.

And there was the bus waiting for him on the corner; his luck was in. He had everything now, everything he would need to inflict quick justice.

Amal boarded the bus and closed his eyes. In his mind he re-lived the funeral he had just left behind. He had been pleased at the huge crowd that accompanied Nasir's body to the grave, not just for the honor shown his family but also for the chance of hiding in the swarm of people with their noisy crying. For himself, he could no longer cry—his face was parched from it. Even in this heat, his eyes felt cold from crying.

The body of his brother had not been washed, nor had the mournful prayers been said at the mosque, because Nasir was a martyr. The body was brought to the cemetery as it had been received, then wrapped three times in white linen for burial. The crowd fell quiet as Hafiz advanced to take his son's body from the hearse. Amal had not been able to look at his father, whose grizzled face had gone white with weakness and who had to be supported by the men from the mosque. Amal had kept his eyes on the corpse and shouldered it along with the other mourners as they made their way to the hole in the pale earth where Nasir would lie, his face toward the holy of holies in Mecca.

Then, at the moment of burial, an unnatural silence came over the crowd as if they had stopped breathing and their hearts had stopped beating. Amal looked up to see a group of men, portly and with graying, short-cut beards, walking from the road toward the party. They were dressed almost identically in sand-colored suits, and each wore the round white turban of an imam. Amal had never seen them before.

The crowd fell back in unuttered respect for these men as they advanced and formed a circle around the grave. Amal was startled when his father took his place as if at the head of the circle. The men began to chant softly.

In the name of Allah and in the faith of the messenger of Allah.

It was time to lower the body into the grave. Amal helped the others position Nasir on his right side, and the men in the circle picked up earth and dropped it gently on the body, muttering prayers as they did so. They withdrew immediately, walking back to the road the way they came, and Amal heard the sound of their vehicles as they pulled away from the cemetery.

Then the keening of the crowd began again; men Amal knew from the neighborhood, as well as men—a little better dressed—whom he had never seen, came forward to embrace him. All at once Amal found in his arms the one he was hoping to find—the one they called al-Muhandis, the Engineer. They had hugged immediately, as if the angels had driven them together in the crowd.

They had not seen each other for many months, even though Amal had walked up the road through the Damascus Gate to visit al-Muhandis many times in the Old City over the years since his adoption. When his uncle abandoned him, he had slept in the house of al-Muhandis, a boy just a little older than himself. It was al-Muhandis who had taught him how to extract toll from the foolish tourists at the Lion Gate. He also enjoyed the chemical tricks al-Muhandis did with gunpowder from shells and a little white fertilizer from the garden shops; moreover, he knew that al-Muhandis had gone on to more impressive, more covert tricks—the kind played on Israeli targets. That's why he was called the Engineer.

There were many boys like him—perhaps hundreds—who called themselves engineers in honor of the fabled Palestinian technician who had invented the martyr's vest, ingeniously embedded with dynamite to send hundreds of Jews to their deaths and the martyr to Paradise. But al-Muhandis was unique: his weapons were dead grass and fertilizer and plastic bags and chunks of paraffin. And he had joked with Amal, months before, about a type of bomb he had used to set fire to an Israeli guardpost. It was so easy, he had said. For that, Amal had wanted to find him today.

They left the cemetery together. Amal had not wanted to go home with his father, had not wanted to sit idle in the heat, the house filled with neighbors, mourning and doing nothing. As they walked through the gate, the women and girls from the town who had watched the funeral from the fence thronged, weeping, around him. It startled him; they looked at him as they had once looked at Nasir.

Then, gratefully, he saw Rabia al-Adawi standing in the shade of a tree, away from the others. She approached and held out her hand to him. Behind her sunglasses her eyes were invisible, but he could tell she was examining al-Muhandis. Amal had taken her hand and thanked her for coming to the funeral.

The bus driver's voice jolted him back to the present.

"We must stop here. Everyone off the bus."

The passengers moaned. An old man protested.

"This bus has been requisitioned. For the evacuation."

Resigned, the old man led the way off the bus, which turned and hummed off toward the west without delay. Amal panicked; he did not know where he was nor how far he had to go. Once in the bright, sun-heated street, the other passengers scurried off like insects for shade, leaving Amal standing alone by the bus stop.

His GeMscreen was unreadable in the sunlight, and he struggled to make out the path he needed to take from this location. Then a radiant purple arrow grew across the screen to show him the way; he clutched his plastic bag under his arm and started down the street in the direction of the arrow. It was unbelievably hot. For courage, he murmured the words the Imam had repeated so many times: *Slay the idolaters wherever you find them.* So many times he had chanted those words without feeling. Now he felt them swelling hard and strong inside his chest. *The Day of Requital will not come until Muslims fight the Jews, when the Jew will hide behind stones and trees. The stones and trees will say O Muslims, O servants of God, there is a Jew behind me, come and kill him.*

He would cry if he thought of Nasir, so he tried not to think of him—of his rich white smile and the intelligence in his eyes. Nasir was gone, Father would soon die, and then he would be alone again. Hafiz had told him he had a mission. Whatever it was, it would be a lonely mission. It was now time to act, to stop playing boys' games. He would start with the family of the man who had killed Nasir.

He arrived at a little house encased in reptilian stucco. He had no idea if the people called Davan were inside; it didn't matter, he would strike anyway. Looking around and seeing no one, he darted under a corner of the house and emptied the plastic bag on the ground. He removed the film from its case, attached it to the house with gum, and unspooled it until it dangled crackling from the corner to the ground. Then he opened a little tin. Inside was a whitish lump of wax, glistening wet in the sunshine. He dug one end of the film into the lump so that it would stay. Now the heat of the day would do the rest.

That was all. For a moment he admired the simplicity of it; then he turned away.

As he did so, two black electric cars rolled almost noiselessly up in the street and stopped. Startled, Amal began to run.

"Amal!" It was the voice of Rabia al-Adawi. "Please stop." He looked over his shoulder and saw her getting out of one of the cars. She was accompanied by two men in tan suits who had attended the funeral, only they had removed their turbans.

"Come back," Rabia called. Amal's instinct was to keep running, but instead he stopped, turned, and walked mystified toward her. The strange little company waited silently for him.

"This is not the way, Amal," she said, reaching for his hands, clasping them tightly. "This is not your father's way."

"But we have a mission. *Slay the idolaters wherever you find them*," he whispered.

"Requital is in the hand of Allah," she whispered back. "You haven't understood. You will have your part in it, but not like this."

She looked up as one of the men approached. He had examined the apparatus Amal had attached to the house. "White phosphorus...still wet," the man said, his voice subdued. "Once dry, it combusts and sets the film on fire. A very intense fire."

"Remove it," she said.

The Western Wall, Jerusalem, 1025h

Rachel Halevy bowed before the dusty yellow stone of the Western Wall and quietly began to cry. *A voice is heard in Ramah, lamentation, and bitter weeping, Rachel weeping for her children; she refuses to be comforted for her children, because they are no more.* Her Casha was no more, but she would soon follow her. It was her only comfort now.

Scarved against the heat, elderly women surrounded her murmuring their *t'khinet,* the prayers of the women, for Israel, for their children, for their husbands, for the brassy sky overhead to be opened, and for refreshing rain from the Lord. She had never seen so many women here. The crisis had filled the square with supplicants, both male and female, and their keening swelled the air. On the northern side of the partition, a sea of *kippehs*; on Rachel's side, a sea of scarves.

Behind her, in a line of Army vehicles, soldiers waited silently for an event no one had defined for them. In their simplicity, they were ready. Just to the south, another line of soldiers guarded the entrance to the Temple Mount. How she would ascend the Mount she did not know, but she would do it. The Lord would do it, and there would be many witnesses.

In the end, it is always the women who save Israel. Rachel, the wife of Israel, who gave her life for her child. Devorah the prophetess, who lured out the oppressor; and then Yael, the wife of Hever, who fixed the oppressor's head to the earth with a stake. And Esther—always Esther, the savior of the people. Her own Casha. Rachel knelt and murmured the *t'khine.*

May the Merciful Father in Heaven, in the power of His mercy, remember with mercy the devout, the righteous, the blameless one who gave her life to sanctify the Name, her who was beloved and pleasant in her lifetime, quicker than an eagle and stronger than a lion to do the will of her Creator.

The strength of women, she thought, is in their stealth. Yael welcomed the *goy* general Sisera to her tent with a cup of milk and then impaled his head while he slept. Esther gave a banquet to entrap the evil one. Casha's plan interlaced in secret the fortunes of the *goyim* with her husband's physics—all to save Israel. Casha would not fail, for Rachel herself would weave her way through the soldiers as if unseen, carrying the undetectable weapon into the heart of the beast. And from that blinding moment, she would study Torah in paradise with the women, saviors of Israel.

She raised her eyes to the wall and kissed the stone. It was the taste of gold to her. *How beautiful is your tent, O Jacob—your dwelling, O Israel.* Soon the hilltop above would be swept clean and ready for the House to be restored. It was time.

She slowly worked her way through the crowd of women and found herself among men, hundreds of them, who had washed and put on white clothes for the prayers of the coming day of Atonement. Many were barefoot. They would neither eat nor bathe until the following night. By then, she hoped, the priests would have stepped forth, like Ezra of old among the ruins of sacrilege, to begin the cleansing of the temple.

At length she stood at the foot of the arched bridge, facing the line of soldiers. She took a step, waiting for a sign. She had come as far as she could; now the Lord must do the rest. But the soldiers stared past her or joked nervously with each other as they watched the throng. She cast another silent prayer into the crowded air.

And then the miracle. From behind the line of soldiers, a young uniformed man stepped forward. Smart in his peaked cap and loden-colored shoulder boards, his bony face concealed behind sunglasses, he brightened at the sight of her.

"Rachel?" he asked.

She nodded, her heart nearly crushing her with its beating. It was an angel, surely.

"Come with me."

The barriers of soldiers parted like the sea and the young officer led her up the ramp. Slowly the blasphemous gold dome rose into view as the surge of white-clad worshipers receded behind her. Fingering the freezing lump in her bag, she wondered if the young man was aware that God had sent him. He wore the badge of the *lulav*, the palm frond to be waved in thanksgiving to God on the feast of Sukkoth. She wondered what was in his mind, and what would happen next with each ascending step. And she wondered if her heart would burst in her body.

At the top of the ramp, the officer politely motioned her inside the security gate and stepped to one side.

After a lifetime lived at the foot of the Temple Mount, she had never climbed it before. Her pulse was blazing; the plain of sun-stricken white limestone blinded her; cypress trees towered like black flames before her eyes.

"This way, please," the officer said in a quiet voice. He gestured toward an empty guardpost that stood between two humming white pylons. She had passed the Flaming Sword! God had brought her through the gate. A whispered *t'khine* streamed from her heart.

Through Your rich mercy I will enter Your House; I will bow to Your Holy Sanctuary in awe of You, O God. I love the House where You dwell, and the place where Your glory resides. I shall bow, I shall kneel before God my Creator. O God, in your rich mercy, you have answered my prayer with Your salvation.

Jezreel Valley, Israel, 1035h

Ari felt the sun melting the muddy sweat on his back as he crouched tight against the car. He had instinctively buried himself in dust to make a less visible target. They had attacked him exactly where he should have expected it—in the middle of a flat field with no cover. He had rolled out of the car into broken stubble the instant the windscreen flew apart from bullet fire. As they surrounded him, he took two men out. The burping of the Tavor alarmed the others and they retreated to their old Army Wolf that now blocked the road.

Ari cursed himself for failing to notice the telltale plume of dust that signaled their approach, but they had come at him from a blind angle down a hill that was now behind them. He had been going too fast, too tense in his confusion. Silently he had crept back to the car, gambling they would not blow it up and create smoke they could not see through. There was not much choice; it was the only cover available. And then he was glad, because a grenade went off like a lightning stroke in the brush behind him.

From their white headbands, it was a Saladin Brigade. He wondered why they would come for a lone old beater flailing down this road—usually they moved against high-value targets such as petrol tankers or machine transports. They were in the sabotage business, striking at the Israeli state like a venomous fly against a horse. The IDF stationed units along these northern roads for a time after every attack, but the Brigades simply waited until the units were pulled out.

So why him? He looked over the tattered car, the tracery of his own blood on the windscreen. Why would they take the risk of coming out in the open for this? Unless, somehow, they knew about him. But they couldn't…

He glanced around the car at the bandits' vehicle. It was all dusty black plates. He could see no one; but they were there. In the distance, children were crying in a bus the terrorists had stopped just in the line of sight. There was no escape. He couldn't run. His GeM was buried in a bag inside the car, but the slightest movement would alert them. He only hoped that someone in the bus had had the chance to call for help.

And then, with disbelief, he saw a woman on the hill behind the terrorists, a woman with a big assault rifle. Her white arms were visible for an instant as she dropped into the low brush.

It was Maryse.

How could she be here? What was she doing? Did she want the terrorists between them, or was she after him too? He looked at the ring he had slipped onto his black finger and for a moment wondered about the range of the Tavor.

He buried his head by instinct at the flutter of an assault weapon. From the shouts in the distance, he knew it wasn't the terrorists; Maryse was on his side.

He risked a glance. Blasting away at the hill, the bandits were diving into the dust in his line of fire and he wasted no time. The Tavor snapped in his hands and two more of them leaped back, screaming.

Now they knew where he was.

They scoured the Mercedes with bullets. Ari burrowed into the roadbed, but knew he had only seconds.

Another burst from the hill spared him. Assault-rifle fire glinted off the Brigade vehicle and drove the bandits back to the ground. Ari got off half a dozen shots before they recovered.

But there were too many of them too eager to die.

With a cry, they rose and charged him, guns flaring. Knowing they wore armor, he fired at the white bands on their heads and saw one of them rip open in a red slash. Another man, shoved forward by the automatic on the hill, crashed into the car and went limp.

Then there was a sharp, disorienting blast from Ari's right and another bandit fell down with shock on his face. Down the road a stranger rushed them, a redheaded man in old fatigues, a flood of fire pouring from a Galil he held waist high. The terrorists' guns raked him across; smiling, he slid into the gravel of the road and was still.

Abruptly, everything stopped. A harsh cry came from the vehicle and the remnants of the Brigade leaped into it. The machine growled to life and skidded backward, crushing the stranger's body, then turned and fled into its own screen of white dust.

Ari raised his head and saw floating up from the south a brace of helicopter gunships. One of them raced over his head in pursuit of the terrorists, guns and propellers cracking the sky while the other closed on him and hovered there. He shrank back under the shell of his car, keeping well out of sight until the helicopter landed a few meters away. Troops leaped from it and scattered before it was on the ground.

Ari crept further under the car, keeping his eyes on the helicopter. At length a helmeted head slowly came upside down into view. "Ari?" asked a muffled voice from behind the flight visor.

"I know you," Ari grunted through a mouthful of dust. "You're the one with the extraordinary nose, the one they call the Miner."

Plaza of the Western Wall, Old City, Jerusalem, 1310h

Toad breathed in the heat and sat down on a stone bench to think. For the hundredth time, "No sign of her," came over his earpiece. Impatiently, he cut off the chatter.

Somewhere in this throng Rachel Halevy was lost, along with an ordinary-looking GeM that had the bizarre capability of turning into anything the owner asked for—including a volatile explosive. It was like Aladdin's lamp, he thought, a talisman that could produce wonders or wreak disaster.

What more could he do? He had thought of impounding every mobile phone in the square, but then realized the heat was affecting his thinking. He had seen her eyes and knew she would never give it up to anyone else. But she had come off the bus hours before and disappeared. Since then Kristall had been in his ear every few minutes: "Where is she? Do you have her? Do I have to come out there myself?" Scores of agents were searching the city with her picture, visiting every shop and house where Temple fanatics were known; female agents stood watch on the prayer wall.

Now he had to think. From his perspective, the golden Dome of the Rock was just visible over the parapets of the prayer wall. He knew the Muslim security force known as the Waqf kept jealous watch on the shrine. Additionally, it had been guarded on all sides for the past twenty-four hours by lines of IDF soldiers and the Flaming Sword detector. It was completely effective against any known weapon or explosive.

Until now, of course—the weapon Rachel Halevy was carrying could pass through the perimeter easily, as it was not a weapon until she ordered it to be one. But so far she had not succeeded in doing so.

Or had she? The only place they had not searched for her was the Mount itself.

He stood and walked more briskly than was usual for him toward the arch that bridged to the entrance of the Mount. Getting through the gathering crowd was already a challenge; by nightfall the square would be jammed with white-robed worshipers. Perhaps she had pierced the defenses and was waiting somewhere on the Mount for the sunset and the beginning of the great Day of Awe.

The line of soldiers looked impassively at Toad as he showed them his badge and the picture of Rachel Halevy. None of them spoke, but a squad leader motioned to their captain to come down the ramp to speak to him. The captain was a solid, aging soldier with sweat cascading from beneath his combination cap. His squad had not seen her, but they had been in position only since noon. His orders were that no one—not even a little policeman with a badge—was to enter the Temple Mount precincts under any conditions. Toad murmured a few words into his GeM.

It took about fifteen minutes for the call to come through to the red-faced captain, permitting Toad to go up the forbidden ramp. He asked for and got an escort of two soldiers.

Watchful, slow, almost casual, Toad climbed the Temple Mount. He had been here once before, as a student in the *yeshiva*. He remembered the caution, the tentativeness of the teachers, who were not sure they should be on the Mount at all. After all, the Rabbinate had forbidden it; but Toad's *yeshiva* was not particularly orthodox. Still, one of the teachers had called continually to the boys to watch where they were walking, although no one knew what they were supposed to be watching for. He remembered this because the teacher had snapped at him when he stepped outside the group for a glance into the long low building where the Muslims washed before prayer. A lone worshiper had looked up at him from a faucet, his hair and hands dripping, and, seeing a Jewish boy, glared icily back at him. At the same moment his teacher had yelped, and Toad had felt the nervousness of both men.

On the same outing, he had encountered a party of American Christians of the type he later knew to be "evangelicals." A smiling man, their pastor, was leading them from the golden Dome as Toad's group approached. He recalled how the ladies had grinned at the "little Jew boys" in their skullcaps.

Now he remembered a passage from Tanakh: *Who shall ascend into the Mountain of the Lord? Who shall stand in his holy place?* It was a forgotten song unexpectedly launched into his consciousness. Probably recited a thousand times and then filed away in a sort of mental cold storage, like so many other things.

He walked through the humming pylons of the perimeter defenses and looked over the dust of the plaza drying in the bright heat. It was empty— no tourists today. The great flagstones under his feet were as white as salt. He surveyed the scaffolded silver tower of Al-Aqsa and then raised his eyes to the golden Dome.

He motioned to the soldiers and they walked toward the Dome. A couple of Waqf men stood in the shade of the entry and watched them, clearly listening to a discussion of their identity and their intentions over their earphones. One of Toad's escorts grinned nervously. "I wish I was them. If somebody blows up the Dome, they go straight to martyr heaven. Doesn't apply to us."

Toad looked blandly at the man. "Shin Bet has no sense of humor about this place."

The soldier's grin disappeared. "Sorry, sir."

Toad nodded at the Waqf men half-hidden in their guard post and entered the sanctuary. It was blindingly dark inside, but after a moment he could distinguish flowers in the green marble of the walls. Shutting off his own murmuring earpiece, he stood silently, thinking, just inside the southern porch.

Toad looked up at the Arabic inscriptions circling the lintels of the Dome, barely visible in the yellowish light of the hanging lamps. When he had come here as a schoolboy, he had watched a young man kneeling on the red carpet, gesticulating in prayer toward the south. The man had stood, then bowed, then knelt, his hands moving gracefully, again and again chanting to his God. There was holiness in this place; Toad understood this intellectually, but that was all. He knew about its drawing power, although it was all ambiguous to him. He was a reader. He needed words more than emotions. And he was irritated that he could not make out the stylized words overhead. The builders had turned writing into illegible art. Everything in this case was connected to this Dome, he sensed—to its unreadable message.

He tried to read what was before him. The shrine was perfectly round and perfectly square at once, seated on an octagonal drum. Eight columns held up the canopy of the dome, its golden gloss only vaguely lustrous in the light from below. Beneath the dome, a high wooden screen encircled and concealed the Rock that was the center of the world. Here they said God had created Adam and Eve, here was the center of the Garden of Eden, here Adam had died and was buried, from here the waters of the flood had boiled up, here Abraham was ordered to sacrifice his son, here Solomon raised the altar of the Holy of Holies at the heart of the Temple. All history began here; all history would end here. It was the irresistible magnet of the spirit.

He suspected nothing would stop Rachel from coming here, not after Catriel's death. There was no other place to go, no other meaning to her life. The Temple had been at the center of her existence. Other women had children, lovers, possessions. She had Catriel, and together they had this vision. For Rachel, there was nothing left but the vision. It was her heart, her contribution, her Sabbath. The conflagration of the Dome would be her lighting of the candles.

He had loved the Sabbath, too, but for a different reason. It was the day of the books.

Rachel would not be able to get in without help. But suppose she could get it? Toad stared at the soldier standing next to him. It would take only one sympathetic IDF officer, perhaps a soldier she knew, or one of those he remembered from the military police who wore the *tallit* with his uniform.

"*Al ha-panim,*" Toad muttered. "This isn't working."

The soldier glanced back uneasily. "Sir?"

"I want to know the names of all the officers on the watch today. Since about 800 hours."

"Yes sir." The soldier spoke quietly to his GeM.

Then Toad walked to the ornate wooden perimeter of the Rock and studied it. Beyond this border was the Holy of Holies where no Jew should walk, he knew. Yahweh would strike him dead if he did, or so it was said. On this rock had once stood the canopy of God, the dwelling, the *shekhinah* or light of the Presence. Here, on the Ark of the Covenant, God himself had reigned from the mercy seat between the golden cherubim, the glory of God filling the Temple. In the books, God had taken Israel for his bride on this rock. *As the bridegroom rejoices over the bride, so shall God rejoice over thee, O Israel.* Rachel would surely come here to give herself. It was a matter of watching for her.

Unless she had already come. Words from the Zohar filtered into his mind like old rays of dust. *The seat of comfort…the canopy of the bride. For the Sabbath is queen and bride. Come, O bride, come, O bride! Receive the lady with the many lighted candles!"*

At once he vaulted up the stairs leading to the Rock and surveyed it anxiously. "Here, give me a torch," he called to the soldiers. Behind them, the Waqf guards ran inside at the sound of his voice, shouting angrily at him. He knew enough Arabic: "Get off!"

He scoured the Rock with the torch and soon found what he was looking for, shoved into a crevice where the Rock met the screen of the enclosure.

The body of Rachel Halevy, bleeding white and dead under a bridal veil.

Shin Bet Headquarters, Queen Helena Street, Jerusalem, 1535h

Without air-conditioning, the blue room was unbearable. Grateful that Kristall had the mercy not to smoke, Ari paused in his story to take a breath and rub the sweat from his face.

"So you think that someone connected with this cabal, this order of Cherubim, has gone rogue," Kristall summed up. "And the Interpol woman is part of it."

"Absurd," Kane interjected. He stood and stared at the blue screen on the wall. "She only heard about them a few days ago."

Ari held up the little ring. "She had this in her possession. She knows about the Order."

"It's fantastic," Didi Mattanyah said. "I've never heard anything about them. A secret cult dedicated to protecting the Temple Mount? And now someone is trying to wipe them out? How do we verify any of this?"

The doors of the stifling, soundproof room had closed only minutes before on Tovah Kristall, her deputies, and the President of Interpol. The news screens surrounding the room were filled with tense, perspiring reporters babbling soundlessly, and a horizontal blizzard of text in Hebrew, English, and Arabic.

"I don't know. I'm only telling you what Maryse told me. She said it was all she knew. It's my theory, not hers."

Didi looked skeptically at him. "Can you explain your theory again? I'm afraid I'm not following you."

"All right. The Order of Cherubim was founded hundreds of years ago to protect the Temple Mount until the Messiah comes…"

"Whoever the Messiah may be," Kristall interrupted. "And Emanuel Shor belonged to this Order."

"Along with Maryse's mentor."

"This…um, Jean-Baptiste Mortimer." Kristall adjusted her glasses to inspect the electronic dossier projected on the wall beside her. Mortimer's small round face smiled out at them.

"Yes," Ari said. "Here's the hypothesis. First Shor is killed. Then Jean-Baptiste Mortimer inducts Maryse into the order to replace him because he's afraid he is going to be next. And he *is* next. The Unknown takes a shot at Mortimer in Rome, but because he wears a bulletproof Caballero suit, he survives."

Kane looked anxious. "That means that Maryse is also in danger."

"We'll have her in momentarily," Kristall murmured. "Did she give you any indication of who the other members of this Order might be?"

Ari shook his head. "She said there would be four, that when one dies the other three come together to choose a successor. Each one is supposed to have a replacement in training."

Kristall shivered as if from a chill, although the room was oppressively hot.

"What's happened to the cooling system?" Ari felt sweat blooming on his skin.

"The government have shut down the new nuclear power station at Dimona and they're dispersing the fuel. As a precaution. So we've lost all our 'nonessential' power supply," Didi explained to him. "They don't want rocket blasts spreading radiation everywhere."

Kane's authoritative voice broke in. "That someone is liquidating these so-called protectors only makes our situation more urgent. It lends substance to this young man's theory about a plot on the Dome."

"Yes," Kristall acknowledged. "And now there are two of those devices out there."

"Two?" Ari asked. "You mean, two of the nano devices?"

Kane explained. "We think Levinsky's wife had the other one. She tried to get access to the Dome sometime this morning, but she was intercepted and shot dead. Your friend Sefardi found her body inside the shrine. The device wasn't on her."

"So they took it."

"Whoever *they* are," Kristall muttered, looking absently around for a cigarette. "This is maddening." She cocked her head, evidently listening to a voice on her earphone, then stood.

"We've located a video I want you all to see," she announced. "It's a clip taken a few years ago by a Technion team in the Negev."

At once the newscasters disappeared from the walls and were replaced by shaky images of a desert valley in the sun. In the distance, a balloon rose from the ground—there was a loud thump followed by shouts, then a weird round bubble of vapor exploded, sparkling like an enormous pearl across the sky. The video froze there.

"What is it?" Ari asked.

"A test," Kristall explained. "The Technion people shot a balloon full of water into the sky and then dropped this designer-atom device into the water by remote control. They ordered the device to transform itself into sodium."

"Number 11 in the periodic table," Ari muttered.

"Yes, Davan." Didi looked strangely at him. "An ordinary enough member of the periodic table of elements, which in its pure form explodes on contact with water." She nodded at the video still. "And you get a tremendous air shock and a pretty, spherical storm cloud."

"So this is how the Unknown proposes to blow up the Dome?" Ari shook his head.

"Technion has done dozens of experiments like this one," Kristall said. "No, a vapor explosion isn't powerful enough. But there are other elements, other combinations they've tried, just to make sure that they're transmuting energy into real matter."

"It's got to end," Kane said quietly, and after a silence, "Can we bring Inspector Mandelyn in now?"

Kristall gave the order, and Maryse was brought in, still in shorts and top and splashed with dust.

"Davan has told us about your ring, and about your association with this secretive group," Kristall said in formal tones. Maryse glanced coldly at Ari, and he stirred restlessly in his chair. "It's a very grave thing, withholding this information from us. As a law officer yourself…"

Maryse interrupted. "With respect, Ma'am, I don't answer to you. I had good and sufficient reasons to keep it to myself." She looked to Kane for support; he returned a brisk nod, but said nothing.

Kristall sighed. "Who else is involved in this…this cabal?"

"I can't tell you because I don't know. I explained all I know to Davan here; he has apparently passed it all on to you." Maryse gave Ari another colorless look.

Kane spoke up. "Clearing away these so-called Cherubim, or protectors, whoever they are, looks to be part of the Unknown's overall plan. Shor is dead. We don't know where Mortimer is—my Intel officer is trying to track him down as we speak. And there are two others. If we could find them, they might lead us to the Unknown."

"Perhaps they're dead already," Kristall proposed. "As we don't know who they are."

Something occurred to Ari. "I don't think so. You said that Rachel Halevy's killer deposited her body inside the Dome. Then he must have taken the

237

device off her, had it there in his hand ready to use. Why didn't he blow up the Dome then?"

"Maybe the Waqf scared him away?" Kristall ventured.

Didi laughed. "The Waqf? He's probably one of them."

Ari went on. "He wasn't ready to destroy the Dome. Not then. There's something unfinished…business to do." He turned abruptly to Maryse. "Where will the meeting be held?"

"Meeting?" Kane asked.

Maryse looked coolly into Ari's eyes and gave him a slow shake of her head. He turned back to Kristall.

"She told me that the Order of Cherubim would be meeting tonight in Jerusalem to replace Shor. But she didn't say where."

"Is that true, Maryse?" Kane asked quietly.

"I don't know where the meeting will be held."

"All this about a meeting is mildly interesting," Didi said, "but isn't it a bit more imperative to find the Unknown as quickly as possible?"

"We've got his face posted on every viewscreen in the city," Kristall answered. "Every IDF trooper, every police officer, and every Shin Bet agent we can scour up is looking for him now. The airspace is secure, the cordon around the Temple Mount is impenetrable, and the Waqf is at full strength guarding the shrines."

"But if we find the meeting, we find the Unknown," Ari interjected. "He's not going to lose the opportunity to light them all up at once, is he? With all the surviving Cherubim in one place?"

Kristall nodded. "It's only logical." At once she broke off, turning her head to listen to her earphone; then she rapidly scribbled a note and handed it to Ari.

"Davan, I've got an assignment for you."

"I thought I was suspended."

"Who said that? Take your team and get on this immediately," Kristall said, pointing at the note. "We might have found the connection we've been hoping for."

King's Garden Restaurant, King David Hotel, Jerusalem, 1615h

Lucien Grammont disliked eating his evening meal so early, but he had been warned that the kitchens would close at sunset because of the holiday. Yom Kippur began then, and for the next twenty-four hours the nation of Israel would fast—along with all guests of the nation of Israel. The sun still slanted through the skylights in the webbed ceiling, so he had an hour or so to enjoy his dinner. And in any case, he would have his hands full with the Order meeting this evening, so it was just as well.

He ordered fish and ate it with a strong white kosher wine, a Binyamina. Although it was not French wine, it was agreeably flavorful and cooling, particularly in this under air-conditioned restaurant. He had brought with him his leather-bound Shakespeare, but didn't get into it, as he was distracted by the diners around him—a small, loud American in a white suit blaring away in his odious accent at his tablemates; Jewish grandfathers in blue suits and skullcaps surrounded by children; families brashly toasting each other, elderly men swaying with full plates from the buffet tables. Israel, he thought, would be ready for the fast.

For dessert, hamantaschen—delicate poppy-seed cakes with honey. He loved them, although he was worried that a seed might make its devastating way into one of his splintered back teeth. Afterwards, he took his book and his coffee to the lobby veranda and sat down to admire the ruined towers of the ancient citadel. Beyond them, the Dome of the Rock reared its golden head.

Although people did not move him, nor did he even attempt to hide the shallowness of his feelings for them, he was passionate about history. The age of the great Dome, its uniqueness, the ambiguity of it fascinated him. Five hundred years older than the Order, its reason for existence had been lost in time even before Richard the Lion Heart and Saladin fought over possession of it. It was not a mosque, it was not a temple, it was not a church—it was none of them, but somehow transcended all of them. A jeweled canopy over the navel of the world. He had grown curious about it over the years, had acquired many old prints of it, and surrounded himself with books about it. With a peculiar possessiveness, he marveled at it.

His GeMphone buzzed tactfully and he spoke into it.

The time and venue for the meeting had changed? He should arrange transportation? This was unexpected. But yes, he would see to it.

He rang off, made a call, and sat back to look at the Dome with new interest. For thirteen centuries it had sheltered the holiest of secrets and held the world together. For how much longer? He wondered. His own Catholicism was august and ceremonial, and he disapproved of the unruliness that had recently come over the Church; but here, at the gates of the Holy City, he felt the forces of history converging and caught a glimpse of the cogency of God. This was the first and the last of places, the beginning and the ending point.

At first Grammont didn't recognize the young man who approached him across the veranda, wearing a black official-looking t-shirt and shorts like a bicycle policeman. Then he remembered.

"Mr. Grammont, we meet again," the young man said, holding an Israeli government credential in his face. "I'm Inspector Davan, and this is my associate, Inspector Sefardi." He motioned to a squat, nondescript man in gray shirt and slacks who stood off to the side—Grammont had not noticed him before. "Please come with us."

"I'm afraid I can't. I have business to attend to this evening, and I was about to arrange a few things."

"This won't take long."

Obligingly, Grammont adjusted his tie and preceded the two policemen into the lobby.

Shin Bet Headquarters, St. Helena Street, Jerusalem, 1720h

"You're not going into the interrogation?" Toad asked.

Ari stretched out in his office chair, for the first time in his memory grateful for this little sanctuary. He was exhausted. Before picking up Grammont, he had had time only for a quick shower and a sandwich.

"No, Kristall and Mr. Interpol wanted to talk to him alone," Ari said, absently rubbing at the bandages on his legs where stones and shrapnel had frayed the skin.

"It's not like you."

"What?"

"To sit here like this. To be…um, excluded."

Ari gave him a drained smile. "I'm tired. Like I've never been."

"I'll leave you alone then."

"No." Ari motioned to him to close the door. "I want to ask you something."

Toad shut the door and sat down. Ari's eyes were closed, and for a moment Toad thought he had dropped off. Then the eyes flickered open again.

"Why would the Saladin Brigade jump the wall to attack one small car on the Afula road?"

"They wouldn't."

"No, they wouldn't."

"Whoever ordered the attack obviously knew who you were—the one responsible for the death of that Palestine Authority officer, al-Ayoub."

"I didn't kill that man," Ari sighed.

"I know. We saw the data this morning."

"So who could have ordered the attack? Who knew where I was?"

Toad's blank face darkened. "We all knew. Everyone here knew. Miss Interpol called her boss this morning, described the car for us. That's why Miner was with that helicopter crew. They were looking for her—and you— on the road south."

Ari called Miner, who appeared almost immediately.

"I didn't get a chance to thank you for saving my poor, hacked-up corpse today."

The big man laughed. "It was the ride of a lifetime."

"And for saving Interpol, too."

"She didn't seem as happy as you."

"She wasn't in the same mess I was in. Even now, I'm not sure what mess *she* was in."

"You two had a tiff, I take it?" Miner smiled. "You didn't have much to say to each other on the chopper ride."

"Nobody could talk over that noise. But I want to ask you. I know why you came out on the rescue, but who sent you?"

"Kristall, of course."

"Was there any talk about the Brigade raid? Did you know what you were up against?"

"Not until we were in the air. Got a call that your car was under attack, so we phoned Wing Four at Hatzor and got that gunship escort."

"Who notified you about the attack?"

"A bus driver who saw the whole thing. Called in from a mobile phone."

"Must have been Maryse's bus driver," Ari muttered. "Doesn't help."

" 'Maryse,' is it?" Miner giggled. "No more 'Interpol'?"

Ari glared at him.

"Bit long in the tooth, isn't she? They're always more grateful, though, I suppose."

Ari grabbed a pencil and jabbed Miner in the rib. Then there was a sudden and authoritative rap on the door. Ari was surprised to see Tovah Kristall standing there. Working her tense lips feverishly, she came inside and slapped the door shut.

"That was quick," Ari said.

"It was outrageous."

"What happened?"

Rummaging through her pockets, Kristall looked hopelessly for a cigarette.

"You're not smoking in here."

She glared at him. "They've let him go. *Ordered* me to let him go."

"Grammont?"

"From the Premier's office directly. No reason, no explanation. How do they expect me to protect this country?" she almost spat. "Our mission is to prevent a bloody Armageddon. We've got a rogue with at least two infernal engines out there, looking to blow up the heart of Islam. How long do they think our Arab friends would hold off their atomics?"

She took a cavernous breath. Ari was afraid she would topple where she stood, but she went on: "And this Grammont is our only lead. Our only connection! He's walking out the front door now."

Ari smiled thoughtfully. "Has the sun set?"

"Yes."

"Then he's in for a surprise." Ari stood and stretched. "I think I'll go for a walk. Want to come, Miner?"

"Sure."

"And bring that special GeM of yours."

"Never go anywhere without it." Miner grinned.

"Toad, you might want to wake up that eye in the sky."

As Ari and Miner left, Kristall muttered, "I just don't want to see the landscape decorated with body parts."

It was her way of thanking them.

∗∗∗

A few minutes later, Ari and Miner stood in the exit from Shin Bet's nondescript building, looking out at Queen Helena Street. A peculiar sight in this heat in his suit, tie, and starched shirt, Lucien Grammont was easy to spot, talking to a policeman on the crowded corner. They got close enough to listen.

"No taxis tonight, sir. Yom Kippur."

Grammont looked around in amazement, taking in the fact that there was no motor traffic in the street. No car, bus, or even motorcycle would desecrate this night in Jerusalem.

"How do I get back to my hotel—the King David?" Grammont asked the policeman, who shrugged and pointed vaguely eastward.

"Walk?"

The policeman turned away. By now the pale gradient of the sky barely lit the street, and people were hurrying home or to synagogue; they fled the intense heat as if it were a storm. Grammont looked confused for a moment, then put his GeM to his ear.

"Can you pick up the call?" Ari asked Miner, who leaned on the building and manipulated his unusually bulky handheld.

"Not possible. He's using his red circuit."

The call was a short one; Grammont rang off and then examined his handheld.

"What's he looking at? Can you see his screen?"

"That I can do." Using a setting that was not supposed to exist, Miner tried pairing the screen on Grammont's GeM with his own. His thumb moved quickly and lightly over the tiny display. "It'll be hard. There are too many active screens…"

Ari glanced around; several pedestrians within a few meters were talking on GeMs as they walked along.

"I think this is his. The display's not Hebrew or English. What is it?"

Ari looked down discreetly into Miner's hand. "It's French. That's it."

"He's looking at a map of the city. The old town. Probably just looking for a route back to his hotel."

The screen illuminated a jumbled lattice of streets with a blue bubble over the corner they were standing on; all at once, a little thread fluoresced purple across the map and ended at a red bubble—the King David Hotel.

Staring at the GeM, Grammont started across the street. Ari and Miner looked at each other, and Ari rang his own GeM. "Toad, do you have a fix yet?"

"Not quite yet. They're still positioning the satellite."

"Grammont doesn't know Miner, so he'll follow him. Once you get him onscreen, don't let go." He rang off.

"I'll stay with him," Miner whispered and padded off behind the erect figure disappearing into the crowd.

Ari had other work to do, and he wasn't pleased about it. An idea had come to him; it was time to see Kristall.

Shin Bet Headquarters, St. Helena Street, Jerusalem, 1830h

"Are you hungry?" Ari asked.

Maryse sat sweating in one of the green interrogation rooms below ground. It was hot and dank, smelling of old effusions of pain.

She had not looked at him when he entered.

"I'm sorry you have to stay here," he said, more gently than he intended. "But how should we know what to do with..." He broke off.

"To do with me?" she murmured.

"I'm only trying to protect my country."

Maryse tensed her lips and stared at the wall.

"Thank you for being on my side today," he offered. "It was brave. Also foolish...but very brave."

The air in the room smothered him—he had always hated closed rooms, small spaces. He wished he could take her out of there, but Kristall had given strict orders—and in part for Maryse's protection. She seemed very pale and slight in the black clothes the matron had found for her.

"Maryse, please. I need to know more from you. This country is at stake..."

"This country," she breathed. "This country. The whole world is in pain because of this country. Has been my entire life. Every day, the oldest drumbeat in the world—'trouble in the Mideast.' "

"We have a right..."

"Yes, I know all about your bloody rights. The rest of us seem to have no rights but to suffer and be terrorized."

Ari sighed and stood to leave.

Maryse shook her head. "I'm sorry. I didn't intend that." She turned her back.

"Maryse, we're caught in a maze with no way out. There's a rogue toying with us out there. We don't know where he is, what he wants, or why he wants it. He seems to be able to go anywhere and do anything he wants— and he's got Jerusalem in his hand."

She turned again and looked coolly at him.

"I won't be interrogated."

"Maryse?" he asked quietly. "You said that each of the Cherubim had a successor, someone to take his place?"

"Yes."

"Then you're to be a successor."

"Yes, to Jean-Baptiste Mortimer. That is, if I want it. And if I qualify."

"Do you know where he is?"

Frustrated, she stood and leaned against the wall. "I don't. I don't. Why can't you just believe me?"

"Because you've held back so much."

Maryse closed her eyes; she was exhausted, he could see.

"What I've held back…it was a promise I made. All right?"

"I'm sorry, Maryse. But I need to know everything you know."

"Everything I know is ancient history."

"Ancient history is what matters here," Ari said. "The mission of the Order of Cherubim is to protect the temple, like guardian angels. How do they do it?

"Originally, with their armies. Today, it's different. Persuasion. Influence."

"What kind of influence?"

"It's a very old story. A sort of chain of influence over the centuries. One old man talking things out with another."

"Old men?"

"As I hear. A Prime Minister gets a call from a former Prime Minister, who was in turn influenced by the one prior to him. The Cherubim keep the chain going."

"They just...talk?"

"They talk. Sometimes they act. When the Israelis took control of Jerusalem in the Six-Day War, a lot of radicals wanted to take over the Temple Mount. One influential rabbi tried to have the Dome blown up immediately. But the defense minister stopped him."

"The defense minister would have been Moshe Dayan."

"Yes. The next day Dayan walked up the Mount and met with the Muslim authorities. They all sat down on the floor together in the Al-Aqsa mosque and talked. Ever since then, you have this modus vivendi—live and let live."

"Are you saying Moshe Dayan was one of the Cherubim?"

"No, but someone had talked to him long before. Chaim Weizmann."

"Weizmann was the first president of the state of Israel..."

"And one of the Cherubim."

Ari smiled at this. A long, quiet conspiracy of peace. A portrait of Weizmann hung on the wall in his parents' home; he had known that grandfatherly face as far back as he could remember. Along with his father's silver menorah and the pictures of forgotten relatives that crowded the house, the portrait connected him to an unnamable longing, a bond in the blood and the heart that he had never broken, despite the detached life he led.

In the same room, another portrait showed a bearded Weizmann making a gift of a Torah scroll to Harry Truman, the American president who in 1948 had enabled the creation of the state of Israel—both grandfathers of his country, beaming with hope even as the world woke from the horror of the Shoah. There was something comforting in the thought of this long, long line of wise men, calm men.

"What about Mortimer? How did he become one of the Cherubim?" Ari asked her.

"At first, the Master of the Templar Order was also—quite secretly—the fourth member of the Cherubim. When the Order was dissolved, the role passed quietly to certain Masters of the Order of Malta, which took over the mission of the Templars. Years ago, Jean-Baptiste succeeded to that role."

Ari nodded. "Maryse, what I'm going to ask you to do—I wouldn't ask it of anyone if I had a choice. I've already cleared it with Kristall."

She looked remotely at the wall. "You need me to draw him out, don't you? You want me to be a decoy for the Unknown."

"We don't have an option. We can't find Mortimer to do it, and you don't know who the other Cherubim are. The Unknown Subject has you all in his sights for some reason—he's trying to eliminate the Cherubim—and the only way we can think of to bring him out in the open is to provide him a target."

A veil of hair hid her face from him. Then she turned and, for the first time, smiled. "I suppose it is my job now. Perhaps, one way or the other, this is how I qualify...to be a guardian angel."

Jaffa Gate Room, King David Hotel, Jerusalem, 1900h

The air-conditioning system, temporarily turned on, pumped and struggled against the heat from television lights and the hundred bodies jammed into the meeting room. Despite the effort, the room was roasting. Nervous, excited, the pilgrims seemed not to care about the heat. "Worse in Texas. Much worse," one of them muttered to another, who nodded.

Lambert Sable wandered on in a sagging white suit, his face gushing with sweat, and stood before a camera. "Folks, this is a direct link back to the End-of-Times network." He was an awkward speaker, but more effective for it. "It'll be Pastor Bob's last TV address, before you and me and him walk back to glory tomorrow morning. Let's make it count."

Cheers broke out as Pastor Bob, also in white but immaculately tailored, strode into the makeshift studio and hit his floor marks precisely.

"I speak to you tonight for the last time. I speak to you from Jerusalem, the city of God Almighty, with my final message and warning to a world on the eve of collapse. It is now only a matter of hours before the Lord takes his church to him in the clouds." There was cheering.

"Thus, before you tonight is this great and final invitation: Accept him now, this minute, or by dawn you will be left behind in this world which is spiritually called Sodom and Gomorrah."

"The prophecy of First Corinthians 15 is about to be fulfilled. *Behold, I'll tell you a secret. We shall not die, but we shall be changed in a moment, in a twinkling of an eye we shall be caught up in the clouds.*"

"Those who are left behind will find themselves in a world turned upside down, where evil is called good and good is called evil, where every kind of sick perversion reigns. When all true Christians are gone, secular-humanist atheists will rule that world for seven years of Tribulation.

"As I stand here, I can look over the towers of Jerusalem. I can see the sights Jesus saw; I also see what he didn't see—that sacrilegious Dome where the temple of his Father stood. The abomination of desolation, just as he predicted in Matthew 24. Well, as the book of Daniel prophesies, after the saints are raptured the Jews will destroy all that and rebuild the Temple. Tonight, this very night, the Jews are observing Yom Kippur all over this dark land of Israel. Soon they will rise up and clear this abomination from the most sacred ground on the planet and fulfill prophecy—the temple of the Jews will stand once again on that very spot I can see from my hotel suite window.

"And then the Anti-Christ, that Jewish incarnation of evil, will stand in that rebuilt temple right here in the city of Jerusalem and declare himself to be God.

"At that moment the wrath of God will fall on this earth. The Islamic hordes will descend on Israel and there will be war like this world has never seen. Millions of Jews will be killed. If God didn't cut the seven years short, not a single Jew would be left.

"Then there'll be earthquakes, fire, and flood. Tornadoes will sweep the earth. Along with the Jew, the Hindu, Buddhist, Muslim, Catholic, Orthodox, the pagan, the witch—all the cultists, the heathens and humanists, the socialists and secularists, the progressives and the pope-worshipers, the gays and God-haters—all of the lost and the lukewarm will be swallowed up together in the prison of Hell, into a lake of fire that burns forever.

"Friend, you'll be with them if you don't join us now. You'll see Hell on earth—breathe Hell, smell Hell, hear Hell! The Bible is clear: *The wicked shall be turned into Hell!*" More exultant cheering.

"You have one chance left to escape the seven years of Tribulation and an eternity of Hell. That chance is now, tonight. You can't afford to wait one minute longer.

"Tomorrow at dawn, through the generosity of Mr. Lambert Sable, myself and hundreds of pilgrims will stand at the foot of the Mount of Olives, dressed in white to welcome the Lord when he comes to take us up. You can be with us in spirit; more important, you can be with us in the clouds."

A gust of cheers from the pilgrims, and it was over.

They overran the lobby, scuttling to the elevators, mothers with children begging to use the swimming pool, elderly women, perspiring middle-aged men with the leftovers of twenty-year-old goatees.

"Americans," Miner thought. "Religion-crazy."

He had taken a chair in the corner of the lobby lounge, and played a game on his GeM while keeping one eye on Grammont and monitoring the babble from Shin Bet headquarters in his earpiece.

Sipping at an effete little coffee cup, reading a small leather-bound book, Grammont sat rigidly at the bar and had not moved for an hour. Miner was unclear who the man was or why he was important; but Ari wanted him shadowed, so Miner complied. Bored, he continued with his game.

The game was called "Inventing Elements." He had been fascinated by Halevy's account of the designer-atom device and was having fun feeding new algorithms into his GeM that would produce elements existing only in theory. He had gone far beyond the sea of unstable heavy elements into an archipelago of solid atoms that seemed dull and slow to die. But now he was inventing something entirely strange, something he hadn't imagined before: single atoms that expire in puffs of air powerful enough to blast away the walls of a building, and iron-like atoms so unstable that they could reproduce out of control and rapidly rip the crust from the Earth and fling it into space. The most hellish atoms had nuclei with 300 or more protons.

Of course, a nucleus that heavy would disintegrate in milliseconds. But he wondered what a gram or so of the material would take with it at the point of its sudden death.

He looked up to check on Grammont. The man hadn't moved, but then he saw approaching him the last person he expected to see.

"Sarah?"

All vertical lines, she had become so thin he barely recognized her; she was still wearing a lab coat, and her hair fell straighter than ever. But she smiled as she sat next to him.

"They told us we could find you here."

"Us?"

An avuncular man in old-fashioned square glasses stood fidgeting nearby.

"Miner, this is my boss, Dr. Rappaport. You weren't answering your mobile, so we rang your friend Ari. I hope it's all right."

"Sure." He was rattled by her presence. "I mean, what can I do for you?"

Rappaport, looking mildly excited, seated himself in front of Miner.

"Um, would you mind leaning a bit to the left? I'm trying to keep an eye on something."

"Oh, of course. I won't turn around or anything like that," Rappaport's eyes glowed. His New York-accented voice was too loud. "You're watching someone."

"Yes. So?"

"Well, Sarah thought it would be best to speak to you about this. She's been very helpful the past few days, ever since I got interested in this problem."

"What problem?"

Rappaport went on in his harsh, horizontal American accent. "Your agency asked us to identify the gene sequence of an eyelash. You know about that—you apparently collected it. Yes. And there was low activity in the MAO-A region. You know, almost non-existent!"

"I'm sorry. I'm not following you."

"Your eyelash is a sociopath!"

"Oh, yes. The gene problem."

Hands in the air, Rappaport was getting more excited. "Then I thought, well, you know—look in the old files! We used random samples of some of those Cohen genes as controls for some of our earliest tests on monoamine oxidase."

Sarah continued. "We found something interesting. For several years, the Centre has been doing tests on people with a certain neurological disorder—we call it monoamine oxidase A dysfunction, or MAO-A. People with this genetic makeup are unusually violent; they seem to have no conscience or scruples. Sometimes we compare DNA samples we've collected from other sources to MAO-A samples—just to see how normal compares to abnormal."

Rappaport jumped in. "And we occasionally run into a control sample that turns out to be not so normal after all. Here."

He held up a tablet showing an image of something like snakes in a writhing embrace. "This is your eyelash—and here's one of our old samples from the Cohanim collection. Notice—virtually identical."

Miner pretended to study it. "So you've ID'd our eyelash?"

"No, not at all. But we've found his father. He was in our control database all along."

"Name?"

"Number 3111," Sarah whispered. "Chandos."

"The father is as great a hazard as the son—if not more so," Rappaport put in.

"Then the father's is the sample missing from the Cohanim database?"

Rappaport nodded.

"I should call Ari Davan with this. Hold on." Miner smiled at Sarah, who smiled back. He touched his GeMphone and looked up at the same moment.

Grammont was gone.

Shin Bet Headquarters, St. Helena Street, Jerusalem, 1950h

"It's out of the question," Kane muttered. "I'm glad I stopped this happening."

"Ari's right. You know he is." Maryse insisted. She stood and came closer to him. "This may be the only way to draw out the Unknown."

"To have you play the stalking horse for an assassin? You still report to me, Mandelyn, and I won't have it."

"Do you have a better plan? The Unknown is not just the key to Acheropita and to clearing Peter Chandos's name. That's the least of it. He could be putting the match to the Dome of the Rock as we speak."

The blue room was alive with news chatter from the wall screens and from Shin Bet intelligence people swarming around the table. Kristall had called in analysts to examine all the evidence Ari's team had amassed, but they were at a loss. The Unsub—the Unknown Subject—had evaporated into the heat of the city. A harsh smell of coffee hung over the room.

In one corner, Toad sat in isolation from the others, staring thoughtfully at the satellite feed and, alternatively, at his own GeMscreen. It was playing a video of a man in a white suit haranguing a crowd of people who at one moment cheered and at another moment seemed to drop into a hypnotic spell. Toad touched his GeM and spoke softly to it: "I need a wiretap authorization."

Kane gave Maryse a dry smile. "The Dome couldn't be safer—it's under the closest surveillance. And things are moving. We've connected the Palestinian Ayoub—who, based on his pinky ring, apparently was a fellow member of your band—to a sinister little crowd here. Group of fanatics called the Flaming Sword. We're bringing the leader in tonight for questioning."

Turning from the fruitless discussion at the table, Tovah Kristall interrupted them. "What have you decided, Kane?" she whispered loudly, her coffee breath souring the air.

"There's no question of it. I didn't bring Mandelyn to Israel to decoy an assassin."

"What did you bring her here for, then?" Kristall was contemptuous.

Maryse burst in. "What about this group—the Flaming Sword, you call them?"

"The Flaming Sword?" Kristall laughed. "You mean Al-Saif? An old men's club? What does Interpol have against them?"

"I was about to tell you," Kane was back in official mode. "The PA cop killed in Rome, Nasir al-Ayoub, he was connected to this 'al-Saif' group through his father."

"And to the Cherubim as well," Kristall said. "That makes sense—keeping the Temple Mount shrines safe is top priority for the PA So to have one of their own in the Cherubim. It follows."

Kane went on. "Unless the Cherubim themselves have been infiltrated. You know there are Muslim radicals who'd like to see the shrines destroyed. It'd galvanize the whole Islamic world against Israel. 'Wipe out the Zionist Entity.' "

"No one knows that better than we do," Kristall said bitterly. "The Zionist Entity is fully aware of it."

"To destroy the Mount, you have to eliminate the guardians or suborn them," Kane pointed out. "Or, even more effectively, infiltrate them."

"Or perhaps all three," Maryse offered.

Kane nodded knowingly at her. "Yes. I hadn't thought of that. It's best to have more than one point of attack."

"So you think the Sword might have something in this?" asked Maryse. "That this Nasir Ayoub, who was a member of both…"

Kane interrupted her. "Ayoub had the ring. He was one of the guardians, and someone eliminated him. How do we know it wasn't his own side? No one is rougher on an Arab than another Arab. Or maybe the Sword is also trying to protect the shrines. I want to know one way or the other."

Ari Davan came in and joined them.

"Miner—um, Inspector Kara—has lost Grammont."

"Splendid," Kristall groaned.

"He was watching him in the bar at the Citadel David. Maybe he just went to his room; Miner's gone up to check. In any case, Grammont could not have left the hotel—it's surrounded."

Something bright flashed on the news panels, and they all looked up at multiple images of a white-suited man with an elaborate slab of red hair gesturing at them. The sound was muted, but a ribbon of text ran across the screens: TV EVANGELIST BROADCASTS WARNING FROM JERUSALEM: WORLD ENDING TOMORROW.

"No joke," Kristall sighed. "At last, a prophet who gets it right."

"He's found him," Ari cut in, listening to his earpiece. "He got room service to deliver something, and Grammont opened the door."

"Superb. Our missing link in this case is having a snack in his hotel room while we wait for the world to end." Kristall could bear it no longer; she lit a cigarette as the others stared her down uselessly.

Ari looked grave. "Isn't it time to give our plan a try? Maryse?"

"I won't allow it," Kane said in a flat voice. "Unsub is a stealth expert—the most precise assassin we've encountered—it's far too dangerous to let Maryse out of here."

"He might not even know about me, that I'm connected to the Order of Cherubim," Maryse observed.

"In that case, there's no point. He won't come after you and it's a wasted effort. But you're not taking that chance."

"It's my chance to take."

Ari looked at her. Pale and determined, she rose from her chair. He didn't fully understand, but Maryse was declaring a kind of independence from Kane.

The Interpol chief gave her a glance, then a resigned smile. "Yes, I suppose it is."

"Miner's back on," Ari's head jolted to one side.

"Put him on the speaker," Kristall ordered.

Miner's voice was a low resonance in the room; the analysts quieted down and stared into the air as if searching for an image. "His GeM's activated. I'm in the fourth-floor lobby near his room, and I've got pairing, so I can see his screen." There was silence for a moment. "He's ringing someone. Damn. He's using the red circuit."

With surprising speed, Kane clicked open his own phone and dictated an order to someone on the other end.

"Tell Kara to link his GeM to mine," Kane whispered to Ari. "Here's the network information and password."

In a few moments, Kane's GeMscreen flickered to life, and he projected it onto the wall: there was nothing to see but a menu of apps and a wallpaper image of a French chateau draped in vines. Miner had successfully patched himself into Grammont's screen.

"What are you doing?" Kristall's voice rasped.

But Kane was listening hard to something on his transparent earpiece. Slowly, a smile cut across his broad face.

"Tell Mandelyn," he said simply, and held his GeM up for Maryse to listen to.

It was a voice she knew well and unhappily. "Good evening, Inspector. The meeting will be held at midnight. In the Dome of the Rock." Intel clicked off.

The Dome of the Rock, Jerusalem, 2050h

"In the name of God, God is the greatest, all praise for God."

Amal listened respectfully and hopelessly, holding up his father as they made their slow way around the circular aisle of the Dome. The old man muttered and coughed as if his throat were dry stone, and Amal wiped the running droplets from his face. It was now an hour since dusk, but unaccountably it was getting hotter. All day he had felt as though his heart would burst; now his head pulsed with heat as well.

His father had insisted on making this journey. As night came on, Hafiz, his face like a gaunt bird's, announced he would walk to the Damascus Gate; he brushed away the mourners in his house who tried to stop him and took Amal with him. But they had not stopped at the entry to the city; Hafiz whispered to him that he wanted to pray at al-Aqsa. So he had supported the old man through the crowds of white-robed Jews toward the Cotton Merchants Gate of the holy mountain.

Near the gate, they entered a tiny, deserted shop stacked to the ceiling with dusty toys—boxes of dinosaurs, soldiers, toy guns with orange barrels, and princess dolls, all plastic, all untouched. There was no shopkeeper, no clerk; only four expressionless men on wooden chairs seated like guardians outside the entrance. The men barely acknowledged Hafiz.

Amal and Hafiz made their way through the maze to the back of the shop, where the old man motioned to the boy to push aside a case displaying hand-knitted baby clothes, yellowed and stiffened with age. Behind the case, he found a utility door double-locked with elaborate, fresh-looking hardware. Hafiz provided a key, and they entered a dark corridor that sloped gradually upward toward a source of light. To Amal's surprise, they emerged inside a bathroom. It was the lavatory worshipers used for ritual washing before going to the Mosque. They were inside the Noble Sanctuary.

At a fountain, Amal cupped water in his hands and held it up so his father could wash his face and the blood from his mouth. Together, they had washed their feet and then moved toward the Mosque for the night prayer.

But they hadn't gone to the Mosque. They went instead to the Dome of the Rock. In the lamplight the sanctuary shone like a garden of gold and jewels.

"Surely God will make those who believe and do good deeds enter gardens beneath which rivers flow; they shall be adorned therein with bracelets of gold and pearls."

Murmuring verses from the Koran, Hafiz gestured to the lustrous mosaics on the pillars. Amal had never noticed them before: royal jewels hanging like fruit from palms of green stone.

"As for those who led the way, the first muhajirin…God is pleased with them…He has planted for them gardens streaming with running waters, where they shall have eternal life…This is the height of exaltation."

Amal understood that his father was not reciting these verses at random; although he only dimly knew why, he repeated them and tried to remember them. As they slowly proceeded counterclockwise around the aisle, the old man spread his hands to the walls.

"We caused to grow gardens of palms and vines for you…And a tree that grows out of Mount Sinai that sheds oil."

Amal knew that his father had every verse of the holy book in his memory, and wondered if he could ever equal him. And to remember the words was one thing; far beyond that was to understand them.

"What is the meaning of the tree that sheds oil?"

Hafiz stopped and smiled weakly at his adopted son. The boy was curious. "It is the oil of anointing. The Prophet, blessings upon him, instructed us to anoint the body with the oil of the blessed tree, for it will heal the seventy nations."

"The seventy nations?"

"Out of Noah came seventy nations to people the earth."

"Heal them?"

"The earth is dark with sin and infidelity, as dark as the Black Stone of Mecca. Here it all began. Here it will end."

"We made a covenant with Adam, but he forgot it, and We found him lacking in faith. And when We said to the angels: 'Bow down before Adam,' they all bowed themselves down except the Shaitan, who refused.

" 'Adam,' We said, 'The Shaitan is an enemy to you…Let him not turn you out of Paradise and plunge you into affliction.

"But the Shaitan whispered to him, saying: 'Shall I show you the Tree of Immortal Life and an everlasting kingdom?' "

Hafiz motioned upward to the arch above their heads. Flowering over the stone, a tree with sinuous branches tipped with fruit fanned out of a jeweled, heart-shaped vase.

"The man and his wife ate of its fruit, so that they saw their nakedness and covered themselves with leaves of the Garden. Thus did Adam disobey his Lord and go astray…Whoever you are, death will overtake you, though you are in lofty towers."

The Sheikh stopped for breath. He leaned back against the wall and closed his eyes. Small bubbles of blood bloomed at the corners of his mouth. After a moment, he opened his eyes again and continued:

"Then his Lord had mercy on him; He forgave him and rightly guided him. Go hence,' He said, 'and may your offspring be enemies to each other."

Hafiz lifted his shaking head and looked into his son's eyes. "That war goes on. I had hoped…but now there is no time. *You* must lead the battle that is about to come upon us."

"I don't understand, Father."

"Do you know what it means…a *sufi?*"

"A holy man. You."

"A *sufi* has taken upon himself the *suf*—the sacred robe, the symbol of his covenant to seek only God. I wear it. And I have also taken the Flaming Sword in my hand. It is said to be the sword of the Prophet, peace be upon him, that carries the trace of the lightning of Heaven. It is now for you."

"What is the meaning of the Flaming Sword? And why is it for me?"

"It has been the burden of our family for many, many years. For centuries. The Sword stands for our willingness to stand against the offspring of the Shaitan, who deceived Adam at the Tree of Immortality. He is our enemy… the Shaitan, the Dajjal…and he is coming here again tonight."

Amal was terrified. What could his father mean by this?

"Where is the Sword then? Why haven't we brought it with us?"

Slowly, trembling, Hafiz led him once more around the circle of arches. At length they paused, and the old man pointed to a pillar opposite them. It was like the other columns upholding the Dome, rising from a square pedestal and capped with a gold crown. But the color of the marble was unique: pale, with a bloody fissure like a shaft of lightning from top to bottom.

"That pillar. It does the same work as the others, but it is unlike them. So are you unlike your brother believers. You…*you* are the Sword now."

His strength nearly gone, Hafiz continued to struggle around the curve of the aisle. Amal was now carrying him. Amal had learned from the imam that the Dajjal must be destroyed before the Day of Requital, that Isa the Prophet would come down and destroy him. Amal could not imagine that he could play any role in such things. What does it mean, *I* am the Sword?

Hafiz seemed to hear his thoughts. "As the stars circle *Yean* the pole star, so do we circle the foundation stone of God," the old man coughed. "God is the Center. The stars cannot stop themselves in their orbit; neither can we escape the curve of the future that He ordains." So they labored on until the old man was satisfied; seven circumlocutions of the holy rock. He could go no further.

"But it's time for sleep. Time to go home," Amal complained. Fatigue had dulled his fear.

And then he was awake again.

A sharp noise of boots on the stonework.

"There will be no sleep yet," Hafiz whispered. "The Dajjal is here."

The Temple Mount, Jerusalem, 2310h

The Dome of the Rock floated overhead like half a golden sun rising from a dark sea.

Maryse walked through the barely visible violet band of the alarm system and felt a slight prickling on her skin; so, this was the vaunted "Flaming Sword"—the supposedly impenetrable electronic barrier around the Temple Mount.

The high-current electron beam flowed from millions of nanoscale pillars embedded in the gates. The artificial intelligence controlling the beam could supposedly detect the most elusive anomaly—a capsule containing milligrams of hydrogen cyanide gas, a miniature printed pistol, a few grains of fentanyl.

As Maryse passed, a high whine issued from the guardhouse at the Moroccan Gate. The Waqf guard touched a screen, shut down the alarm, and inspected her weapon. Ari and Kane went through the same routine.

On the other side of the barrier, they were met by an Israeli officer. Maryse looked hard at him. He was lean and short, smart in a uniform the color of sand. Ari snapped a few words at him in Hebrew, and the man produced a card—Ari held it up to the light to validate the man's identity.

The lieutenant led them in a straight march across the plaza toward the Dome. Maryse looked around nervously, her hand on her weapon, staring into the distance made darker by the floodlights on the dome. She thought she saw writhing shapes outside the pool of light; perhaps waves of heat or the twitching of her eyes from exhaustion.

At Shin Bet headquarters, Ari had encouraged her to rest for a while, but she couldn't sleep on the hard bunk they gave her in an underground room. Dozing in the heat, she had dreamed about hanging from a speeding bus in the desert; a panicked mob ran alongside the bus, shouting for help, as the sun grew more intense and the landscape whitened to the color of bone. Then a pillar of smoke boiled into the sky; across the plain, thousands of people dried up along with their shadows.

Startled awake, she had found Ari standing over her; David Kane, dressed in a black commando uniform that was almost elegant, waited in the doorway. They would all three attend the meeting of the Cherubim uninvited.

"This is the plan... in the broadest possible sense, of course," Kristall had said in her accustomed ironic voice. "If we're going to draw Unsub out, we'll need to keep our presence minimal but maintain absolute security at the same time. If the Cherubim really are his target, we'll have our precision instrument—Davan—waiting for him inside the Dome. Inconspicuously." She eyed him and he nodded.

"I'm going in too," Maryse had said almost involuntarily. "I'm another possible target—more incentive for Unsub. And I can handle myself."

Kristall looked skeptical.

"It's too dangerous," Ari shook his head. "And it's not necessary now. We have the Cherubim to decoy him."

"Dangerous for whom? I'm a far better shot than you."

Ari grinned at her; he had to admit it.

"If you're going into the Dome, I'm going as well," Kane had announced, and Kristall did not object.

Maryse sighed imperceptibly with relief as they arrived at the gate of the Dome and entered. An ethereal quiet came over them. The lieutenant departed, his heels snapping on the stone into the distance, and they were alone in the building.

As planned, each of them silently moved into position next to one of the gates. A fourth gate would be unguarded, but under surveillance. Maryse was assigned to the south gate and, finding a secure place behind a marble pier, she sat down on the floor to wait. From here she could surveil the entry without being seen.

Lamplight washed over the walls of stone and the red carpet on the floor. The patterned gray marble on the piers rippled upward like streams of milky sand. Inlaid medallions of the moon and sun alternated with ten-pointed stars. They reminded her of the star, moon, and sun cards of the Tarot deck. Roman arches topped the pillars that held up the dome, and beyond them Maryse could just glimpse starry golden galaxies spiraling around the base of the dome. It was like the observatory at Cambridge that she had once visited, a round cavity of a ceiling with a keyhole to the universe.

She thought of the labyrinth at Chartres, of the maze stone at Glendalough— of the eternal re-imagining of the round heavens, the reaching for the center that should unite rather than divide.

In the near-silence, she could still hear the tinnitus of the crowds outside the Mount. Passing through them, she had looked round quickly at the Jews sweating in their white robes, praying nervously, expectantly, as floodlights played over the plaza fronting the Western Wall. Severe heat made the worshipers restless, and they all kept one eye on the Dome, willing it to disappear—and fearing that it might. The night was made grimmer by the mournful chanting of the Kol Nidre, the hymn of yearning for atonement that the Jews sang on Yom Kippur. And among them those American pilgrims, too excited to sleep away their last hours, roaming the square, loitering smugly until the End.

Then Miner's voice came clearly into her earpiece. "Grammont has left the hotel on foot. We'll keep you informed on his progress." She heard Ari and Kane acknowledge, and she did the same.

Maryse stood up quietly to observe the shrine. She had hoped the interior of the Dome would be cool; instead, it was hot as a greenhouse. The sacred Rock was invisible behind a circular wooden screen inside the colonnade of piers; palm-like columns marched around it. As her eyes adjusted to the pale light, she could see the veined purple porphyry of the columns and began to make out bunches of golden grapes coiled in mosaic over the green marble soffit overhead, elaborate fruits and foliage dripping like jewels from every surface. For a moment she imagined the vines on the walls coming to life, the fruit ripening in the heat. These stylized plants inlaid in the marble meant something, of course: This was Eden, guarded by the Cherubim at the command of God. This was the garden of Adam and Eve. Where so many others outside waited for the ending, Maryse caught a breath of a beginning.

To her historian's eye, it was a strange building—unlike any church or temple she had ever seen. No altar, no cross, no image. Nor was it like a mosque. From where she stood, she could see the *qibla*—the niche in the south wall indicating the direction of prayer—but the building was not oriented toward it. The *qibla* seemed almost an afterthought. Despite the monumental Koranic inscriptions, the Dome soared curiously beyond any particular idea of God, and yet centered on Him.

She heard a footstep, and her heart bumped in her chest. Would it be Jean-Baptiste? How could he get through the maze of security around the Mount? Then she remembered what Kristall had said.

"The Waqf seem to know about this meeting tonight."

"What do you mean, they *seem* to know about it?" she had asked.

"We've had a little talk with them, and they don't say yes, they don't say no. They never really communicate with us unless they're angry about something. So, we've given our orders. If someone comes toward a gate and the Waqf let them in, so be it."

They would have plenty of notice if anyone approached the Dome. And someone was approaching—it was the hard click of the lieutenant's footsteps.

But this was wrong. He shouldn't be returning.

She heard the west door open; then a shout in her earpiece and a simultaneous echo. Then nothing.

"Ari?" she whispered. No answer.

"David?"

Kane's voice hissed in her ear. "Sh. I'm coming."

Instinctively Maryse flattened herself against the pier, keeping the colonnade toward the west door in sight and her pistol ready.

She held her breath forever, but there was nothing.

Then someone emerged from the lamplit gloom. Walking calmly toward her, a curious look on his face—Ari.

She glanced behind her. Kane stood by the *qibla*, and she breathed again.

One relaxed second was too long.

She only had time to glimpse the face, to recognize it.

Too late. Her neck exploded with pain. Then darkness.

CHAPTER 5

MONDAY, OCTOBER 11, 2027

Beit Horon, near Jerusalem, 0010h

Inside the van box, the darkness was almost complete, except for an occasional flash of light from the crack around the lid. Ari knew from the roar of the engine that the van was climbing rapidly.

He gulped air from the bare opening and tried to think, tried to make sense of what had just happened.

From his crouch behind a pier in the Dome, he had wondered why the IDF man was returning and kept his weapon ready. The door opened, and the lieutenant entered calmly enough; too late, he saw it was not the same man in the sandy uniform. In the gloom, the face was unclear. The instant he knew he was looking at the twin brother of Peter Chandos, the man disarmed him with a swipe to the hand and a smooth, simultaneous blow to the chin.

Cursing himself as Chandos confiscated his GeM and earpiece, he heard a whispered instruction—there was a nine-millimeter pointed at his head—he was to remain completely silent and walk forward.

Chandos had been smart enough to stay out of Ari's reach. At a certain point, he was told to stop and stand still. The gun trained on him, Ari was forced to watch as the man crept up on Maryse in utter silence and struck her in the neck, a knifelike blow. She dropped without a sound onto the red carpet. The next moment, Chandos did the same to him.

On waking, he had still hurt from the methodical blow he had received to the vagus nerve. Lying on the carpet alone, he could see neither Maryse nor Kane, but Chandos stood over him pointing a black pistol at his eye. "Get up," the man whispered.

And that was all he said. From a small cabinet he extracted a tunic and cap of a Defense Force officer, then motioned to Ari to put them on. He pocketed the gun and marched Ari out the door and across the moon-stained plaza, down steps, toward a warren of corridors he knew to be the Cotton Merchants' Gate. Ari knew better than to make any signal at all to the

265

two Waqf guards who stood at the Gate; they motioned them through the electronic cordon without a second look. Once beyond the gate, he ordered Ari to drop the disguise. Under a dim stone arch beyond the cordon, a group of sleepy IDF men rustled to attention at a salute from Chandos.

After a helpless forced walk through shadowy alleys, they had come to Dung Gate, the south entrance to the old city, where an ancient van sat waiting. Chandos wordlessly ordered him into a large box in the van bed and locked him down inside it.

Now the van was on a sudden decline and picking up speed. The faint wind did nothing to cool the box—the heat was like a force pressing on Ari's body. He tried to think, but couldn't for the memory of Maryse lying on the blood-colored carpet. He had to force her out of his mind; she was probably already dead, along with Kane. Chandos was so smooth, so calm, so conscience-free, as logical as a dancer in his motions.

The van stopped and Ari heard the driver getting out. This might be his only chance—to overpower Chandos when he leaned over the box to unlock it.

It was useless. The lock clicked electronically, and Ari peered out to see Chandos standing well away from the van, a remote control in his hand.

"Stand up," he motioned with his head, the nine-millimeter aimed exactly at Ari's left shoulder.

Ari stood and looked around quickly. He couldn't tell where they were— some dry road in the desert. From the length of the drive, he estimated a place within ten miles of the city. A three-quarter moon tarnished the horizon; by its rusty light, he could see they were near a precipice.

With this disciplined an enemy, Ari knew his only chance was the haphazard—and talk his only weapon.

"I know who you are."

Chandos never took his eyes off Ari; there was no amusement in them. He removed his officer's cap and for the first time, Ari noticed the man's resemblance to himself: the same cable-like limbs, the trim head with dark cropped hair, the eyes.

A gold ring on his finger shone with sweat.

"Your name is Chandos, and you are an assassin. You murdered the Pope, you murdered Emmanuel Shor, you murdered Tempelman and Rachel Halevy and Catriel Levine."

Calmly, Chandos rummaged in the cab with one hand and pulled something from it.

"And you murdered your own brother."

Chandos tightened his lips, unwrapping the parcel he had taken from the van.

"Disguised as Rome police, you pulled inspection duty in the Sancta Sanctorum. You hid, removed the icon in the middle of the night, and when your brother came to look things over the next morning, you shot him and traded places with him. You even put a Cherubim ring on his finger. Why? To cast suspicion on the Cherubim?"

Ari paused.

"An hour or so later, it was you who went with the Pope into the chapel. When he knelt to pray, you maneuvered the gun into your brother's dead hand, fired shots at the Pope, and left the gun there. You threw off your robe. When the police stormed the building, you mingled back in with them."

Chandos was expressionless.

"At first I didn't understand. But when I saw the blood spatter on the altar, I knew. It was a ritual killing. The red sash around his head, the blood sprinkled seven times—your brother was a sacrifice, a scapegoat."

Chandos spoke at last. "Exactly right. To you I am the cliché, the evil twin." His voice was infinitely remote. "Cain, the envious stock character in a thousand bad movies, curling my mustache, coiling to strike at my poor, victimized brother Abel. But you have that part exactly wrong."

Ari was pleased; Chandos was talking.

"My brother was a false priest, groveling to a false pope, an abomination in the temple of God. An Unholy Father who turned the Vatican into Sodom. So I knocked off his crown."

"That profane, wicked prince of Israel," Ari encouraged him.

"I, on the other hand, I am a true priest like my father."

"Like your father? Who is he?"

"I'm a son of Aaron, a son of Levi. Yes, I made the offering. I did it to make atonement for the whole sinful Church. "

Ari wanted to keep him going, and not just to buy time. "So you collected the blood from the wound and sprinkled it seven times with your finger…"

Chandos nodded. "Leviticus. Chapter 16."

"But the ritual isn't finished yet."

"No." For the first time Chandos smiled, looking at Ari with a glimmer of admiration. "It isn't finished."

"Because it's the tenth day of the new year, the Day of Atonement. The priest has more to do. There must be *two* sacrificial victims. One of them is already dead."

"There must be three, actually," Chandos said simply, and he tossed something at Ari, which he caught instinctively. It was a skein of wool.

"What's this?"

"You will wrap that wool around your head now."

In the pale light it was hard to tell, but the wool had a blood-soaked look. Ari understood.

"It's red." He tried to recall his father's recital of Leviticus. "The priest lays hands on the second goat and confesses over it all the wickedness of Israel. A red cord is tied around the goat's head to represent the blood of the sacrifice, and it is sent into the desert to carry away the guilt."

"You've been well instructed."

"My father is a rabbi of sorts. And your father—what does he do?"

Ignoring this, Chandos repeated, "You will wrap the wool around your head now."

"And this place. It's the ancient sacrificial place, isn't it? The place called Duda'el? Where the scapegoat was pushed off the cliff."

Chandos stared at him silently.

Ari went on, "You're the priest. According to the ritual, you need to lay hands on the scapegoat to transfer your guilt to the creature, *l'azazel*."

"That's the work of the high priest, and he has already done it."

"You mean at the Temple? While I was…asleep?"

"Yes."

Ari was more curious than afraid. "So you're the messenger priest, not the *high* priest, the *kohen gadol*. That person would be your father?"

Immovable, Chandos stared at him. Ari shifted his feet as if under the scrutiny of a camera continuously re-focusing.

"What is your father doing now? Is he still in the Temple? The ceremony isn't over."

"Now you will wrap the wool around your head."

Ari dropped the skein on the ground. "That you will have to do yourself."

"Then I will shoot you first."

"You can't do that. The ritual requires a healthy living victim. And I am not going to be marched off the cliff like a lamb to the slaughter."

Chandos smiled again, but this time with a trace of uncertainty. Ari now knew that the man's discipline was also his weakness. Chandos would not violate the ritual; he would have to approach Ari to carry it out.

Ari watched him intently but was still unready.

In a flash, with a simple Krav Maga kick, Chandos dropped Ari to the edge of the cliff. Ari's kneecap collapsed like broken stone. Chandos crowned him with the red thread and in the same motion flicked him almost lightly off the precipice.

As he fell, Ari instinctively tightened his elbow around Chandos's ankle and pulled him over with him. Both men grabbed for the cliffside and found the same sharp spur of rock to arrest their fall.

Then the pain struck. Ari's knee froze; trembling, he pushed off the spur with both arms to get distance from Chandos, slid a few meters and stopped, grasping a nubbin of crystal rock with one hand.

Steadying himself, Chandos darted like a spider across the rock face toward him.

Ari kicked at him with his good leg and made contact. But it was like kicking hard ice; Chandos grasped his leg in the upsweep, and Ari involuntarily pulled his enemy toward himself.

Chandos pirouetted over his body and landed flat against the cliff, attaching himself to the limestone by his hardened fingers. Now he was on the side of the bad knee, and Ari had nothing to fight with. He could neither kick out nor punch.

He wedged himself into an angle of the cliff that opened like a book beneath him and waited, hoping to use Chandos's moves against him.

But Chandos made no move. For an instant they hung there together, matched and checked. Ari could sense his enemy's odorless breath, feel him thinking and measuring machine-like the possibilities before him.

Ari's left leg was useless; his only chance was to get away. He twisted his body around like a door against the cliff and reached back desperately for a new handhold—the rock was rotten. With an agonizing thrust, he jammed his left heel into the crumbling stone to keep from falling. Instead he slid, his feet plowing into the cliff, his fingers searching wildly for a grip. Then, just above a sheer drop, his right foot found a shard of hard rock and he balanced on it like a bird frozen in flight.

He looked up; Chandos was snaking carefully toward him, almost on him, his officer's boots mirroring the moon. He reared back to give Ari a final head kick that would send him plunging into the jagged talus at the foot of the cliff. With one free hand, Ari reached for the boot and jerked down on it with all his strength.

But Chandos had counted on this. In a flood of scree, he skidded down next to Ari, jammed his left hand into a crack, and raised his right elbow, ready to slam it into Ari's face.

By reflex, Ari snapped his right fist into the man's eye. The tissue around the eye melted into black blood, the blinded head sprang back.

And Chandos fell. He swirled downward without a sound, scrabbling helplessly at the cliff, and smashed full against an obelisk rising from the talus below.

Coughing hot dust, Ari trembled, his arms spread-eagled over the rock.

For a long time he lay there, breathing without thinking. Gradually, the dead heat and darkness relaxed him, and his heart slowed. But he could not stay there; he feared the torpor because he knew he was going into shock.

Levering off his right foot, he turned and hugged the cliff like a bed, and then began to edge his way upward. His practiced fingers discerned tiny, soft cracks in the stone, almost invisible, and bit by bit he wound his body diagonally up the run-out toward a harder surface. The exertion got his blood running again, but nausea came with it. He choked it back and willed himself toward the verge of the cliff.

At last he could see overhead a sharp break between sheer blackness and the smudge of sky. With a final push, he manteled over the edge and fell to the ground.

"My God," he whispered. It was not a curse.

He allowed himself to rest only for a moment. There was more to do. Much more.

Ari struggled up on his good leg and hobbled to the van. Leaning against it, he massaged the thigh above his injured knee, watching as the corroded moon slipped behind the hills in the distance. Now it was truly dark.

He pulled himself into the driver's seat. From the dash a small clock glowed: 0111. Next to it a digital thermometer keyed to Fahrenheit: 78°. It was an old vehicle with a manual transmission and a petrol engine, the kind he could start without a key. Fumbling in the dark for the wires, he made the contact and the engine jolted to life. The light from the dashboard revealed a mobile phone on the seat next to him.

Ari ran his fingers over the surface; it was the size of an ordinary GeM but covered with a net made of some light metallic substance, brush-like to the touch. A menu bar blazed a dull blue across the top, but the rest was featureless black plastic. At the base, he found a tiny, glowing red spot and debated whether to touch it.

"Is it done?" the voice asked. It was electronically scrambled, monotone, unrecognizable.

He hesitated, and then, "This is Davan. Who are you?"

Now there was hesitation at the other end.

"Then he is dead," came the voice, a muted hum.

"Yes. Chandos is dead."

Another silence, and then: "I have Mandelyn. You will return to the Dome immediately. You will speak to no one."

Grimly, Ari realized that he would obey the voice.

Dome of the Rock, Jerusalem, 0139h

Her first impression was beauty.

Pulsing, jeweled light filled her eyes as she crept back through a maze of winding, straggling memories toward consciousness. Hot mist drenched her body; she was sweating, trembling with pain, nauseated with shock.

She imagined herself in a nest of plants and trees, gazing up as a vast rose spun slowly around, beyond the forest, in a bright orbit veined with red and gold. Involuntarily, her arms reached for it. Far away at the apex of the circle, there was a single symmetrical golden star—the center of the sky— she fixed her eyes on it, and gradually the wheeling sphere around it slowed and stopped.

Where was she? Chartres? The Holy of Holies?

She remembered.

The Dome of the Rock.

Maryse gazed past the marble pylons with the mosaic palms that signified Eden into the dome overhead and counted the ripples of gold leaf and crimson, all converging on the central star. On the rock beneath it Adam was created; here Abraham brought his son Isaac to be sacrificed; here Christ died. The world began here, and it would end here.

Reaching reflexively for her neck, she massaged the point of pain where someone had struck her so hard it had nearly blinded her. She remembered the rocklike blow of that hand and shivered.

There was a sensation on her leg—something there—a device like a wristwatch with a plain gray brand encircling her calf. It was an electronic tag used to keep track of convicts; it would detect even a millimeter of motion. She touched it lightly and felt the galvanic patch that would give the alert if the device were tampered with. Someone had made her a prisoner.

She lay quietly thinking, willing away the pain in her head. Her weapon, her GeM—all gone. Whoever attacked her—it had been total, crushing surprise. Who had done it? What had happened?

Why was she alone?

Risking detection, she crept carefully to her knees trying not to move the banded leg. She had been lying on a carpet that edged the wooden screen around the holy rock; pulling herself up against the screen, she immediately felt the blood drain from her head. On all fours, she breathed hard, and soon her sight returned and the pressure in her head normalized. She inched her way up and peered over the screen into the sanctuary, then caught herself before she cried out.

Propped on the rock, soaked in light from the lamps overhead, stood the *Acheropita*, its silver frame flashing with jewels, the brown eyes of Jesus staring eastward in eternal calm. Her first reaction was relief—it was intact.

Then shock. At first, she couldn't make it out. Positioned centrally on the rock, in front of the picture, was a metal bowl with heavy gold handles. She had dreamed of it, searched the world for it, cursed it. She knew it as she knew her own face. The Ardagh Chalice. Stolen in Dublin years before.

A ring of lighted candles surrounded these objects as if arranged for some bizarre ritual. What was happening? What did it mean?

From somewhere in the Dome, someone spoke.

"How shall I lie through centuries, and hear the blessed mutter of the Mass, and see God made and eaten all day long, and feel the steady candle-flame."

She recognized the voice. "Jean-Baptiste Mortimer," she said aloud.

"No, Robert Browning."

Mortimer's disembodied voice echoed from somewhere beyond the rock, directly across the shrine.

" 'The Bishop Orders His Tomb.' Not one of Browning's best, but apt for the occasion, I hope."

"Jean-Baptiste, where are you? What's going on?" Maryse asked the walls. "What is all this about?"

"It's all about twenty centuries of Western civilization coming down round our heads."

"I don't understand."

"It's a very, very long and complex story, Maryse. You've heard only the beginning. Unfortunately, you are now present for the ending."

"The ending."

"Yes, like a bad disaster movie. No poetry. No sense of wonder. Just a big explosion preceded by lots of poor acting, really."

"Jean-Baptiste…where is David Kane?" She hesitated. "And Ari Davan?"

"Your Romeo, your Antony, your Porphyro? Dead by now, I imagine. At the hand of the jealous lover."

"Stop playing with me and tell me what's going on."

There was a heavy sigh. "Maryse, open the book around you and read it for yourself."

It was the old game, she thought; he would tell her nothing until she stumbled through her own translation of the text.

She tried to reset her mind to understand the story. Where to start?

"It's all in where you stand." Mortimer's voice was almost gentle. "Look around you."

Beyond the screen lay the rock the Jews called *eben shetiya,* the foundation of the cosmos—an unremarkable outcropping of stone, as bare as the moon, formless, ominous as a frozen drift of the sea. Here Abraham had bound Isaac, here the lamb without blemish was offered up and slain. *On this rock,* she recited half consciously, *I will build my Church…*

"It's the cosmic altar at the center of the universe," she said. "And on the altar, the sacrifice?"

"Thus the image and the cup," Mortimer replied eagerly. "You're beginning to work it out."

"It's the Holy of Holies again."

"Precisely. The Sancta Sanctorum in Rome was the temple transplanted, but now the Presence, the Acheropita, the Image of the universal sacrifice, is returned to its source. Where it belongs."

"And the cup?" she asked. There was dread in the question.

"For the blood of the sacrifice."

"Whose blood?"

Mortimer was silent for a moment. "Now…look up. Read."

Shaking off the thought of blood, she gazed up into the dome.

Shapes, angles, cubes, and spheres—the geometry of the cosmos. Hexagonal walls rising into the four-sided tympanum overhead, the spherical cupola above.

"The circle squared," she announced.

"Yes, a symbol of the transcendent. Go on."

The cupola above was bright with serpentine lines of red and gold, all converging on a central sunburst. The lines reminded her of something. Of what? The rippling pathways of a maze…

"The labyrinth!" she breathed. "The labyrinth at Chartres. Leading to Jerusalem, the rose at the center of the earth."

Mortimer laughed. "The labyrinth traces history from the beginning to the end. And it ends in Jerusalem, at the Dome of the Rock."

"But this is an Islamic shrine, not a church."

Mortimer's voice softened. "My dear, why do we Cherubim guard this Dome? It is more than an Islamic shrine. It is not a mosque. Not a church. Not a synagogue. It is a great book in which we can read the meaning of atonement. It is the very symbol of the oneness of the faith of Abraham, and of the oneness that eludes the children of Abraham—Jews, Muslims, and Christians, fragmented in turn into multiple sects and schisms. But no matter where one starts, if God is the true quest—not power, not gain, not glory— one will arrive here."

Maryse now understood.

A schematic of the shrine materialized in her mind. The building wheeled around her, as symmetrical as the sky. She pondered aloud, "Four gates, equidistant from each other, each aligned to a cardinal point on the compass. North, south, east, west. So there are four Cherubim."

"And on the pillars?" Mortimer asked.

Great round medallions…globular moons of granite, golden sunbursts.

"And the stars overhead."

"Think of the Tarot deck," Mortimer pressed her. "What comes after the Star, the Moon, and the Sun?"

"The Last Judgment. And then the Redemption. The second coming of Christ."

"You have it, my dear. The pure sons of Levi are about to offer unto the Lord an offering…for the last time."

Hints of the scripture echoed in her mind. Was it Isaias? She tried to remember, but Mortimer recited it word-perfect.

"Who may abide the day of his coming? For he is like a refiner's fire. He shall purify the sons of Levi, he shall purge them as silver and gold, and they shall offer unto the Lord offerings in righteousness."

"It's insane," she breathed. "You're trying to coax God down from Heaven."

"*I?*" Mortimer laughed. "*I'm* trying? You still haven't understood, have you?"

There was a rustling noise behind her. And then another voice—a voice she knew so well—pierced her through like a shock of lightning.

"Jean-Baptiste is not responsible. I am."

Beit Horon Junction, near Jerusalem, 0210h

Ari struggled with the unfamiliar clutch as the old van groaned through the hills on the divided highway toward Jerusalem. The complete absence of traffic unnerved him; he felt utterly alone in the darkness. Pounding loudly, the powerful motor made the night hotter, and Ari scraped with one dirty hand at the sweat that scorched his eyes. The ache in his knee had become nearly unbearable.

He couldn't think about it now.

Soon the van lumbered into the suburbs, and he made his way through a maze of back streets to avoid checkpoints. It would take longer this way, but not so long as getting permission to proceed toward the Old City. He could not explain himself to anyone—not to his friends, not even to Kristall.

In the dark curve of the road just west of the Dung Gate, he cut the engine and sat quietly for a moment scanning the night. His knee vibrated with pain. How would he get to the Dome—through the crowd of worshipers, through Security, filthy as he was and with one shattered leg?

It would have to be done.

He grasped the GeM and stared at it. It was his only prospect, the only way to communicate with the devil at the other end, the only advantage he had. And what it could really do, he barely understood.

He turned it over and over in his hands, baffled at its unmarked surface. Under his thumb, the lattice felt soft and brushy, like the skin of a starfish. He touched the blue-lit menu bar, and it gave a slight, interrogatory pulse, as if waiting for a command.

"Gold," he said to it, and immediately felt foolish. Nothing happened. No gold appeared on the surface. Had he really expected anything? At the very least there would be a login code, a password. The thing would be totally secured from fools like himself.

He leaned his head against the steering wheel, trying not to let despair in. The Dome was surrounded by the most sophisticated defense force on the planet, the most advanced of security systems, but it was all for nothing. And what could he do about it, even if he made it inside? The Dome would be destroyed and hell itself would descend on his home. He had killed the man he thought responsible, only to face alone a far more inscrutable enemy behind an impenetrable wall. Alerting Kristall would not help, although he knew he should do it. And there was Maryse Mandelyn.

He thought of the first time he saw her, in the posture of a saint, gazing up at that bouquet of a ceiling in the Sancta Sanctorum. She was so curious, like a young girl, unintentionally fragile; but also old in her way, maternal. She could have been one of the holy figures painted on the wall. There was a deep root of love in her, spiraling up without branches, with nothing to connect to; a sad kind of love, reaching and at the same time detached.

He knew then that he would try to make it into the Dome.

Alongside the van a group of white-clad Orthodox men walked along, floating past like a flock of pale fish—nine of them, looking for a tenth to make a *minyan* for prayers. He listened to their muttering. They stopped at the gate, and then, startling himself, he called out to them.

"Let me pray with you."

They turned and stared back at the van. Two of them, tall adolescents, approached him; he opened the door and, grasping the GeM, he swung his legs out and gasped with pain.

"You're hurt," one of the men said. He looked doubtfully at Ari, all at once conscious of his torn, dusty clothes.

"Yes, I hurt my leg. I've been sitting in that van for a long time."

"Let us take you to the infirmary," another said, as the rest of the group closed in on him.

"Yes, yes. But first let me pray with you."

The men made a stretcher with their hands and carried him through the gate and into the plaza. Weak with fasting and praying, thousands of worshipers lay chanting, reading, or dozing hypnotically on benches and on the stony ground. The floodlit Western Wall rose before them like bleached coral under a sea of heat. Gently setting him down, the two tall boys supported him as the ten of them formed a circle and prayed.

Yitgaddal v'yitkaddish sh'meh rabba

"May the great Name of God be exalted and sanctified…"

V'yamlikh malkutah

"May He establish his kingdom; may His salvation blossom; may His anointed come near in your lifetime and in the lifetimes of all the house of Israel speedily and soon. Amen."

Ari's leg was an agony, even though the boys were strong and held him carefully. From dust and pain, the image of his own father condensed in his mind. He knew the old man was praying the *selichot*, even now, between nightfall and dawn, mourning for the sins of others unrecognized and

278

unconfessed, phylacteries around arm and forehead, crying for the loss of the Temple and the unrelenting brokenness of the world.

And for his own aimless son.

Ari could barely remember the solemn Hebrew. He would lose a word, and then the whole phrase disappeared like ashes in the wind. After a few moments he stopped trying and listened to the confident, smooth tenor of the voices around him. And these voices focused the masculine song from thousands of worshipers, a chanting tide that rolled across the square and swelled like the sea against the stone walls of the Temple Mount. Such a crowd could take the lost Mount, swarming over the army and at last pitching the flag of the kingdom of God themselves. As Emmanuel Shor and Nathan Levinsky had aimed to do.

Shor. Levinsky. The prayer. *Hebrew.*

That was the answer.

Ari could hardly wait for the prayer to end. When they finished, the nine young men looked awkwardly at the tenth, who was clearly anxious to go. "Please. Could you take me to my friends? They should be near the Cotton Merchants' Gate." They shrugged and lifted him through the crowd, back to the exit from the Temple Mount he had left only hours before.

The chief of the guards recognized him. "Back again, Davan? You look pretty roughed up," the officer said, eyeing the young men who carried Ari.

"It's all right. I fell. I just need to sit down for a moment."

The officer waved some soldiers off a bench to make room for Ari. Ari thanked the boys, who set him on the bench and left.

He sat quiet for a moment, eyes closed, until the officer's attention was elsewhere; a shrouded woman had approached to speak to him. Then, nearly fainting from the pain, Ari stood and hobbled slowly through the gate, toward the stairway to the Mount. He leaned against the wall and dragged himself halfway up the stairs, where he collapsed in the shadows, and, fighting back the sour taste of pain in his mouth, nestled the GeM in both scratched hands and whispered into it.

"Zahav." The Hebrew for "gold."

Nothing.

"Zahav, Zahav," he repeated. *"Zahav!"*

The blue strip of light was steady. No change at all. Gold. The one element that made sense. The element powerful men would pay anything to possess, to control. Enough of it could buy the Temple Mount itself. His chemistry came back to him: gold, the heavy, the malleable, the eternal. Can't be oxidized. Element 79. Every element has a number for the protons and neutrons in the nucleus, even the elements without names. Gold. Element 79…

"Zahav. Shiv'im tishah!" he whispered. *Gold. Seventy-nine!*

Something happened. The blue light wavered. The lattice shimmered; a luminous rectangle formed before his eyes.

He rubbed it with his thumb. It was cool, heavy, yellow even in the dim shadows. A thin slab of gold.

The Grotto beneath the Dome of the Rock, 0250h

"Everything is quiet here," Kane spoke into his secure GeM. "We still have Grammont in custody, along with the old man and his son."

Kristall was relieved. "Are you sure you don't need help? Perhaps we should move them out. Maybe the whole thing is over, and he's been scared off. No one has gone in or out except the guards."

"I don't know what to anticipate now; I certainly expected more than this. It might be best to wait till daylight."

She grunted. "A French antiquarian and an elderly Palestinian lawyer. It's like going out for shark and coming back with herring."

"None of them have anything to say, and I don't speak Arabic in any case."

"I could send Sefardi up. He speaks Arabic."

Kane hesitated. "No. The less we disturb things the better, as we still have a subject to flush out of the trees. We might have the minions, but we don't yet have the Moriarty."

"Fine. We'll wait for daylight. Kristall out."

Kane sat back in his camp chair and glanced at Grammont, who stood in the corner of the cave as if made of marble. The old man lay curled like a cat on the floor; incredibly, he was asleep, although the boy, crouched next to him, stared wide awake back at Kane and, occasionally, at the nine-millimeter pistol Kane kept poised at his elbow.

Kane sat quietly next to the stairs that led up to the sanctuary in order to be unseen from above. He had set up a kind of command post by the *qibla* in the wall. The only sound was the pebbly rhythm of the old man's breathing. Kane stood and stretched.

He felt oddly dissatisfied. He had hoped for more from this night. It was dark and hot and as empty as other nights. The one he had expected had, of course, not made an appearance—not yet. At dawn, undoubtedly; then Maryse would see at last what heroism he was capable of.

"So, Mr. Grammont," he said at length, "you know the legend of this cavern?"

The Frenchman was motionless.

"We're under the famous Rock here. There it is." He pointed up at the stony, irregular ceiling. "It is said that when Mohammed ascended into Heaven, the Rock yearned to follow him, and this hollow space we are standing in is the result."

Grammont might have been part of the wall. Except for a tiny pear-shaped drop of sweat on his temple, the man paid no notice.

"We all have this hollow space inside of us, Grammont. Even you."

The small grotto was empty except for two prayer stools and a bulbous lantern suspended from the ceiling. The light made a star-shaped shadow on the floor. Kane briefly examined his GeM's dim projection on the marble-white casing of the stairs. In the center of the screen, the octagonal shape of the Dome dominated a cloud of swirling red smoke—it was the heat signature of the Temple Mount as seen by the Eros satellite far above them.

Kane turned back to Grammont.

"I understand you were an officer in the Foreign Legion with Mortimer. Hard life. Militant. Strengthens you, toughens you. But you're not strong now. You were once; not now. The stoicism of the army. It was a way of filling the hollow, but you found that it's inexhaustible. So you tried the conventional approach of your countrymen—books, wine, art. Civilization. But civilization is like you—just an aging man with bad teeth."

He motioned to the boy who sat taut on the floor. "Muslims. They pour their anger into that space. Like an eagle dropping from the sky on its prey. Implacable." The boy clearly had some English; his fists tightened and his sharp chin rose abruptly.

"You see, Grammont? And then there are the Jews. Upstairs you can hear them. Two thousand impotent years of wailing and hoping, studying forever and never getting the answer. Bawling like an old cow in a field waiting for the slaughter."

Kane's GeM signaled him, and he peered at the projection on the staircase. From the corner of the screen an isolated figure moved slowly into view, making small eddies in the heat cloud. Whoever it was circled around a line of cypress trees and slowly approached the Dome's eastern portal. Kristall's voice crackled over the GeM. "Someone coming."

"Yes," Kane answered. "It appears that our friend has decided to show up. Sooner than I had expected." It was time to move.

The Dome of the Rock, 0320h

Ari Davan limped from the cover of a tree toward the Dome. He had successfully made his way past the Flaming Sword because he was carrying no conventional weapon; the little GeM meant nothing to the electronic barrier. Now the pain was returning to his knee, but he had just enough strength to make it to the door. He turned the tiny lattice to nitrogen—the freezing seventh element was so cold that, just by waving it near his knee, he numbed it and stopped the swelling.

A half dozen quick experiments had turned up nothing he could use as a weapon, and he dared not speak any numbers past 114 into the GeM's little receiver. He did not know what those elements might be or how dangerous they were. He did know that number 94, plutonium, would kill—but not fast enough. It would take days, perhaps hours, after exposure to the radiation, if it worked at all. His only hope was to get close enough to the Unsub— whoever it was—to threaten him with the plutonium.

But if he was dealing with a terrorist who was ready to die anyway, there was no hope.

Slowly he pushed the great door open and rolled inside, the GeM at the ready. All was quiet. He inched forward on the red carpet, and pulled

282

himself up so he could peer over the wooden screen into the lamplit sanctuary of the Rock itself.

A laser beam blinded him.

"Welcome back, Mr. Davan," a familiar voice echoed across the chamber.

As his sight slowly returned, he made out a vague figure, all in white, standing on the Rock opposite him. The laser sight of a nine-millimeter pistol played over his face; he froze where he stood.

"Kane?" he whispered, looking away.

"Ari!" another voice called out. It was Maryse's voice.

"Where are you, Maryse? Are you all right?"

"I'm here. Yes, I'm all right." And now he could see her, sitting bound on the Rock, her back leaning against the screen next to the giant figure of Kane.

The President of Interpol stood astride the Rock, dressed in the white robes of the high priest Israel. Behind him was propped the missing image from Rome, the Acheropita, its silver frame glinting in the lamplight. A great metal chalice had been placed on the Rock before the image.

They were the swirling images of a nightmare.

"You were the only one who came close to an understanding of the true situation, Davan, so in a way I'm glad you're here for the winding up."

"Kane? What is all this?" Ari hissed.

"You were right—well, partly right. Our little talk Friday at the airport, remember? There was a plot to destroy the Dome. But it was not the Mishmar's plot. It was mine."

"You? Destroy the Dome?"

"Absolutely. It must go. Secretly, everyone wants it to happen. It's the great friction point, the keystone of this miserable world. And once it gives, the whole world order comes crashing down at last."

"That's insane. No one wants that."

Kane smiled. "Of course they do. The Jews must build the Temple here, so it must go. The Muslims must rise in fury against Israel, which they've

283

wanted to do for decades. Then, and only then, when Israel is about to be destroyed, is the Messiah free to intervene. Only then can the prophecies be fulfilled."

Maryse shouted, "He's mad, Ari! Somehow we've got to alert the guards."

"He knows he mustn't," Kane broke in. "The moment he does any such thing…well, the Dome becomes history. Known only in photograph, song, and story." He held up the other GeM in his right hand.

Ari's mind flashed back to the cliff, to his helplessness there. As then, his only weapon was talk.

"You could let Maryse go," he said. "She doesn't have to die here. Surely you don't want her to die."

"She won't die here. She'll be taken up in the Rapture of the saints, which I will at last bring about. She won't have to face what will happen to this old world as soon as I've finished my work here, believe me. Besides, she must stay. She's the witness."

"The witness?"

All at once, another voice rose out of the dim circular aisle to the right.

"The Magdalene. She was at the Cross. She was at the Tomb. She was the only one who understood." It was the voice of Jean-Baptiste Mortimer.

"Mortimer? So you're a part of this too? I thought you were a guardian of this place, one of the Cherubim."

"My dear young man, unfortunately, I'm not in a position to carry out my guardianship just now. I'm afraid my friend Grammont and I are bound, too."

Ari made his way along the wooden screen, hand over hand, slowly around the aisle toward the north portal, keeping Kane in sight. There they were, both men. Mortimer, short and rotund; Grammont, tall and correct. Both were handcuffed to a marble pillar just inside the door.

Jean-Baptiste smiled resignedly. "I came here tonight ready to expose him. So hard to believe one of our own…a traitor."

"One of your own?"

"Yes. Mr. David Leonard Kane here." He nodded toward him. "Leo. The Lion of England, the Cherub of the West."

"And Grammont?"

"He is Secretary of our Order. Keeps our records. Carries out our determinations. Maintains our anonymity."

Grammont cleared his throat and bowed slightly.

"And Maryse?" Ari asked. "You said something about a witness? The Cross? The Tomb?"

"Yes. You should know your Christian history, Davan. Mary Magdalene was the only one who stayed near Jesus through his Passion. She witnessed it all—the tortures, the crucifixion. And she was rewarded by being the first to encounter the risen Christ."

"Just as Maryse Mandelyn will be the first to encounter the returning Christ," Kane announced from the Rock. "It will be her privilege."

Jean-Baptiste chuckled involuntarily. "Maryse Mandelyn. Mary Magdalene. The similarity *is* striking, isn't it? What do you think, Grammont?" He lowered his voice, still in a theatrical tone. "But there's more to it. Maryse has, shall we say, a certain appeal for Mr. Kane."

"He's in love with her," Ari said.

"Ah, yes," Jean-Baptiste sighed. " '*Madeline, sweet dreamer! Lovely bride!*' Keats."

"It's a pretentious habit," Kane called to Mortimer. "Quoting poetry."

There was a hopeless silence while Ari searched for more questions. He had to keep Kane talking without antagonizing him.

"So…there are four Cherubim. Jean-Baptiste Mortimer…"

"Yes," Mortimer interjected. "I am the Angel, the Cherub of the North."

"And Emmanuel Shor was your third."

"The Ox. The Cherub of the East," Mortimer explained. "The first Cherub of the East was Moses Maimonides, Saladin's trusted physician. To begin with, the charge was passed down in his family from father to son. Eventually, after many generations, it devolved on Chaim Weizmann, the first president of the State of Israel. He and his successors carefully watched over the Dome after the Turks lost Palestine."

"And that's why the Israeli army withdrew from the Temple Mount after the Six-Day War?"

"Precisely. The Cherubim have maintained contacts at the highest levels in your government since the independence of Israel in 1948."

"But who watched over the Mount before that?" Ari asked.

Kane interrupted them. "Don't imagine I don't know what you're doing, Davan. You want to keep me mentally busy, sparring for time. But you needn't worry. Nothing will happen till dawn. We have about two hours, so we might as well enjoy some conversation."

"What happens at dawn?" Ari asked.

Kane looked around and sighed. "This Dome will disappear. Your death will be…spectacular. Then the Islamic states will attack the state of Israel in full force—and the result, a nightmare. But for the saints, God will step in. He must. He will rapture them, catching them up to his presence, and his appearance will be glorious."

"You're deluded," Ari answered him. "When Kristall hears nothing from us, she'll suspect. She won't sit quietly for two hours with no contact."

"Oh, Kristall and I are in constant contact. I merely call in periodically to reassure her. But you had a question, Davan. Let's hear a little more history—it's fascinating." He gestured toward Mortimer with his gun.

"Ah, yes," Mortimer was startled. "You wanted to know who guarded the Mount before 1948? Over the centuries, all of the Cherubim have more or less been true to their callings"—he stopped to give Kane a long, cold look—"until now. But the primary task for many generations lay in the hands of a powerful Muslim family with ancient connections to the Mamelukes and then to the Ottomans. From the time of Saladin, actually. Let me introduce you to the current holder of that honor…"

Across the sanctuary, Ari heard the faint clink of handcuffs. He advanced closer to the screen and saw an elderly man in the shadows by the south portal, his beard ragged, a white head cloth covering most of his face. Next to him stood a handsome youth, shackled by the leg to a pillar, holding the old man by the shoulders.

Kane took over the introduction. "This is Hafiz al-Ayoub, the Eagle, the Sword of the Prophet, the Cherub of the South. Linguist, lawyer, Sufi scholar, diplomat. He and I have staved off a good many problems in the Middle East."

The old man gazed at Kane thoughtfully, as if he were examining a witness in court.

Next to Hafiz, Amal strained at his chain; he was staring not at Kane but at Ari. "There he is, Father. That is the man who killed my brother. I recognize him!"

"Peace, Amal. That man did not kill your brother—*he* did!" Hafiz pointed at Kane.

"It had to be done," Kane said calmly. "Your brother Nasir was a very brave and skillful policeman. He was dangerously clever...dangerously close to uncovering my purpose. My heart hurts for him."

"Your heart? *Your* heart hurts for him? *My* heart is shattered for him!" Amal cried.

"You must understand," Kane answered him calmly. "I have lost a son also. Two sons, in fact." He glanced at Ari. "What you call the Day of Requital cannot come until this Temple Mount is restored to God. The one you call the Prophet Isa—the One I call Jesus the Messiah—they are the same. Only he has the right to reign. Only he can restore the true Temple. But it is our task to prepare the way. For more than forty years, I have worked and planned for this day, and your brother was trying to stop me."

"It isn't true," Amal shouted. "You are not the hand of God. In your dead white robes, with your white hair and your flaming eyes, you are the *dajjal*, the devil himself!"

"Peace," the old man held up his hand. "Study him carefully, Amal. 'Surely those who guard against evil, when the Shaitan visits them, they become mindful. Behold! They see!' You may learn more about your task in a night from watching this man than you will learn in all the years to come."

Kane smiled, almost sadly. "For him, there are no years to come, Hafiz. Only hours."

"If it is the will of Allah," Hafiz waved a dismissing hand. "I understand now. More than forty years ago, I stood guard over this place. My uncle, the Eagle, had alerted me that an attack on the Dome was imminent. We captured three bombers who tried to mine the Dome; a fourth escaped. He was young, a strong runner, a climber. That fourth man was you."

"I had only a partial view of things then," Kane replied. "I was in the Marines. A soldier in the Holy Land. Lebanon, Palestine. I saw unspeakable things—women, children ripped up by bombs. Hatred, death everywhere. My old teacher, Maryse's father, had given me such a romantic idea of the place. The reality was quite different."

Hafiz regarded Kane meditatively. "All these years I've wondered—intensely at first, only idly since—what became of the fourth man. And you were one of us all along." He called out to Mortimer. "Cherub of the West, how did you know the Lion was a traitor?"

Mortimer's chuckle echoed through the Dome. "When Shor was killed, I began wearing armor for fear someone was trying to eliminate us. Someone who knew of us. Thanks to the efficient work of our friend Monsieur Grammont here"—the tall Frenchman bowed imperceptibly—"that would be very, very few people. Then I asked Maryse to investigate the background of Peter Chandos, the papal secretary, wondering about his connection with our little band. When she reported that a page of the Great Book was missing—from the section dealing with the Chandos family—I knew who our antagonist was. It could only be David Kane, the successor of the Chandos, trying to erase that link."

Hafiz coughed. "And so it was. I too wondered. I sent my son Nasir to Haifa directly I heard of Shor's death, to gather what intelligence he could. I should have shared my concerns with you, Jean-Baptiste, but I was unsure of you."

"And I of you, old friend," Mortimer called back in a weary voice. "I'm sorry. If the Cherubim cannot trust one another...well, apparently we cannot." He looked up coolly at Kane, who had listened until now without emotion.

"Father," Amal cried. "What can we do? *We've* got to stop him."

Hafiz hushed his son. "We have done all that can be done. It is in God's hands now." He turned to Kane. "You fell in with a cult...the Lifta group..."

"Yes, I was reading everything in those days and came across a tract by a man named Shlomo Barda. On my leave days, I joined him. He had a vision that all the religions would come together at this Temple Mount. That the Muslims had desecrated the spot by building the Dome here. That if the

Muslim shrine were destroyed, Jesus would return. He proved it from the Bible, that only Christ Himself could put an end to this misery.

"You all stood in the way. I'd met Sir John Chandos, made friends with him; he saw me as the son he'd never had. He was old and babbled the whole thing. The Ox, the Lion, and so forth. I even learned your names, collected your photos, and gave them to Barda."

Kane grew excited and walked to the center of the Rock. "But Barda didn't realize there is a proper time. That was not the time. He was captured along with the others—of course, they were all sent to the asylum. But I remained free. I searched, I studied, I prayed. I even took steps to become one of you. Gradually, things came clearer to me. Who I really was. What I was to do. The timetable..."

"October 11, 2027," Mortimer intoned from his hiding place by the north portal. "Of course, you had much to do to prepare for this crucial day. You discovered that you were the high priest of Israel, the true pontiff, the only one who could fulfill the prophecies."

"What prophecies?" Ari asked.

" 'Who may abide the day of his coming?' " It was the fading voice of Hafiz al-Ayoub. " 'For he is like a refiner's fire. He shall purify the sons of Levi, he shall purge them as silver and gold, and they shall offer unto the Lord offerings in righteousness.' Scrawled on the walls of the old shrine in Lifta."

Kane smiled at the old man. "Before the day of his coming, a true son of Levi—a high priest of Israel—must offer up a righteous offering. A true offering. A temple offering! That is the key."

"The high priest of Israel," Maryse said slowly as if to herself. "Yom Kippur. The Day of Atonement. The blood offering in the Holy of Holies. You offered up your own son in the Sancta Sanctorum at Rome. Peter Chandos was your son! And you sent his twin brother to perform the sacrifice, to scatter his blood on the altar."

Kane looked tired. He glanced up at the windows, as if searching for the light of dawn, but it was still dark outside.

Mortimer continued, "You insinuated yourself into the confidence of Sir John Chandos, the Lion, the Cherub of the West. He needed a successor. He prized you, married his daughter to you, never suspected you until it was too late, so you killed him."

Maryse was still thinking aloud. "And there were twins. You left one of them—Peter—with his mother and took the other…"

"Elias," Kane sighed, glancing again at Ari. "His name was Elias."

" 'The one shall be taken, the other left.' " Maryse recalled the Bible verse Rafqa had quoted to her.

"It was ordained. She needed punishment anyway…" Kane trailed off.

"Punishment for what?" Maryse cried. "What could she have done to you that you would cause her this kind of pain? Abandoning her, stealing one son and turning him into the killer of the other?"

"Never ask me," Kane spat at her. Then calmly, "It was a useful sin in any case."

Maryse drew back, horrified, whispering. "So you raised Elias with one purpose in mind—to prepare for this Day of Atonement. You trained him to do your exact bidding. To climb walls, to steal, to use a weapon commando-style, to kill without mercy. To force his mother to drink the blood of atonement. To murder his own brother and coldly sprinkle his life's blood on the holy altar."

"To make the blood offering, yes."

Maryse shook her head. "But you're not a priest. You're not a son of Levi, you're not even a Jew."

All was clear to Ari now. "He is a Jew. He's one of the *cohanim,* the descendants of the house of Levi with rights to the priesthood. Emmanuel Shor verified it for him, and he sent Elias to force Shor to give up the Chandos DNA samples so there would be no trace of them."

"My father was a Jew," Kane explained in a matter-of-fact tone. "Leonard Kane was his name. He was an American, an athlete, turned my mother's head when he played a tennis championship in Britain. Then my mother's oh-so-English parents found out; that was the end of the marriage; it was annulled. In their eyes, I was not only illegitimate, but Jewish as well."

"Yes," Mortimer assumed his pedantic voice. "Cohen, Kahane, Kane— all variations of the same name. A *kohen* was a priest of Israel; and as I understand, their bloodlines have stayed relatively pure for two thousand years."

"I am the *kohen gadol*," Kane murmured. "The last true high priest of Israel. My bloodline is the pure one from Aaron, the brother of Moses. I felt it. I always felt it, and Emmanuel Shor verified it for me. It was like a death sentence on myself."

"But why kill Emmanuel Shor?" Ari asked.

"Shor, Tempelman, Catriel Levine, Nasir al-Ayoub, Rachel Halevy—they all had to die for the same reason," Mortimer explained. "To protect the great plan of our friend here. Each one knew too much, or danced a bit too close to the flame. Therefore, the necessity of murdering me—although I foiled him there—and the other Cherubim, the very men tasked with guarding the Dome. Nothing could be allowed to interfere with the plan."

"Correct," Kane said. "Nothing must prevent the sacrifices of this Day of Atonement. Nothing and no one."

"Thus the white linen, the ritual robes of the priesthood," Mortimer added. In the lamplight Kane looked majestic, his single garment moon-white and flowing in folds from his powerful body. "And the magnificent chalice. And the singular image known as the Acheropita. His purpose? To replay the sacrifice of the temple, to offer up the sacrificial blood before the Real Presence. And on the very site the high priests used in the time of Solomon."

Suddenly, Maryse nearly leaped at Kane. Her body shook in the bonds, she writhed toward him. "The Chalice! The Ardagh Chalice. Your son stole it. Your son killed Father. The shot was not for me, it was for him! *You* killed my father! He loved you, did everything he could for you. And you had him killed." She choked out tears.

Kane was almost tender. He seemed relieved to let it all out. "I loved him, too. I tried to explain to him what I had found out, what my destiny was. He was the only one I thought I could speak to and share what I knew. But he was shocked…he withdrew from me. I was afraid he would tell you. No, Maryse, it was no accident. You had to be here, tonight, to play the role of the Magdalene, the witness. It was all ordained long ago. As I said, nothing, no one must prevent it."

"So…whose blood will fill the chalice now?" Maryse asked, no longer struggling, staring up at him with swollen eyes. "For your last sacrifice?"

Hesitating, he raised his hand toward Ari.

"No," Maryse said firmly.

Mortimer barked with rage. "It's poetic! Abraham will at last finish the task, here on the Rock of Ages. A son of Abraham, bound once more on this very place, his throat slit and his blood poured out on the rock. The last sacrifice of the last priest to call down the final fire from Heaven."

"It was to have been Elias." Kane gazed at Ari. "Elias was to take the scapegoat to the cliffs and end it there. Then he would return."

"But it has been ordained otherwise," Mortimer announced in a disgusted voice. "Elias Chandos played the scapegoat and Ari Davan is to be the last great sacrifice."

"You mean you would have cut the throat of your own son?" Maryse sobbed at Kane's feet.

"He knew it was to be. He was prepared for it. He was given me for that purpose."

"You're insane," Maryse whispered, and bent her head prayerfully to her knees.

Kane gazed up around the clerestory of windows. They were still dark.

Ari challenged him. "As I said to your henchman earlier tonight, I am not going like a lamb to the slaughter. And I didn't. He did."

"But you will, Mr. Davan," Kane replied, holding up the GeM in one hand and the nine-millimeter in the other.

"What is that thing?" Mortimer asked, then turned to Grammont. "Is it the GeM you told me of, the one that turns into gold?"

Kane held it up in his fingers—it was identical to the one Ari had, rectangular, faceted like a black diamond. "On my command, it will become anything—any element you can name, as well as elements you can only dream of. And some of them are blinding explosives, believe me."

"Hm. You do have a Jesus complex, don't you," Mortimer sniffed. "Turns water into wine, does it?"

The hoarse voice of Hafiz came from across the room. "No. His machine makes gold, but not bread or wine. Not even water."

Ari grinned at Kane. "You won't shoot me. Again, as I said to your son, the ritual requires a healthy, living victim. Unblemished."

Kane pointed the pistol at Maryse's knee and answered Ari with pain in his voice. "You will be whole and healthy. Others may not be."

A loud, startling buzz emanated from the GeM in Kane's hand; he glared at it.

"This is Shin Bet ringing," Kane growled. "If any of you make any sound at all, I will let this nine-millimeter do some work on her leg. I have no reason not to. She rejects me." Keeping an eye on Ari, he turned and spoke low into the instrument. Ari could not hear what he was saying, but by the tone of his voice, he was reassuring Kristall that all was well.

When he rang off, everyone remained quiet. There was no more to be said. The heat grew more intense. With Grammont's help, Mortimer arranged his shackles so they could both sit by the pillar they were chained to. Grammont, however, chose to stand. Maryse crouched on the rock in a posture of hopeless prayer. Al-Ayoub, taking little choking breaths, sank to the floor and laid his head down in the lap of his son, who began to cry covertly over him.

Ari bent like a tiger over the wooden screen, never taking his eyes off Kane. His nerves electrified by pain, he waited, alert, desperately watching the madman watching him. He weighed every reckless remedy he could think of. Fly at him? There would be no time; the bomb would go off in his hand. Trick him? Try to talk him out of it? Ari smiled grimly despite himself; he remembered something Miner had told him just tonight about the father of Elias Chandos.

Make him angry? How?

Talk about Maryse!

"So, Kane. Mr. President of Interpol, sworn to uphold the law of nations." Ari started fencing with him. "You planned this thing beautifully. Of course, you're very sure of yourself and your theories. But how many murders to bring it off? Starting with Sir John Chandos...ten? A dozen? And one of them Maryse's father. It was a sniper job, I understand?"

Maryse looked up with hard eyes at Kane, who turned away.

Ari went on. "She always spoke of you as 'David'...her protector, her mentor. A second father. She didn't realize you were a lying religious nutter with no honor and no respect for human life. Even the lives of your friends."

"Your baiting me will make no difference," Kane replied, sweating, his voice taut.

"It's true, Lion," Mortimer broke in with his sing-song voice, waving the golden ring on his hand. "You have no honor. Your oath—*donec venire cuius est iudicium*—you have betrayed it. Your word is worthless. What do you say, Grammont?" He looked up at the secretary, who stood taut and silent against the pillar. "You see? Grammont agrees with me."

"I *have* honored the oath," Kane spat. "Better than you. With me in charge, every asset of Interpol has been dedicated to protecting the Dome 'until he comes whose right it is to reign.' But now he is about to come, and I am here to welcome him."

Ari tried to keep him on track. "Maryse didn't know about the manipulations, the deceits. She respected you, admired you—maybe even loved you a little once. The way a young girl feels about the big man in her life. But you were using her all the time…years and years of cold, careful manipulation."

Kane snarled audibly at Ari. He had ignited something in the man, now gushing sweat in the intolerable heat.

Ari smiled. "After you killed her father, she withdrew from you. But you didn't worry; when it came time for her to play her part, you would entice her back to you. Imagine the nights you lay awake thinking about Maryse, dreaming about Maryse, about drawing her in with such care she would never suspect you were laying such elaborate traps for her."

"Traps?" Maryse asked, looking sadly at Ari.

"Most recently, an eyelash. A blood spatter. A gold ring. Just enough trace to trick us along. But this scheme started long, long ago." Ari kept his eyes on Kane. "You trained her, you brought her up in your business. You sent her to Mortimer; you convinced him to teach her and eventually bring her into the Order."

"Then the theft of the icon from the Holy of Holies. She could never resist it. Too curious, too interesting a mystery. You knew she would follow it anywhere. The reports from Lebanon that you engineered. You knew she would find it—and so she has. And when she found it, she would also find you. She would discover what you are."

"And what am I?" Kane retorted. "She sees me as I am: the great high priest. The fulfillment of prophecy!"

"No," Ari laughed at him. "A leering swine. A sadistic murderer. Just another potty terrorist gone round the bend on religion. And she—above all—knows that now."

Kane turned to Maryse. "A terrorist? I, who've been fighting terror all my life? You fought beside me. Is that what you think of me in your heart?"

Her voice was quiet, bitter. "My heart doesn't matter. You've taken a father from your own grandchild. You've ripped a beloved husband from a woman you could have loved as a daughter. You turned one son into a cruel, thoughtless killing machine who had no qualms about murdering his own brother. And you abandoned and destroyed the wife who loved you."

Struggling to her feet, soaked in sweat, Maryse raised her face to Kane's. "She was right. Rafqa Chandos *Kane* was right. You are not a priest, not a servant of God. Just the contrary. You are *Phosphoros*. You are Lucifer. You are a devil," she spat at him.

All at once, Ari knew what to do.

He gripped the GeM of Elias Chandos hard in his hand, feeling for the red-circuit button, hoping for the right degree of temperature.

Kane stood quiet for a moment, staring down at the Rock. Then, with a gasp of rage, he clutched Maryse by the throat. She thrashed about for breath; her shackled hands swept up reflexively and knocked him backward.

"Maryse, get away from him!" Ari shouted.

The massive Kane seized her arms, wrenched her around with one hand, and held her tight by the neck under his arm. He was crushing the life from her.

Ari was frantic. Then he noticed something.

"Kane!" he cried, pointing skyward. "It's time!"

Everyone looked up. Dawn smoldered like faint ash in the windows overhead.

Kane glanced up, hesitated; Maryse tumbled out of his grasp, scrabbling her way across the Rock toward Ari.

Indeed it was time.

Ari jammed his finger into the red-circuit button and shouted into the GeM. *"Fosforos! Khamisha asar!"*

A percussive flash.

Kane's hand erupted in white fire. Then the linen robe, then his whole body blossomed into liquid flame, and he fell like a meteor against the Rock.

Astonished, Maryse crouched at the wooden screen and grasped at Ari with her manacled hands. Mortimer yelped with surprise. Hafiz and Amal averted their faces. They all looked away, blinded, as the body of David Kane crumpled to the ground and burned to a bright cinder.

The Temple Mount, Jerusalem, 0625h

The rays of the sun ascended over the Mount of Olives.

"What better way to neutralize the Cherubim than to become one of them?" Jean-Baptiste Mortimer said, released from his manacles and rubbing his wrists. "What do you say, Grammont?"

The little group, clustered in the shade on the west side of the Dome, watched the medics tending to Ari. They had laid him on a stretcher and were binding his knee with a brace. Another medical man bent over Hafiz al-Ayoub while Amal stood by anxiously. A team of police silently and methodically worked inside the building; leaving them, Miner came out the door and shook his head at Ari in disbelief.

"And now, Davan, you must explain what happened in there," Mortimer asked. "I imagine it wasn't fire from Heaven that just saved us."

"I see how it was done," Miner grinned. "Stunning."

Ari winced as the technician locked the brace on his leg. "It was Maryse. She gave me the idea."

Everyone glanced at her.

Unhearing, curled up against the pearly stone of the entrance, Maryse Mandelyn looked diminished, the shadow of a long agony crossing her face. Despite the heat, she held herself tightly, like a vine drawing back from the ice of winter. The men looked at her and felt the distance that men always feel from a suffering woman.

" *'The serpent beguiled me,'* " Mortimer whispered.

Seeing her over his shoulder, Ari felt a deep relief that he had saved her, but knew he couldn't shield her from the past. The weight of it had settled on her. He wondered if she would ever again be able to see beyond the desolation she felt.

An officer came up with bottles of cold water; the medic tipped some into Ari's mouth. The water felt sweet and silver in his throat. "Give some to her," he waved the officer toward Maryse, who took the bottle without looking up.

"I'll have one of those." Mortimer grasped a bottle and emptied it in one long swallow. "So. Now, tell us, Davan."

Ari turned his head on his pillow and looked back at Maryse. "Later," he muttered.

"I'll tell you how he did it," Miner was chuckling. "It was the red circuit, wasn't it."

"Not now, Kara." Ari's voice startled Miner, who had never heard his boss call him by his real name. Ari continued, "The director will want a full report. You will want to get it to her as soon as possible."

"Sir?" Miner looked puzzled; Ari nodded at him, and then he withdrew back into the shrine.

A small group of Waqf guards approached, accompanying a woman in sunglasses and a rainbow-colored shawl over a white medical tunic. When she saw Hafiz and Amal, she ran to them and inspected them all over.

"Hafiz, Hafiz," she cried repeatedly, and then seemed to scold him—all in Arabic. They exchanged a few words, and the woman stood and advanced toward Ari.

"Rabia al-Adawi," she introduced herself, kneeling by his stretcher. Her voice was deep and impressive. "I am the doctor for Hafiz." Her professional eye looked him over with concern.

"Thanks," Ari said, "but I think the medics have things under control."

"Sure. I want to thank you for what you've done," she replied quietly, examining the brace on Ari's knee. "It appears we owe you a great deal."

" 'We?' "

"We of the Flaming Sword," she whispered. "For protecting the Noble Sanctuary. And for saving my friends."

She stood. "We have been worried for hours." She spoke in English to Hafiz and Amal. "When you didn't return in the middle of the night, when we heard nothing, I came to find you. Of course, they wouldn't let me in." She tossed her head at the Waqf guards, who shrugged.

"You needn't have worried," Hafiz replied. The bottle of water had revived him. "We only came to worship—sometimes it takes all night."

"We met him. The Dajjal who killed Nasir!" Amal whispered loudly to Rabia. "And he fell in a pillar of fire. God struck him down."

"Yes," Hafiz sighed. "The Sword prevailed once again—as it has so many times before."

"What Sword? We didn't have the Sword! We stood like sheep, chained to the wall," Amal reproached him.

"It's time you understood," Hafiz said, annoyed but still gentle. "The Flaming Sword is in the hand of Allah. We followers of the Sword are not great warriors or mighty men ourselves. We are merely those who have faith in His hand."

"So we never fight?"

"We fight if—and when—the Sword comes into our hands. Tonight He placed it in the hands of another. Our task is to do what can be done; afterward, we are only witnesses."

"Witnesses? Of what?"

Hafiz smiled and sank into the stretcher, gazing up into the center of a bottomless blue sky. " '*At all times God walks with the lost-hearted, who see nothing and from a distance cry, O God!*' "

Maryse Mandelyn stirred from the portal, stepped to Hafiz's side, and knelt on one knee next to Rabia. She touched the thin hair on his head; his eyes fluttered and closed. Amal looked up questioningly at Rabia.

"He looks very ill," Maryse whispered.

Rabia's face told her all.

The medics put an oxygen mask over his face and carried him away; Amal followed along behind like a small boy.

Maryse watched them go, her face reddening with tears for the first time. "Will the young man be all right?"

"He has a long path ahead, and we'll help him along it. His brother was prepared all his life for it. Now it's for Amal to choose."

Maryse put a hand on Rabia's and nodded. "You were a friend of Nasir al-Ayoub."

Rabia said nothing, but gave Maryse a faded smile and walked after her patient. Then she turned. "We had hoped he would be the last."

Once again, Miner appeared at the door of the shrine and asked Ari, somewhat stiffly, "For the record now, Inspector, I need your statement on how you, um, on how the situation was defused."

Ari smiled painfully at the police-speak and glanced up at Maryse, who nodded and sat down cross-legged on a tiled stone in the shade.

Ari spoke into Miner's recorder. "All right. I knew the nano devices were paired—that if the red circuit was open, they communicated with each other. I'd found out earlier how to activate the device, so I opened the red circuit, which automatically rang up the device in Kane's hand, and ordered it to…change into something."

"Into what?"

"That was the idea Maryse gave me. She called Kane a devil. And in Greek…"

Baffled, Miner shook his head.

"Phosphorus! The Greek word for Lucifer!" Jean-Baptiste Mortimer, who had been listening closely, was exultant. "Brilliant. Positively brilliant! If the ambient temperature is high enough, white phosphorus explodes. And there was just enough of it in his hand to put an end to his scheme."

Miner, still playing the professional, spoke up. "Of course. Favorite trick of terrorists, actually; we've dealt with white phosphorus before."

"So you had to wager that it was hot enough in there to blow up the stuff." Mortimer smiled proudly at Ari.

"I didn't know. I hoped." Ari tried to remember. "Thirty-four degrees, I think."

"Thus the freezing temperature in Nathan Levinsky's lab. To keep from accidentally blowing up volatile elements like phosphorus," Miner added. "Now, how does it work?"

"The code for the device is to speak the name of the element into the receiver, but you also have to add the atomic number. From the periodic table. Phosphorus is number 15."

"And the added twist," Mortimer whispered excitedly, "it understands only Hebrew! Think of it, Maryse. Phosphorus, number 15. The same number as the Devil's card in the Tarot deck!"

Maryse trembled, wiped her hand heavily across her forehead to clear away the sweat and to push back at the painful exhaustion she felt. "I keep thinking about the women. About Rafqa Chandos. Fatima, who loved Peter for so long. And this woman we just met."

"Don't exclude yourself, my dear," Mortimer added. "The Devil has a peculiar agony in mind for certain women…they anger him because they love so much." He caught sight of a wisp of white smoke emanating from the shrine and murmured. " *'Lucifer from Heaven, brighter once among the host of angels than the stars themselves.'* Milton."

Miner gestured to the medics, who hoisted Ari's stretcher and began carrying him toward the waiting ambulance. The others followed.

"Now for breakfast," Mortimer intoned, rubbing his hands together. "I'm famished. But perhaps a nap first. What do you say, Grammont? Long night?"

The Royal Suite, King David Hotel, Jerusalem, 0645h

Pastor Bob Jonas tipped the hotel barber at the door, then turned and gave the silhouette of the Old City a last look through the paneled windows of the Royal Suite. Pretty view, he thought, picking up a slim black case and shutting the door quietly behind him.

In the lift, he regarded himself in the arched mirrors—sunglasses, blue golf shirt, khaki shorts, a close haircut that barely showed the dark red cast of his hair. The descent was only six floors, but it seemed much farther. He had only to make it across the lobby; the car he had paid exorbitantly for would be waiting; a half-hour to the airport. Simple.

A nightmare that seemed eternal had kept him awake all night tossing in his bed. He had rehearsed in half-sleep every moment of the journey to come, and after a few hours gave up on the night and got up to watch for dawn. He was glad when it came at last.

No one would be raptured into the sky this morning, he thought. No one but himself—by a British Airways flight to London and then to Nassau.

When dawn had broken in London moments before, the titanic assets of the Global e-Manager Corporation transferred automatically into the electronic coffers of the Left-Behind Foundation. Then, in seconds, through a complex series of transactions, another account in the Bahamas absorbed a payout from the Foundation sufficient to keep a single man in unimaginable luxury the rest of his life. It would take an army of experts months to untangle the mess, and even then, the account in Nassau was untouchable. This is how to make gold from air, he chuckled edgily to himself.

The lift doors opened on a lobby that was strangely quiet. A barefoot worshiper in white silk sat in one of the sumptuous chairs poring over a book. Two uniformed young men conferred at the concierge's desk, and the people at reception were buried in their work. Jonas imagined their whispers echoing from the high ceilings were about him, although he knew better. Willing himself invisible, he stepped lightly through the lobby toward the exit.

The pastor knew his followers would still be out in the plaza after the wakeful night, holding hands, embracing each other watchfully at the Wall, mothers grasping their sleepy children as they stared up at the empty sky. He also knew they would now be turning things over in their minds. Dawn had come. The sun had risen over the Mount of Olives just as it did every day. Just as it had always done. Perhaps, by now, some of them were even beginning to think.

He quickened his pace. There, outside the exit in the driveway, the metallic-black car was waiting. He had paid far more than the usual fare for a ride to the airport on Yom Kippur, when none but emergency vehicles were supposed to be on the roads. He was relieved to see that the driver had, as arranged, put a counterfeit blue police light on the roof of the car.

Jonas breathed more easily as the lobby door closed behind him and he reached the car, noting with relief the deep tint on the windows. He slid into the seat behind the driver.

"Perfect," he said to the driver, adjusting his safety belt. "I know you're not supposed to be on the roads today, so there will be a lot more for you if we can stay clear of the police."

The driver's dull face, visible in the rearview mirror, twitched upward to signal that he had understood.

Jonas sank into the seat, shut his eyes, and smiled at the past he was leaving behind for good. He had grown up in the business, apprenticed to some of the best TV evangelist fundraisers, and had hosted his own Pastor Bob cable show at twenty-two. But no one had done what he had done. Now, he realized, he had the means to make a real difference for the Lord. This would be the end of the fakery. He would disappear, he reminded himself. His monumental fortune would fund real missions in places that really needed them. Africa, he thought. That's the place. Africans always need help. And he would no longer have to work at it, pretending so hard for so long not to care for the things of this world. Temptation can't touch the man who already has it all. He would now wrap himself in the luxury he had craved all his life and never have a single worry ever again. Not even about his own salvation. His money would take care of that for him.

The electric car made no noise at all, and the motion made him sleepy. In the window he watched the yellowing walls of Jerusalem pass by and hoped no one would be out in the streets this early to toss an angry stone at the car. He couldn't tell where he was, but then the driver was probably following a special route.

Sleep was gliding over his mind when a fragment of his dream stung at him. He visualized looking down at a crowd of people, mostly women dressed in white, who were staring into the sun, going blind without realizing it. Some people might call him a deceiver, but he didn't think so. From his point of view, what he had done did not descend to the level of a lie. After all, he keenly believed that the Rapture would come someday; and the logic of October 11, 2027, seemed plausible. Why not today as much as any other day? It may even happen yet—the day's just starting.

Then, without warning, the car turned into an underground parking garage and stopped. Jonas woke up.

"What? Why are we stopping?"

The driver turned to him and removed his sunglasses. "Mr. Jonas, I'm Sefardi of State Security. This is our headquarters. You will come with me, please."

"State Security? The police?"

Two robust uniforms appeared and motioned Jonas out of the car. They walked him rapidly into a dim chamber and set him in a metal chair.

"Why am I here? What do you want me for? I...I'm an American citizen."

"Yes, sir," Toad responded in his monotone. "Your consulate has been notified." He looked the American up and down almost without interest, fingering his GeM in one hand. The two officers did a quick, professional search of Jonas and stepped back.

A door opened, and more officers came trooping in with someone else in tow, a squat, disheveled man in white clothes. It was Lambert Sable.

"Pastor Bob? Is that you?" Sable looked baffled.

"You've arrested Lambert Sable?" Jonas asked, incredulous. "Do you have any idea who this man is?" He raised his voice to Toad.

"I know who both of you are," Toad replied without emotion.

"What do you want with us?" Jonas was defiant. "We're just tourists. Is this how you treat tourists?"

"I'm arresting you both for conspiring against the security of the State of Israel."

Sable looked desperately at Jonas, who moments before had hoped he would never see the rumpled, sweating former billionaire again. Jonas turned on the ugly little policeman.

"It's ludicrous! Conspiring against the security of...how?"

"By arranging for the theft of some valuable State property—a device for generating designer atoms."

"Theft?" Jonas shouted. "Designer atoms? What on earth...?"

"Before you say anything more, Mr. Jonas, you'll want to have your consul and a lawyer present."

Jonas went silent and dropped back into his chair next to Sable. Toad blinked at the two men, tried to read their character, and then decided there wasn't much to read after all. The soul of an American, he thought—thin as a plastic credit card.

Then something spilled out of him, something he didn't recognize in himself. The image of Catriel Levine hung in his mind. His voice shuddered. "You, and others like you—your religion is a game. A Disneyland fantasy. A circus for children in your own country, but when you play your games with *my* country…"

Then he stood and retreated, muttering, to a corner of the room. "People die. Serious people. People with souls."

St. Peter's Square, Vatican City, 1415h

Antonio Bevo sat in the Vatican security center next to the Commendatore of Vatican Police, as they watched together on a dozen flat screens the sodden crowd in St. Peter's Square. Any moment there would be an announcement. Everyone had seen the white smoke from the Sistine Chapel and knew that a Pope had been chosen; soon the new Holy Father would appear on the Cathedral balcony to be acclaimed.

The two officials kept their eyes on the viewscreens.

But Bevo's mind was elsewhere. Only hours before, he had heard of David Kane's death—a heart attack while supervising Interpol operations in Jerusalem. Now what would become of him? He had made a few inquiries, as judiciously as possible, but no one at Interpol seemed to know anything about Kane's recruitment of him.

The request had been so simple. "Give it out that the Israeli agent Ari Davan was the one who killed the Palestinian. It's important to our plan to capture the real culprit."

Bevo had seen immediately through this. Kane merely wanted Davan out of the way for some reason. "I'm reluctant to do that, Signor President," he had said. "It is very much out of order."

"Signor Bevo, your position with the Rome Police is tenuous, I hear, since the papal assassination happened on your watch." Kane was smooth. "But we can solve that. We're always looking for good police executives at Interpol."

"I'll see to it," was Bevo's reply.

Since then he had put through several calls to follow up with Kane, who was staying at the Via Condotti. Nothing. He had kept his part of the agreement, but now Kane was dead.

The Commendatore shouted into his headpiece: "They're coming out now. I want all eyes on the crowd." Each of dozens of police scrutinized his own little segment of the piazza.

"It looks under control." Bevo sighed with indifference.

"It looked under control ten days ago, too." The Commendatore was cold.

Staring angrily at the screens, Bevo saw nothing. "If I were you, I'd retract that statement."

"I have already retracted your identification of Inspector Davan as the killer of Nasir Ayoub," the Commendatore whispered, his gaze never wavering from the panel in front of him. "That is the only retraction you can expect from me, Bevo. The Minister of Justice has asked for my recommendations regarding you. You can imagine what I will have to say to her."

A distant rumble from the crowd. The balcony drapery moved.

"Here they come," the Commendatore called. The voice of the Cardinal Dean rang out across the Piazza:

"Annuntio vobis gaudium magnum;

habemus Papam:

Eminentissimum ac Reverendissimum Dominum,

Dominum Emmanuelem

Sanctae Romanae Ecclesiae Cardinalem Estades

qui sibi nomen imposuit Emmanuel I."

To the immense crowd, the name of the new pope meant virtually nothing; still, shouts and applause thundered across the square with a noise like a waterfall. Flowery hand-lettered "Z3" signs—calling for another Pope Zacharias—wilted underfoot. An Irish claque cheering for Cardinal Tyrell fell silent and looked around bewildered, not understanding the name that had been announced. Nuns fell to their knees. Everywhere people screamed with joy, and at the same time called to each other in fifty languages: "Who?"

Within the curtained balcony doors, Tyrell looked, stunned, at his friend Manuel Estades, who was taking the embraces of his brothers in turn. It was the second shock of the day: David Kane, dead in Jerusalem. The invulnerable, iron Kane, who had blackmailed him for decades over Rafqa Chandos, who had thrust Peter onto him to raise up in the Church hierarchy. He had learned to love the son and to hate the father. In one hour, his greatest fear and his greatest ambition had died within him. He felt his soul collapsing, his spirit within his stony frame crying the tears of a child—of anguish or relief, he himself could not say.

Smiling expansively, buried in the white and golden robe of the papacy, Estades—now Pope Emmanuel I—raised his hands in blessing and passed through the veiled doors to greet the City and the World.

Only moments before, the election had ended in a way no one had anticipated. All the tensions of the previous days at once vaporized. A glow of interest in Estades had ignited immediately after the ardent sermon given by his protégé at the beginning of conclave; it grew among the bishops who looked uncertainly at Cardinals Tyrell and Stone; it bypassed the haughty man from Manaus. At last, in the early hours of Monday, like a flame of warm wind over the conclave, the choice spread and gently toppled all opposition.

Estades nearly fainted. "*Accepto*," came his astonished whisper when he was informed of his election. "What else can I do?" He shrugged up at Tyrell.

Immediately, the Cardinal Archpriest John Paul Stone, his face frozen, asked Estades what name he would choose to rule by. "My own?" he responded. "I can't think of another."

Since that moment, Pope Emmanuel's quick, generous mind had blazed a path through the tangle of conflicts that surrounded him. He knew exactly how to begin his work, and thanked God silently for it.

Smiling down at the people in the square, so many of them, he intoned the age-old blessing *Urbi et Orbi*—to the City and the World. Traditionally, the new pope would then leave the balcony; Emmanuel chose to stay. He spread his arms, reached for Cardinals Tyrell and Stone, who stood on opposite sides of the balcony, and drew them toward him. With the raising of his hand, he calmed the sea of cheers and spoke again into the microphone.

"Today our friends of the Jewish faith devote one full day solely to reconciliation, as Leviticus commands: '*Upon the tenth day of the seventh month shall be the day of atonement; it shall be most solemn, and shall be called holy.*' For them, this is Yom Kippur, the holiest day of the year. In English it is called the Day of Atonement—the day when all debts are forgiven, all differences put aside, and all people become 'at one' with each other and with God, embraced together in the love of God.

"May God grant that this new day become for us all a Day of Atonement, a day of forgiveness, of understanding, of embracing one another's differences—not in sacrifice of principle, but in upholding of brotherhood. Not with an unyielding mind, but in remembrance of the yielding knees of Our Lord, who Himself knelt to wash the feet of the Apostles."

Emmanuel embraced Stone and then Tyrell, who whispered, "It was you who wrote those words."

"My brothers," he said privately, firmly to the two of them, "we will not tear the Church in two. We will work hard together, and we will love each other. And we will be One in the end."

The new pope then turned back to the congregation below and cried out a Psalm. "*Behold how good and how pleasant it is for brethren to dwell in unity.*"

Situation Room, Shin Bet Headquarters, St. Helena Street, Jerusalem, 1430h

"You're holding Lambert Sable? The head of GeM Corporation?" The Prime Minister was incredulous.

"Yes, we're holding him for conspiring against state security," Kristall answered, with an official sniff.

She smiled at the air. Across the conference table, Ari sat in a comfortable briefing chair, his knee in a brace, while Miner played with the GeM Ari had taken from Chandos. Toad was at a flatscreen in the corner of the room, completing the paperwork on Lambert Sable and Bob Jonas. The Prime Minister's voice filled the room.

"You must release him immediately."

"Sorry, sir. He's already been charged. You'll have to take it up with the judiciary."

There was a gagging noise from the speakerphone. "First the head of Interpol, and now this. Sable is one of the most powerful businessmen in the world. On my own authority, I order you to release him."

"But not even his Board of Directors want him released. They want him right where he is."

"His Board of Directors?"

"They're unhappy with his recent conduct. Apparently, a large piece of the GeM Corporation disappeared this morning into a bank account in the Bahamas. They're going to seek a few charges of their own against Mr. Sable."

The Prime Minister rang off without another word. Ari and Miner laughed.

"Toad, what put you onto Sable?" Ari asked.

Toad looked up absently from his monitor. "His name was in the contact list of her GeM."

Ari grinned at Miner.

"*Her* GeM? You mean, Catriel Levine's GeM?"

"Yeah, who else?" Toad seemed irritated.

"She was a cold customer," Miner said softly.

"She had strong convictions," Toad sighed. He pushed himself away from the monitor and rotated his chair. "She was one of those people who talk only to themselves—and to God. She went to Sable with the nano device because she knew he was interested in the Temple. With enough of his backing, the Arab powers might be bought off and the Mount opened to the Temple.

"Then, a few days ago, Sable had second thoughts and tried to shut down the deal. Catriel insisted, so he independently hired Catriel's contractor to get the device for him. What neither of them realized was that the contractor was working against them both."

"Elias Chandos," Ari said, his smile gone.

"Right. Known to them only as 'the Arab.' He had his own purpose: to get his hands on the nano devices so that his father could use them to destroy the Dome."

"But what was her connection to Elias Chandos?" Kristall asked.

"Sable confessed the whole thing an hour ago. He's talkative. Catriel Levine told him she'd had to use the Arab to…eliminate her uncle because she found out he was working against the Mishmar, trying to prevent the building of the Temple. She considered him a traitor."

"That makes sense," Ari said. "Shor was one of the Cherubim sworn to protect the shrines on the Mount."

"Right, and I've been formulating a theory about that," Toad went on in his dull voice. "It occurred to me yesterday, when you told us about the Order of the Cherubim—that each member was responsible for recruiting his own successor. What if Shor tried to recruit his niece Catriel Levine to succeed him? Who would be a more natural choice? She was smart, well connected, deeply religious. And one of the family. But it would be appalling to her— it would mean renouncing everything she believed in. For her, the Dome had to be removed so the Temple could be built. And Shor was head of the Mishmar."

"So Catriel Levine hired the Arab—Chandos—and it was all over for Shor," Kristall offered.

"For her, too. Chandos's father couldn't afford any loose ends to snarl up his plans. No one could be left alive who knew anything about the murder of Emmanuel Shor and the connection to the nano device. So Elias Chandos was sent to dispatch her."

"And Tempelman," Ari added. "If I know him, he had worked things out and intended to blackmail her. That was his way."

Agitated, Kristall stood and began walking aimlessly around the conference table. "A bloody, wasteful mess. And to think—for more than forty years, that madman Kane schemed and plotted for just this day. Using his own son as an instrument of murder. Tentacles everywhere."

Ari sat back and closed his eyes. In that moment, he felt both relieved and dejected. So much death, so much anger. Deep down, it alarmed him to think of the big, distinguished man with his white hair, who had listened with such apparent sympathy to him. The alien nature of Kane's heart frightened him.

Ari murmured to the air. "It must have been Kane who tipped off our enemies about the danger to the Dome."

"And tipped off the Saladin Brigades about you," Toad added. "He must have contacted them directly he heard from Maryse Mandelyn that you were on the road to Jerusalem. He wanted you out of the way."

"And out of Mandelyn's life," Kristall said briskly. She continued her pointless wandering around the room. Ari opened his eyes, glared at her, and closed them again.

"How far back? Did you say *forty years*?" Ari shook his head at the intricacy of Kane's scheme, his endless patience, his careful maneuvering into one position of power after another, the murders that seemed random but all fit into one bizarre picture—the apparent suicide of Sir John Chandos once Kane was in his confidence, his induction into the Order of Cherubim to replace Sir John, his careful vetting of one son as a lethal weapon and the other at the center of power in the Vatican. Every chance and opportunity he turned to benefit his scheme. And no one who got close to the scheme could be allowed to live. No one except Maryse.

"It's my fault, in a way," Kristall said quietly. She continued her orbit around the table. "Kane slipped out of our hands long ago. It was…I can't remember exactly. We cornered the Lifta gang on the Temple Mount, but the athletic one escaped. After we put the others away, we lost interest in him. But the Waqf never forgot him. And it's sad."

Ari was surprised at her tone. It was not like her.

Kristall went on. "Sad that Nasir Ayoub was helping us all along and we didn't realize it. He obviously figured out who Elias Chandos was long before we did, and then went after him."

"How did he figure out Elias Chandos?" Miner asked.

"That's clear from our surveillance," Toad said. "Nasir was trying to find out what had happened to that terrorist Bukmun. We listened in on Nasir's conversation with the owner of the shop where Bukmun was killed. The shopkeeper said that Bukmun was after 'the man in Rome.' Naturally, we assumed the 'man in Rome' was Nasir, who attended the security conference there—but it was actually Elias Chandos."

"I don't understand."

"It was on television," Toad was patient. "Bukmun had seen video of Nasir Ayoub's meeting with the Vatican officials in Rome. In the video, next to Nasir, was Peter Chandos, who looked exactly like Elias. Bukmun mistakenly assumed that Peter *was* Elias—the man who had bought two contraband Hawkeye rockets from him to destroy Jewish holy sites. When Elias used one of them on the Great Synagogue, he was happy. But when another struck al-Aqsa, he felt betrayed. That's why he rang Nasir Ayoub—he wanted to tell him about the 'man in Rome.' "

"So Nasir didn't kill Bukmun." Miner was beginning to see. "Elias Chandos did."

"But Nasir made the mental leap. He realized that 'the man in Rome,' who was now dead, must have a living twin. He tracked the twin to Rome, which ended up fatal for him." Toad shrugged, turning back to his monitor.

"And that's the sad part," Kristall said. "We were chasing the same ghost, we and Nasir Ayoub. But there's so little trust between us and the Palestinians that even now, we can't talk to each other."

"Why did Elias attack the Great Synagogue *and* the Mosque?" Miner wanted to know.

"To whip up hatred on both sides," Toad answered simply. "To raise the alert level to red so that a threat to the Dome would be more likely to ignite a war."

Someone knocked at the conference-room door. "Where's my assistant?" Kristall grumbled as she stalked over to open it.

"He took the holiday off," Ari laughed.

"Holiday? What holiday?" She let in Sarah Alman, who walked past her and took Miner by the hand.

"And who's this?" Kristall asked, miffed.

"You don't remember your own staff? This is Sarah Alman—used to work in the lab," Ari said.

"I'm taking the rest of the day off, if it's all right with you," Miner asked Ari. "Sarah's invited me to break the fast with her family."

Ari looked questioningly at Miner.

"I've got Dr. Rappaport's permission to lead a new project." Sarah was shy. "We have a new lead on Tay-Sachs. Gene therapy on chromosome 15. A promising study."

"Go," Ari grinned, waving him away.

Sarah smiled at Miner and they left together.

Kristall moved quickly around the table once more and reached to grasp a note from her desk. "That reminds me. Davan, you're invited to break the fast tonight at the Royal David." She held up the invitation. "A formal request from Jean-Baptiste Mortimer."

"Hm," Ari was noncommittal.

"Inspector Mandelyn will be there," Kristall added, as she started another stroll around the table.

Ari changed the subject. "Why are you wandering the room like this? Usually, you're never out of your chair."

"Nerves. I've given up smoking for Yom Kippur."

At that, even Toad smiled.

The King's Garden, King David Hotel, Jerusalem, 2030h

A slight fall wind, just enough to stir the white candles on the table, breathed past as Maryse gazed out over the Old City. The Dome of the Rock rose above the ancient stone walls like a bright planet. Reflexively, she stroked with dismay the unfamiliar gold ring on her fourth finger. The voices around her, like the breeze, seemed to come from nowhere; she still felt infinitely remote from them.

"Some of this sour cream cake, my dear?" Mortimer nudged her. "It's exquisite."

She looked down at the delicate cake on the plate before her, smiled at him, and shook her head.

She felt utterly alone, without connection. Blunt images of her father and David Kane had pounded in her mind all through this blinding day. She couldn't bear the sight, even in her imagination. In her room she had tried to sleep, but a sharp diagonal light fell through the curtains onto the bed and, as she stared at it, faded first to red gold, then to purple—and at last, like an anesthetic, darkness approached.

She must have slept then, because she remembered the dream. It was Eastertime. Once again, a boy, suntanned, supple as a spider, skittered by the ends of his fingers over the rocks of Glendalough while she sat watching in her pool of shade by the lake. She yearned to be with him, to share his strength and courage and cunning, to join him and live alongside him among the cliffs.

Then a sound had awakened her. What was it? Mourning? A horn throbbing in the distance, resonating up from the streets, through the open windows. It was truly dark now. As if after surgery, a sensation of pain pressed on her: she knew who the boy had been. Easter. David Kane always visited at Easter. She hadn't imagined it after all.

He had brought Elias with him.

Her past life drained away from her as if history had lost its meaning.

It was not long before her GeM rang and Mortimer ordered her down to dinner. "Maryse. The white thread and the black thread look-alike. The *shofar* has sounded! Time to break the fast!"

She had risen, dressed, and descended automatically to the restaurant. The little group was already seated at a round table on a veranda beyond French doors. They had a view of the old city, framed by a lone black palm hanging over one side of the table and an isolated black cypress on the other. Beyond them, the walls of the citadel shone in the yellow light like the frayed teeth of a skull.

Jean-Baptiste Mortimer, in full knightly evening dress, stood as she approached and settled her into a chair. Between Mortimer and Grammont sat Dr. Rabia al-Adawi, her face sober, strained. Ari sat next to Maryse.

The dinner was quiet. Grammont ate artistically, savoring the pear crèpes and the whitefish with a frail radish salad, commenting on each course to no one in particular. Mortimer had double helpings and tossed off bits of poetry.

" 'Now I see all the bright-eyed Achaeans, but not the two leaders, Castor and Pollux, both my brothers.' So said Helen of Troy. The Iliad. Castor and Pollux were dead, you see? The Gemini? They were the twin sons of Zeus, who seduced their mother Leda in the body of a great swan. What do you say, Grammont?"

The Frenchman was contemplating the texture of the whitefish. "I haven't the remotest idea what you're talking about."

Mortimer piled more of the succulent radishes onto his plate and munched for a while. Then he held up his fork. "Now I see. Do you remember, Maryse, I've always wondered why the Gemini were in the wrong place on the Zodiac Window at Chartres. It's simple, and it's all wrong. The Chandos twins. They were never intended to be Cherubim."

Ari smirked at the old man, who paused for another bite. "I see you shaking your head and smiling at the incoherent old fool, Mr. Davan. But when I say I'm still learning to read the Cathedral, perhaps you'll understand how great—and unfathomable—a book it really is."

Eventually, dessert was cleared and tea and coffee brought. Maryse asked Rabia with pain in her voice, "How is Dr. Ayoub?"

Rabia glanced up from her plate, and then at the horizon. "He is resting. I've given him medication." She gave Maryse the hint of a hopeful smile. "I think there will be time."

"Time?"

"To educate another son."

Ari sighed and pushed himself away from the table. "To what end? Maybe the time of the Cherubim is over." He picked up his wine glass. Staring into it, he asked, "Will anyone ever trust the Cherubim again?"

Grammont looked alarmed enough to put down his fork.

Rabia laid her hand on Mortimer's. "Oh no, the Cherubim must continue. The flaming sword burns on as long as there are people who want peace. Do not be despairing. Remember, 'At all times God walks with the lost-hearted.' "

Mortimer smiled back at her and finished the verse from the Koran. " 'We who see nothing and from a distance cry, O God!' Wise, just like your father. You're right, of course. We blunder along, thinking the whole show depends on us, when in the end we are only witnesses after all."

"Witnesses?" Maryse looked coolly at him. "Witnesses of what?"

"Of love," Rabia whispered.

"Love?" Maryse stared across the city at the blinding globe of the Dome of the Rock. She felt that the whole long labyrinth of her life had led her to that empty temple on the hill, only to find nothing at its heart. She remembered Ezekiel—the withdrawal of the *shekinah* from the temple of Solomon. "It's a long time now since God left us. If you love someone, you don't abandon them."

Mortimer sipped his wine and, after a slow silence, touched his lips with a napkin. "There was once a King of England. A very noble, memorable king, he mourned the loss of the Order of Templars, the protectors of the Mount of God in Jerusalem. An evil plot had destroyed that order, leaving the Mastership vacant and the knights scattered or dead. So he built a new order of guardian knights, the Order of Gardeurs. The twenty-four knights of the Gardeurs symbolized the twenty-four angels of the Apocalypse who guard the throne of Christ.

"The King was hopeful. But then he lost his beloved eldest son, the master of the order in whom he had invested the guardianship of the future. The father despaired. His other sons were quarrelsome, wasteful; none of them was worthy to guard Christ's throne.

"But the dead prince had a bosom friend, a noble young man who loved peace and honor more than life. He stood before Edward III, and the King loved Sir John Chandos and privately made him the Lion of England, the Master of the Temple.

"A long line of successors stayed faithful to that charge, even after the Order degenerated into a shallow honorary fraternity and its name was corrupted to 'the Order of the Garter.' "

Mortimer leaned forward with sudden intensity and spoke to Maryse. "We have not lost that faith. We serve that throne as knights should. When one falls, another is raised up. We are tested, yes. Tried and tested like fire right down to our bones. And the test consists of this: will love die in us, or will it flame up again and make us one?"

Maryse gazed into the colorless wine in her glass.

"You're a witness too. You saw it today," Mortimer urged. He gestured toward Ari. "The sons of Abraham, Arabs and Israelis, were saved once

315

again. Israel is bound to that Rock, to that altar, but only through love is he ever redeemed."

"I don't follow," Maryse said, hesitating.

"Why did this young man, this Ari Davan, come back alone this morning? Why didn't he alert the whole Israeli Defense Force and let them do the job? Hasn't it occurred to you yet?"

Maryse turned and looked intently at Ari, burned, bronzed, and thin in his linen suit, his face abraded by sharp rocks, his injured leg bent to one side. The boy on the mountain…

She felt hot tears in her eyes, stood and went to the wall overlooking the trees of the garden. Ari struggled to his feet and followed her, clumsily. Together they gazed past the palms and the cypresses at the deepening glow of the Old City. In the distance, tiny figures in white were leaving the citadel as the traffic picked up in the streets. Jerusalem had survived the day.

"It's over. Yom Kippur," Ari said, leaning on the wall. He pictured Tovah Kristall in her chair at headquarters, wrapped in a tobacco fog, relieved that the crisis had passed. "The last prayer for the Day of Atonement is the *Neilah*. It's the one prayer I remember because after that we could go home and eat." He laughed softly. "Neilah means 'locking.' When the gates of the Temple were locked for good, long ago, there was despair. The Neilah is a plea to God to unlock the gates again."

Timid, she touched his hand and looked at him, eyes newly open.

Mortimer approached with two rings in his palm. "This one belonged to the late Emmanuel Shor, the faithful Ox." He held up a simple, worn circlet engraved DVCEI. "Some say it is a relic of Maimonides, the great defender of the faith of Israel. I don't believe it, do you?" He slipped it onto Ari's finger.

"And this," he held up a massive ring emblazoned with a golden lion and a royal crown athwart a world globe. He put it in Maryse's hand. "The Lion. I saved it from the ashes. My dear, from the day Kane sent you to me in Chartres, that day you turned up a starving, dirty, dizzy adolescent, I suspected you were the one. It was in the cards."

He put his hand to her cheek and then turned back to the table. "Now, they say the lioness is the fiercer of the breed. What do you say, Grammont?"

The Frenchman primly swallowed his coffee. "But you are the Angel, and you are seventy-five years old. Who will replace you?"

Mortimer shrugged and winked at Ari and Maryse. "I don't need replacing. Not yet."

Rabia al-Adawi held up a glass of tea. "There's a saying of the Prophet. '*I swear by the One who holds my soul in His hand that you will not enter paradise until you believe. And you won't be believed until you love one another, and until you spread the 'salaam' among you.*' "

"In that case, *Salaam aleykum*," Mortimer intoned quietly, raising his glass. "Peace be with you."

"*Shalom*," Ari smiled at Maryse. "Peace."

THE END

ABOUT THE AUTHOR

Breck England juggles writing thrillers with composing classical music, French cooking, teaching MBA's in the world-class Marriott School of Business, ghostwriting for authors such as Stephen R. Covey, and (formerly) singing in the Mormon Tabernacle Choir. He is the author of *The Tarleton Murders: Sherlock Holmes in America*, published by Mango. He holds a PhD in English from the University of Utah. Breck lives with his wife Valerie in the Rocky Mountains of Utah among nearly innumerable grandchildren.

Im Salon der Königsloge kann man – zumindest in klaren Vollmondnächten – das Schloss Neuschwanstein wie eine märchenhafte Erscheinung vor den Bergen erleben (oben); man kann aber auch, wie König Ludwig im Maurischen Kiosk, sich in weichen arabischen Pfühlen wälzen.

Der großartigen Aussicht auf See und Berge entspricht in der Königsloge der Blick hinunter auf die Bühne, etwa auf den endlosen Horizont der Berge bei der „Schlittenfahrt" im 4. Akt des Musicals.

Das Foyer im 2. Rang mit seinen mobilen Bars und seiner Fernsicht hat den Charme eines Promenadendecks auf einem Überseeschiff.

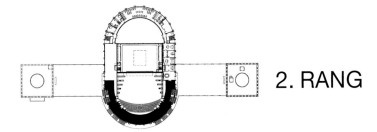

2. RANG

Alle Plätze im ansteigenden Parkett werden bequem vom Erdgeschoss aus erschlossen. Die vier vorderen Eingänge (rechts) haben ein königliches Maß: Sie sind 5,25 Meter hoch.

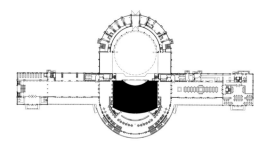

AUDITORIUM

Das Deckenbild, das König Ludwig II. für das Speisezimmer von Schloss Linderhof bestellt hat, taucht zweifach im Theater auf: mit einer Möwe in der Mitte am Boden des Hauptfoyers (oben), mit einem Adler in der Mitte an der Decke des Zuschauerraums (rechts), die Vögel sind Zutaten in Anlehnung an Kaiserin Sissis Gedicht von Adler und Möwe (2. und 5. Akt). Die Beleuchtungsschlitze um das Adlerbild, die man von der Bühne aus sieht, sind von den Plätzen im Zuschauerraum aus nicht zu erkennen.

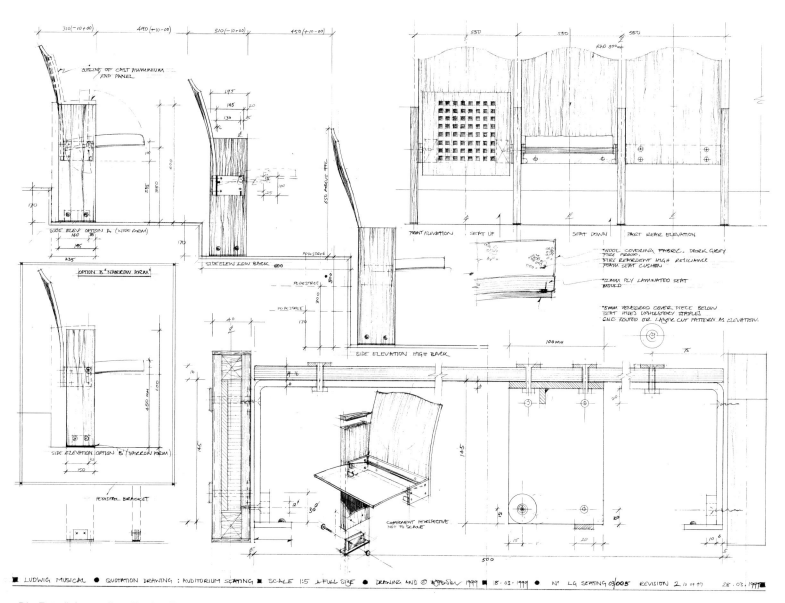

Die Entwürfe von Ben Fowler für die Sitze im Zuschauerraum und für die ornamentalen Seitenwangen an den Enden der Sitzreihen zeigen, dass das Haus – und besonders der Zuschauerraum – als Gesamtkunstwerk konzipiert wurden. Von den Podien über den Eingängen grüßt Ludwig herunter.

60

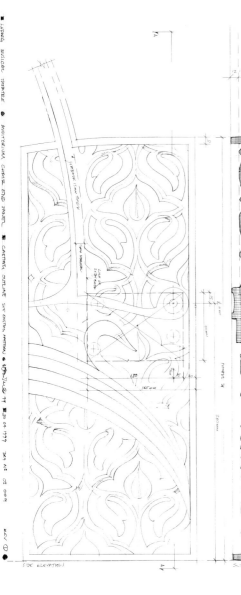

■ LUDWIG MUSICAL THEATRE ● ● ● ● ● ● ● ● ● ● ● KEY ⊕ ●

SIDE ELEVATION   SECTION

Die Drehbühne mit ihren 28 Metern Durchmesser ist die zweitgrößte in Deutschland (hier zwei Aufnahmen aus den Tagen der Montage). Der Blick von oben, vom Bühnenturm herunter (rechts), zeigt die versenkbare Wasserwanne, die im Finale des Musicals als Starnberger See, als Ort des Sterbens und als Triumphbrunnen fungiert. Am oberen Rand sind der Eiserne Vorhang und daneben der Orchestergraben zu erkennen.

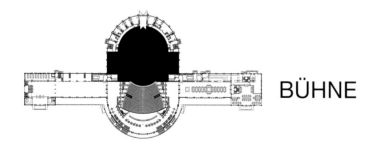 BÜHNE

Im Bühnenhaus, in der Maschinerie der Theaterträume: Wir blicken über den „Starnberger See" hinweg in die Kulissen des Spiegelsaals und hinauf in den Schnürboden (oben links); werfen einen Blick in den Rollenboden hoch oben im Bühnenturm (oben rechts) und schauen von der Drehbühne aus über den Spiegel des „Sees", in dem die versenkten Nymphenrösser auf die Schluss-Apotheose warten, in den Zuschauerraum hinein.

Das Wandbild „Klingsors Zaubergarten" aus dem Sängersaal von Neuschwanstein ist im 4. Akt des Musicals in ein mehrschichtiges Bühnenbild über-setzt (oben rechts). In der „BierWirtschaft" hängt das Bild an der Stirnwand und kommuniziert mit den Insignien der bayerischen Wirtshaus-Seligkeit.

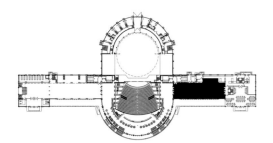 BIERWIRTSCHAFT

Die großen Spiegelwände im „RomantikRestaurant" sind selber wieder ein Reflex auf den Kissinger „Spiegelsaal" im 2. Akt des Musicals (oben rechts).

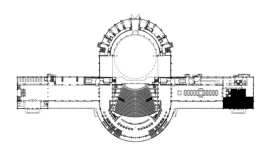

ROMANTIKRESTAURANT

Die Natur ist der wichtigste Partner im Gesamtkunstwerk des Musical Theaters. Im Gartenlabyrinth des 2. Akts blüht die Liebe auf (oben links).
Im Gartenparterre vor dem Theatergebäude – es wurde von Cornelia Pechtold gestaltet – spazieren und sitzen die Zuschauer zwischen den Figuren des Stücks herum (oben rechts). Im „PanoramaSaal" im ersten Stock des Restaurant-Pavillons liegt die Voralpenlandschaft den Besuchern zu Füßen.

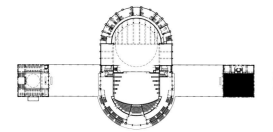 PANORAMASAAL

In den Treppenhäusern und Fluren des viergeschossigen Personal- und Garderobentrakts, der sich im Halbkreis um die Drehbühne herumzieht, kehren die ruhigen Farben aus den Foyers wieder: ein tiefes Königsblau, ein helles Weiß und verschiedene Stufen von Grau.

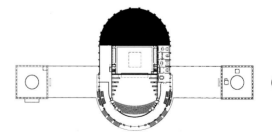

GARDEROBENHAUS

In den Räumen des Garderobentrakts kann kein Gefühl der Enge aufkommen: Hier eine Künstlergarderobe, ein Perückenraum und die Probebühne.

Nächste Seiten: Die Kantine hat eine ähnlich luxuriöse Lage wie die „Königsloge" am anderen Ende des Theaters; sie wird zum Aussichtsrestaurant.

DATEN UND FAKTEN

Ludwig II. – Sehnsucht nach dem Paradies
Musik: Franz Hummel
Text: Stephan Barbarino
Bühne: Heinz Hauser

Regie: Stephan Barbarino
Kostüme und Maskenentwürfe: Joachim Herzog
Bewegungs- und Co-Regie: Barbara Karger
Choreographie: John Carrafa
Musikalische Leitung: Bartholomew Berzonsky
Lichtdesign: Thomas Roscher
Sounddesign: Wolfgang Ellers

1994: Idee von Stephan Barbarino

11. Februar 1996: Bürgerentscheid für das
Musical in Füssen

10. Juni 1997: Bekanntgabe des Bauplatzes
im Forggensee

Nacht vom 14. auf den 15. Mai 1998:
Gießen der Bodenplatte mit 1700 m³ Beton

25. August 1998: Grundsteinlegung am
153. Geburtstag von Ludwig II.

23. April 1999: Richtfest

25. März 2000: Hauseröffnung

7. April 2000: Uraufführung

Die Ludwig Musical AG & Co. Betriebs-KG hat
über 200 Mitarbeiter
davon Mitarbeiter im Theater: ca. 170
Königswelten GmbH (Gastronomie): ca. 100
Berufssparten: ca. 20
Darsteller: 45 (drei- und vierfach besetzt)
pro Show: 28, 1 Kind, 2 Pferde und 18 Musiker

Tickets & mehr:
0 18 05/58 39 44
www.ludwigmusical.com

Kosten
Die Ludwig Musical AG & Co. Betriebs-KG
ist rein privatwirtschaftlich finanziert, d. h. ohne
Subventionen oder öffentliche Gelder.
Für das Gesamtprojekt inklusive Theater-
produktion lagen die Finanzierungskosten bei
ca. 82 Millionen DM.

Baukosten
Erschließungbeiträge: 800 000 DM
Konstruktion und Ausstattung: 32 245 000 DM
Technische Anlagen: 18 325 000 DM
Außenanlagen: 1 585 000 DM
Baunebenkosten: 8 752 000 DM

THEATER

Bauzeit: 18 Monate
Länge: 159,80 m
Tiefe: 78,00 m
Höhe: 31,25 m
Grundfläche: 5725 m^2
Nutzfläche: 11 600 m^2
Umbauter Raum: 76 000 m^3
Zuschauerraum: 842,87 m^2
Fensterfläche: 1927 m^2
Geländer: 478 laufende Meter

Grundstücksfläche ohne Gebäude: 45 000 m^2
Aufschüttung: 215 000 m^3 Kies
Drei Monate sind täglich 480 Lastwagen-
ladungen Kies aufgeschüttet worden.

GARTEN

Mutterboden: 6000 m^3
Großbäume: 250
Sträucher: 3200
Bodendeckende Gehölze: 5000
Bux: 3200
Blütenstauden: 5000
Blumenzwiebeln: 9000
insgesamt: 25 650 Pflanzen
Rasen: 23 000 m^2

ENERGIEHAUS

Länge: 17,28 m
Tiefe: 17,28 m
Höhe: 8,14 m
Es enthält Lagerräume der Gastronomie, Patis-
serie, Notstromaggregat, Brunnenwasser- und
Heizzentrale, Elektroanschlussräume

BÜHNENTECHNIK

Bühnenbreite: 40 m
Bühnentiefe: 35 m
Durchmesser der großen Drehscheibe: 28 m

Drehgeschwindigkeit: 1,2 m/sec.
am Scheibenrand
Durchmesser der kleinen Drehscheibe mit
Pferdelaufband: 6 m
Länge des Wasserbeckens: 22 m
Breite: 11 m
Wasserbecken: 90 000 Liter
Gewicht: 120 Tonnen (90 Tonnen Wasser)
Portalhöhe: 11 m
Portalbreite: 15 m
Zugstangen: 50, max. Breite 22 m,
belastbar mit 350 kg je Stange
Eiserner Vorhang: 4,5 Tonnen
Zwei Spiegelwagen: 10 Tonnen
Nutzfläche je Wagen ca. 80 m^2
Fahrweg: 13,5 m
Fahrgeschwindigkeit: 0,02–0,6 m/s
Hauptspielfläche: ca. 530 m^2
Gesamtbühnenfläche: ca. 1100 m^2
Raumvolumen der Bühne: 23 600 m^3
Schnürboden: 30 m breit und 18,20 m tief
Im 32 m hohen Bühnenturm befinden sich
fünf Arbeitsgalerien, die über Treppenhäuser
auf der linken und rechten Seite oder einen
geräuschlosen Schnellaufzug zu erreichen sind.

BÜHNENBILD

Entwurf von Heinz Hauser
29 Bühnenbilder, angefertigt in Werkstätten
aus ganz Deutschland
Die ca. 22 m langen Prospektanlagen sind
7-mal aufgehängt. Die Aufhängelaschen sind
so auf den Rohren verschweißt, dass auf allen
Prospektzügen Flugwerkwagen fahren können.
Alle Prospekte (Szenenhintergründe) sind
handgemalt. Bewusst wurde auf alte traditio-
nelle Bühnenmalerei und Bühnenarchitektur
zurückgegriffen, um das Thema aus dem
19. Jahrhundert auch im Stil des 19. Jahr-
hunderts zu erzählen.
Die Prospekte wurden von den Theatermalern
Werner Schmidbauer aus Unteregg und
Winfried Mayerhofer aus Ihringen angefertigt.

LICHT

Scheinwerfer: 180, davon 35 Scanner
(Movinglights)
Sternenschleier: 2000 Lämpchen
Lampen: 15 bis 5000 Watt
Über 200 Lichtstimmungen

TON

Lautsprecher: ca. 40
Leistung: 20 000 Watt
Mikroports: 30
Einspielung über zwei Festplatten-Rekorder
Das Steuerpult ist rein digital mit 128 Kanälen.
Ein einziges Glasfaserkabel verbindet das Pult
mit der Bühne.
Bei Stromausfall funktioniert das Pult noch für
10 Minuten autonom, automatisch schaltet
sich das Notstromaggregat ein, mit dem die
Vorstellung bis zum Ende gefahren werden
kann.

KOSTÜM

Kostümbildner: Joachim Herzog
Herstellungsleitung: Viola Lindenau
Gesamtzahl: 190 Komplettkostüme
pro Show: 101 Komplettkostüme auf der Bühne
Komplettkostüm heißt:
Herren-Hemd, Halswäsche, Hose, Weste,
Jacke, Accessoires, Schuhe, Handschuhe.
Damen-Korsett, Krinoline, Unterrock, Rock,
Taille, Accessoires, Hüte, Schuhe, Handschuhe.
Alle Kostüme sind Maßanfertigungen für die
jeweiligen Darsteller.
z.B. Sissis Ballkleid: 350 Arbeitsstunden
Ballkleider Ensemble: je 250 Arbeitsstunden
Die Ballroben sind aus ca. 30 m Stoff genäht
und wiegen ca. 12 kg

Die Stoffe wurden zum Teil eigens für das
Musical nach Entwürfen von Joachim Herzog
gewebt.

PERÜCKENABTEILUNG

Die Masken wurden nach historischen
Vorbildern von Joachim Herzog entworfen.
pro Vorstellung 65 Perücken
Um eine Perücke herzustellen, werden
60 bis 80 Arbeitsstunden benötigt.
Die Perücken sind Maßanfertigungen,
d. h. für jeden Darsteller wird nach seiner
Kopfform eine eigene Perücke aus Echthaar
handgeknüpft. Die Sissiperücke hat offen
1 m langes Haar.

KÖNIGSWELTEN

Der Begriff „Königswelten" bezeichnet alle
künstlerischen Projekte und Ausstattungen in
und um das Musical Theater Neuschwanstein,
sowie die Gastronomie und die Gartenanlage.
Der Bühnenbildner Jürgen Kirner und die
Architektin und Bühnenbildassistentin Tanja
Götz haben die Ausstellungen der „Königswelten" innerhalb des Gebäudes und auf dem
Gelände des Musical Theater Neuschwanstein
konzipiert und realisiert. So zum Beispiel die
Gestaltung der etwa 150 Vitrinen. Dank der
fruchtbaren Zusammenarbeit mit dem „Ludwi-
gologen" Jean Louis Schlim können hier
einzigartige Originalstücke gezeigt werden.
Die Ideen und Motive der Königsweltenausstat-
tung sind aus dem Bühnengeschehen bzw. aus
der Geschichte von Ludwig II. unter Mithilfe
des Dramaturgen Jan Linders entwickelt
worden: Das Deckengemälde im Zuschauerraum, die Bodengemälde im Erdgeschossfoyer,
der blaue Nymphenriss vor der „Champagner-
Bar", die Gestaltung der Kunstbeete im Garten,
die Lichtbeete auf den Terrassen u. v. m.
In den Vitrinen befinden sich u. a.
die letzte Zigarette von König Ludwig II.,
Modelle des Bühnenbildes,
eine Modelleisenbahn mit Stationen aus dem
Leben von König Ludwig II.
und Bühnenschmuck von Kaiserin Sissi.

ENTWURFSPLANUNG
Josephine Barbarino architeam, München
Mitarbeit: Katrin Preiswerk

INNENARCHITEKTUR
ENTWURF & AUSFÜHRUNGSPLANUNG
architeam – www.architeam.co.uk
Nico Rensch, Sussex (GB)
Ben Fowler, East Sussex (GB)
Josephine Barbarino, München

TECHNISCHE PLANUNG DES BÜHNENBILDES
Zimmermann Ideen & Projekte, Bayreuth

BÜHNENTECHNIK
Walter Huneke + Partner GdbR,
Bühnenplanung, Bayreuth

PLANUNG „KUNST AM BAU" (Ausstellungs-
konzeption und -umsetzung der Königswelten)
Jürgen Kirner, Berlin
Tanja Götz, München

FREIANLAGENPLANUNG
Cornelia Pechtold, München

ELEKTROPLANUNG/AUFZÜGE
Ingenieurbüro Knab GmbH, München

HEIZUNG / LÜFTUNG / SANITÄR &
BAUÜBERWACHUNG
Josef Bauer, Ingenieurbüro für Haustechnik,
Unterschleißheim

AUSSCHREIBUNG/
TRAGWERKSPLANUNG I
Storr Architekten Ingenieure, München

AUSFÜHRUNGSPLANUNG/
TRAGWERKSPLANUNG II
Dyckerhoff & Widmann AG, München

RAUM- und BAUAKUSTIK/IMMISSIONSSCHUTZ
Müller-BBM, Planegg bei München

BAUGRUNDBERATUNG
UNTERSUCHUNG & VERMESSUNG
Prof. Dr.-Ing. Weinhold, München
Büro für Geotechnik, Blaichach

AUSFÜHRUNGSPLANUNG
AUFSCHÜTTUNG & PARKPLATZ
Ingenieurbüro Dieter Greif, Kempten

BRANDSCHUTZGUTACHTEN
Dipl.-Ing. Detlef Laspe, München

PLANFESTSTELLUNGSVERFAHREN
Kling Consult Ingenieurges. f. Bauwesen und
Raumordnungsplanung mbH, Krumbach

PROTOTYPEN-HERSTELLUNG
Fowler and Company, Scott Workshops,
East Sussex (GB)
Andrew Ramsay Design, East Sussex (GB)
Patrick Letschka, East Sussex (GB)
White Eagle Foundry (Andrew Shaw),
East Sussex (GB)

BAUKÜNSTLERISCHE LEITUNG
Josephine Barbarino, München

BAULEITUNG/AUSSCHREIBUNG
INNENAUSBAU
Amtsberg & Partner, München

BAULEITUNG
Dyckerhoff & Widmann AG, München
Storr Architekten Ingenieure, München

BAULEITUNG ELEKTRO
Ingenieurbüro Körbl + Feneberg, Füssen

OBJEKTÜBERWACHUNG
RKW Rhode Kellermann Wawrowsky GmbH &
Co. KG, Düsseldorf/Frankfurt/Füssen

GENERALUNTERNEHMEN
Dyckerhoff & Widmann AG, München

BAUHERR
Ludwig Musical AG & Co. Betriebs-KG,
München/Füssen

GENEHMIGUNGSBEHÖRDEN
Stadt Füssen – 1. Bürgermeister
Dr. Paul Wengert,
Stadtbaumeister Theo Fröchtenicht
Landratsamt Ostallgäu – Staatliche
Bauverwaltung, Marktoberdorf
Wasserwirtschaftsamt Kempten
Regierung von Schwaben, Augsburg
Kreisbrandrat für Landratsamt Ostallgäu

PRÜFSTATIK
Ingenieurbüro Dr. Helmut Kupfer, München

FINANZIERUNG
LfA Förderbank Bayern, Bayerische Landes-
anstalt für Aufbaufinanzierung, München

Bayerische Hypo- und Vereinsbank AG,
München

Bayerische Landesbank Girozentrale, München

Berliner Bank AG, Berlin

SchmidtBank KG aA, Hof / Saale

Bankhaus Hermann Lampe KG, Hamburg

AN DER AUSFÜHRUNG BETEILIGTE FIRMEN

ABSCHOTTUNG HEKU Brandschutz GmbH, Kissing · AUFZÜGE : Kone Aufzug GmbH, Augsburg · AUSSCHALARBEITEN: A. F. Bau GmbH, München · AUSSENANLAGEN/UFERBEFESTIGUNG: Schuster GmbH, Dirlewang · Thormeier Garten- & Landschaftsbau GmbH, Füssen Weissensee · AUSSEN-TRANSPARENT: Werbehaus GmbH/Ulli Seer Studios, München/Rosenheim · BAUSCHILD: XYLO Wolf GmbH, München · BAUSTROMANSCHLUSS: Elektrizitätswerke Reutte/EWR GmbH & Co. KG, Füssen · BESCHICHTUNG: Bamer Brand- und Bautenschutz GmbH, Birkenau · BESTUHLUNG: artcasa GmbH, Albershausen · BETONBOHRARBEITEN: FIDAN Betonbearbeitung GmbH, Mehring bei Augsburg · BETONKOSMETIK: Concrete Service, Imst und BAU-TEC GmbH, Crinitzberg · BETONLIEFERUNG: J. Dachser GmbH Allgäu Beton, Marktoberdorf · BETONSTAHLARMIERUNG: Michael Fries GmbH, Memmingen BETON-/STAHLBETON-/MAUERARBEIT: Bautech Slawomir Bochenek, Nysa (Polen) · BEWACHUNG: Wach- und Sicherheitsdienst Göbel, Lechbruck BLITZSCHUTZ: M + K Blitzschutzmontagen GmbH, Friedrichshafen · BÜHNENBELEUCHTUNG: ADB Gesellschaft für Lichttechnik und Elektronik mbH, Mühlheim/Main · BÜHNENBODEN: Bühnenbau Wertheim GmbH, Wertheim-Urphar · BÜHNENBILD: Gerriets GmbH, Volgelsheim (Frankreich) und A.M.F. Theaterbauten GmbH, Erdmannshausen · BÜHNENMALEREI: Werner Schmidbauer, Unteregg und Wilfried Mayerhofer, Ihringen · BÜHNENTECHNISCHE ANLAGEN: BBB Bayerische Bühnenbau GmbH, Weiden i. d. Opf. · DACHDECKERARBEITEN: Gebr. Haas GmbH/Spenglerei, Spiegelau · DAMMBALKENVERSCHLUSS: EKO-System Kossbiel GmbH, Pirmasens (Biebermühle) · EDELSTAHLVERKLEIDUNGEN: Fa. Heindl, Bad Abbach · ELA-ANLAGEN: SAAVS, Friedrich Salzbrenner GmbH, Hallstadt · ERDBAUARBEITEN: Driendl Erdbewegungen, Füssen · ESTRICHARBEITEN: Weber Estrich GmbH, Neubeuern · ESTRICHSCHLEIFARBEITEN: M. Paulus GmbH, Nalbach · ESTRICHTROCKNUNGSARBEITEN: Fa. Auer Trocknungs- und Abdichtungstechnik, Emmering · F-30 BESCHICHTUNG: Termer Decotec, München · FASSADENARBEITEN: Alu-Fenster srl, Caselle di Selvazano (Italien) · FERTIGTEILE: Dyckerhoff & Widmann/GBW Büro München, Werk Aresing, Aschheim · FILIGRANPLATTEN: LFT Lindermayr Fertigteilwerk GmbH & Co. KG, Friedberg-Derching · FLACHDACHABDICHTUNG: Rudolf Schweiger/Abdichtung und Isolierbau, Gräfelfing · FLIESENARBEITEN: Enzensberger Baukeramik GmbH, Schongau · FOLIENABHÄNGUNG: SA-NE Baugesellschaft GmbH, Berlin-Schönefeld · GASBETONARBEITEN: Greisel GmbH, Feuchtwangen · GERÜSTBAU: Gerüstbau Gemeinhardt GmbH, Poing · GRUNDLEITUNGEN: Koch & Co. Baugesellschaft mbH, Schongau · GRÜNDUNG: Fa Schmid + HOCHTIEF AG GUSSGELÄNDER: Fa. Castro Massari & Neumann ohg, Augsburg · HEIZUNGSANLAGEN: Erdgas Schwaben GmbH, Augsburg · HEIZUNG UND SANITÄR: Max Doser GmbH & Co. KG/Haustechnik, Füssen · HOLZINNENTÜREN: Schreinerei Unglert GmbH, Marktoberdorf · HYDROPHOBIERUNGSARBEITEN: Hydro-Tech GmbH, Bobingen · INDUSTRIEBÖDEN: Skomsek GmbH, Peißenberg · INNENAUSBAU: Bachuber GmbH, Dietersburg; Fa. Huber, Triftern-Neukirchen und Fa. Engel, Stetten-Erisried · KERTO-FASSADE: Lipp Holzbearbeitung, Nesselwang · KÜCHENAUSSTATTUNG: Lohberger, Mattighofen (Österreich) · LEUCHTEN: I Guzzini, München und Osram Light Consulting GmbH, München · LÜFTUNGSANLAGEN: Dietrich GmbH/Lüftungs- und Klimatechnik, Aitrang · MALERARBEITEN: Maler Partner GmbH, Germaringen · MAUERWERKARBEITEN: HARRY GmbH, München · METALLZARGEN: Strehle Schreinerei, Wallerstein · MÖBLIERUNG (lose): Habitat Deutschland GmbH, Stuttgart; Toprail Systems Ltd., Twickenham (GB); Topdeq GmbH, Pfungstadt; KARE-Workhaus, München · MRS-TECHNIK: Hörburger & Partner/Schaltanlagen GmbH, Waltenhofen · PUTZARBEITEN: EPG GmbH, Ebersbach · REINIGUNGSARBEITEN: Wolfgang Himmler, München · ROHBAUARBEITEN: SC CORA Internat. Group S. A., Frankfurt a. M. · RÜCKENFORMTEILE: Längle + Hagspiel GmbH, Höchst · SCHALLSCHUTZTÜREN: Stahltürenbau Buchele GmbH, Ebersbach/Fils · SCHLIESSANLAGEN: Fa. Atterer, Marktoberdorf · SCHLOSSERARBEITEN: Metallbau Knauer, Marktoberdorf · SCHREINEREI: Demmler GmbH, Willofs/Allgäu · STAHLTREPPEN: Schmid & Pröbstl Bau- und Kunstschlosserei, Füssen · STAHLTÜREN: Riexinger Türenwerke GmbH, Eching · SOCKEL-PUTZ: Holger Rußbach/Maler Akustik Fachbetrieb, München · SPRINKLERANLAGE: Minifax GmbH/Brandschutz+Sicherheitstechnik, Achim · STAHLBAU: Stahlbau GmbH, München und Metallbau Knauer, Marktoberdorf · STARKSTROMANLAGEN: Elektrizitätswerke Reutte GmbH, Füssen und Reutte (Österreich) · STUCKARBEITEN: Fa. Stevensons of Norwich Ltd · SYSTEMSCHALUNG: Peri GmbH, München · TROCKENBAUARBEITEN: Termer Decotec Meisterbetrieb, München und Strehle Schreinerei, Wallerstein · VERFUGUNGSARBEITEN: VBI ISOFUG GmbH, Kempten · VERSIEGELUNGSARBEITEN: Epowit Bautechnik GmbH, München · WC-TRENNWÄNDE: SANA, Weiden/Gröbenzell · ZÄHLER-VERTEILERSCHRANK: Hubert Geiss Bauunternehmung GmbH, Marktoberdorf-Hattenhofen ZIMMERARBEITEN: Lehrwerkstatt der Dyckerhoff & Widmann AG, Lohhof und viele andere

DANK

Ein Theater zu bauen, gehört sicher zu den schönsten und positivsten Aufgaben, die einem in meinem Beruf widerfahren können. Wie schwer es auch heute noch für eine Frau ist, bei einem solch großen Projekt die „Oberhand" zu behalten, habe ich in den letzten 6 Jahren zu spüren bekommen. Dass dieses Projekt überhaupt zustande kam, ist vielen Glücks- und Zufällen, vor allem aber den Visionen und dem Durchhaltevermögen meines Mannes zu verdanken. Dass er mich, zu allen anderen Schwierigkeiten, auch noch mit seinem Glauben an mein Können als Architektin durch- setzen konnte, und während der gesamten Zeit unerschütterlich an meiner Seite stand, ist der Hintergrund für die erstaunliche Tatsache, dass „dieses Theater zum Erstaunen aller von einer Frau erbaut wurde". (Prolog für Ludwig II. – Sehnsucht nach dem Paradies)
In den ersten Jahren, in denen die Vorarbeit für jegliche Art von Finanzierung geleistet werden musste, haben uns unentgeltlich, und nur mit „Aussicht" auf einen eventuellen Auftrag, Freunde geholfen und beraten. Für die Archi- tektur waren dies vor allem der Bühnenbildner Heinz Hauser, um dessen Bilder herum ich das Theater entworfen habe, Gero Zimmermann, der Technische Direktor in Bayreuth, der uns bühnentechnisch beriet, Horst Babinsky, der erste Kosten und Genehmigungen ermittelte, und dessen Technischer Zeichner Erwin Kaindl, der die ersten Computerzeichnungen meiner Entwürfe erstellte. Mein Dank auch an die Brüder Saurer, die viel Vorarbeit leisteten, als das Theater noch ein Holzbau werden sollte. Fast von Anfang an dabei waren auch mein Bruder Nico Rensch und der Möbeldesigner Ben Fowler; in dieser langen Zeit bestätigte sich die aus früheren Projekten bewährte, kreative und immer positive Zusammenarbeit. Die morali-

sche Unterstützung, die ich von den beiden erfahren habe, ist in jedem Fall unbezahlbar. Als dann nach drei Jahren die LfA (Landes- anstalt für Aufbaufinanzierung) die ersten zwei Millionen für die Projektentwicklung zur Verfü- gung stellte, konnten Fachingenieure hinzu- gezogen werden. Viel gelernt habe ich, wenn auch leider nicht all unsere akustischen Pläne verwirklicht werden konnten, in der Zusammenarbeit mit Prof. Müller. Von Anfang bis zum Schluss immer kompetent und hilfs- bereit waren Oliver Knab und sein Mitarbeiter Thomas Benesch bei der Elektroplanung. Als gleichbleibend freundlich und tüchtig erwies sich Herr Veeh vom Büro Bauer (Heizung & Sanitär). Meine Außentreppen als Ersatz für abgeschlossene Treppenhäuser setzte Herr Laspe durch. Schnelle und kreative Rettung erfuhr das Projekt durch Jo Storr und sein einsatzfreudiges starkes Frauenteam. (Ihr habt uns mindestens vor einem Jahr Verzug, wenn nicht vor Schlimmerem bewahrt.) Ein unver- gessliches Erlebnis war für mich die Nacht vom 14. auf den 15. Mai 1998, als von der Firma Hoch-Tief die Bodenplatte in einem Stück gegossen wurde.
Mein Dank gilt auch Prof. Robert Hausmann für die richtigen Worte zur „rechten" Zeit; dem Füssener Stadtrat (der von Anfang an für das Projekt war) und allen genehmigenden Behörden, die schnell und unbürokratisch gehandelt haben, und mir oft mit gutem Rat beiseite standen; Cornelia Pechtold für die Umsetzung meiner Gartenträume und Walter Huneke für seine Theatererfahrung (auch wenn schließlich alle Eisenteile grün gestrichen waren, obwohl sie doch grau sein sollten). Einen besonders großen Anteil an der Realisie- rung des Baus hatte die Dyckerhoff & Widman AG München, hier möchte ich mich ganz

besonders bei zwei Abteilungen bedanken, zum einen bei Erich Lechner und seinem gesamten Planungsteam, die immer versucht haben, meine Wünsche und Vorstellungen zu realisieren, zum anderen bei dem Fertigteil- werk in Aresingen, die meine „unmöglichen Forderungen" – „thermisch getrennte, scharf- kantige … nach 3 Tagen sandgestrahlte Betonfertigteile" – möglich machten (siehe Fotos rechts, von Ullrich Haas, der den Bau bei Tag und Nacht, in allen Phasen, und bei jedem Wetter fotografierte). Apropos Wetter, meine höchste Anerkennung verdienen alle Bauarbeiter, die in den beiden harten Wintern 1998 und 1999 während der nur 18-mona- tigen Bauzeit trotz meterhohem Schnee und hartem Frost weiterarbeiteten.
Immer in meinem Herzen bleiben wird die Richtfestsonate, die Franz Hummel für mein Haus spielte.
Wichtige Wegbegleiter waren für mich Florian Hintermeier (immer ruhig), Jürgen Kirner (immer tröstlich) und Jan Linders (jeder Archi- tekt sollte einen Dramaturgen an seiner Seite haben). Besonders mutig verhielten sich mir gegenüber in schwerer Zeit Herr Ertel vom E-Werk Reutte und Herr Feneberg.
Zum Schluss möchte ich mich bei Helmut Orterer bedanken für die immer erfreuliche Zusammenarbeit mit unseren Sponsoren und dafür, dass er mich immer „fragt", bei unseren Kommanditisten, die mich ohne Einmischung arbeiten ließen und sich an dem Ergebnis mit mir freuten, bei der Musical AG und allen Mitarbeitern, die mir geholfen haben, diesen unseren „Traum" zu verwirklichen und natür- lich beim Publikum, das den Bau so positiv angenommen hat.

Josephine Barbarino

BILDNACHWEIS

Brinkhoff & Mögenburg, Geesthacht: 18, 52 l., 68 r.
Fotodesign U. Haas, Füssen: 11, 21, 24, 27, 29 r., 31, 32 l., 34 l., 36, 42, 43, 44 l., 46 r., 47 l., 55 l., 56 l., 58 l., 62, 64 l. & r., 65, 66 l., 69, 72, 73, 74 l. & r., 75, 79, 83 o. & u.
Rainer Lafeld, Hamburg: 10, 22
Roland Rasemann, Leutkirch: 63
Gregor M. Schmid, Gilching: 6, 28 l. & r., 29 l., 38 l., 40 o.l., 48 r., 50 l., 66 r., 68 l., 70 l. & r.
Ulli Seer, München: 40 o. r.
Leigh Simpson, Simpson Photographic, Lewes (GB): 26, 30 l. & r., 32 r., 34 r., 38 r., 40 l. & r., 41, 46 l., 50 r., 52 r., 54 r., 56 r., 58 r., 61 r., 67, 71, 76
Dyckerhoff & Widmann AG, München: 47
Thomas Dix, Grenzach-Wyhlen: 44 r.
Landesvermessungsamt München: 9
Modellfoto, Deutsches Theatermuseum, München: 4
Verlag J. Schoierer KG, Nürnberg (aus: Seidel, Klaus J.: Das Prinzregententheater, 1984): 2, 13, 14, 16
Architectural Review Juni 1994, S. 42: 15 l.
Achim Bunz, München: 48 o.

Die Deutsche Bibliothek – CIP-Einheitsaufnahme

Knapp, Gottfried:
Ein Theater für den König : Josephine Barbarinos Musical Theater Neuschwanstein. Schauplatz des Ludwig II. Musicals /
Gottfried Knapp. – Regensburg : Schnell und Steiner, 2001
   ISBN 3-7954-1414-8

1. Auflage 2001
© 2001 by Verlag Schnell und Steiner GmbH, Regensburg
Leibnizstraße 13, D-93055 Regensburg

Technischer Anhang: Elisabeth Gutjahr
Pläne & Zeichnungen: Ben Fowler, D & W, Cornelia Pechtholt, Storr Architekten und Ingenieure
Layout: Josephine Barbarino
Satz und Lithographische Bearbeitung: MultiByte, München
Druck: Erhardi Druck GmbH, Regensburg
Printed in Germany – ISBN 3-7954-1414-8